THE FATE OF FENELLA

VALANCOURT CLASSICS

THE

FATE OF FENELLA

A NOVEL

BY

Helen Mathers	A. Conan Doyle
Justin H. McCarthy	May Crommelin
Frances Eleanor Trollope	F. C. Philips
"Rita"	Bram Stoker
Joseph Hatton	Florence Marryat
Mrs. Lovett Cameron	Frank Danby
Mrs. Edward Kennard	Arthur A'Beckett
Richard Dowling	Jean Middlemass
Mrs. Hungerford	Clement Scott
Clo. Graves	George Manville Fenn
H. W. Lucy	"Tasma"
Adeline Sergeant	F. Anstey

Edited with an introduction and notes by
Andrew Maunder

Kansas City:
VALANCOURT BOOKS
2008

The Fate of Fenella
First published in 1892
First Valancourt Books edition 2008

Introduction and notes © 2008 by Andrew Maunder
This edition © 2008 by Valancourt Books

Library of Congress Cataloging-in-Publication Data

The fate of Fenella: a novel / by Helen Mathers ... [et al.] ; edited
with an introduction and notes by Andrew Maunder –
1st Valancourt Books ed.
p. cm. – (Valancourt classics)
ISBN 1-934555-42-8 (alk. paper)
1. Wives – Fiction. 2. Paramours – Crimes against – Fiction.
3. Murder – Fiction.
I. Mathers, Helen, 1853-1920. II. Maunder, Andrew.
PR3991.A1F28 2008 823'.8–dc22
                                            2008003892

Design and typography by James D. Jenkins
Published by Valancourt Books
Kansas City, Missouri
http://www.valancourtbooks.com

CONTENTS

INTRODUCTION

On 2 October 1891, *The Birmingham Post* introduced its readers to a new development in the world of popular fiction:

> Miss Helen Mathers is to write the first chapter of a serial story for *The Gentlewoman*, the remaining chapters of which will be contributed by many well-known novelists without consultation or any plan being arranged. "The Fate of Fenella," as the tale is to be called, will have among its authors Mrs. Lovett Cameron, Mrs. Edward Kennard, Miss May Crommelin, Miss Florence Marryat, "Rita," Mr. F. C. Philips, Mr. G. M. Fenn, Mr. J. H. McCarthy, Mr. Bram Stoker, Mr. Conan Doyle, and Mr. Richard Dowling; and it will commence to appear in the Christmas number.[1]

This "experimental" work of fiction, symbol of the fast-paced literary marketplace of the 1890s, was the brainwave of publisher Joseph Snell Wood. It was a project that assumed notoriety as a literary gimmick but which today can be said to occupy a uniquely interesting place in the history of nineteenth century fiction. A "curious mosaic,"[2] each chapter being written by one of twenty-four different novelists, *The Fate of Fenella* symbolized the growing professionalization of novel-writing, the sense that fiction was a business and writing a trade. At a time when, as Frederick Greenwood noted, novels were becoming "ordinary commodities ... [to] be sold at the drapers, & with pounds of tea,"[3] anything which helped a novel stand out from the crowd was an important matter for publishers; then as now novelists and books were sold in a competitive marketplace. Collaboration seemed to some to be one solution. In 1892 a writer for *The Bookseller* decided that "a collaborative novel gives the reader good measure for his money," not least because he (or she) got two, three, four—or in this case twenty-four—novelists for the price of one. A "curiosity of collaboration," will, he noted, "be read irrespective of its merits...." Later, *The New York Times* noted that collaboration with better-known people could do a real service to young writers wanting to build reputations. This was despite the fact that collaborative works were rarely well-planned. The same paper compared the multi-authored novel to a rickety stagecoach with "many wheels, all of different diameters, and it kicks and jolts and lumbers" with its horses—or authors—seeming to "kick, rear, gallop, trot and stumble" all the while.[5]

How then, did *The Fate of Fenella* come about? It was the brain-child of an energetic London publisher, Joseph Snell Wood (1853-1920). He was a recent figure on the Victorian literary scene, a man with little influence of his own but a relentless networker, go-getter, and entrepreneur. Wood began as a journalist but by 1892 he was the editor and co-proprietor of a new magazine, *The Gentlewoman*, one of a number of cheap magazines and papers which flooded onto the market in the 1890s, many of which were aimed at women.[6]

Written "by gentlewomen for gentlewomen"[7]—or so it boasted—*The Gentlewoman* was an illustrated weekly (price six-pence; circulation 250,000) which mixed topical items assumed to be of interest to mothers and their daughters—fashions and the "gentle art of Beauty," the household, the theatre, celebrities, royalty, careers, advice, gossip, together with stories from the fash-ionable writers of the day and the chance to win what were vaguely described as "valuable competitive prizes." Like many other mag-azines of the day, *The Gentlewoman* also ran serialised novels by well-known authors (its first was the domestic saga "Other Peo-ple's Children" by John Strange Winter [aka Henrietta Stannard]). The magazine's readers lapped these stories up thirstily.

The magazine market was a fierce one and in an attempt to distinguish itself from its rivals—*The Ladies Pictorial, Woman, The Queen, The Ladies Fashionable Repository*—*The Gentlewoman* prom-ised not only better value but classier material. "Bright reading by the best writers" was its tag line and this self-described "newspa-per *de luxe*, indispensable to every Gentlewoman" was designed to appeal to the socially aspiring housewife who, even if she was never going to get an invitation to take tea with the Princess of Wales, liked reading about those who did. It also—in keeping with Wood's commercial bent—made money by carrying advertise-ments, hundreds of them: perfumes, corsets, cookers, hats, cosmetics, beef tea, and laxatives. *The Fate of Fenella's* depiction of modern marriage amongst the upper classes, and of pure—and not so pure—womanhood and material greed appeared alongside adverts for Holloway's "World Famous Restorative Pills," Dickins and Jones' latest tea-owns, Liberty's new silks, Pears' soap—a heady cocktail of sensational fiction mixed with consumer porn.

How Wood came up with the idea of *The Fate of Fenella* is not, however, clear. The project was presumably part of an attempt to generate some extra excitement for the magazine in the face of stiff competition. As an element of book publishing, collaborative novels were not themselves new and the topic of collaboration had been the focus of a good deal of discussion by the likes of Walter Besant[8] and Brander Matthews.[9] As a way of working, collaboration was intricately entwined with the late-nineteenth century's changing attitude to authorship itself and the ways in which a writer could work. Collaboration could happen for various reasons—one author might take over from another in the event of illness or death. However, by the 1890s there was also a belief that far from being a romantic solitary experience, the writing of fiction could be shared into a series of distinct tasks. This method had been undertaken with some success by Charles Dickens and Wilkie Collins in stories and plays of the 1850s and 1860s including *The Frozen Deep* (1856) and *No Thoroughfare* (1857) in which Dickens tended to provide ideas and act as editor whilst Collins did the bulk of the writing. This was the format followed by James Rice and Walter Besant in the 1870s, with Besant taking on the Collins role. Working from detailed outlines, Besant later finished Collins' last novel *Blind Love* when the older novelist died in the middle of its serialisation in 1889. In the United States, Mark Twain and Charles Warner shared the writing on *The Gilded Age* (1873). Novels with more than two authors were rarer. The best known example seems to have been an epistolary novel, *La Croix de Berny* by Emilie de Girardin, Théophile Gautier, Jules Sandeau and Joseph Méry, published in France in 1857. Later *Six of One by Half a Dozen of the Other* (1872, with Harriet Beecher Stowe, Adeline Whitney plus four) and *The Miz Maze, or, The Winkworth Puzzle: a Story in Letters* (1883; Charlotte Yonge, Christabel Coleridge plus seven), were paradigmatic examples of how such projects might work. Another influence may have been another attention-grabbing serial, *His Fleeting Ideal; or, A Romance of Baffled Hypnotism* which appeared in an American magazine, *The Boston Globe*, in July 1890. Billed as "the great composite novel," it boasted the boxer John L. Sullivan, the showman P. T. Barnum and the detective Thomas Byrnes, as well as nine other celebrity authors.[10]

However, the most immediate source for *The Fate of Fenella* lay closer to home. *The Gentlewoman* had already run a similar collaborative venture with some success. In July 1890 it had launched a competition in which it challenged readers to take on the writing of successful instalments of one of its serials, "A Novel Novel," the first chapter of which had been written by Lady Constance Howard. The magazine explained:

> As a new and audacious venture in the direction of curiosities of literature we offer to our literary minded friends a share in the construction of our twenty-chapter novel, by a score of different writers. . . . Frequently authors working in collaboration consent to a series of what might be called successive "go as you please chapters" before they write the closing scenes. Our own notion is of course of a purely fantastic sort, and we offer it as an experiment, perfectly conscious that it may turn out a very monster of fiction, or it may be a humorous study of the quaint nature of the popular drawing-room game known as "consequences."

A prize of three guineas was offered to the reader who sent in the best instalment each week. Submissions poured in and the magazine got a serial story very cheaply.

So successful was this venture that, in the summer of 1892, Joseph Wood appears to have decided to take it one step further. To enlist not four but *twenty*-four professional authors—twelve men and twelve women—none of them knowing how the story was to turn out—would make Wood's project bigger and better than anything that had gone before, add excitement, and bring publicity to the magazine. It was also a way of getting busy, popular novelists—"toilers" in the field of literature as the *Birmingham Daily Post* described them,[11] who didn't have the time to commit to a full-length serial—associated with the magazine. Arthur Conan Doyle,

Mary Kennard, and Margaret Hungerford all had large followings. Helen Mathers and Florence Marryat were spectacularly popular with women readers; "Frank Danby" (Julia Frankau), "Tasma" (Jessie Catherine Couvreur), and "Rita" (Margaret Humphreys) were daring and modish in their exposes of "high society," whilst George Manville Fenn had a strong male fan base on the basis of his thrilling stories of crime and tales of derring-do. The others were a mixed bunch—the women good all-rounders, representatives of the legion of "lady" novelists "without end,"[12] as "Tasma" put it; the men, examples of what Clement Shorter rather disparagingly termed "the great little men who were flourishing in the nineties";[13] sociable, clubbed men like Bram Stoker, F. C. Philips, and T. H. Lacy, for whom novel writing was a useful sideline.

Serialized between 29 November 1891 and 7 May 1892, *The Fate of Fenella* was thus the product of high-profile writers. But despite this, we have very little knowledge of how it was written; few of the contributors refer to the work in their letters, and scant mention is made in biographies or memoirs. The exception is a 1905 biography by Winifred Stephens of her friend Adeline Sergeant, who was one of the contributors. In the book—an old fashioned piece of late-Victorian hagiography—Stephens claims that, true to its publicity, the novel was indeed "developed chapter by chapter, without any collaboration and any pre-concerted plan." Stephens speculates: "It must have been a matter of regret to our author that, when her turn came, her pet shipwreck incident had already been introduced into the story by one of her predecessors; she contrived however, by the adoption of another favourite sensational device, the anonymous letter, to still further darken the already frowning fate of Fenella."[14]

These assertions do not shed much light on the planning or composition of the novel—but they are a reminder—as, of course, is the novel's title—that *The Fate of Fenella* was a work deeply imbued with the populist literary culture of its day. The novel's origins lie very clearly in the realm of sensation fiction made famous by the likes of Wilkie Collins, Mary Braddon, and Ellen (Mrs. Henry) Wood in the 1860s and 1870s. This was a provocative form of writing which took its label from the contemporary theatre's "sensation drama," and drew on the techniques of popular melodrama and newspaper reports of criminal trials in order to bring murder, mystery, adultery, bigamy, illegitimacy, madness, and sexual deviance into the confines of the respectable middle or upper-class drawing room. In *The Fate of Fenella*, the world of Fenella Ffrench is quite literally destroyed when her lover, the Austrian Count de Mürger, is found stabbed to death in Fenella's hotel room in genteel Harrogate and she is charged with his murder. Although she is acquitted, the "stain" upon Fenella's life means that she is shunned by "respectable" society. It also means that she is judged an unfit mother for her young son, Ronnie. Whilst technically a "free woman," "the laws of her country [having] . . . given her back her liberty," she is forced to leave England and inhabit a castaway's existence—a kind of female Robinson Crusoe—taking on the role of what is "other," subversive and marginal.

As this brief summary implies, in keeping with the sensation genre—but also with the demands of serialisation and the need to keep readers "hooked"—the resulting novel is heavily plot-driven and dependent on cliff-hanger instalments. Some critics thought the novel "unnatural and extravagant" for this very reason. *The New York Times* noted that because "each man or woman was bent on making their own chapter end with a climax there are precisely twenty-four *coups de théâtre*."[15] Other critics questioned whether *The Fate of Fenella* is really a collaborative novel at all. They discerned not a spirit of co-operation but competition; a popular analogy was the idea of the novelist as pool player, each one attempting to leave the next with as difficult a shot as possible. As *The Spectator* noted:

> Either stirred by a spirit of emulation or anxious to make matters difficult for the unlucky contributor who follows them, they pile incident on incident. . . . At the end of their chapter they send off the personæ dramatis on long journeys, scattering them to the ends of the earth, and then their immediate successor has to persistently rake them together again before any more progress can be made.[16]

Seen in this light, *The Fate of Fenella* seemed more of a literary sport or game—a narrative which, as Lillian Nayder puts it, is deliber-

ately teasing: "the contributors pursue mystery for mystery's sake
. . . challenging each other with unexpected and bizarre twists and
turns in the plotline, and contesting or revising the claims of those
whose chapters precede their own."[17]

All these elements conspire to make *The Fate of Fenella* an exaggerated version of the popular middle-brow fiction of the day.
Indeed, so exaggerated are its plotlines that it is possible to see
the novel as a deliberate parody or pastiche or as a self-referential
commentary on the 1890s sensation novel. Certainly many of the
characters have their basis in particular narrative conventions of
plot and genre and in their similarity to characters in other fic-
tions. Lucille de Vigny—"[t]hat foreign woman"—resembles any
one of a number of cut-price *femme fatales* on the make who pop-
ulate late-Victorian fiction and melodrama. Oscar Wilde's Mrs.
Cheveley in *An Ideal Husband* (1892) is a notable example. Other
significant elements are also familiar. The use of altered states of
consciousness, together with the concept of dual personalities and
the sense that the self was capable of splitting, which are reflected
in the novel's treatment of Frank Onslow, also recall Robert Louis
Stevenson's *The Strange Case of Dr. Jekyll and Mr. Hyde* (1886) and
Oscar Wilde's *The Picture of Dorian Gray* (1891). The idea of crimes
committed by a "lesion of the will,"[18] that is to say, whilst a person
was not in full control of his or her senses, was also a popular fictional device, featuring in a number of lesser-known novels of the
period. In Florence Severn's *The Pillar House* (1888) a wife murders
her husband's employer whilst sleepwalking; in Florence Marryat's
Blindfold (1890), a young woman under hypnosis is programmed to
push a man over a precipice in the Alps, whilst Iza Duffus Hardy's
A New Othello (1890) reveals how a hypnotist compels a young girl
to enter a man's room in the night and poison him.

Although sensation fiction is one context for the case histories
of Frank and Fenella Onslow, it is sensation fiction re-worked in
such a way as to engage with issues in 1890s culture and society
more generally. It is easy to think of the end of the Victorian
period as one of confidence in Britain's role as "the workshop of
the world," as imperial power and as the prosperous centre of
"self-help," "industriousness," and "civilization." Britain was "the
heartbeat of that great Empire on which the sun never sets," as

Bram Stoker put it.[19] Yet this view of the period as one of stability and "prosperity" can be misleading. There were plenty of people for whom this prosperity sat uneasily with powerful feelings of loss, decline, and uncertainty. A sense that "olde England" had gone for ever, that there were no certainties any more (not even religious ones) was mixed with a feeling that this was a country of mass-produced mediocrity and self-satisfied inhabitants. Overcrowding, poverty, poor standards of national health, widespread unemployment, the increasing momentum of the woman's movement, falling birth rates, and alcoholism fostered a sense that *fin de siècle* Britain was in the throes of a deep-seated malaise. For others, the trappings of civilisation merely hid a crude barbarism. Events such as W.H. Stead's exposé of child prostitution in "The Maiden Tribute of Modern Babylon" (1885), the "Jack the Ripper" murders of 1888, and the Cleveland Street Scandal in 1889, which revealed a homosexual brothel, had uncovered a darker side to the city. Elsewhere, economic, commercial and political competition on the world stage from the USA and Germany, together with the difficulties in maintaining Britain's imperial rule, helped foster a sense that the country was being exhausted by colonial expansion. A sense of Englishness "gone bad" also raised questions about "whose England"?

Out of all these anxieties, the most important context for *The Fate of Fenella* is the urgency with which late nineteenth century writers debated the figure of "Woman." The 1880s saw the emergence of the so-called "New Woman" (a type of "advanced," independent young woman), together with the resurgence of the "The Woman Question" including questions and viewpoints about female emancipation, about a woman's rights to education and professional training and to earning and keeping her own income and property, her ability to make her own decisions, her right to be recognised as an independent legal entity and British subject, and her right to be able to petition for custody of her legitimate children. These developments were seen by some as threats to the presumed stability of Victorian patriarchal culture. As Lynda Nead has noted, the construction of the separate spheres ideology—which assigned woman her proper role as guardian of home and children—and around which so much of Victorian society had been founded, "was part of a wider formation of class identity, nation and empire. . . . International leadership and the domination of foreign competition were believed to depend directly on the existence of a stable domestic base and social stability."[20] But by the 1890s there was a feeling that modern woman was, as Lyn Pykett puts it, "in flight from motherhood, family responsibility and domestic existence."[21] In "Modern Women" (1895), the German feminist Laura Marholm wrote of a "new phase in woman's nature."[22] The following year a writer for *The Era* noted that: "The old-fashioned idea that woman is born to be a kind of domestic breeding animal and a submissive dependent on man is steadily dissolving away; and in its place the notion is growing up that she is intended as a companion, a friend and an ally." Furthermore, "the old fashioned ideal of the superficially accomplished, carefully-caged, and conventionally tutored woman is being abandoned. . . . restrictions removed, woman is capable of meeting man on his own ground and being a very respectable rival."[23]

Yet whilst the position of women had begun to change—in 1894 *The Quarterly Review* noted that "women are now graduates in half a dozen professions and disciples in all"—the ideology of many commentators moved at a much slower pace.[24] *The Gentlewoman* for example, admired intelligent, practical women. Interviewed in 1893, Joseph Wood explained that his contributors were under strict instructions to "regard woman as an intelligent creature, with a soul above *chiffon* merely."[25] Yet at the same time, the magazine also impressed upon its readers the importance of careful household management in terms reminiscent of those to be found in John Ruskin's "Of Queen's Gardens" (1865) which, with its emphasis on the home as a "temple," had helped elevate Victorian married love thirty years earlier.[26] Elsewhere, conservative commentators raged against the ambitious "New Woman" and the "Wild Woman"—the latter characterized at the time by Eliza Lynn Linton as "a woman who does anything specially unfeminine and ugly."[27] The response of many writers to what Grant Allen in 1894 discerned as "that blatant and decadent sect of 'advanced women' who talk as though motherhood were a disgrace and a burden, instead of being as it is, the full realization of woman's faculties, the natural outlet for woman's wealth of emotions"[28] was to try to prevent women from deviating from existing moral codes and seek to re-contain them in a more domestic definition, a pre-lapsarian view of women and one which sustained hard-won masculine identity.

Readers of 1890s literature do not have go very far to realise just how far writers of the period were preoccupied with the issue of "woman": the "monstrous" woman, the adulterous woman, the emancipated woman who committed the cardinal sin of "unsexing" herself by personally rejecting marriage and sacred motherhood altogether. When taken in the context of the "Woman Question," *The Fate of Fenella*—a text of different male and female voices vying for our attention—has quite a powerful dimension to it, becoming a kind of mixing bowl of ideas about woman's "proper" role and allowing us to see how the simultaneity of different positions could exist in practice. The early chapters of the novel set up the sense of romance and intrigue, but they also feed off *fin de siècle* fears about the collapse of moral standards and the future of marriage. In chapter one, written by Helen Mathers, which takes place well before the murder of the Count and the public trial, which destroys Fenella's reputation, there are indications that this noisy, upper-class young woman is not only "loose" but unstable, intemperate, with few sexual scruples and little sense of propriety. "I like a free hand," she says joyfully of her separation from her husband, and she jokes loudly of "picking up" Frank, suggesting her excess of feeling, her instability, her need to be the centre of attention, her immaturity, and her delight in challenging her estranged husband's authority and reputation. As Mathers comments, in what seems to be a deliberate challenge to the sexual double standard: "It couldn't be supposed that because Lord Francis Onslow kicked up his heels rather more than was exactly pretty, Lady Francis Onslow was to be allowed to follow suit."

In a recent study of literary collaboration Jeffrey Masten has suggested that collaboration should be viewed as a space in which the single authoritative voice is broken up rather than reinforced. As he puts it: "to reverse the aphorism: two heads are different from one."[29] Masten is writing about the Renaissance but his comments are relevant to an understanding of the dynamics of *The Fate of Fenella*. Helen Mathers, as a reviewer for *The Spectator* noted, had "invented" Fenella.[30] Yet whilst the twenty-three contributors who followed Mathers had to take her description as their starting point, they did not have to endorse it completely. Thus some of them demonstrate a much more ambivalent relation to the heroine's representation and to the issues of gender and female subjectivity this involves. Notable is chapter ten by Bram Stoker, "Lord Castleton Explains," which forms part of the middle section of the novel. It focuses on Fenella's exile and is striking for its inscription of some of the anxieties he and his society sometimes felt in regard to transgressive women. Not least of these anxieties is the figuring of the unruly woman as a dangerous presence, one troublesome to the stability of the social structure presided over by men. For Lord Onslow and his friend, Lord Castleton, Fenella's very notoriety is, of course, a sign that she is no better than she should be. In contrast, the story of Clitheroe Jacynth's sister, Helen Grandison—as related by F. C. Philips in chapter six—reminds us that respectable women have no story: they stand quietly in their proper place on the side-lines of the action. So while Stoker describes how the trial has "softened" Fenella, he also has her husband's close friend, Lord Castleton, cast doubt on Fenella's brave display of "wifely devotion" in shielding her husband from a charge of murder. Far from being a heroine, Castleton believes that Fenella is no better than she should be, that she took the blame for her husband's crime to cover up a more horrible crime: her own adultery. "Where, then," asks Lord Castleton, "was Fenella's heroism after all?":

> [S]he had taken the blame on herself; but might it not have been that she was morally guilty all the same? Why then had she taken the blame? Was it not because she feared that her husband might have refused to screen her shame; or that she feared that if any less heroic aspect of the tragedy were presented to the public, her own fair fame might suffer in greater degree? Could it be that Fenella Onslow was not a heroine, only a calculating woman of exceeding smartness?

Within the context of the novel, Lord Castleton's dismissive reaction to Fenella's self-sacrifice illustrates the misogyny inherent in the ways in which men respond to women. Fenella falls and hence becomes a threat to the stability of society, which is based on the control of women's sexuality. She is presented by Stoker without apparent irony as a sexually compromised woman and to *The Gentlewoman's* more impressionable women readers there could hardly be a stronger deterrent to transgressing than the misery which informs the disgraced Fenella's sense of herself as an outcast, sent "mad" with shame before collapsing into a near-fatal attack of brain fever. This, together with Stoker's comments on "the protective feeling which is part of a woman's love," makes it possible for the novel to be interpreted as a discourse on the process of constructing gender identities and the binary oppositions which sustain them. Surrounded as he is in the pages of *The Fate of Fenella* by a number of progressive "New Women" women writers—amongst them "Tasma," Mary Kennard, and Clo Graves—Stoker depicts the stereotype of the unruly woman with a degree of distaste, while at the same time positioning the heroine so that we feel some sympathy for her, particularly in light of the entrenched (hypocritical) male attitudes she is up against. He and the other more conservative novelists—F. C. Philips, Clement Scott, Emily Lovett Cameron, Margaret Hungerford—position us as readers so that we become voyeuristic spectators of Fenella's misery.

The second part of *The Fate of Fenella* is also concerned to stress the kinds of negotiations that any woman might be expected to undertake in order to meet society's expectations. Most of the contributors—even a supposedly risqué novelist such as "Frank Danby"—use the heroine's enforced separation from her son and her solitary exile under a false name to rehearse a fairly predictable idealization of motherhood and female passivity:

> He had spoken to her of her boy, and the cold emptiness of her heart ached with the sudden rush of emotion as she cried out, with outstretched arms: "My boy! Bring me my boy!" To press the child in her arms, to feel the soft down of his cheek against hers to hear the lisping "Muzzer, muzzer dear!" from his lips, to have his arms around her—this, this would save her reason. She felt her reason going, felt her mind darkened, the path before her no longer clear.

Fenella's punishment—her "fate" as it were—and her resulting hysteria is an upper-class version of the fate that befalls the majority of "fallen" women in nineteenth-century fiction—intended to serve as a powerful object lesson in the necessity of self-control and of accepting things as they are. But at the same time, the novel reveals how masculinist structures, which depend in part on the subjugation of women, are made possible. Whilst its contributors do not offer an explicit feminist critique of their society in the way that for example, outspoken "New Women" writers of the 1890s such as George Egerton or Mona Caird do, it is difficult to read some of the chapters without noticing that they are clearly interested in the underside of domesticity, in female lives lived in a male dominated society, and the indoctrination and victimization which this may involve—as well as the chances for escape. When it comes to keeping Fenella in her proper place, ideological inscription is supplemented by male coercion and by a powerful display of masculine moral superiority and activity—of the kind some commentators of the day claimed was sorely needed. Seen in this light—and despite the fact that Fenella seems as egotistical at the novel's end as she is in the beginning—it could be argued that *The Fate of Fenella* can be read as an exposé of the way in which a patriarchal society manages to keep women in a slave-like position at the same time as fostering in them the belief that their own desires are sinful and in need of policing. Fenella is transported off to Guernsey, given a small allowance and separated from her son ("for his own good") by the novel's stock chivalric hero, Jacinth Clitheroe, in order that she should not further "stain" her son's and her husband's lives. Not only has she forfeited any chance of gaining a place in "respectable" society but also she is no longer deemed a fit nurturer of children. The message seems to be that Fenella has destroyed her very reason for being, her very self.

Throughout the novel Fenella is described as a woman of "impulse and recklessness" and this cannot go unchecked. What seems to unite the novel's authors is a wish to show how destructive Fenella's undisciplined behavior is to her happiness. It is only by reining in this tendency that she achieves contentment. There is considerable emphasis on the necessary acceptance by women of the social structures against which they might be expected to rebel, together with the recurrent spectacle of what Katherine Blake describes as "male dominance as a fact and a wish."[31] The male in this case is the hard-working professional, Clitheroe Jacynth. There is also something very *déjà vu* about the middle chapters charting Fenella's decline into a life-threatening collapse and illness. Hers is the kind of conveniently vague illness which many Victorian novelists found so useful. Fenella herself may become incoherent but her own story is actually very tidy. She emerges from her illness with a restored identity created by her realization of the possibilities inherent in being "a happy wife and mother." Seen in this light *The Fate of Fenella* is escapist but it also propagates a number of ideological messages for *The Gentlewoman's* readers. Alongside the exposé of upper-class excess and indolence, it is most obviously a text designed to remind its female readers of their social responsibilities, of the joys and privileges of the cult of motherhood and of the fact that motherhood is woman's primary duty as a citizen. Simplicity, self-abnegation, nurturing, passivity, these are touchstones of Fenella's new "feminine nature," rather than the insensate love of pleasure which characterizes her at the beginning of the novel. So whilst the novel is suffused with chapters where readers are invited to question the various punishments meted out to the heroine, these narratives are, as in a good many other sensation novels of the time, constantly elbowed out of the way by a more conventional preoccupation with "women's sphere" on the part of the novel's more conservative contributors, and perhaps, it may be said, by *The Gentlewoman's* editor, Joseph Wood. Fenella ends up making do with less, but in settling for less she will be, it is hinted, entirely contented.

Publication and Reception

It is difficult today to re-capture the impact of *The Fate of Fenella*. Almost all of the novelists who contributed to it have become forgotten. The story itself can strike the modern reader as clichéd, implausible and sentimental, with its heavy-handed morality, its conventional emphasis on its heroine who needs rescuing, and its idealized, precocious golden-haired child. At the heart of the novel there is an appreciation, albeit troubled, for women—and men—

marriage and motherhood and the merits of English culture. It can also be useful to see it as the product of a particular community—heavily class-conscious and seemingly snobbish—and of a particular time and place. This is not just the community of Joseph Wood and his authors—many of whom moved in the same middle and upper-class social circles of London—but the "imagined community" (to use Benedict Anderson's phrase)[32] of the *Gentlewoman* with its genteel, domesticated accents and shared interest in "proper," "lady-like" behaviour.

How though was it received? Was it a success? Despite being trumpeted by *The Gentlewoman* as "the most extraordinary novel of modern times,"[33] as a serial the novel did not receive much ongoing criticism. Its impact was sometimes reported as "tremendous" in the literary columns of provincial papers but there is not much sense that it grabbed the public imagination in the way that Joseph Wood had hoped. It wasn't until the novel appeared in volume form in May 1892, near the end of its serial run, that British and American reviewers gave it much consideration. In Britain its price was set at thirty-one shillings and sixpence (a sizeable sum of money in those days). Its British publisher Hutchinson had marketed it aggressively, "puffing" its authors' literary pedigrees. The first print run sold respectably enough, the bulk of its copies going to the metropolitan circulating libraries. The firm then issued a one-volume six shilling edition in September 1892. In North America Cassell brought out a one volume edition for $1.00. Later in the year, the Leipzig firm of Tauchnitz, the leading publishers of cheap reprints for continental readers and tourists, brought out another edition. By 1895 the novel had reached a fifth edition.

Whilst the novel was not the best-seller Wood had hoped for, the evidence of the periodical press shows that the literary reviewers took *The Fate of Fenella* seriously, although praise was muted. *The Academy* pronounced it "an ingenious success,"[34] but the country's other influential literary journal, *The Athenæum*, was cautious in its praise, calling the novel "a somewhat startling experiment" but suggested that it did not live up to expectations: "of collaboration in the real sense there is none . . . . comparison of the styles of the different contributors to the story night be interesting and amusing, had not individual peculiarities and mannerisms been, with one or two exceptions, almost wholly subordinated to the common cause."[35] The fastidious *Spectator* likewise reckoned the multi-authoring of the novel its selling point but also its downfall, for "the homely adage of the broth that was spoiled by too many cooks may be applied to literature as well as to the kitchen." "The plot is ridiculous; the characters waver and change from chapter to chapter," whilst "the absence of any preconceived plan must have robbed the writers themselves of any interest that they might otherwise have taken in the characters with which they had to deal—for what interest could they take in a personage when they did not know whether he would live through three volumes and be happy ever afterwards, or whether he would not be killed in the very next chapter?" The result was "a fairly readable novel" albeit telling "an extremely silly story."[36]

Other reviewers, however, found *The Fate of Fenella* not merely ridiculous but also distasteful. The novelist George Moore called it a "literary crime,"[37] whilst in the United States, *The New York Times* called it "a precious mess." The objections were not to its content but to the project itself which was seen to be bringing the "Art" of novel-writing into disrepute. "It seems a pity that some of the literary people who have reputation at stake, should have stooped to this kind of thing," continued the *Times* and implied that the better writers were simply prostituting themselves in a kind of literary freak show.[38] To other observers, the novel represented a move away from a pure (romantic) vision of authorship incorporating the solitary genius towards a new unromantic writing in which the author was simply a hand for hire. Moreover, the project was symptomatic of the "catch-penny side of literature," where writing was a question of money rather than art. According to *The Graphic*: "Four and twenty authors, nearly all of more or less distinction, have been found to insult their art. . . . The practical result is the use of their names and autographs to advertise a proof that two dozen clever people may collectively be equivalent to a single imbecile."[39] In Ireland, the *Belfast Newsletter* reviewed the novel alongside Rudyard Kipling's *Barrack Room Ballads*. *The Fate of Fenella*—"a patchwork that can scarcely be read with pleasure expect by persons whose ideal novel is of a very humble type"—not surprisingly suffered by comparison—being a project of staggering "vulgarity." "Our American friends have a covering which they call a crazy quilt. 'The Fate of Fenella' is a literary crazy quilt."[40]

Where then should we place *The Fate of Fenella* today? Although the impact of *The Fate of Fenella* rested almost entirely upon the reputation of its contributors rather than any critical acclaim, the project brought together important ideas as well as interesting writers. Since then it has remained one of the most marginalized works of late-Victorian literature, a work that barely registers with historians of the novel. Yet, it is a more intriguing novel than it first appears. Joseph Wood's choice of particular writers and the mixing of their ideas reveal a lot about literary culture of the 1890s. Clearly, not everyone wanted to read Henry James or Thomas Hardy. Despite the novel's seeming conventionality and place within the Anglo-centric and rigidly class-based culture of its time, one of the things which makes *The Fate of Fenella* a more intriguing novel than it first appears, is the way in which it enters into a fluctuating relationship with the cultural values it appears to espouse. It engages with some of the most absorbing topics of the 1890s: marriage and separation, the sexual double standard, male and female sexuality, masculinity, motherhood. As Pamela Gilbert points out in a recent study, popular Victorian writers are often writers who "exemplify Victorian popular literary tastes, and yet who are under-read" despite the fact that they "offer a rich complexity . . . on the culture they represent and create."[41] *The Fate of Fenella* also offers the reader a range of ideological positions and as twenty-first century readers we inevitably question some of them. The novel collaborative origins add to this sense of ideological schizophrenia feel, but part of the novel's interest is the way in which its can seem revolutionary and reactionary at the same time. As a starting point for rediscovering some of the main concerns of 1890s popular fiction, *The Fate of Fenella* is good value.

Andrew Maunder
University of Hertfordshire

January 24, 2008

NOTES

1 [Unsigned Notice], "London Correspondence," *Birmingham Daily Post* (2 October 1891).

2 [Unsigned Review], "The Fate of Fenella," *Bookseller* (3 June 1892), 518; [Unsigned Review], "New Novels," *The Academy* (23 July 1892), 68.

3 Frederick Greenwood, "Looker On," *Pall Mall Gazette* (1898), quoted in Philip Waller, *Writers, Readers and Reputations: Literary Life in Britain, 1870-1918* (Oxford: Oxford University Press, 2006), 61.

4 Unsigned Review, "The Fate of Fenella," *Bookseller* (3 June 1892), 5186.

5 Unsigned Review, "Four New Novels," *New York Times* (5 June 1892), 19.

6 See Peter D. Macdonald, *British Literary Culture and Publishing Practice 1880-1914* (Cambridge: Cambridge University Press, 1997).

7 Editorial, "The Gentlewoman's Curtsey," *The Gentlewoman* 1 (12 July 1890), 1.

8 Walter Besant, "Of Literary Collaboration," *New Review*, 6 (Feb. 1892) 200-209.

9 Brander Matthews, *With My Friends. Tales Told in Partnership.* (New York: Longmans, Green, & Co., 1891).

10 Ella Wheeler Wilcox, Pauline Hall, P. T. Barnum, Inspector Byrnes, Howe and Hummel, John L. Sullivan, Mary Eastlake, W.H. Ballou, Alan Dale, Maj. Alfred Calhoun, Nell Nelson, and Bill Nye, *His Fleeting Ideal, A Romance of Baffled Hypnotism* (New York: J.S. Ogilvie, 1890).

11 "London Correspondence," *Birmingham Daily Post* (27 April 1888), 7.

12 "Tasma," "Literary Notes from Paris," *Australasian* (16 April 1881), 5.

13 Clement Shorter, *The Sphere* (15 May 1915).

14 Winifred Stephens, *The Life of Adeline Sergeant* (London: Hodder, 1905), 225-226.

15 Unsigned Review, "Four New Novels," *New York Times* (5 June 1892), 19.

16 "The Fate of Fenella," *Spectator* (28 May 1892), 751-752.

17 Lillian Nayder, "Decadent Detection: *The Fate of Fenella* (1891-92) and Mystery for Mystery's Sake" (Unpublished paper delivered at the Victorians Institute Conference, 1999), 4. I am very grateful to Professor Nayder for making available a copy of her paper.

18 Joel Eigen, *Unconscious Crime* (London: Johns Hopkins University Press, 2003), 11.

19 Bram Stoker, *Personal Reminiscences of Henry Irving*, 2 vols. (London: William Heinemann, 1906), I, 342.

20 Lynda Nead, *Myths of Sexuality* (Oxford: Blackwell, 1988), 91.

21 Lyn Pykett, *The Sensation Novel* (Plymouth: Northcote, 1994), 45.

22 Laura Marholm, "Neurotic Keynotes" (1896), in Angelique Richardson (ed.) *Women Who Did* (London: Penguin, 2002), xlix.

23 Unsigned Article, "Women and the Stage," *Era* (May 16, 1896), 3.

24 William Barry, "The Strike of a Sex," *Quarterly Review* 179 (1894), 294, cited in Richardson, *Women Who Did*, xxxvii.

25 Joseph Hatton, *Pens and Pencils of the Press* (London, 1893), 471.

26 John Ruskin, "Of Queen's Gardens," in *Sesame and Lilies, Unto This Last and The Political Economy of Art* (1865; London: Cassell, 1909), 73.

27 Quoted in Sally Ledger, *The New Woman: Fiction and Feminism at the Fin de Siècle* (Manchester: Manchester University Press, 1997), 16.

28 Grant Allen, *The Woman Who Did* (1895), Oxford: Oxford University Press, 1995), 94.

29 Jeffrey Masten, *Textual Intercourse: Collaboration, Authorship and Sexualities in Renaissance Drama* (Cambridge: Cambridge University Press, 1997), 19.

30 "The Fate of Fenella," *Spectator* (28 May 1892), 751-752.

31 Kathleen Blake, *Love and the Woman Question in Victorian Literature* (London 1983), 82-86.

32 Benedict Anderson, *Imagined Communities. Reflections on the Origin and Spread of Nationalism* (London: Verso, 1983).

33 "Literary Notices," *Freeman's Journal Dublin* (23 November 1891), 8.

34 Unsigned Review, "New Novels," *Academy* (23 July 1892), 68.

35 Unsigned Review, "New Novels," *Athenæum* (28 May 1892), 693.

36 Unsigned Review, "The Fate of Fenella," *Spectator* (28 May 1892), 751-752.

37 Cited in Joseph Hatton, *Pens and Pencils of the Press* (London, 1893), 472.

38 Unsigned Review, "Four New Novels," *New York Times* (5 June 1892), 19.

39 Unsigned Review, "New Novels," *The Graphic* (9 July 1892).

40 Unsigned Review, *Belfast Newsletter*.

41 Pamela Gilbert, *Disease, Desire and the Body in Victorian Women's Popular Novels* (Cambridge: Cambridge University Press, 1997), 7. See also, Nicola Thompson (ed.), *Victorian Women Writers and the Woman Question* (Cambridge: Cambridge University Press, 1999).

A Note on the Text

The Fate of Fenella was first published in serial form, in *The Gentle-woman*, from 29 November 1891 to 7 May 1892. It was first published in book form in April 1892 by Hutchinson in Britain and Cassell & Co. in America. There are slight variations between the British and American first editions. Most of the changes are trivial and none of them affect the development of the story. Most are matters of spelling and phrasing. The present text is based on the first one-volume British version, published by Hutchinson in 1892.

The Fate of Fenella

EDITOR'S NOTE

THAT twenty-four well-known writers should each be able to affirm "I wrote a twenty-fourth part of that Novel" is sufficiently striking even in these days of literary collaboration. But that each should further be able to say that "I did so without any collaboration whatever, without a word exchanged, or a reference made, to my fellow-workers" will, I think, be regarded as somewhat startling.

That I have survived to write this note is attributable to the fact that there was no collaboration in the ordinary sense of the word. Had it been otherwise the ten months of patient labour involved in the matching off a dozen pairs of authors and authoresses must have produced a literary "Frankenstein" which would have fallen upon and pulverized me, as soon as life was breathed into it, by twenty-four persons discussing plot, plan, and characters from twenty-four points of view.

Mr. Walter Besant has said, in reference to collaboration in novel writing,[1] that there must be one dominant mind responsible for the production of the work of two or more collaborateurs. It would be a little difficult to apply the story in this case, where the novel has been developed chapter by chapter, without plan. I leave it to the intelligent reader to discover the "dominant mind" in the "Fate of Fenella."

This is the first appearance of the Novel in book form, though the story has been told week by week in the pages of *The Gentlewoman*, for which journal it was specially written.

J. S. WOOD
Howard House,
Arundel Street,
Temple.

April 1892.

THE FATE OF FENELLA.

CHAPTER I.

"FENELLA."

BY HELEN MATHERS.

"And dinna ye mind, love Gregory,
    As we twa sate at dine,
How we changed the rings frae our fingers,
    And I can show thee thine?"[1]

HER hair, gloves, and shoes were tan-colour, and closely allied to tan, too, was the tawny, true tiger-tint of her hazel eyes. For the rest, she was entirely white save for her dark lashes and brows, the faint tint of rose in her small cheeks, and a deeper red in her lips that were parted just then in a spasm of silent, delighted mirth. She stood on the top steps of the Prospect Hotel, Harrogate,[2] waiting for the coach to come round, and looking across the hotel gardens to the picturesque Stray[3] beyond, upon which an unique game of cricket was just then going forward, to the intense diversion of all beholders. Two little boys had evidently started it on their own hook, and a variety of casuals had dropped in to bear a hand, the most distinguished of these being a nigger minstrel,[4] who, in full war-paint, and with deep lace ruffles falling over his sooty hands, was showing all his white teeth, and batting with a prowess that kept the whole field in action.

"I hope Ronny won't get his pate cracked," said the girl, half aloud, as the four greys drew up with a flourish, and the usual bustle on the steps began. "Good morning, George!" and she nodded brightly to the good-looking driver, who beamed all over, and touched his hat, for the girl had clambered to many a pleasant drive beside him during the past fortnight.

"Box-seat again!" snapped a spiteful female voice behind her. "I *wonder* she is allowed to monopolise the best seat as she does, day after day!"

The girl laughed, as giving a brief glimpse of a soft mass of whiteness above silken hose, she swung lightly up to the perch that was indeed wide enough to accommodate three persons, though the privilege of occupying the third lay entirely within George's jurisdiction, and was never, save to an old favourite, accorded.

"Where are we going to-day?" she said, as she settled herself comfortably, and unfurled a big tan-colour sunshade. "Not to any of those tiresome show-places, I hope? I'm *so* tired of them!"

"No, miss," said George, who refused, even in the teeth of Ronny, to recognise her as anything but a slip of a girl, "we're going for a drive of my own; just dawdling about a bit like, and nowhere in particular."

"Jolly!" she said, sniffing up the pure air as if she loved it, and with that delightful quality of enjoyment in her voice which acts like an elixir on surrounding company. "Do you know, I mean to come up here every year to drink the waters, for I've got to *love* the place!"

George looked delighted as he glanced round to see if all his cargo was aboard, but as usual everyone was waiting for the inevitable person who is *always* late, and who will probably be late for his own funeral if he can possibly manage it.

"Most people who come here once come again, miss," said George, twisting the lash of his whip into a knot. "There's one gentleman who never misses a season, and I was going to ask you, as a favour, if you'd mind his coming on the box-seat this morning? He 'most always had it last year. I told him I must ask a lady's consent, so we're to pick him up outside the Pump-room⁵ if you're quite agreeable."

"Is he fat?" said the girl dubiously, and feeling that her drive would be quite spoiled.

"He's as slight as a poplar," said George, his face lightening up, "and he's a gentleman, miss, and you can't say more than that. There's so few of 'em about nowadays!"

The cargo was now complete. The miscellaneous crowd that daily assembled to witness the departure of the coach fell back, the horses stretched out into a gallop, and skirting the hotel garden, with its lounging seats, and cheerful awnings, rounded the corner with a flourish, emerging on the Stray with a musical horn-blowing that made Ronny, in the distance, hold up his little flushed face to his mother, and wave the bat he was so very seldom allowed to use.

The girl waved and kissed her hand lovingly to the boy, and the nigger, appropriating the compliment to himself, and promptly returning the same, while he also tried to combine business and pleasure by hitting a ball, lost his balance, and sat down in a large puddle. Quaint and varied were the aspects of life afforded by the Stray, that curious piece of ground secured to the townspeople for ever, that in some parts almost resembles a fair; while in others, ancient trees shut in stately houses that have all the dignity and peace of a cathedral close.

In the open a band was playing, nigger minstrels were performing, children played, old maids cackled, pigeons flocked, fortune-tellers plied their craft, and old couples sat side by side like puffins, warming themselves in the sun. Even the inevitable groaning Salvation Army lasses and lads were there, combining piety and health with that astuteness which is so distinguishing a feature of their peculiar religion.

And the thoroughly English scene, so full of human life, and steeped through and through with such a glory of September air and sunshine as even summer had never dared to promise, or even tried to fulfil, gave extraordinary pleasure to the heart, making one feel, with Lucretius, that "he who has grown weary of remaining at home often goes forth, and suddenly returns, inasmuch as he perceives he is nothing better for being abroad."[6]

Down the steep incline in George's smartest style, past the Crown Hotel,[7] that should surely be at the top of the hill, not the bottom, and so to the Pump-room, where with a clash and a clatter he draws up, scanning the crowd of people, who, having drunk their nauseous doses inside, are dawdling and gossiping in true Harrogate fashion before they disperse.

The girl does not take the trouble to look at any of them, not

even when George touches his hat, and says, "Here, my lord."
Then there is the sensation as of a person ascending the coach, on
her side, she indignantly notes, so that she hastily whispers,—

"Couldn't he go on your other side, George?"

"Very sorry, miss, but couldn't drive that way," and then she
draws her skirts close to her with head turned aside, as her unwel-
come coach-fellow swings himself into the seat beside her.

She is so slight, so small, that after all there is ample room and
to spare, especially as he answers to the graceful description of
him furnished by the driver.

"Do you call this a new drive?" she says to George, as they rattle
past the lovely Bogs Valley Gardens,[8] and up the steep ascent to the
Spa. "Why——"

"*Fenella!*" breathlessly exclaimed a voice beside her.

"*Frank!*"

Two aghast, petrified young faces looked into each other; then
the girl, recovering herself first, said,—

"Pray, how do *you* come here?"

"And what brings you?" he retorted.

"Gout. What are you laughing at?" she said airily; "haven't I
got ancestors? Didn't they drink October ale by the hogshead, and
old port by the gallon? And *I've* got to pay the piper, for I never
heard of the liquor hurting *them*. But talking of ancestors, I've
got such a lovely story to tell you. There is a frightfully fat, vulgar
woman at our hotel, and you know there are only two things in
this sinful world that give me real fits—humbug and vulgarity.
Well, this woman never for one single meal lets anybody forget
her progenitors, and bawls out at the top of her dreadful voice,
'*All* my people are cavalry people!' And what do you think? Her
uncle keeps a pork-shop not far from here, so after all she's perfectly right in her boast, only the cavalry are—Pigs!"

Frank laughed.

"You are as bad as ever, I see," he said, and then glanced at the
driver, who had averted his head as much as possible.

"George," said Fenella, putting a coaxing little face round his
shoulder, "could you—*would* you mind putting a bit of cotton
wool in your ear on this side, because I want to talk to—to Lord
Francis? I've got a bit in my pocket somewhere, I know!"

George's face flickered, as he expressed himself quite agreeable, but was rather surprised, as blue-blooded people usually talk before their inferiors as if they had no more hearing and understanding faculties than tables or chairs. When the wool was produced out of a smart little pocket, he proceeded to plug his ear gravely, and even rammed it down hard to show that his intentions were strictly honourable. This business over, Fenella turned round and showed a little laughing face that seemed to have caught all the sunshine of the day, ay, and held it fast.

"I always carry a bit in my pocket for Ronny," she said, "as he gets a touch of ear-ache sometimes. What's that? They can hear us behind? Oh! no, the trot of the horses' feet swallows up our voices. Let them talk. They will say I picked you up!"

"So you did. Do you know any of them?"

"Heaven forbid! A woman, my dear, who *never* sits in the drawing room with the other ladies," said Fenella, adroitly mimicking a sour female voice, "there *must* be something wrong about her. And so there is," she added, below her breath, and for a moment the little face grew hard.

"How is Ronny?" said Frank.

"He is very well," she said, nonchalantly. "Poor wee man, isn't it a good job he isn't a girl? And he hasn't begun to grow ugly and horrid and masculine yet—he is all mine, mine!"

The mother's love in her rang out triumphantly, and her face grew very tender.

"We have such good times together, he and I," she went on happily; "he is not with me to-day, because he is playing cricket at the present moment. We go down to the Stray with the bat and stumps, and forage round for a scratch team. I took a hand myself the other day, and actually bowled out a butcher's boy!"

Frank laughed, then shook his head. "You are quite as mad as ever," he said. "Where is your companion?"

"I *hope*," said Fenella calmly, "that she is dead. I didn't try to polish off any of the other ones, because they meant well in spite of their aggravatingness, but she was downright *wicked*. So I led her a life," she concluded, looking as triumphantly happy as a child who plays truant on a glorious day with a pocketfull of pennies and burnt almonds.

Frank shook his head sadly.

"Why won't you be good, Fenella?" he said. "You could be so easily."

"I always am," said Fenella promptly, and nodded her curly head close to his nose. "I take sulphur baths,[9] and regularly *sneeze* sulphur. I get up every morning at half-past seven. Just think of that! It's a fearful scramble, because Ronny never will wake up. He sleeps just like you, for ever and ever." She stopped, and coloured vividly, then dashed on again breathlessly, "And of course it takes some time to dress him."

"You have no nurse, no maid?" he exclaimed, in amazement.

"No," she replied with great *sang-froid*, "I like a free hand, and no woman can have that, with a female detective tripping up her heels, and wearing her silk stockings. And I love to wait on Ronny—to wash and dress him, and make him look sweet. Of course," she added anxiously, "he isn't *always* clean—the dirtier a boy is, the nicer he is—but he is *perfectly* happy! You should see us run down the hill to the Pump-room, though everyone has done long before we get there! And then we eat *such* a breakfast. We've got a dear little fat waiter who simply devotes himself to us, and steals for us all the newest eggs. But he had an awful accident yesterday," said Fenella, turning tragic eyes on Frank; "what do you think it was?"

"He fell in love with you?"

Fenella began to laugh in that low gurgle which was so like the sound of a cheerful, overfull brook.

"Do you remember you said that about my hairdresser? And how I said I thought it would really have come cheaper in the end if I *had* married him? I always thought that rather neat myself. But I never told you what the accident was. He broke four hundred plates yesterday!"

"Very greedy of him if he did it all at once."

"It *was* all at once. The strap of the lift broke as he was hauling them up!"

"Poor devil!" said Frank absently.

They were quite away from the houses now, and the brisk, pure air, the pleasant scents from the hedgerows, and the swift movement to the music of the horses' feet, and perhaps some other sources of satisfaction within, brought a light to Fenella's eyes, and a rose-soft colour to her cheek that made her altogether enchanting and sweet.

"And pray," said Frank, looking at her eagerly, unwillingly, as at forbidden fruit that sorely tempted him, "do you *talk* to any of the fellows at the hotel?"

"No," she said airily, "they talk to me. You see, they are all so fond of Ronny."

"No doubt," said Frank, curtly and significantly.

"But I pretend not to hear. Stay—there is *one* man whom I talk to——"

"Who is he?" said Frank, grimly, and looking straight between the horses' ears.

"Oh, nobody in particular," said Fenella, rather faintly; "but you see he has a small nephew here, and it seems he and Ronny met at the Grandisons in the country, and are quite old friends. So the barrister and I have got quite pally."

Frank sat mute as a fish.

"He is of the type I rather admire," she said, with a suspicious note in her voice. "You know, Frank," she lifted a naively impudent, grave little face to his, "I always *did* like a dark, clean-shaven man!"

Frank himself was as dark and clean-shaven as it was possible to be, and the corners of his mouth trembled at her audacity, as he turned away.

"He told me such a delicious story yesterday," she went on, her face breaking up into dimples. "It was about a little girl upon whose mother a horrid old woman was calling. When the old woman got up to depart, she said to the child, 'You'll come and see me, my dear, won't you?' 'Oh, yes!' said the child. 'But you don't know where I live?' 'Yes, I do,' said the child, nodding. 'I know who is your next-door neighbour.' 'Who is that?' says the old woman. 'Why, *mother* says you are next door to a fool!'"

But Frank did not smile. It is curious that a man's sense of humour is usually entirely in abeyance when matters of stern import engross him, while a woman's is usually at its keenest when tragedy is in the air.

"What do people think at the hotel?" he burst out in the undertone both had maintained throughout the conversation.

"That I am a widow," she said, coolly; "that is to say, if they turn up the hotel list of visitors."

"What name have you inscribed?" he said coldly.

"Fenella Ffrench. I suppose I have a right to my own name?"

"And the child's?"

"Ronny Onslow."

"What are your trustees about?" he broke out, with subdued passion.

Fenella shrugged her slender shoulders, and laughed. "I was twenty-four years old yesterday," she said, with apparent irrelevance; "did you remember?"

"I remembered," he said curtly.

"Talking of trustees," she said, "will you ever forget the talk, and fuss, and documents that day at Carlton House Terrace? I couldn't help thinking of Lady Caroline Lamb,[10] and how, when she and her husband were required to sign the deed of separation, the pair of them could nowhere be found! When discovered at last, Lady Caroline was on her husband's knee, feeding him with bread and butter! But, though they parted, he loved her all the time," went on Fenella, the little mocking voice grown suddenly wistful; "and it was on *his* faithful breast that she pillowed her dying head at last, and his kind voice that sped her on her way!"

"Yes," said Frank, in a strained voice; "her faults were more of head than heart. But some women have not even hearts for faults to be bred in. Why did you do it?" he said suddenly, with a mist before his own eyes that hindered him from seeing the tears in hers.

"Hi! Onslow! I say, *Onslow!*" shouted a voice that seemed to come from beneath the horses' feet, and both the young people peeped over to see a fat little man in white linen clothes, standing on tiptoe in the road, and blowing out his cheeks like a cherub's.

"Why, Castleton!" cried Frank, "what are you doing there?"

"Walking down my fat, dear boy. I was looking heavenwards, and saw you coming. Where do you hang out? Beastly water— rotten eggs, rusty iron, and a dash of old Nick. Oh, I say!" (catching sight of Fenella, not quite hidden by her sunshade) "is that really—well, you know, really—I *am* astonished—and delighted, *too!* I always said——"

"Drive on!" roared Frank, and on they went upon the instant, and Frank turned to look at Fenella. She was very pale, and very angry, with all the summer gladness gone out of her eyes and lips.

"Frank," she said, "never, *never* will I submit to be made ridiculous. By to-morrow this time, the story will be all over the London clubs. Drive back to Harrogate with you I will not, and either you get down, or I will."

Frank never moved.

"George!"

"Yes, my lady."

She stamped her little foot.

"How dare you call me that?" she said, in a furious under-breath. "Put me down!"

George never budged an inch. The trot-trot of the horses' feet maddened her, and she sprang up.

"Fenella," said Frank, winding his arm round her waist, "if you don't sit tight, I'll put you on my knee, and keep you there, and then I'll *kiss* you."

CHAPTER II.

KISMET.[1]

BY JUSTIN H. MCCARTHY, M.P.

"But, ah, that Spring should vanish with the rose,
That youth's sweet-scented manuscript should close."
OMAR KHAYYAM.[2]

"HULLOA, Jacynth!"

Jacynth awoke from his reverie with a start and stared at the speaker. He had quite forgotten where he was. Through the grey smoke of his cigarette he had conjured, as from some magic vapour, an enchanting face—a girl's face—with hazel eyes and wonderful tan-coloured hair. He had been in dreamland, and now he was only in the gardens of the hotel, and instead of his exquisite vision he found facing him a fat little man in white linen, who looked very hot and very jolly.

"I say, Jacynth, don't you remember me?"

Jacynth did not remember, at least fully. He had a dim consciousness that the fat little figure ought to be familiar to him, but he could not remember where or why. He had not quite collected himself yet, and he was slightly annoyed at the interruption to his day-dream. Also he was annoyed at being annoyed and being discomposed by anything. No perplexing witness, no hostile counsel, no antagonistic judge had ever been known to ruffle Clitheroe Jacynth's imperturbability. But then no vision with tan-coloured hair and hazel eyes had ever come into court with him. He looked at the fat white figure, and shook his head gravely.

"But I say, hang it all, Jacynth, don't you remember that night in Cairo, and the dancing girls and the hasheesh den, and the row and all the rest of it?"

Memory asserted herself in Jacynth's mind. He did remember a night in Cairo when a party of young fellows from Shepheard's[3] set out to see something of the queer Cairene slums. The fat little man was of the party; he was in white then, too, Jacynth remembered. He remembered, too, how hugely the little man had enjoyed everything, from the—well, the eccentricities of the dancing girls to the fumes in the hasheesh den, and even to the final scrimmage in the gambling hall, when Jacynth by a timely stroke saved his fat companion from being knifed by a Levantine[4] rogue who had been detected in cheating. There was an awful row. afterwards; he remembered that, too, and an awkward business before the authorities next morning, but the names of his friends and his own legal reputation settled the matter. Yes, he remembered the fat little man now. He got up with a smile on his dark, clean-shaven face and held out his hand.

"How are you, Lord Castleton?"

Lord Castleton laughed. That was his way. He went through life laughing, as if everything were the best joke in the world.

"I'm glad you haven't forgotten me," he said. "By Jove! I haven't forgotten you, and that turn of the wrist which sent that Levantine devil's toothpick spinning. Well, and how are you?"

The men had sat down beside each other on the garden chair. Castleton produced a cigarette-case almost as fat as himself, on which a daintily-painted ballet girl disported.

"Try one!" he said; "they are ripping. Bingham Pasha sent them to me himself. He got them from the Sultan."[5]

Jacynth took a cigarette, lit it from the end of his own, Castleton watching him all the time with the most jocular expression.

"You're not looking very fit," he said. "Those confounded courts, I suppose. By Jove! I shouldn't like to be a lawyer."

"Oh, I'm all right," Jacynth said; "I'm not taking the waters here. My sister lives here, and I've a festive little nephew. I only came here for a rest. I don't quite know why I came here just now though. Kismet, I suppose."

As he spoke that same vision of face and hair and eyes floated up before him.

Castleton laughed more boisterously than ever.

"Ah! Kismet, the dear old word. Yes, I suppose it's fate that makes us do most of the things which we seem to do for no particular reason."

"Has Kismet brought you here?" Jacynth inquired. "You seem fit enough, at all events."

"Fit, my dear fellow? Not at all."

It was one of Castleton's little jocularities with life to consider himself likely at any moment to become a confirmed invalid. "I was up in Bagdad, and I picked up an English paper which said that Harrogate was looking lovely, and somehow I felt homesick and seedy, and all that sort of thing, so I just cut the East and came slap on here."

"Do you know," said Jacynth gravely, "that there are moments when I feel much more inclined to cut the West and go, as you say, 'slap on' to some sleepy Eastern place—Bagdad perhaps, or Japan—and dream away the rest of my life."

"The rest of your life? You talk as if you were ninety!" And Castleton slapped his fat little leg merrily.

"Don't you know what the man-at-arms says in Thackeray's ballad?" Jacynth replied. "'Wait till you come to forty year.'⁶ Well, I have come to forty year, pretty nearly. I was thirty-nine three weeks ago—and do you know, Castleton, there are times when I'm tired of the whole business."

"By Jove! what would the judges say if they heard the famous Clitheroe Jacynth talking like this?"

"My dear fellow, I'm not famous, and if I were, what's the good of being famous at the price of becoming a fossil?"

"Do you know," said Castleton, with a grin, "I believe you must be mashed on somebody or other, by Jove, I do, if you talk——"

Before Castleton had finished his sentence he became aware that Jacynth was not paying him much attention. In fact, Jacynth's gaze seemed to be directed very intently toward the end of the garden, and Jacynth's mind appeared to be giving no heed whatever to Castleton's amiable garrulity. So Castleton, following the direction of his friend's glance, saw in the distance a woman's form—a form that was familiar to him; a form that he had already seen that day.

"By Jove!" said Castleton to himself softly. He had no time to say more, even to himself, for Jacynth had jumped to his feet and was bidding him good-bye.

"Glad to have met you; hope to see you soon again." These

were the words Jacynth was saying, with a confusion curiously at variation with his habitual composure. He shook Castleton warmly by the hand, and moved away so rapidly that Castleton's "Why, my dear boy, of course you will; I shall stop here for ever so long," was delivered to the empty air.

"By Jove!" Castleton said again, this time aloud, as he watched Jacynth's rapid advance in the direction of the girl. "By Jove, he's struck, like all the lot. Poor devil! I'll stay here and give him a hint presently. Oh, poor devil, poor devil!" And Castleton's jolly face expressed as much honest commiseration as its ruddy plumpness permitted.

In the meantime, Jacynth, walking rapidly, had met the girl. She smiled a welcome to him, and stopped as he stopped. Her face seemed troubled, he thought, in spite of its enchanting smile.

"How grave you look!" he began, for want of anything better to say.

"How grave you look!" she retorted, with a flash of the familiar enchanting audacity, as she looked up into his grave dark face.

"I have something to say to you," said Jacynth. The remark was commonplace enough, but he felt his voice fail as he said it, and he knew by the sudden heat in his face that the blood was filling his pale cheeks.

The sound of his voice evidently impressed the girl, for she looked up at him with a sudden start, and her reply was queerly girlish and puzzled.

"What is it?" Then, as if she felt suddenly conscious of a blunder, or of unexpected knowledge, she tried to add other words,—

"I mean, of course—I do not understand—I am looking for Ronny."

"Ronny is quite safe," said Jacynth, gravely. "He is still at cricket with Harold. What I have to say does concern him, though, a little."

"Concern Ronny!" There was a genuine note of alarm in the girl's fresh voice, and she looked up at Jacynth with a wistful trouble in her eyes. "Concern Ronny! Why, what have you to say about Ronny?"

"Can you give me a few moments?" he asked. "It is quiet here."

He pointed to a pathway more secluded than the rest; a pathway with a rustic garden chair—a deserted pathway. "Shall we sit here for a minute?" he said, and they walked to the rustic seat, and sat down side by side. There was a curious look of alarm in the hazel-coloured eyes, but Jacynth did not notice it, for he was looking down, tracing a word upon the ground with his stick, and the word that he traced was the word he had used but now—Kismet.

"What do you want to say to me?" He could hear a hard ring in her voice, and looking up he saw a hardness in her eyes, and his lips trembled.

"We have been very good friends," he began, and faltered. She caught him up.

"We have been good friends," she said. "If you wish us to be good friends any more you will not say what it is just possible that you may think of saying. There are some words which will estrange us for ever."

Jacynth looked at her despairingly. How exquisitely lovely she looked, like some angel of youth, some vision of summer in that autumnal garden. His heart seemed to be beating very fast, his eyes were hot and his lips dry, and his hands trembled feverishly.

"Listen!" he said, and as he spoke his own voice sounded far away and unfamiliar, like the voice of some shadow encountered in a dream. "Listen! I love you with all my heart. Hush! let me say what I have got to say"—for she had turned to him, half appeal-ing, as if to interrupt his declaration—"I daresay you may think it very audacious of me to love you—or, at least, for I could not help loving you, to tell you so. I know that you are beautiful enough and good enough to be addressed by better men than I. I should have been content with my secret love, and held my peace. But I couldn't—I couldn't!"

He paused for a moment. She laid her hand on his gently, and he trembled at her touch. "I am very sorry," she began, but he went on again wildly,—

"I am not quite a fool. Men who are not quite fools either say that I have a great career before me. I have made something of a name as it is, although I may still almost speak of myself as a young man. You shall be proud of me, indeed, I promise you that, if you will only let me serve you. Life is all a game of chances, but if you will take this chance, I do not think that you will regret it. Your lover will not be quite unworthy of your love."

"I am very, very sorry," she said, "but you have said the words which must divide us. I did like you, I do like you very much, but we cannot be friends any more."

"You cannot love me," he said slowly.

"I cannot love you—and I know we cannot be friends. You are not that kind of man. It would tear your heart to pieces. Better one wrench at once, and be done with it. And I am not the kind of woman to accept a friendship that I knew was only a mask for love."

"You cannot love me?" he asked again monotonously, like a man repeating some set formula.

"I cannot love you. I have played with my life in my own way, and as I have played so I will pay. Now, good-bye, I know you too well and I trust you too well to fear that you will trouble me at all. You will go away, I suppose?"

"Yes," said Jacynth moodily, "I will go away."

"Thank you, and good-bye." She moved away swiftly, and he stood there staring after her until she disappeared inside the hotel.

Jacynth walked moodily back into the garden and stared sullenly at the bright sky. If the autumn day, so warm that it might have been midsummer, had suddenly changed to winter, it could not have looked colder or more dismal to his eyes. He shrugged his shoulders. "So that's all over," he said to himself bitterly; "you have played your stake and you have lost, and now you must remember that it is your duty to play the man and not the fool." Thrusting his hands into his pockets he began to walk slowly down the garden path, feeling very dull and dizzy, like a man who has had a heavy fall. He was thinking, or trying to think, of things which interested him so deeply once, and which now seemed so strangely uninteresting, when his meditations were interrupted. He found himself confronted by Castleton, who was eyeing him sympathetically.

"Old man," said Castleton, "you saved my life once, and though it wasn't much worth saving, I'm devilish grateful to you all the same. So I'd like to do you a good turn now if I can."

"You can't do me any good," Jacynth answered; "there's nothing the matter with me. Don't talk rot, there's a good fellow."

"There's a great deal the matter with you, and I can do you good," Castleton answered. "I can tell you all about that woman."

CHAPTER III.

HOW IT STRIKES A CONTEMPORARY.[1]

BY FRANCES ELEANOR TROLLOPE.

"But this case is so plain . . . that nothing can obscure it,
but to use too many words about it.—JEREMY TAYLOR.[2]

LORD CASTLETON, doubtless, did not literally believe that he could
tell his friend "all about" that woman. But he probably was possessed with the conviction that when he should have said what he
had to say, there would remain little more worth telling. We smile
with a kind of fatigued contempt at the venerable classical joke
of the fool who, wishing to sell his house, carried about a brick
from it as a specimen. We know better how to judge of houses.
But we are willing—sometimes—to pick off a very small fragment
of human life, and to exclaim knowingly, "Look here, I'll tell you
what it is made of!"

Lord Castleton's well-meant offer was not received with
gratitude.

"What woman?" growled Jacynth, taking one hand out of his
pocket to tilt his hat a little more over his eyes.

"Why, Mrs.—Miss—Lady—by Jove, I scarcely know what to
call her!"

"That's a good beginning," said Jacynth sardonically.

"No, no, my dear fellow, I really do know all about her; only
it's—it's a little puzzling where to begin."

"Why begin?"

The fat little gentleman reddened and frowned. Then his good
nature, and his sense of obligation to the other man, and his pity
for him (which, perhaps, rendered the sense of obligation easier to
bear), conquered the momentary irritation.

"The fact is, Jacynth," he said, "I consider it my duty to tell you the story of Fenella Ffrench. No one knows it better than I do. You may hear it told by a score of men in town, who will be a deuced deal harder on the girl than I am. I have no animosity against her, poor little fool—none in the world. In fact, I rather like her."

"Very gratifying to the lady; but—excuse me—not of palpitating interest to me. Good-bye. I think I shall go for a long spin."

"Stop a moment, Jacynth! Did you never hear of Lady Francis Onslow?"

Jacynth turned round sharply and looked at him. "Lady Francis Onslow?" he repeated, putting his hand to his forehead and looking as though he were trying to recall some half-effaced recollections.

"Lady Francis Onslow. She was a daughter of Colonel Fortescue Ffrench, of Crimean[3] celebrity, and she married Frank Onslow when she was only seventeen, and three years afterwards they were separated."

"Is that the woman?"

"That is the woman."

"She looks such a child!"

"I told you she was married when she was only seventeen."

"But he—Lord Francis—he is alive?"

"Very much so! At least he looked alive enough when I saw him about half an hour ago."

"He is *here?*"

"Yes. Look here, Jacynth; just let us take a turn somewhere; here, this is a quiet path, and——"

"No; not there!" said Jacynth, drawing back roughly, as Lord Castleton laid his hand on his arm. It was the pathway where he had just been speaking with Fenella. "I don't know why I should listen to you at all. What does it matter? Nothing you can say will do any good."

Nevertheless, he did listen. What man would not have listened? That he should believe it when it was told was another matter. Jacynth was a clever man—a man of brilliant talents and rising reputation in his profession. He had also certain special gifts which were not so generally recognised. He had a keen and almost intuitive insight into character, and a steady power of incredulity as to a vast proportion of the stories circulated in the "best society" on the "best authority."

At first sight this may seem no very extraordinary power. And perhaps it is not extraordinary, but it is certainly not common. The gossip of the smoking room, the tittle-tattle of the clubs, penetrate, as a fine drizzling rain penetrates one's clothing, into the consciousness of most men.

Men may declare that they give no heed to that sort of gossip; but, as a rule, their minds are porous, and do not resist it. With persons who pride themselves on knowing the world, credulity has almost come to signify believing good of men's neighbours. But Jacynth had often been cynically amused by the childish credulity with which a knot of men at his club would swallow evil stories, intrinsically improbable, and supported by no tittle of evidence that he would have dared to offer to the least enlightened of juries, merely because they were evil. For these gentlemen "knew the world." Something he dimly remembered hearing of the separation which had taken place between Lord and Lady Francis Onslow; but nothing clearly. He had not lived in their world; he did not now live in it.

He had a poor opinion of Lord Castleton's intellect, but he believed him to be as truthful as he knew how to be. Jacynth was quite capable of disbelieving a story against a woman, even though she were young, beautiful, full of impulsive high spirit, and separated from her husband, and even although he had not happened to be in love with her. He did not intend to break a lance on her behalf. He was not given to such breaking of lances, for he also "knew the world." But neither was he going to accept Lord Castleton's statements with the undoubting faith that Lord Castleton seemed to expect. Nevertheless he listened.

"She was an only child, you know," said Lord Castleton, hooking himself on to his companion's arm, so as to speak confidentially in his ear as they walked up and down, "idolized by her father. Her mother died when she was a small child, so she was left to take pretty much her own way ever since she was six years old. Ffrench got some old woman or other to look after her as she grew older—a kind of duenna, you know. But as to controlling her, it was a mere farce. Fenella did as she pleased with the Colonel, and the Colonel did as he pleased with everybody else, for he was a Tartar, and never allowed any member of his household to contradict him—always with the one exception, you know; and so the end of it was that every man, woman, and child about the place had to be Miss Fenella's very humble servant, or had to go. She was the wildest little beggar; used to go tearing about the country on a little Arab horse she had. Once she took it into her head to ride to hounds, and, by George, sir, she went flying over everything that came in her way and was in at the death! The only woman there; just think of that! A child not fifteen riding to hounds quite alone, for the old groom who used to trot about after her could no more keep up with her than if he'd been mounted on a tortoise."

A vision of the slight, straight, fearless young creature, with a wave of tawny hair floating behind her, the wonderful hazel eyes shining, and the delicate cheeks glowing like roses, came vividly before Mr. Jacynth's mind as he listened.

"I know that story's true," continued Castleton. "Old Lord Furzeby, who was Master[4] at that time, and had been hunting the county for twenty years, told me it himself; and said he'd never seen anything like it. However, he called next day on her father, and then Ffrench did put a stop to the hunting. He wouldn't quite stand that."

"Well?" said Jacynth, after a pause.

"Well, that's just a specimen of the way she was brought up. But there were worse things than the hunting, a deuced sight."

"What things?" growled Jacynth, flashing a dark side glance at his companion's round rubicund face.

"I—upon my soul, I think they may be all summed up in one word—flirtation! Of all the outrageous, audacious, insatiable little flirts that ever were born for the botheration of mankind, I suppose Fenella Ffrench is about the completest specimen."

"Poor mankind!" sneered Jacynth, drawing down the corners of his mouth.

"My dear fellow, she began when she was in short frocks. I've no doubt the man where she bought her hoops and dolls was in love with her. And when she began to grow up it was a general massacre."

"Not of the innocents, however," muttered Jacynth.

"Ffrench's place was in Hampshire, not quite out of reach by a drive from Portsmouth, although it was a long pull by road.

And before she was sixteen, Fenella had bowled over the whole garrison.[5] I believe the local chemist expected a wholesale order for prussic acid[6] the day her engagement to Frank Onslow was announced," said his fat little lordship, chuckling at his own wit.

"Where did she meet him?"

"At a garrison ball in Portsmouth. It was supposed to be a case of love at first sight. Regular Romeo and Juliet business, don't you know?"

"Oh! she loved him?" said Jacynth, between his set teeth.

"God knows! she said she did, any way; and made him believe it. As for him, he was desperately mashed."

"And so—and so they married, but didn't live happy ever after."

"No, by George! It didn't last long. For the first year or two, it was all billing and cooing. They took a little place in Surrey, and gave themselves up to rurality and domestic affection. Old Ffrench used to spend half his time there with 'em. And when Fenella's boy was born, they had a story that the Colonel was seen wheeling a perambulator about the garden, and administering a feeding-bottle. It did seem as though Fenella had begun to put a good deal of water in her wine, as the Italians say. They hadn't been married three years when Colonel Ffrench died suddenly. I was not in England at the time. I was in a very low state—all to pieces! In fact, Sir Abel Adamson has since confessed that he thought my nervous system—— However, that will probably not interest you. I set off on a long sea voyage, which they said was my best chance. And, in point of fact, I prowled about for more than a year and a half. It was in Japan that I got hold of an old *Times* with the announcement of Ffrench's death. O-ho! thought I to myself. My Lady Francis Onslow will come in for a nice little pile. She had something when she married. And, of course, Ffrench left her everything he had in the world."

"Then Lord Francis Onslow hadn't made a bad thing of it?"

"A very good thing of it!—from the financial point of view, that is. He was a duke's son; but I needn't tell you that a duke's fifth son——"

"Can't expect to marry a lady from Chicago or New York with millions of dollars in pigs or petroleum.[7] Of course not! That's reserved for his seniors," said Jacynth.

Lord Castleton laughed. But he did not quite like this little speech. He considered himself the least bumptious of men about his rank. But there was something in Jacynth's words—a twang, not only of bitterness, but of contempt—which Lord Castleton inwardly pronounced to be "bad form." But Jacynth was sore, poor wretch,—terribly sore! However, his lordship compressed his narrative somewhat, as being very doubtful what venomed criticism might be lurking in the barrister's mind.

"Well, the main point of the story is what happened after the Colonel's death, and when Frank Onslow and his wife went up to town. Only I thought it well to give you a glimpse of the madcap sort of life the girl had been allowed to lead, because it, to some degree, explains a good deal of her reckless way of carrying on."

Lord Castleton fancied he heard Jacynth mutter under his breath, "Poor child!" But the clean-shaven, firmly moulded jaw looked set and grim when he glanced at it; and a countenance less expressive of any "compunctious visitings" of sentiment than the countenance of Clitheroe Jacynth, barrister-at-law, as it appeared in that moment, it would be difficult to imagine.

"Lady Francis made one of the biggest sensations I can remember, when she began to get into the swing of London society. She had been presented on her marriage, of course.[8] But then Frank had carried her off to the cottage in Surrey, and the world had seen no more of her, so that now she appeared as a novelty. And she is—well, you know what she is to look at. I know dozens of women handsomer by line and rule. But there's something fetching about Fenella that I never saw equalled. And then the old game began again. Fellows were mad about her, and she flirted in the wildest way."

"The Romeo-and-Juliet passion having meanwhile died a natural death?" said Jacynth, staring straight before him.

"Oh, I suppose so. The fact is, she is a butterfly kind of creature that no man ought ever to have taken seriously."

"And the husband——?"

"Frank was—well, the fact is, Frank acted like a fool. He was very young, too, you know. They were like a couple of children together, and used to squabble, and kiss, and make it up like children. Frank never had the least suspicion of jealousy about her, though. Never—until——"

"Exactly!" exclaimed Jacynth, with a nod of the head.

"Well, whether his aunt, old Lady Grizel, put it into his head, or whether he saw something for himself that he didn't like—the fact is, Frank made a scene one night when they came home from a ball at the Austrian Embassy, and Fenella—who is the Tartar's⁹ own daughter when she's roused, I can tell you; dynamite isn't in it!—flared up tremendously, and there was, in short, the devil to pay. Fenella, it seems, had been secretly bottling up a little private jealousy on her own part. There was a certain Madame—her name don't matter; and she has returned to Mongolia or wherever she came from long ago—a certain woman, pretty nearly old enough to be Frank's mother, but a fascinating sort of Jezebel, whom you met about everywhere that season. And Fenella turned round and declared that Frank had been making her miserable by his goings-on with that vile woman!"

"All her foolish fancy, of course!" said Jacynth, suddenly looking at the other man with a penetrating gaze from beneath his frowning black brows.

"Oh—well—you know—— Oh, I dare say Frank had, to some extent, been making an ass of himself. But, of course, the case was totally different."

"Oh, of course."

"Fenella talked like a wild Indian, you know. It couldn't be supposed that because Lord Francis Onslow kicked up his heels rather more than was exactly pretty, Lady Francis Onslow was to be allowed to follow suit. He had taken exception to a certain man—military attaché to one of the Embassies—and forbade Fenella to dance with him or receive him in her drawing room. Needless to say that Fenella made a point of waltzing with him the next night, and of giving him a standing invitation to five o'clock tea. More rows. Family consultations. Aunt Grizel volunteering as peacemaker; I think that was the last straw. Fenella insisted on a separation; she was as obstinate as possible. She would take her boy and leave him. As to the money, he might keep it all. And that sort of wild nonsense."

"But she carried her point? She left him? How was it possible that he let her go?"

"My dear friend, the idea of talking of 'letting' or not letting Fenella Onslow do anything she had set her will on is refreshingly *naïf.* She threatened them that if they did not consent to an amicable arrangement she would bring legal proceedings (on account of the Mongolian fascinator!), and make a scandal. Well, the Onslows hate the name of a scandal as a mad dog hates water."

"Or as a burnt child dreads the fire," put in Jacynth.

"At any rate, among them they cobbled up the deed of separation; and there is poor Frank with a wife and no wife, and the boy—he was devoted to the little chap—taken away from him, at any rate for some years."

"And there is Lady Francis Onslow with a husband and no husband."

"Upon my soul, I believe she's happier without him; upon my soul, I do! All she cares for in life is to flirt; to decoy some wretched fellow into a desperate state about her, and then to turn him off with an impudent little assumption of innocence, and declare she meant nothing. People said there was more in that affair of the military attaché than her usual coquetries. But I don't know. I don't believe she has it in her power to care for any man. However, very few of those who saw the little drama being acted before their eyes take a lenient view of Fenella's conduct. I felt bound to open your eyes, Jacynth. The woman is as dangerous as a rattlesnake. Of course she's gone and made a hideous hash of her own life; but she has done worse than that to other people's lives, and she'll go on doing it. I saw her just now sitting up on the box-seat of the coach beside her husband, and——"

"Beside *whom?*"

"Beside her husband, Frank Onslow. There's nothing she hasn't impudence enough for! It wouldn't surprise me if they were to come together again."

"And that," said Jacynth, walking away by himself, "is what Castleton calls telling me 'all about that woman!' I don't know whom she loves, nor whether she loves anyone at this present moment. But that there are depths of feeling in that girl of which old Castleton is about as well able to judge as a mole of the solar system—— But what's the good of it? I have played my stake and lost it. I—I must get out of this place if I'm to keep any hold over myself at all. How could a raw lad like Frank Onslow value her or understand her? Of course, he was selfish and unreasonable and dull to all the finer part of her nature, like a boy as he is—or was, at any rate, when he married her!" He went up to his room and dragged out a portmanteau. He must get away. There was no use in parleying or delay. Flight—instant flight—was the only thing for him. But when he had opened the portmanteau, and dragged out a few clothes from the chest of drawers, he sat down by the bedside, and buried his face in the pillow. "I love her! I love her!" he moaned out. And then he hated himself for his folly.

At this moment a little childish footstep was heard tramping up the stairs; tap—tap, tap—tap, climbing up with much exertion, but with eager haste, and then a sweet little childish voice said, "Mr. Jacymf, Mr. Jacymf! Are you there?"

Jacynth opened the door with a wildly beating heart. Could she have sent him a message? "What is it, Ronny, my man?" he said, looking down upon the child's curly, tawny hair and bright, innocent, hazel eyes that were so like his mother's.

"Halloa!" cried Ronny, surveying the portmanteau and the litter of clothes on the floor, "are you going away?"

"Yes, old boy."

"Is Grandison going too?"

"No; not Grandison. What do you want, Ronny?"

"I want you not to go away!"

"Anything else?"

"Yes. Why can't you come with us, if you *are* going away?"

"Come with you? Where?"

"With me and Mummy. Mummy says we shall go to a nicerer place than this. And I may play cricket. I wanted you to come and play with me and Grandison. But I s'pose you can't if you're packing your clothes. Ain't they in a jolly mess?"

Jacynth lifted the child up in his arms and kissed him. "Goodbye, Ronny," he said, in a queer, choking voice; and then he set the little fellow outside the door and shut it.

Ronny prepared to make the descent of the staircase, holding tight to the banisters. He put one little chubby finger up to his cheek and looked at it. "Hulloa!" said he, very gravely, "my face is all wet!"

CHAPTER IV.

"BETWEEN TWO FIRES."

BY A. CONAN DOYLE.

"Happier is he who standeth betwixt the fire and the flood,
than he who hath a jealous woman on either side of him.—
Fourth Veddah.[1]

THE single short drive on the Harrogate coach had re-awakened all
Frank Onslow's dormant passion for the capricious and beautiful
woman whom he had made his wife. His weak and pliant nature
was one which could readily forget, and after a few weeks of dull
pain his separation had ceased to be a grief to him, and he had
devoted himself to the turf and the green table with an energy
which had driven his matrimonial troubles from his mind. That
Fenella had at the least been indiscreet in the case of the Count
de Mürger was beyond all question. Further, she had allowed her
indiscretion to be known and commented upon. Domestic unhappiness is ill to bear; but worse still is it to see pitying eyes turned
upon one in society, to read snappy little two-edged paragraphs in
gossiping papers, or in a club smoking-room to see heads incline
towards each other while a swift malicious whisper passes from
man to man. All this is bad to bear; and yet it had been Lord Francis's lot to bear it. It had soured his mind and hardened his heart at
the time of his separation.

But every wound will heal, and this one also had skinned over.
When in the morning he had seen the girlish figure of his wife
perched upon the box-seat, with her yellow hair curling from
under the dainty hat, and looked into the hazel eyes which still
shone with the old provoking, mischievous, challenging twinkle,
he had felt his heart go out to her, and had loved her once more
even as he loved her on that first night when he had plighted his
troth to her after the Garrison Ball at Portsmouth. It maddened

him now to find that, with all the fire of his love, he could not kindle any answering spark in her. Had she turned away from him, treated him coldly, or upbraided him for his conduct, then indeed he might have had hopes. A quarrel might lead to a reconciliation. But that she should treat him as an everyday acquaintance, gossip with him about trivial matters, and break small jests with him, that was indeed intolerable. In vain, through the long drive, he strove to pass the barrier. At every allusion to their married life, or to their quarrel, she either retired into absolute silence or else with quick feminine tact turned the conversation into other channels. If he had forgiven her there was no sign that she in turn had forgiven him.

And who was there who knew better than himself that there was much to forgive? If her name had been coupled with that of the Count de Mürger, had not his been equally and even more openly associated with the notorious Madame Lucille de Vigny? He might have doubts as to his wife's guilt, but he could have none as to his own. If he had been subjected to the degradation of the pity of his fellow men, had not she undergone as much, or more? He remembered now with grief and compunction how day after day, and evening after evening, he had deserted his wife in favour of the society of the fascinating Frenchwoman. He remembered, too, how patient she had been at first; then how her patience had gradually changed to surprise, surprise to suspicion, suspicion to anger, and anger to revenge in the shape of the flirtation which had brought about the separation. Who was he, to blame her? He had himself been the first to sin. Now he was the first to forgive. Would she follow him in the one as in the other?

Alas! it seemed that she would not—that the breach was too broad to be ever again bridged over. Through the bright summer morning, as they rattled past the lines of beech trees, and through the pleasant Yorkshire lanes, he chafed and fretted, but in vain. His sin had been too deep to be forgiven. As he handed her down, when they arrived once more at the Prospect Hotel, he pressed her little hands in his feverish grasp, and looked appealingly into her hazel eyes. There was no answering softness in their glance— nothing but amusement and something akin to contempt. He turned away with a sigh, and wandered slowly off in the direction of the gardens, walking with bent head, and the listless steps of a melancholy man.

Had his eyes not been downcast he might have noticed that he was not alone on the gravelled, hedge-lined walk, which curved down through the pleasant Harrogate gardens. A woman was walking toward him, moving slowly through the rich yellow sunshine, and glancing from right to left with the air of one who is a visitor and a sight-seer. Her light cream dress, her dainty pink sunshade, and her broad shady hat, with its curling snow-white feather, made a pleasant picture to the eye, which was by no means diminished by her approach, for she was a woman of singular beauty. Though past her first youth, the lines of her figure were as graceful and perfect as an artist could desire, while her face, with its dark Southern beauty, its clear-cut, delicate features, and imperious eyes, spoke of a passionate and impetuous nature, such as is seldom to be found among our cold and self-contained Northern races.

Approaching from different ends of the walk, the two had almost passed each other before Lord Francis looked up, and their eyes met. He sprang back with a cry of surprise, and of something approaching to dismay, while she stood quietly looking at him out of sombre, deeply-questioning eyes.

"Lucille!" he gasped. "You are the last person whom I expected to see in Harrogate."

"But I am not surprised," she answered, speaking with a slight French lisp, which added a charm to her rich, deep voice. "I knew that you were in Harrogate. That is why I came."

"But why do you wish to follow me, Lucille? What good can come of it?"

"What good? All good. Is not love good? And do I not love you? Ah, Frank, you taught me to love you, and how can I unlearn it? It is happiness to me to see you and to speak to you."

"But see the misery that it has caused. We must part, Lucille. If you truly love me you will help me to retrieve my life, and not to wreck it further."

"Ah!" cried she, with a quick flash in her dark eyes. "You have seen her. You have been speaking with your wife again."

"Yes, I saw her to-day."

"By chance?"

"Yes, by chance."

"And you are friends again?"

"No, not friends."

"Ah, you wished it, but she would not have it. I can see it in your face. Oh, Frank, how could you humble yourself to such a woman? How could you? To hold out your hand to her, and to be refused! *Quelle dégradation!* See how she has treated you—she, who is not worthy to be the wife of any honest man."

The colour sprang to Onslow's pale cheeks. It was one thing to know his wife's faults, and it was another to hear about them.

"That is an old story," he said curtly. "We may let that drop."

"An old story? Why, she was with De Mürger last week in London."

"Fenella was?"

"Yes, I saw them with my own eyes riding together in the Row."[2]

Lord Francis started as if he had been stung. "Come here!" he said. There was a garden bench in a little recess, and he threw himself down upon it. Lucille de Vigny seated herself beside him, and a triumphant smile played over her dark and beautiful face as she marked with a sidelong glance the anger and chagrin which convulsed her companion's features.

"Is this true?" he cried.

"I tell you, Frank, that I saw them with my own eyes. It is not my custom to say what is not true."

"They were riding together?"

"Yes."

"And talking?"

"Talking and laughing."

"By heavens, I will see that fellow De Mürger. I will shoot him, Lucille! It is not our custom in England to duel. But he is a foreigner. He will meet me. I have wished to avoid a scandal, but if they court one why should I spare them? In the Row, you say?"

"Yes, and just when all the world was there."

"Heavens! It is maddening." He sank his face in his hands, and groaned aloud.

"And what matter, after all?" said she, laying one delicately gloved hand upon his wrist. "Why should you trouble? What is she to you now? She is unworthy, and that is an end. *Tout est fini.* You are a free man, and may let her go her way while you go yours. Which way will be yours, Frank?"

The blood throbbed in his head. He felt her warm, magnetic hand tighten upon his wrist. Her soft, lisping voice, and the delicate perfume which came from her dress, seemed to lull the misery which had torn him. Already, in her presence, the fierce longing for his wife which had possessed him was growing more faint. Here was a woman, beautiful and tender, who did indeed love him. Why should his heart still dwell upon that other one who had brought unhappiness and disgrace to him?

"Which way will be yours, Frank?"

"The same as yours, Lucille."

"Ah, at last!" she cried, throwing her arms about him. "Did I not know that I should win you back?"

A sharp cry, a cry as from a stricken heart, and a dark shadow fell between the pair. Lord Francis started to his feet. Fenella was standing in front of them, her hands thrown out, her eyes blazing with anger.

"You villain!" she gasped. "You false villain!" She put her hands to her throat, and struggled with her words like a choking woman. Lord Francis Onslow looked down, while the blood flushed to his temple. Madame de Vigny stood beside him, her hands folded across each other, and a look of defiance and anger upon her face.

"I came out here to tell you that I had forgiven you. Do you hear? That I had forgiven you. And this is how I find you. Oh, I shall never forgive you now—never, never, never! Why were you so nice to me this morning, if you meant to treat me so?"

"One word, Fenella!" cried Onslow. "Answer me one question, and if I have wronged you I will go down on my bended knees to you. Tell me truthfully, and on your honour, were you in the company of De Mürger last week?"

"And if I were, sir?"

"Were you or were you not?"

"I was."

"You were with him in the Park?"

"I was."

"Then that is enough; I have no more to say. Madame, let me offer you my arm!" He walked past his wife with her rival, and the dresses of the two women would have touched had Fenella not sprung back with a cry of disgust, as one who shrinks from a poisonous thing. Madame de Vigny laughed, and her proud sparkling eyes told of the triumph which filled her soul.

Fenella Onslow stood for an instant in the middle of the sunlit walk, her little right hand clenched with anger, her gaze turned towards the retreating figures. Then a sudden lurid thought flashed into her mind, and she started off as rapidly as she could in the direction of the railway station. Clitheroe Jacynth's train did not leave for ten minutes. Ronny had told her of the hour of his departure. The barrister was standing, moody and disconsolate, upon the platform, when he felt a light touch upon his shoulder, and looking round, saw a flushed little woman with sparkling eyes looking up at him.

"Fenella!" he cried.

"Yes; you must not go."

"Not go?"

"No, you must come back."

"You bid me?"

"Yes, I bid you. You must come back to the hotel."

"But it was you who this very morning drove me away from it."

"Forget it. Many things have happened since then. Will you not come?"

"Of course, I will come."

"Then give me your arm."

And so it happened that as Lord Francis Onslow and Madame Lucille de Vigny stood at the door of the Prospect Hotel after their walk, they perceived Lady Francis and a gentleman whom neither of them had seen before coming toward them arm-in-arm, and engaged in the most intimate conversation.

CHAPTER V.

COMPLICATIONS.

BY MAY CROMMELIN.

"Weep not, my wanton, smile upon my knee,
 When thou art old, there's grief enough for thee.
  The wanton smiled, father wept,
  Mother cried, baby leapt,
  More he crowed, more we cried,
   Nature could not sorrow hide."

GREENE (1560-92)[1]

"I've wired for him!" Fenella imparted in a startling burst of confidence. "Ronny and I got up early and ran down to the telegraph office."

"My *goodness!*" Jacynth stared in resentful dismay at her sparkling eyes. "Well! you have made a nice complication, now."

The girl laid a beseeching hand on his arm.

"Don't look so furious; and do—do stand by me in everything as you promised. Remember you are my only friend here—except Ronny."

"I have promised," he said solemnly. "But you might consult me as a friend. And why do anything so rash—mad?"

"Because all my life I have taken my own way; because if he comes here to vex me, when we are all quite happy"—she set her small white teeth—"and flaunts *that creature* before my very face, I will show him the red rag he hates worst! Sauce for the goose is sauce for the gander."

"Not always. Take care."

"Besides, I want to convince you—every one—that on my side there is nothing to blame, nothing—while Frank—oh, there!"—with a pathetic little break in her voice that makes Clitheroe wretched—"after having forgotten this miserable business very nearly, I hardly slept last night—thinking."

"You are fond of him still, then?" said Jacynth, very low.

"No! no! I hate him now," she exclaimed passionately, apostrophizing the rocks and trees around. "I should like to divorce him, and—and—see that poisonous serpent crushed alive."

"Come, don't say such terrible things. And divorce is no such easy matter."[2]

Jacynth's heart beat hard as he soothed the headstrong girl. If she were indeed free! Down, down, wild hope! Was he not her true friend and faithful counsellor? "So this accounts for your silence as we drove here. You meant to spring this surprise on me."

Fenella nodded, mischief simply brimming over in her suddenly transformed little face.

"If I get into a scrape, you've got to get me out. It's a duel, you see, between four of us, with you and Lord Castleton for seconds, and I come of a fighting family," her feet breaking under her into a few steps of war dance. "O—o—h, *look there!*"

Her shriek rang far and shrill through the Knaresborough[3] rocks, as, stiffened suddenly to stone, she stood with outstretched arms, her straining eyes gazing up at the cliff. A small object had hurtled through some brushwood overhead, and, rolling downward, was now stopped half-way. It was a little boy, clinging desperately to a bush at which he had caught.

Before the last sounds had left her parted lips, Jacynth bounded forward, and was clambering, springing as best he could, up from foothold to ledge. Many holidays of mountain-climbing stood him in good stead. Higher still—Ah! there! The bush is giving way slowly at the roots. A little shower of earth falls down on Fenella's upturned face; she has somehow tottered with quaking knees onward.

Safe—safe! Just as the terrified child feels his hold giving way, a strong arm catches him round the waist.

"Thank God!" exclaims a well-known man's voice. Fenella feels a little group about her, summoned by her echoing shriek; but her filming vision sees nothing till Ronny is placed, pale but plucky, in her arms. Presently, with the boy hugging her neck, and her own tight grasp proving he has no bones broken, she turns to find Frank, looking strangely excited, holding out a hand to Jacynth.

"Let me thank you. That was splendidly done. You saved

the boy's life, and I am—I——" he stammered and stopped, reddening.

"No thanks are needed. I could not tell but that it was my own little scamp of a nephew. Where is Grandison?" Jacynth frigidly answered, looking round. He had driven Fenella and the two boys out here, because she wished to avoid meeting her husband and his probable companion. And, lo! tricksome fate had drawn these two hither as by some irresistible attraction.

Lucille was meanwhile looking on with intense apprehension. The child—the child was the sole remaining link between this man and wife, but that one how strong! She must interfere rapidly.

Next moment she had dropped on her knees beside Ronny, who now stood leaning against his mother, and had tenderly lifted his hand.

"Poor infant—*chéri!* He is bleeding, see!" And she softly wiped some trickling drops from a graze on the chubby, childish fist.

"How dare you? Leave my child alone!" blazed out Fenella, withdrawing as if from the touch of a reptile.

Lucille rose with an air of dignified humility, and looked full at Onslow, with surely a sudden moisture in her beautiful dark eyes.

"I have made a mistake, it is true. But I am a woman, and only remembered that a child was hurt—your child!" The last words were murmured only for his ear.

"Come away," said Onslow briefly, but consolingly.

⋆ ⋆ ⋆ ⋆ ⋆

A very thunder-cloud, charged with electricity, overhung the end of one of the long dinner tables in the Prospect Hotel that evening.

Lord Castleton presided at the foot, the post of honour. On his right hand, seated thus low, as befitted new guests, were Lord Francis Onslow, and, "by Jove! Madame de Vigny herself." To his left, Jacynth, faithful to his place beside Fenella, who had asked the head-waiter some days ago not to move her seat higher, in usual hotel progression, opposite a sour-faced set of ladies, with side-ringlets and warming-pan brooches, who whispered innuendoes about herself that palled as a diversion. She had then innocently preferred new arrivals. So Castleton looked at four freezingly expressionless faces, four pairs of eyes bottling up lightnings.

"In for a storm!" he chuckled to himself, rubbing his plump hands under the table. "But who is my lady keeping that empty place for on her other side?"

Just then a slight young man, with blond curls clustering thickly on his head, well-waxed moustaches, and a slightly foreign military air about the cut of his clothes and the stiffness of his shoulders, came down the long room with a buoyant step. Fenella's eyes gleamed as she held out her hand in greeting, which the newcomer pressed with that mingled homage and effusion betraying a stranger to English customs.

Onslow's dark face grew suddenly livid with passion. He made a movement as if about to rise, but was restrained by an imploring touch on his arm, and a murmured entreaty from his companion to be calm.

"You see! I obeyed your message on the instant," said the new comer to Fenella, in an undertone, audible in the fell silence around. "Last week you said don't come—it is *stupeed*. Now you say, come!"

"Ah, but we have had some new visitors since then, and it is *much* more amusing."

After which really impudent remark, Fenella leant back, and with a look of infantile innocence on her piquant face, indicated Jacynth.

"I want to make you two acquainted. I like my friends to like each other. Mr. Jacynth—Count de Mürger."

The two men's eyes met. Clitheroe's gaze gravely observant, De Mürger momentarily taken aback, then bowing with gay readiness, as who should say, "A rival? Come on! measure swords."

Next he looked across and started.

It was only a slight start, yet Castleton's cheeks at once puffed with suppressed mirth. Lucille gave the faintest inclination of her handsome dark head. But Onslow, laying his arms on the table with a cool superiority that in a less well-bred man might be offensive, stared at his enemy full, not stirring a muscle.

The cut was direct, cutting De Mürger short in an instinctively-begun bow of politely cold recognition. A brilliant smile instantly lightened the young Austrian's face. He had suspected a trap, but now he knew his ground.

An awkward silence ensued. Then Castleton demanded, in nervous accents,—

"What fish *is* this, waiter—eh?"

"*Tom Dory*,[4] milord," answered the recently imported Teuton with suave readiness.

A little buzz of talk began at once; the spell was loosed. Under cover of this Castleton bent forward, irresistibly thirsting to confide in Jacynth.

"I say, what a game! Would you think De Mürger is one of the greatest gamblers going, and a tremendous duellist?"

"That boy! He looks as if dancing was his strong point."

"So it is. He is a favourite leader of cotillons[5]—invented that figure for Lady Birmingham's ball of shooting with Cupid's bows and arrows—you know."

"No, I don't. I am too old for much ball-going," answered the barrister curtly.

Meanwhile, though Fenella never once looked his way, she felt that her husband's eyes were stabbing her with glances like daggers. It hurt; but she had the sweet revenge of knowing she was wounding his pride in return, though the false Circe by his side might try to pour in balm. So looking a picture of girlish sweetness in her delicious white gown, so simple seemingly, so costly—a white bud of a little creature in contradistinction to the darker, maturer charms of her handsome rival, she listened with apparent eagerness to De Mürger.

"Yes, I should regret not going to Vienna this summer, if I were not *here*. You do not know it. Ah, how I should like to show you our Prater.[6] And the life, the gaiety. How you would enjoy it!"

"Do you know Vienna?" asked Madame de Vigny of Onslow, in clear tones, as if her neighbours were dummies. "It is—how do you say it in English?—*la ville la plus dévergondée*[7] in Europe."

At the inference that this abandoned capital will suit herself, in Madame's evident opinion, Fenella's pale small cheeks take a sudden rosy tint, her tawny eyes gleam with quite a tigerish flash. She throws up her head, challenging Onslow mutely to dare countenance the insult. But Frank's French is that of Eton,[8] and he merely ejaculates an "Ah!" impassively.

("Quarrels are so upsetting to one's digestion," was Castleton's thought. Yet not for anything would he have missed the human interest of the scene, which was "as good as a play." Still the lull of talk was ominous, so he desperately addressed the only person from whom no explosion was to be feared.)

"What is coming next, waiter?"

"Suckie-pig,[9] sir," responded the gentle German.

Ronny's curly pate appearing on a level with the tablecloth, and nestling between his mother and Jacynth confidingly, was a welcome diversion. All eyes turned with relief on the rosy, roguish face, alone unconscious of hidden trouble among them.

"It will soon be dessert-time; I may stay, mayn't I, mummy?" coaxed the child confidently.

Then, to beguile the time, he produced some glass marbles from his pocket, aiming at the salt-cellar, where his friend Jacynth fielded and sent them back. With her arm round her son, Fenella was chatting animatedly to De Mürger, rejoicing inwardly in her immense superiority over her opposite foes in possessing Ronny. A vagrant ball escaping the latter's fingers, cannoned off a dish, and flew straight into Madame's lap. With a secret honeyed glance at Ronny, she feigned to detain it.

"No, you mustn't! That would be stealing, and then you would be put in prison," remonstrated the child. Then looking at her with the sweet familiarity of one of Raphael's cherubs, "*Were you ever in prison?*"

Madame de Vigny, who was just lifting a full glass of claret to her lips, started, so that some wine was spilt. She raised her delicate brows, with a glance of charming dismay at Onslow's gloomy face.

Castleton and Jacynth, noticing the accident, exchanged furtive, surprised looks; but Ronny, no more heeding that red splash than if he had slopped over his glass of milk, announced in joyous tones, "Because I was—very nearly. Grandison and me were very naughty once, and his nurse tried to give us to a p'leeceman, but we pulled at her dress so hard she couldn't; and the p'leeceman shook his finger at me and said, 'Next time!'—Oh, I say!"

Suddenly diving, so that his little body eluded Fenella's grasp, to her surprise he rushed round the table and flung himself against Frank, who had annexed the truant marble, and was ostentatiously secreting it in his own pocket.

"Give it me! It's mine! You must! Please!"

Frank held the treasure nearer, then embracing the boy's shoulders with one caressing arm, stooped and deliberately kissed the sweet, childish face.

"Take it, there. Why, you will soon be old enough to go to school."

Raising his head, he looked straight at Fenella with such defiance that the wrathful jealousy, boiling within her at so flagrant a show of authority, suddenly cooled.

With a shiver at the warning, she nevertheless had spirit to retort with cool, decisive command, "Ronny, come here. You must stay by me, dear, and not go to—other people." Then she rustled from the table with superb displeasure at Frank's unwarrantable liberty. Both De Mürger and Jacynth sprang up, too, in quick rivalry, as her bodyguard. They were soon followed by Castleton, who found it poor fun to watch only Onslow's lowering face, and Jezebel,[10] as he secretly politely designated Madame de Vigny.

Before the hotel door the night was still and cool; stars had begun to twinkle in the "blue vaults, magnificently deep."

"So you have to suffer such insults?" De Mürger impetuously whispers in Fenella's ear. "Let me avenge you. Ah! you did right to send for me."

"No, no, you must not take your own way to help me. Wait— I must just ask Mr. Jacynth to do something for me. Then I will come back and talk *to you*," murmurs Fenella, frightened, therefore sweetly deceitful. Then drawing her mentor apart, while Castleton eagerly fastens on the prey she has left, she entreats: "Help me. Keep the Count and Frank from fighting; anything but that!"

"For goodness' sake get rid of De Mürger. He is so *embroiling*," counselled Jacynth.

"How can I? After bringing him here a long journey to-day, can I whistle him away to-morrow?" she responds with naive indignation. "It is as bad as putting back the bottle-imp."[11]

"Then you—some of us must leave. The situation is too strained."

"You advise flight; and I, who am just spoiling for a fight, as the Irish say"—she was actually laughing again; it was too bad.

"If you will stay, let me make you acquainted with my sister Helen, Grandison's mother," said Jacynth, softly, pity stirring his heart-strings for this young creature. "She is a good sort—a genuine woman."

"Thank you," said Fenella, absently looking round. "What is the Count about? and where is Ronny?"

CHAPTER VI.

A WOMAN'S VIEW OF THE MATTER.

BY F.C. PHILIPS.

THE next morning Jacynth called upon his sister and explained to her that he wished her to extend a helping hand to Lady Francis Onslow. He had told Fenella that his sister Helen was "a good sort—a genuine woman," and he was, therefore, disagreeably surprised when he found the view that lady took of the situation.

"Lady Francis Onslow?" she said, raising her eyebrows. "She is separated from her husband, is she not?"

"Yes, but it is not her fault," answered Jacynth quickly. "Onslow treated her very badly."

"I remember something about it," said his sister. "I think there was a kind of shuffling of the cards and a new deal. Lord Francis took up with a Frenchwoman, and his wife consoled herself with Monsieur de Mürger. Is not that the story?"

"It is a garbled account of it. Lady Francis was perfectly innocent," said Jacynth hotly.

"I have no doubt, but all the same I think I would rather have nothing to say to her. It is always a foolish thing to interfere between husband and wife."

"I do not ask for your interference, Helen," said her brother. "I merely ask you to let me introduce you to Lady Francis, and I should like you to be kind to her."

"Why are you interested in her?"

"Because I think she has been badly treated, and because she is an impulsive, reckless little woman who will benefit much from your advice."

"I dislike impulsive, reckless little women," said Helen, "and I would much rather not know her."

"You are very unkind, dear, and quite unlike your usual self. Lady Francis has got herself into a fix, and you must really get her out of it—to please me."

"What fix has she got herself into?"

"Well, I will tell you. Her husband is here, as of course you know, and immediately after his arrival Madame de Vigny appeared on the scene. Poor Lady Francis, who is naturally outraged at his conduct, telegraphed to De Mürger to come down, and this will, of course, make things look black for her if you do not give her your help and moral support. She does not know any ladies here, and of course she has acted imprudently."

"Yes, she has acted imprudently and stupidly. It only confirms my impression that I would rather not know her," said his sister.

"But, Helen, she is very young, and she has no one to advise her."

"She has you to advise her," laughed Helen; "and as you are a clever, rising barrister, I should have thought you would have been wise enough to have prevented her telegraphing for her lover."

"He is not her lover;" shouted Jacynth, loudly.

"As to her extreme youth," pursued his sister, unmoved at his interruption, "she has a child old enough to play cricket on the green with the tinkers and the tailors and the butcher boys of the place. She must surely be out of her teens! And if she does not know how to behave herself now, I am afraid she never will."

"Why are you so hard, Helen?" he asked, looking at his sister in surprise.

"I am not hard," she answered, "but I really fail to see why you require my aid. Lady Francis seems quite able to take care of herself. The fact is, Clitheroe," she continued, "you must know as well as I do that the lex talionis¹ does not apply to husbands and wives. It is only in quite the lower classes that the wife throws back the sugar basin at her husband when he has aimed at her with the teapot. Men have a certain license with regard to flirtation which has always been denied to women. It may be wrong—I daresay it is—but I am not going to head any movement to bring about a change."

"I think she would listen to you if you would ask her to send M. de Mürger back to town," said Jacynth. "As it is, they fear there may be a duel."

"And you want me to mix myself up in all this unsavoury business?" she exclaimed. "Really, Clitheroe, you are very unreasonable."

"I am very sorry for Lady Francis," he said, in a low voice.

"And I suppose you are in love with her. Nothing else could explain your strange persistency. You are very foolish, and you are wasting your time. If the woman cares for any one, I suppose it is for her curly-headed attaché. It is evident that you are only being made use of, and I am certainly not going to follow your ridiculous example. Lady Francis possesses no possible interest for me. I consider her unladylike, wanting in *savoir vivre* and tact, and quite the last person for whom I could have any sympathy."

"She has been cruelly treated," said Jacynth.

"So have thousands of other women, but they manage to bear their cruel treatment and behave with better taste than Lady Francis."

"What am I to say to her?" said Clitheroe, almost angrily. "She is waiting in the garden. I told her that you would call upon her this afternoon."

"Then you took a very unwarrantable liberty," said his sister. "I will not call upon her. I should advise you to tell her to send De Mürger away at once."

"And then will you call upon her?" he asked eagerly.

"No, I won't," answered his sister. "I detest fuzzy-headed little women who get on well with any man except their husbands. There will be an *esclandre*² one day, and I don't mean to be mixed up in it."

"I had no idea you were so uncharitable," he said, with genuine surprise.

"I am not the least uncharitable," she said, "but you must admit that Lady Francis has everything against her."

"Appearances may be against her," he said doubtfully.

"And appearances in society count for everything," said his sister. "If women wish to be original, and what you call reckless and impulsive, they must give up society, for you may be quite sure that they will meet with the cold shoulder wherever they go."

"You have certainly shown it to Lady Francis," he said bitterly.

"For the reason I have told you. As for your sentimental rubbish about her ill-treatment from her husband, she cannot have suffered so very dreadfully, as she has always had Count de Mürger to console her."

"Thank you, Helen; you have said quite enough. I am sorry I

attempted to enlist your sympathy, and I am doubly sorry that I mentioned you to Lady Francis. I don't know what I shall say to her. You have placed me in a very awkward position."

"You have placed yourself in one," she said. "Why not leave Harrogate at once? You are only being made a tool of, and you had better let the *partie carrée*³ sort itself as best it may."

Jacynth felt terribly perplexed, and he could scarcely help feeling that there was a certain amount of truth—a certain amount of worldly wisdom—in what his sister had said. Of course Fenella did not care for him, and never would. Every one had warned him against her, and it was very foolish of him to indulge a wild dream which could never be anything but a wild dream. He was perfectly convinced of her innocence with respect to De Mürger, but evidently it was difficult to get others to share his credulity. And why should they believe that she was innocent when she allowed the man to come and stay in the hotel with her, in defiance, not only of her husband's wishes, but also of all the laws of society and good taste? His sister's words had been very severe and uncompromising, but he almost felt as if he must agree with her, and this feeling added to his annoyance and depression.

What could he say to the poor, little, misguided woman who was waiting for him to extricate her from her difficulties? How could he possibly explain to her that his sister had refused to make her acquaintance, when he had told her that she might count upon her assistance and sympathy? He walked out of the house in a furious frame of mind. He was angry with his sister, and still more so with himself for being influenced by what she had said. He went straight to his rendezvous with Lady Francis, and when she caught sight of him she started up, and came forward with outstretched hands. At once his doubts disappeared. It only needed one look from her pleading brown eyes for all his old confidence and infatuation to be restored.

"How kind you are!" said Fenella, with gratitude beaming in her face. "Have you been all this time with your sister? When am I to see her?"

Then Jacynth felt extremely uncomfortable, and looked down and kicked about the gravel, unable to answer the questions which were put to him.

"What did your sister say?" pursued Fenella. "Did you explain everything to her?"

"Yes, I explained everything," he said, awkwardly.

"But not so well as I can explain it," she continued; and then, "I am sure I shall like your sister—that is to say, if she is like you."

"She is not like me," he said moodily. "She is altogether different."

"Never mind," she said brightly; "I shall like her all the same."

"I am afraid——" he began.

"Yes? What are you afraid of?" she asked.

"You see, my sister is going away very shortly; in fact, she may leave any day," he answered, confusedly.

"Oh, I am so sorry," she said, simply.

"Yes," he continued, desperately, "and, of course, as her stay here is going to be so very short, she thinks—I mean she fears——"

"Well, go on," said Fenella calmly.

"She fears that she could not be of much assistance to you."

"But I myself am not going to stay long," she said. "But it will be very kind of her to let me see something of her before she leaves. It will silence the evil tongues."

"She feels that it will be scarcely worth while to make your acquaintance," said Jacynth, with a final violent kick at the gravel.

"I understand," said Fenella, in altogether a different voice, and the light went out of her face.

"I can assure you——" said Jacynth, but Fenella stopped him.

"You need say no more," she said. "Your sister refuses to know me. I dare say she is right."

Then there was an awkward silence. Jacynth could find no excuses ready, and Fenella was inwardly very indignant. At last she managed to subdue her emotion sufficiently to say to him,—

"I must thank you for the effort you have made on my behalf; you have been very kind, and whatever happens to me, I will never forget your kindness."

Jacynth still found nothing to say, and, scarcely before he had realised it, Fenella had turned from him and was hastily running towards the hotel.

CHAPTER VII.

SO NEAR—SO FAR AWAY.

BY "RITA."

"I never think but to regret
I know too much——"

THE hush and silence had fallen over the outer world beyond and about the great hotel, and something of its hush and mystery brooded too in the deserted corridors and vacated public rooms of the building itself. Perhaps one or two of its inmates—so strangely thrown together—would have given almost every earthly possession for the power to gaze unknown—unseen—into one of those locked chambers; a room where a woman sat alone, with all the light and laughter and mischief gone from her face, and the shadows of suffering and regret resting like sombre memories in her veiled and sorrowful eyes.

This was not Lady Francis as the world knew her—as the men whom she bewitched and tormented and flirted with in so audacious a fashion knew her. No, this was a woman maddened by self-reproach and unavailing regrets, fired with jealous hatred of a rival, and filled to the heart's core with the memories and the longings that one voice, one face, alone in all the world, had power to awaken, and had awakened to-day.

She had thrown on a loose muslin wrapper, and the soft lace and pale tinted ribbons seemed to cling lovingly around the lissom figure, the snowy throat and arms. The long glass opposite reflected her as she raised her drooping head with its wreath of unbound hair, and the sorrowful eyes that met her own struck sharply on her senses as a surprise—so unlike they were to the eyes she was used to see. "Oh, what a fool I have been!" she cried, with an impatience and intolerance of herself that was the more maddening by reason of its vain remorse. "And yet I suppose I should do it again to-morrow under the same circumstances; yet, oh! Frank, Frank, how I loved you once—how you *seemed* to love me!"

She looked down again at the table by which she was seated. On it lay an open photograph case containing a photograph. The dark eyes smiled at her—the handsome, gay, young face looked radiant in its happy youth and supreme content with life.

Her own intent gaze seemed to drink in thirstily every line, every feature, well as she knew them all. "He doesn't look happy—now," she said, and a little sob broke from her.

Impatiently she closed the case, and began to pace up and down the room in a stormy, impetuous fashion—dashing the tears from her wet lashes, though they only thronged back fast and swift in very mockery of her efforts to deny their weakness.

"How could I expect it to be different? Isn't it always the same—always, always?" she repeated, passionately. "Love doesn't last; it can't. And there were so many temptations; and then the excitement of conquest, and the vanity of wishing to show him I could still charm others, though he seemed to think I had no right to try. But it was all so false, so—so foolish. If he had only trusted, if he had only spoken gently, kindly—as he used to speak! And then that hateful woman, that French serpent—fiend—adventuress. Heavens! how I hated her; how I hate her still. If I thought he cared, *really* cared—if I thought he had ever held her to his heart—kissed her as he used to kiss me—if—— Oh! I could *kill* her!"

She broke off abruptly, pressing her hand to her heart, while the blood rushed in a crimson torrent to her face. "Oh! he can't!" she moaned, throwing herself face downward on the cushions of the couch. "And yet I believed it—once; and I've never even let any man's lips touch my hand; never, with all my whims and follies and vagaries, allowed myself to forget that I am Frank's wife. But he doesn't care any longer. How could I expect it? And yet if he had only spoken one word to-day—one little word, I would have thrown myself at his feet and said, 'Oh! Frank, I love you—I've never ceased loving you. Oh! take me back, and let us forget all this miserable mistake.' Frank!" She raised her head and shook back the rich, soft hair impatiently, and stretched longing arms out to the empty silence. "Frank," she whispered more loudly, "why don't

you come to me? Why don't you feel I want you as—as surely—
sometimes—you want me. Frank——"

She rose unsteadily, supporting herself by one hand that rested
on the back of the couch.

Her face had grown strangely white, her eyes had a look of
intensity that spoke of strained mental force. "If I dared go to
him," she said, still in that strange whisper. "I've never said I was
wrong—or—or sorry, but I am, Frank—God knows I am. Don't
drive me desperate; I'm too happy and too reckless to be always
patient. But if you swear you never loved any other woman, Frank,
I—I will swear I never loved or thought of any man save you.
Never, dear heart—never."

Still with that strained look, intense and far off as that of a sleep-
walker, still with face deathlike in its rigid whiteness, she moved
across the room. The loose shower of hair seemed to annoy her
by its weight. She paused an instant before the table, and took up
a curious-looking silver dagger. Then, hastily twisting the hair into
a thick coil, she fastened it with the dagger and turned towards the
door.

* * * * *

"Will she read it?" muttered Lord Francis to himself, as he
looked at the closely-covered pages of the letter in his hand. "Oh,
if she would only believe; if she would only let me know what she
really feels. It is maddening to be placed in such a position, to see
her playing fast and loose with reputation; to have no more right
to kiss her lips or touch her hand than the veriest stranger. To be
here now, to-night, the same roof covering us, not half a dozen
walls dividing us, and yet not dare——"

He broke off abruptly; his eyes grew dark with stormy passions. The pain and fever of aroused memories throbbed wildly
in his heart, and thrilled his veins anew with love and longing, as
once her light step and sweet low laugh had thrilled him.

"Fenella!—wife!" his heart cried. "Oh, God! are our lives to be
for ever wrecked and spoilt by this miserable folly? Child, surely
you know I love you, that all other women are but as shadows to

me. Oh, how my heart aches for you! Surely you feel it—you can't have forgotten—you *can't!*"

He looked again at the letter, then placed it in an envelope and sealed it hastily.

"I will go to her—I know her room. I can slip it under the door if—if she is asleep; but, perhaps——"

He did not finish that thought audibly. Only opened the door and looked down the dark and silent corridor beyond.

How still it was! He heard a clock striking, somewhere in the silence, two hours after midnight. A strange chill—a feeling of half shame, half uncertainty—held him there on the threshold. There seemed something guilty and wrong about the simple action he intended.

"To think," he muttered to himself, "that a man should actually feel there was something improper in leaving a letter at his own wife's door. Yet, if I were seen, who would believe it?"

He drew the door after him. The whole corridor was in darkness. At the further end stood a marble statue surrounded by tall palms. He had noticed it already during the day. The room next to it was the one he had seen Lady Francis enter.

He moved softly down the long passage. Suddenly he paused, and shrank back into a doorway close at hand. That door beside the statue and the palms was thrown open; a slender white figure stood revealed by the light within the room. At the same moment another figure—the figure of a man—advanced rapidly, and spoke in a low, hurried voice.

The watcher stood as if turned to stone. He saw the woman retreat backwards, step by step, into the room she had just quitted; he saw the man attempt to follow her. The door shut; again all was darkness and silence.

For one hateful, throbbing moment, that seemed to hold a lifetime of agony in its passage, Lord Francis stood there, gazing at the closed door. At last, with trembling limbs and face bloodless as the dead, he staggered back to his own room, and sank down on the chair where he had written that letter, with its pleading for love and reconciliation.

"Too late!" he cried. "Oh, Heaven! to think my own eyes should be the witness of my own eternal shame and—hers!"

His head fell on his arms. He was as one dazed and stunned by the consciousness of misery undreamt of, despite those cold and silent years.

Moment after moment passed. One hour and then another dropped into the gulf of time that is no more. Still he never stirred. Consciousness of anything besides his own misery—besides the living recognition of his own shame—was dead within him; dead as youth was dead, and hope, and truth, and all things fair and sweet in life—slain by a woman's hand.

* * * * *

The dawn was brightening into daylight as at last Lord Francis roused himself from his long stupor.

"What had happened?" he thought confusedly. "Had he been ill? Had he done anything?"

A hideous dread seized and appalled him. In those brief hours he seemed to have lived a lifetime.

"Why did I not kill him?" he muttered, lifting his haggard young face up to the faint rose light that filtered through the curtains. "Kill him!—ay, and in her arms—kill him and her too! Heaven!——" a strange, hoarse laugh escaped him. "I shall go mad if I stay here—under the same roof with them."

He began to move about confusedly, putting things together, and tossing his clothes into his portmanteau. He was possessed but by one idea—to leave a place made hateful by this discovery, to get away from these men and women, with their jeering tongues and malicious smiles, who all guessed or knew of his disgrace. It had been so public, so shameless. She had summoned this man to her side. She had flaunted her preference for him before his very face, and now——

He cursed her in his heart, as still, with fevered haste and strange, impetuous movements, he gathered together his few possessions. Then he locked his box, and wrote a hurried note to the manager of the hotel, enclosing a cheque, and stating that the portmanteau would be sent for later on. A hurried glance around—a glance which passed over the letter he had written but a few brief hours before. It lay where it had fallen from his hand when he sank into the chair by his writing-table—lay there so innocent, yet so fraught with power to work remorse or retribution in days that were to come.

The grey light of the early dawn gleamed like a pale phosphorescence over the shadowy corridor, and lit with spectral mystery the white statue and the dusky palms. He shuddered as his eyes fell on them. How significant they had become!

Then, with a smothered oath that breathed vengeance for the future, he rushed down the staircase and past the sleeping porter in the entrance hall, and in another moment was standing in the fresh, sweet atmosphere of life and light that God and Nature have so freely given to the thankless, sated eyes of men.

★ ★ ★ ★ ★

How that day passed Lord Francis never knew. It seemed to him, when his senses grew clearer, that weeks and months must have gone by since the awful moment that had brought to him the full and complete knowledge of his wife's perfidy. Yet there had been a strange and consistent purpose in all his actions. He had walked for miles and miles before taking the train. He had reached London, and driven straight to his chambers, to the no small dismay and discomfiture of his man, who had been inaugurating a brief spell of leisure not as wisely as he might have done. He had given orders to this man to pack up clothes sufficient for a long journey, paid his wages, arranged with his usual caretaker to remain in the chambers, then departed for Charing Cross¹ to catch the tidal train *en route* for Paris.

All this he remembered afterwards. Remembered vaguely, impassively, as if every action had been performed by someone apart and outside of himself; as if he had been spectator instead of actor. Remembered, even as he remembered the crowded station, the flashing lights, the hoarse cries of the porters, the bustle and confusion on the platform, and high above all the shrill voices of the newsvendors crying out the news of the evening papers—*"Pall Mall! St. James Gazette!* or *Star!*² Latest edition! Mysterious murder of a foreign count in a hotel! Latest special!"

He threw himself back on the seat of his carriage. What mat-tered murders or tragedies to him? In heart he knew himself a murderer by desire and fierce hatred—in reality, his life had turned to tragedy deep and bitter and terrible, with a hopelessness that the coming years could never brighten, and the dawn of Hope would never bless.

The shrill whistle of the engine sounded above all the clamour. The train moved slowly out of the station, and still clear and distinct those words reached him like a meaningless echo: "Murder of a foreign Count! Mysterious occurrence! Special edition! Special edition!"

CHAPTER VIII.

THE TRAGEDY.

BY JOSEPH HATTON.

"Out, out, damned spot!"—*Shakespeare.*[1]

IT was during these hours that had "dropped one by one into the gulf of time" that the miserable Count had been done to death by as fierce a murderer as had ever mutilated Nature's handiwork, albeit unconscious of his sanguinary deed.

While mind and body had, so far as Lord Francis knew, been absorbed in sleep, both had been cruelly awake under a strange mesmeric or electro-biologic influence.

The wrong by which his soul was vexed had carried him out of himself, and brought him under the control of what unsophisticated people call sleep-walking, with suicidal or murderous impulse. Scientists have found in this hypnological condition new examples of unconscious evolution of the mind; but it is not our business to describe or investigate the various discoveries which, in the direction of hypnotic trance or mesmeric constraint, have of late occupied public attention; we have merely to record the facts that in this present history are stranger than fiction.[2]

Illustrations of the possibilities of a dual existence have been given to the world in the case of Hyde and Jekyll, but sleep-walking is as old as the hills; and, give the hypnological subject the original impulse of a bitter wrong sufficient to excite a vengeful desire, then such a deed as that which was proclaimed by the newsboys—as Lord Francis left his chambers to take the tidal train to Paris—is quite conceivable.

The victim of the dream in action, the sleep-walker—the subject of the mesmeriser—comes out of his trance oblivious of his hypnotic adventures.

And thus it was with Lord Francis. But what a crime he had

unconsciously committed! And with what heroic self-denial the wife had taken upon herself all the responsibility of the criminal's vengeful act!

The male figure which Lord Francis had seen stealing toward his wife's room was the Count de Mürger. In this Lord Francis was not mistaken, but Fenella was. We know how at the moment her heart was yearning for its rightful lord; but De Mürger little thought that Lady Francis had taken him for Frank. Her feelings had been so wrought up to the pitch of hope, that leaving her room to find her husband, and throw herself at his feet, she fancied him in a similar frame of mind—as indeed he was—and love interpreted the approach of the Count into that of her husband.

Alas! if she had only resented the presence of the Count in the hearing of Lord Francis; if he could have heard the overwhelming rebuke of the true wife as the truculent lover flung himself upon his knees before her, what a world of misery had been spared him and her!

Not that the death of the Count was any loss to society or the world; it was not. There was no redeeming feature in his character. He had worked his way into Fenella's confidence by subtle lies; he had won his position in society, such as it was, by the meanest arts; not to mention the replenishing of his purse on more than one occasion by doubtful play at cards, even when invited to the best houses. In short, the Count was an unscrupulous man, but he was fascinating to women, and could boast, and did, of his many conquests.

Such perfidy as this may be successful for a time, but it not unfrequently has a violent ending.

In the case of Count de Mürger his career was cut short at the moment when he was, as he thought, on the eve of his most daring and villainous success. If his death cast a shadow upon the reputation of Fenella, since it occurred in her chamber, it threw around her the halo of a wifely devotion not unworthy of the classic days of classic virtue.[3]

It is only the reader, however, of the present history who can understand all that is meant by this revelation of wifely atonement and love. Fenella, like many another wife, had sought to amuse herself with a would-be lover; she had also played him off against the supposed indifference of her husband in a careless rivalry of his harmless flirtations.

When the police entered the chamber of Lady Francis Onslow, they found the Count lying dead on the floor. Looking to her for some explanation, she drew herself to her full height, and, flinging upon the body the silver-hilted dagger she said, "This man attempted my life, and I killed him."

It is curious how situations of a kindred character often inspire similar explanations. It will be remembered by many that when the Deputy in "The Dead Heart"[4] drew the attention of the guard to the dead Abbé, he did so in words quite similar to those used by Lady Francis Onslow.

It was a most pathetic figure—the slim, pale woman, as she drew her brocaded gown about her, and fixed her expressive eyes on the police.

Lord Francis Onslow little dreamed what had occurred as he fled from the hotel. And yet it was he whom his wife was shielding in her strange confession. It was Lord Francis himself who had slain the Count, and in her presence.

It is known that great discoveries have been made during so-called sleep. Men have made long journeys in their dreams, and awakened unconscious of their travels. Others have arisen refreshed with a new sense of knowledge and power. Louis Stevenson has confessed that he dreams his stories, and then writes them out.[5] There was in a recent Academy the picture of a young girl walking with closed eyes amid poppies and hemlocks.[6] The present writer has experienced, in his own career, an incident of hypnotic sleep or mesmeric trance, during which he went forth in very truth with knife and pistol to commit, as it seemed, some great crime, and was only prevented by the kindly guidance of a loving arm, that held his own, and led him back to the couch from which he had risen.

And thus it was when Lord Francis exclaimed, "Too late! Oh, Heaven! to think my own eyes should be witness of my own eternal shame, and—hers," the hand of Fate was stretched out against the intriguing and vicious Count de Mürger. For as Lord Francis staggered back to his room, dazed, stunned, the cold tears welling up into his eyes, his head on his arms, his whole form limp with shattered nerves, a new and terrible power was created within him. He fell into a chair, entirely overcome, and for a little while appeared to sleep. But it was the sleep that awakens, the mesmeric sleep that walks and acts, the dream-sleep that takes possession of body and mind;[8] such sleep as that which afflicted Lady Macbeth after the murder of Duncan.

Hardly had De Mürger surprised the startled Fenella, than Lord Francis arose from the chair and retraced his steps toward his wife's room. While all that he knew of himself was asleep, Nature, in one of its strangest freaks, propelled him forth.

"Back, sir! How dare you come here?" Lady Francis was exclaiming as he entered the room.

De Mürger had just risen from his knees, and in Fenella's hand was a gleaming dagger.

"But, my dear Fenella, listen," said the Count.

"Back, I say! Touch me, and I will kill you!"

"Oh, this is foolish bravado," the Frenchman answered.

"Another word, and I will alarm the house."

"That would only be to ruin your reputation," said the daring lover.

"God knows I have not much reputation to lose in the eyes of the world, since it seems I have given you sufficient encouragement to bring you here."

"Well, then, why be cruel now? You know I love you dearly!" As he made this last appeal, Fenella stood transfixed, her eyes no longer upon his, but gazing, as it seemed, on vacancy.

"Hush," she whispered, her eyes fixed, her figure rigid with fear.

She saw her husband steal ghost-like into the room; noted his blanched face, his lips blue, his eyes piercing bright. He seemed to glide towards her like an animal creeping towards its prey.

"Ah, you relent," said the Count, approaching her with loving action, at which the apparition of the avenging husband paused. For a moment Lady Francis thought it was an apparition, the unreal creation of her fears; but as it came crouching on again, as if ready to spring, she realised the dreadful situation, and in response to the Count in his fool's paradise, she whispered, "Hush! your hour has come, and mine. And, O Heaven, he will never know I am innocent!"

The next moment the stealthy figure rose up and seemed to smite the Count as an anaconda might. There was no noise, no thudding blow; but a great iron grip held him by the throat, and in a moment later the dagger was taken from the hand of Lady Francis, and was thrust into the heart of the already dying man.

Presently the deed was done, and the murderer stood face to face with his wife. He looked at her as if he saw her not. She spoke; he did not seem to hear her.

"I am innocent, Frank," she said, "but oh! kill me, too, for you can never believe me! I was seeking you when he came to me; I had upbraided myself, and determined to ask your forgiveness for my neglect of you. But, oh! for nothing more, as Heaven is my judge! But kill me; you can never again think me a true and honest wife."

For a moment the somnambulist stood and gazed at her, but surely saw her not.

"He is mad!" she said, "mad! Or have I lost my senses? Frank, Frank, I will save you! Begone! I am to blame! I will accept the responsibility! Begone!"

She did not move as she spoke, nor did he. They both looked steadily at each other. She thought he was about to answer her, when he moved away, retracing his steps from the room as stealthily as he had entered it. She watched him with a strange fascination, and without the power to move until he disappeared. Then, with a moaning cry, she sank upon her knees, and put out her hand towards the ghastly heap upon the floor, in the hope that she was only dreaming, and that all she had seen was mere phantasy. The carpet was wet, and there was blood upon her hand.

"Why did I not kill him?" he had exclaimed, as we know, when he had returned to his own room and passed out of his sleep to life and consciousness.

He knew nothing of the murderous scene in which he had played so terrible a part—knew nothing of the crumpled, bleeding body lying in a hideous heap, with its pale companion looking down upon it, and the light stealing through the curtained window, wan and ghost-like.

Fenella watched the first sentinels of the morning, pointing airy fingers here and there; one trembling sun-glance falling upon the silver hilt of the red dagger; another seeking, as it were, to find out the hideous face of the dead man. But she uttered no word, only stood there still and quiet, like some strangely sculptured statue waiting to be called to life—as she was presently called by an inspector of police and the manager of the hotel.

Aroused to action, she took upon herself all the odium of her husband's deed—took it upon herself with the queen-like dignity of an avenging angel.

"This man attempted my life, and I killed him!"

And they knew, those common men, that when she said her life she meant her honour. To her that was her life, and they were conscious of her great beauty, even as she stood before them, pale as a ghost, and with hot, burning eyes.

The officer noticed that there was no evidence of a struggle; not a curtain was awry. No chair was out of its place. The carpet was unruffled, the room neat and trim as if nothing unusual had taken place. Before touching the body he wrote these facts down in his book; then, laying his hand upon the bundle of clothes, he exposed the dead face of the Count, and requested the hotel manager to admit his two attendant constables. One he dispatched for a doctor; to the other he confided the custody of Lady Francis Onslow.

"I charge you formally, madam, with the murder of this man on your own confession, which I have written down; and I warn you that anything else you may say will be given in evidence against you."

"Yes," said Fenella; "he attempted my life and I killed him."

"You are my prisoner, my lady," said the inspector; "but you may call in any friend you wish to see. At the same time, I again warn you that anything you may say will be taken down and may be given in evidence against you. I will do my duty as considerately as possible, but I have a duty to perform, and that of course you will understand."

The first editions of the newspapers gave conflicting reports of the Count's death.

For a time the public did not understand whether the Count had been murdered in his bed by burglars, whether he was the victim of Nihilistic vengeance,[9] or whether he had committed suicide;

but on the morning following the tragedy they were regaled with all the strange story, and much more besides.

The confession of Lady Francis Onslow was a text upon which everybody had a sermon to preach. But it was speedily a point of comment that the marks upon the throat of the dead man suggested a more powerful grip than that of Fenella. There was something in the condition of the body which puzzled the experts. This was no ordinary murder, everybody agreed; nor indeed was it, as we know.

At the inquest the medical testimony showed that death might have been caused either by strangulation, or by the deep fierce stab wounds that disfigured the body.

It seemed to the experts that the man had been done to death by some person far more powerful than the prisoner. The marks on the throat were almost as strong, and the bruises and depression of the windpipe as great, as would be caused by hanging. The man had been gripped by a powerful hand, while he had been stabbed with a force that had left an impression of the dagger's handle upon the flesh. The witnesses were few, but they were sufficient to show that a murder had been committed, though the jury and the public had evidently grave doubts about the criminality of the prisoner, Lady Francis Onslow.

One of the jurors had asked a pointed question as to the possibility of the deceased having committed suicide. This was, however, only a kindly suggestion in the direction of Lady Francis Onslow's innocence. The Count had been killed by other hands than his own. There was no doubt about that.

What irritated the public in regard to the first day's inquiry was that, while there were hints at scandal, nothing came out that might be called piquant.

Of course, there was the fact that the Count was in Lady Onslow's bedroom at midnight; but none of the details that led up to this piece of audacity—if it were audacity—were disclosed.

The coroner, in a mild rebuke administered to the foreman of the jury, said the Court was assembled to inquire into the death of Count de Mürger, but it was not a court of social investigation; it was not an inquisition charged with a mission to unravel scandal or to exploit the life and manners of a section of Her Majesty's subjects. While he would take any evidence that bore upon the case, however painful that evidence might be to the private feelings or public reputation of even the highest in the land, he would not allow that Court to be unduly inquisitorial in matters that could only satisfy the prurient and licentious taste of that wretched section of the public which found its chief amusement in French novels[10] and the scandals of Vanity Fair.[11]

Poor coroner! He lived to regret those words. Even some of the very best newspapers condemned them; and the worst called for the coroner's instant dismissal, as a panderer to the aristocracy, and unfit to preside over a court of any kind.

On the first day of the inquest the coroner asked why Lord Francis Onslow was not present. The question created an expectant hush, which was maintained while Mr. Jarrow Cook, of the firm of Cook, Son & Lovett, the family lawyers of the Onslows, explained that Lord Francis was somewhere abroad—where, they did not know.

"When did Lord Francis quit the hotel where the Count was killed?" asked the foreman of the jury.

"I do not know," was the lawyer's reply.

"I believe he left very early and suddenly for London, and then went on to Paris. Is that so?"

"I really cannot say," was the lawyer's answer.

"I do not know that these questions are in order, Mr. Foreman," said the coroner.

"Maybe not, Mr. Coroner," replied the foreman, "but there is a good deal, it strikes me, in the conduct of Lord Francis Onslow in this matter that requires explanation."

"Mr. Coroner," said the lawyer, "if you will permit me to say so, Lord Francis will, I am quite sure, be quite ready to answer any questions that this honourable court may desire to ask him; but I think in his absence that——"

"Certainly," said the coroner, interrupting Mr. Jarrow Cook, of the firm of Cook, Son & Lovett. "I am sure the foreman will feel that it is not within our province at the moment to refer to the conduct of Lord Francis Onslow. His lordship will, no doubt, present himself before us in due course, if wanted. If necessary, I will order his attendance."

At this there was some applause in Court, and Mr. Jarrow Cook rose to remark with all deference that he thought the coroner's observation uncalled for; whereupon the coroner reminded Mr. Jarrow Cook that he was only there by courtesy, and that he must request him not to offer any further criticism of a personal nature in regard to the conduct of the Court.

Mr. Jarrow Cook bowed, and the proceedings went on without any further interruption.

The prisoner, who was dressed in a quiet gown of grey cashmere, sat placidly in an armchair near Mr. Jarrow Cook. She was pale, but quite self-possessed. The evidence of the police inspector seemed to interest her very much, as he related with careful regard to detail how he was sent for, and what he saw and heard in the prisoner's room; how he cautioned her, and what he said when he took her into custody.

An observant reporter thought he detected a peculiar smile pass over the mobile features of Lady Francis Onslow, when the first medical witness suggested the impossibility of a woman having made the marks on the throat of the dead man; but no doubt, when the case comes to be sifted to its very dregs, and the prosecuting counsel has to reply to this medical criticism, he will be able to adduce instances of the enormous strength that comes with passion, or is the outcome of some great act of revenge, and so on.

That is, if Lady Francis Onslow should have to take her trial for wilful murder; though the coroner's inquest ended with her condemnation, the case has still to go before the police magistrate; and already public opinion has decided that if Lady Francis Onslow did kill the would-be Tarquin,[12] she is only guilty of manslaughter. By her own confession, upon which she was originally charged, the man sought her life, and she killed him. It was remarked by many that in America she would have easily found bail if she had been arrested, and that if she had ever come before a court for trial she would have been promptly acquitted. "Justifiable homicide" is a verdict not unknown to the English law, many wise persons also remarked.[13]

Meanwhile Lady Francis Onslow was on her way, in a police-van, to be charged in the police-court, and a detective had been told off at Scotland Yard[14] to keep his eye upon Lord Francis Onslow.

CHAPTER IX.

FREE ONCE AGAIN.

BY MRS. LOVETT CAMERON.

"And my soul from out that shadow that lies floating on the floor,
Shall be lifted—Nevermore!"[1]

SHE was free—free to go where she pleased—to do as she liked. The hideous nightmare of the trial was over; a jury of her countrymen had brought in a verdict of "justifiable homicide." The laws of her country had given her back her liberty, and Fenella was a free woman.

Perhaps the jury had not been altogether unimpressed by the pale loveliness of the unhappy girl who had stood before them as "prisoner in the dock" during those two terrible days; perhaps the sight of the small pale face, of the piteous brown eyes, of the childish rosy lips that quivered a little, yet that never swerved in that one statement that they repeated through all the weary examination and cross-examination, may have influenced those rough men, who held her life in their hands, more than they had any idea of.

"I confess it. I killed him; he attempted my life, and I killed him in self-defence."

"When you say your life, you mean probably more, do you not?" inquired the barrister who was examining her; and she answered, simply, "I do—I mean that which to a woman is dearer than life itself;" and at the words a sort of shiver of suppressed excitement ran through that packed and crowded Court—a shiver that made as though one heart's throb of sympathy and of admiration. But more than all else did Fenella owe her salvation to the man who stood up for a whole hour to defend her.

Clitheroe Jacynth, it was said afterwards, made his professional reputation over the defence of Lady Francis Onslow. He had been known to be clever, he had been reckoned among the rising men of

his day, but never until now had the world quite realised the power
that was in him. He had all the eloquence, the fire, the passionate
pleading of a man whose whole soul was in the cause that he advo-
cated, and his arguments carried all before them by the sheer force
of will and talent. No one who saw the dark, passionate face—the
eyes that shone with righteous wrath—who listened to the strong,
sinuous words, that seemed to burn into the hearts of his hearers
as they fell like living fire from his lips, ever forgot Jacynth as he
was that day. And when, at the last, he looked round the court,
and, after a moment of silence, more eloquent than words, began
with a deep and low-voiced impressiveness: "I see around me here
a crowd of men—fathers, husbands, and brothers—men who have
women they love at home, and whose honour lies in the hands
of those women. Which of us, my brothers—my fellow-men," he
cried suddenly aloud, stretching forth his right arm in a passionate appeal to those before him, "which of us all, did those women
whom we love stand where my unfortunate client stood upon that
fatal night, alone in the darkness, with no arm to defend her, no
ear to hear her cry, with nothing but a certain and a shameful dishonour before her—which of us, I say, would not desire that the
women we love and hold sacred, you and I, and every true man in
all England, should do as this woman did; and save her honour at
all costs?"

There was a murmur of applause that ran round the Court as
he sat down. Then the judge summed up strongly in her favour.
There had been no evidence to contradict the prisoner's own statement. No eye save her own had been in that chamber of death in
the darkness of the night. Something, indeed, had been said about
signs of more force having been used than it was in the power of a
woman's frail hands to employ, but there had been no evidence in
support of that theory. Not a vestige of any other presence in the
prisoner's chamber, save that of her would-be destroyer, had come
to light; and the jury must bear in mind that a desperate woman
is often given an almost miraculous strength in such moments of
horror and of fear, and that if the blow with the silver dagger had
been, as it appeared, struck first, the victim would necessarily have
become much weakened, and was probably in a partial state of
collapse.

There was much more of it, but it was all in her favour, and almost before the jury retired it was felt that their decision was a foregone conclusion. No one could righteously condemn a woman to death for murder who had taken a man's life under such circumstances as these. So the horror of it all came to an end, and Lady Francis Onslow was told that she was free; that she could go where she pleased, and do as she liked.

One thing there was, however, that not all the judges and the juries in the land could do for her: they could not wash the stain of blood from her hands.

It was when Clitheroe Jacynth came that night to visit her, at her hotel in Dover Street[2] (she had left for London immediately after the trial), that this terrible fact first came home to her in all its dreadful reality. As he entered the room, she ran gladly to meet him, impulsively reaching out both her small hands to him.

"It is to you I owe my life!" she cried; "it is you who have saved me. How can I ever repay you, or ever thank you enough?"

But Jacynth stood with a grave, sad face, and downcast eyes, and arms folded together across his breast, and took no notice whatever of those little white hands stretched out to him.

A dull sense of dismay crept over her; something—she hardly knew why or wherefore—struck a cold chill to her heart, and her hands sank nervelessly down again to her side.

"Won't you shake hands with me, Mr. Jacynth?—you, who have just saved my life?"

"If I have saved you, it is because it was my duty, and because—because—alas, I love you, Fenella! and I shall love you to my dying day! That is why, if I can serve you, I will do so, if I can be of use to you. You can command me now, and always, but I cannot take your hand, for there is blood on it!" and he averted his face gloomily.

There was a moment of terrible silence between them. In the old days Fenella would have flamed out at him—would have heaped abuse and rage and anger upon his head; but now she said not one single word—not one. The events of the last month had broken her down, and crushed her to the earth, and her tongue was tied. She could not deny the charge, nor tell the truth. She had taken this blood-guiltiness upon her soul to save him she loved—

and to the end she must bear it—to the end! Only, she had not realised before how dreadful it would be to bear. That Jacynth, who had worshipped the very ground she stood upon, should refuse to touch her hand was very terrible to her.

She sat down. There was a moment of intense silence, then dully, spiritlessly, she asked,—

"Why have you come here, then?"

"To see you—to help and advise you, if you will take my help, and to tell you about Ronny."

"Ah—Ronny!" she cried, looking at him with a sudden eagerness, while a pink flush flooded her pale cheeks. "Where is Ronny? I must have him. Will you bring him to me now—at once—this very night?"

"My dear Lady Francis, I want you to be very reasonable and sensible, and to listen to me."

"I never was reasonable and sensible in my life," she began, with a little pout and a shrug of her shoulders that reminded him almost too painfully of her own wayward self—"but I will listen if you like," she added humbly.

"I want you to let Ronny be where he is—for the present at least. He is with my sister Helen, and with Grandison, her boy, his old playfellow. I think it would be good for them both to be left together. My nephew has an excellent tutor, and Ronny can share his lessons. My sister has taken them both down to the country, to her home in Sussex. She was very hard to you, Fenella, but she is not really a bad-hearted woman, and she was very, very sorry for poor little Ronny when—when it all happened—and when—you were taken from him. Let Ronny be where he is."

"But I want him—I want him!" she cried. "He is all I have on earth—why should I be parted from him?"

"For his own good, Fenella!"

"It is best for a child to be with his mother."

He looked at her fixedly, but very sadly and seriously.

"Do you think so," he asked slowly—"in this case?"

Then she understood. Understood that, because of the brand of Cain[3] upon her brow, the world would not think it good for her boy to be brought up by his own mother!

Her cup of woe was indeed full. She bowed her head—the

bright brown head that he would have died to serve—upon her hands, and wept aloud.

"Don't," he said, a little unsteadily; "don't give way; be brave, as you always have been, my dear. Live down this story—this stain upon your life; go to other countries, where no one will know you; make new friends, who will have heard nothing. The world is before you; leave England, and do not come back to your boy till time has covered up with its kindly mantle this wretched episode of your life. Ronny shall be well cared for. I will look after him, and write to you constantly about him. Only—for his own sake—separate yourself entirely from him, until he is old enough to know and to choose."

He waited for a moment, looking at her yearningly and anxiously, but the bowed head never stirred. Then, in the silence and gloom of the bare and half-lit room, he turned, and left her alone in her sorrow and her desolation.

Thirty-six hours later Fenella stood by herself upon the deck of a Channel steamer, watching the white cliffs of England as they receded farther and farther into the distance. She was quite alone in the world—she had not even taken a maid with her. She had made up her mind that she would break every connection of her former life, and start entirely anew. There should not be even a servant about her to remind her of her past. It was for this reason that she had decided to go to the Channel Islands⁴—for a time at least, until she could settle her further plans. Guernsey was a quiet and comparatively secluded place, and she was not likely to meet any of her former friends and acquaintances there, and it would be easy to go on to France from there, should she feel inclined to do so.

Jacynth entirely approved of her idea, and went down himself with her to Weymouth to see her off. To be with her in so close a friendship, and yet to be unable even to take her hand as a friend should do, was inexpressibly painful to him; yet he did not shrink from sacrificing his own feelings in order to serve her, whom, in spite of everything, he still loved and admired more than any woman on earth.

"I have treated you very badly," she said to him once in the train; "I led you on, and flirted with you, and made you fall in love with me, and all for nothing but the pleasure of making an empty conquest! I played with your heart as I have done with that of dozens of others; but I think you will allow that I have been punished for it."

He could not answer her. The punishment her own folly had brought upon her was indeed terrible. And yet he did not know one half of the burden she had to bear; nor did he guess at her hopeless and helpless love for the husband for whose crime she was suffering, that seemed to have sprung up into new life in her heart during these last three weeks of peril and of well-nigh despair.

Where was he for whom she had suffered so much, for whose sin her own life had been in jeopardy? This was the question she asked of herself, wildly and despairingly, as she leant over the bulwarks of the steamer, and watched the green waves, as they hurried by, and dashed themselves into foam against the side of the vessel.

Who that had known the wild, reckless girl of old, the Lady Francis who had flirted, and laughed, and danced; who had shocked her acquaintances, and terrified her best friends, by her mad and foolish frolics—who would have recognised Lady Francis Onslow in the sad-eyed "Mrs. Orme," in her dark and Quaker-like simplicity of dress, who stood mournfully alone upon the steamer, and looked her last upon her native shores?

It is a week later. A little furnished house, standing in a garden that runs down to the edge of the cliff, about a mile out of St. Peter's Port,[5] has been taken by a quiet but very lovely little lady, who apparently is a widow, and who has given her name to the house agent as "Mrs. Orme."

She has engaged a couple of maids, and filled her tiny house with the flowers for which Guernsey is famous, and that are so cheap that not to have flowers in every corner is not to have the very breath of life. The window of her little sitting room looks over the blue sea that is bluer than any other sea in English waters. Out there is the low land of Herm, and all the little rocky islands glittering and shining like jewels set in the blue; and far away the long straight line of Sark, with her steep cliffs and jagged rocks filling in the picture on the horizon; whilst in the foreground there are countless little sails of snowy whiteness that move to and fro upon the crisp and azure waters. "Mrs. Orme" sits watching it all from her garden lawn. It amuses her vaguely and quietly, but she has nothing to do, and it is very dull and quiet at Prospect Cottage. It gives her quite a little excitement when a beautiful schooner yacht turns into the bay, with all her sails set, and makes as straight as wind and tide can take her for the entrance of the harbour.

Fenella thought she would run down to the quay to see her come in. She was glad of an excuse to go into the town, so she started off quite in good spirits, having attired herself quickly in a smart little sailor hat and a trim serge jacket.

"I can call at the Post Office, and see if there are any letters from Jacynth or Ronny," she thought; and so she started off, little knowing that she was starting to meet a new complication in her fate.

The beautiful yacht came in, nearer and nearer, to port—her sails came down with a ringing noise, and from the shore one could hear the cries and the songs of the sailors upon the deck. Fenella stood among the crowd upon the quay watching her.

"What yacht is that?" she asked of a respectable-looking individual, in the blue serge garments of a sea-faring man who stood next to her.

"She's the *Seamew*, a hundred-and-twenty-ton schooner," replied the man.

"And to whom does she belong?"

"To Lord Castleton."

Fenella started. "To Lord Castleton!" she repeated blankly.

"Ay, ay! but he ain't aboard her now; he have lent her, I hear, to a friend who has had her for the last six weeks. She started from this very port, did the *Seamew*, six weeks ago, bound for Madeira and the Canary Islands, where she have been cruising about ever since, and now she have come home again, to the very day as she was expected to do."

"You are quite *sure* Lord Castleton is not on her?" inquired Fenella, earnestly.

"Sartin sure, Miss"—they always called her "Miss," she was so young and girlish!—"his lordship was off to the South of France the werry day she started, and that's how he came to lend his schooner to his friend."

Fenella breathed anew. "And the friend's name?" she inquired, after a minute; but her acquaintance had already moved away from her side, and was talking to some cronies of his own farther on.

The yacht had settled down to her moorings in the dock. The crowd began to disperse—there seemed nothing more to wait for, and Fenella, with the rest, moved away.

She had an errand or two to do in the town before going home, and so she clambered up the steep irregular picturesque little street, and went about her small shoppings. Just as she was about to turn into a baker's shop, half way up the hill, a man's tall slender figure, in a blue serge suit[6] and peaked cloth cap, suddenly darkened the narrow doorway.

"Frank!" she gasped, falling back a step.

"My God—*Fenella!*" he said; and for a moment they stood there—pale, speechless, petrified, gazing with horror and despair into each other's faces.

CHAPTER X.

LORD CASTLETON EXPLAINS.

BY BRAM STOKER.

LORD FRANCIS ONSLOW lifted his cap. The action was an instinctive one, for he was face to face with a lady; but he was half dazed with the unexpected meeting, and could not collect his thoughts. He only remembered that when he had last seen his wife she was opening the door of her chamber to De Mürger. For weeks he had been schooling himself for such a meeting, for he knew that on his return such might at any time occur; but now, when the moment had come, and unexpectedly, the old pain of his shame overwhelmed him anew. His face grew white—white till it seemed to Fenella that it was of the pallor of death. She knew that she had been so far guilty of what had happened—that the murder had been the outcome of her previous acts. She knew also that her husband was ignorant of his part in the deed; and her horror of the man, blood-guilty in such a way, was fined down by the sense of her own partial guilt. The trial, with all its consequent pain to a proud and sensitive woman, had softened her, and she grasped at any hope. The sight of Frank, his gaunt cheeks, which told their tale of suffering, and now the deadly pallor, awoke all the protective feeling which is a part of a woman's love.

It was with her whole soul in her voice that she said again, "Frank!"

His voice was stern as well as sad as he answered her,—

"What is it?"

Her heart went cold, but she persevered.

"Frank, I must have a word with you—I must. For God's sake, for Ronny's sake, do not deny me!" She did not know that as yet Frank Onslow was in ignorance of De Mürger's death; and when his answer came it seemed more hard than even he intended.

"Do you wish to speak of that night?"

In a faint voice she answered,—

"I do." Then looking in his eyes and seeing the hard look becoming harder still—for a man is seldom generous with a woman where his honour is concerned—she added,—

"Oh, Heaven, Frank! You do not think me guilty? No, no, not you, not you! That would be too cruel!"

Frank Onslow paused and said,—

"Fenella, God help me! but I do," and he turned away his head. His wife, of course, thought that he alluded to the murder, and not to her sin against him as he saw it, and with a low moan she turned away and hid her face in her hands. Then with an effort she drew herself up, and without a word or a single movement to show that she even recognised his presence, she passed on up the street.

Frank Onslow stood for a few moments watching her retreating figure, and then went across the street and turned the next corner on his way to the Post Office, for which he had been inquiring when he met his wife. At the door he was stopped by a cheery voice and an outstretched hand,—

"Onslow!"

"Castleton!" The two men shook hands warmly.

"I see you did not get my telegram," said Lord Castleton. "It is waiting for you at the Post Office."

"What telegram?"

"To tell you that I was on my way here from London. I went in your interest, old fellow. I thought you would like full particulars—the newspapers are so vague."

"What papers? My interest? Tell me all. I am ignorant of all that has passed for the last six weeks." A vague, shadowy fear began to creep over his spirits. Castleton's voice was full of sympathy as he answered,—

"Then you have not heard of—— But stay. It is a long story. Come back to the yacht. I was just going to join you there. We shall be all alone, and I can tell you all. I have the newspapers here for you." He motioned to a roll under his arm.

The two went down to the harbour, and finding the sailor waiting with the boat at the steps, were rowed to the yacht and got on board. Here the two men were all alone. Then, with a preliminary clearing of his voice, Castleton began his story.

"Frank Onslow—better get the worst over at once—just after you went away from Harrogate your wife was tried for murder and acquitted."

"My God! Fenella tried for murder? Whose murder?"

"That scoundrel De Mürger. It seems he went into her room in the night and attempted violence, so she stabbed him——"

Castleton stopped in amazement, for a look of radiance came over Frank Onslow's face, as he murmured "Thank God!" Recalled to himself by Castleton's silence, for he was too amazed to go on, Frank said. "I have a reason, old fellow; I shall tell it to you later, but go on. Tell me all the facts, or let me read the papers. Remember I am as yet quite ignorant of it all and I am full of anxiety!"

Without a word Castleton handed him the papers, and, lighting a fresh cigar, sat down with his back to him, and presently yielded to the sun and fresh air and fell into a doze.

Frank Onslow took the papers, and read carefully from end to end the account of the trial of his wife for the murder of De Mürger. When he had finished he sat with the folded paper in his hand, and his eyes had the same far-away look in them which they had had on that fatal night. The hypnotic trance was on him again.

Presently he rose, and with stealthy steps approached his sleeping friend. Murmuring, "Why did I not kill him?" he struck with the folded paper, as though with a dagger, the form before him. Castleton, who had sunk into a pleasant sleep, and whose fat face was wreathed with a smile, was annoyed at the rude awakening. "What the devil!" he began angrily, and then stopped as his eyes met the face of his friend, and he realised that he was in some sort of trance. He grew very pale as he saw Frank Onslow stab, and stab, and stab again. There was a certain grotesqueness in the affair—the man in such terrible earnest in his mind committing murder, while his real weapon was but a folded paper. As he stabbed he hissed, "Why did I not kill him? Why did I not kill him?" Then he went through a series of movements as though he were softly pulling an imaginary door shut behind him, and so back to his own chair, where he sat down, hiding his face in his hands.

Castleton sat looking at him in amazement, and then murmured to himself,—

"They thought it was some one stronger than Fenella whose grasp made those marks on the dead man's throat." He suddenly looked round to see that no one but himself had observed what had happened, and then, being satisfied on this point, murmured again,—

"A noble woman, by Jove! A noble woman!" He called out,—

"Frank—Frank Onslow! Wake up, man!" Onslow raised his head as a man does when suddenly awakened, and smiled as he said,—

"What is it, old man? Have I been asleep?" It was quite evident that he had no recollection of what had just passed. Castleton came and sat down beside him, and his kindly face was grave as he asked,—

"You have read the papers?"

"I have."

"Now tell me—you offered to do so—why you said 'Thank God!' when I told you that your wife had killed De Mürger?"

Frank Onslow paused. Although the memory of what he had thought to be his shame had been with him daily and nightly until he had become familiarised with it, it was another thing to speak of it, even to such a friend as Castleton. Even now, when it was apparent from the issue of the trial that his wife had avenged so dreadfully the attempt upon her honour, he felt it hard to speak on the subject. Castleton saw the doubt and struggle in his mind which was reflected in his face, and said earnestly, as he laid his hand upon his shoulder,—

"Do not hesitate to tell me, Frank. I do not ask out of mere curiosity. I am perhaps a better friend than you think in helping to clear up a certain doubt which I see before me. I think you know I am a friend."

"One of the best a man ever had!" said Frank impulsively, as he took the other's hand. Then, turning away his head, he said slowly,—

"You were surprised because I was glad Fenella killed that scoundrel. I can tell you, Castleton, but I would not tell anyone else. It was because I saw him enter her room, and—God forgive me!—I thought at the time that it was by her wish. That is why I came away from Harrogate that night. That is what kept me away.

How could I go back and face my friends with such a shame fresh upon me? It was your lending me your yacht, old man, that made life possible. When I was by myself through the wildness of the Bay of Biscay and among the great billows of the Atlantic I began to be able to bear. I had steeled myself, I thought, and when I heard that so far from my wife being guilty of such a shame, she actually killed the man that attempted her honour, is it any wonder that I felt joyful?"

After a pause Castleton asked,—

"How did you come to see—to see it. Why did you take no step to prevent it? Forgive me, old fellow, but I want to understand."

Frank Onslow went to the rail, and leaned over. When he came back Castleton saw that his eyes were wet. With what cheerfulness he could assume, he answered,—

"On that very night I had made up my mind to try to win back my wife's love. I wrote a letter to her—a letter in which I poured out my whole soul—and I left my room to put it under her door, so that she would get it in the morning. But"—here he paused, and then said, slowly, "but when in the corridor, I saw her door open, and at the same moment De Mürger appeared."

"Did she seem surprised?"

"Not at first. But a moment after a look of amazement crossed her face, and she stepped back into the room, he following her." As he said this he put his head between his hands and groaned.

"And then?" added his friend.

"And then I hardly know what happened. My mind seems full of a dim memory of a blank existence, and then a series of wild whirling thoughts, something like that last moment after death in Wiertz's picture.[1] I think I must have slept, for it was two o'clock when I saw Fenella, and the clock was striking five when I crossed the bridge after I had left the hotel."

"And the letter: what became of it?"

Frank started. "The letter? I never thought of it. Stay! I must have left it on the table in my room. I remember seeing it there a little while before I came away."

"How was it addressed? Do not think me inquisitive, but I cannot help thinking that that letter may yet be of some great importance."

Frank smiled, a sad smile enough, as he answered. "By the pet name I had for Fenella—Mrs. Right. I used to chaff her because she always defended her position when we argued, and so, when I wanted to tease her, I called her Mrs. Right."

"Was it written on hotel paper?"

"No. I was going to write on some, but I thought it would be better to use the sort we had when—when we were first married. There were a few sheets in my writing case, so I took one."

"That was headed somewhere in Surrey, was it not?"

"Yes; Chiddingford, near Haslemere.[2] It was a pretty place, too, called 'The Grange.' Fenella fell in love with it, and made me buy it right away."

"Is any one living there now?"

"It is let to some one—I don't think that I heard the name. The agent knows. When the trouble came I told him to do what he could with it, and not to bother me with it any more. After a while he wrote and asked if I would mind it being let to a foreigner? I told him he might let it to a devil so long as he did not worry me."

Lord Castleton paused awhile, and asked the next question in a hesitating way. He felt embarrassed, and showed it.

"Tell me one thing more, old fellow—if–if you don't mind."

"My dear Castleton, I'll tell you anything you like."

"How did you sign the letter?"

Onslow's face looked sad as he answered,—

"I signed it by another old pet name we both understood. We had pet names—people always have when they are first married," he added with embarrassment.

"Of course," murmured the sympathetic Castleton.

"One such name lasted a long time. An old friend of my father's came to see us, and in a playful moment he said I was a 'sad dog.' Fenella took it up and used to call me 'Doggie,' and I often signed myself 'Frank Doggie'—as men usually do."

"Of course," again murmured Castleton, as if such a signature were a customary thing. Then he added, "And on this occasion?"

"On this occasion I used the name that seemed full of happiest memories. 'Frank Doggie' may seem idiotic to an outsider, but to Fenella and myself it might mean much."

The two men sat silent awhile, and then Castleton asked softly,—

"I suppose it may be taken for granted that Lady Francis never got the letter?"

"I take it, it is so; but it is no matter now, I refused to speak with her just before I met you. I did not know then what I know now—and she will never speak to me again." He sighed as he spoke, and turned away. Then he went to the rail of the yacht and leaned over with his head down, looking into the still blue water beneath him.

"Poor old Frank!" said Castleton to himself. "I can't but think that this matter may come right yet. I must find out what became of that letter, in case Lady Francis never got it. It would prove to her that Frank——"

His train of thought suddenly stopped. A new idea seemed to strike him so forcibly that it quite upset him. Onslow, who had come over from the rail, noticed it. "I say, Castleton, what is wrong with you? You have got quite white about the gills."

"Nothing—nothing!" he answered hastily. "I am subject to it. They call it heart. Pardon me for a bit, I'll go to my bunk and lie down," and he went below.

In truth, he was overwhelmed by the thought which had just struck him. If his surmise were true, that Onslow, in a hypnotic trance, as he had almost proved by its recurrence, had killed De Mürger, where, then, was Fenella's heroism after all? True that she had taken the blame on herself; but might it not have been that she was morally guilty all the same? Why, then, had she taken the blame? Was it not because she feared that her husband might have refused to screen her shame; or because she feared that if any less heroic aspect of the tragedy were presented to the public, her own fair fame might suffer in greater degree? Could it indeed be that Fenella Onslow was not a heroine, but only a calculating woman of exceeding smartness? Then, again, if Frank Onslow believed that his wife had avenged her honour, was it wise to disturb such belief? He might think, if once the suggestion were made to him, that his honour was preserved only by his own unconscious act. Was it then wise to disturb existing relations between the husband and wife, sad though they were? Did they come together again, they might in mutual confidence arrive at a real knowledge of the facts, and then—and then, what would be the result? And besides, might there not be some danger in any suggestion made as to his suspicion of who struck the blow? It was true that Lady Francis had been acquitted of the crime, although she confessed to the killing; but her husband might still be tried,—and if tried? What then would be the result of the discovery of the missing letter on which he had been building such hopes?

The problem was too much for Lord Castleton. His life had been too sunny and easy-going to allow of familiarity with great emotions, and such a problem as this was to him overwhelming. The issue was too big for him; and revolving in his own mind all that belonged to it, he glided into sleep.

He was wakened by the sound of oars and voices drifting in through the open port.

CHAPTER XI.

MADAME DE VIGNY'S REVENGE.

BY FLORENCE MARRYAT.

"Revenge is sweet—especially to women."—*Byron.*[1]

PERHAPS of all the visitors who were in the Prospect Hotel on the night of De Mürger's murder the one to be most perplexed was Lucille de Vigny. To her, Lord Francis Onslow's mysterious disappearance was (at first) inexplicable. Yesterday he had been her lover, full of protestations of affection, and ready, as she believed, to fly with her anywhere. To-day he had flown by himself, and without leaving a word of explanation behind him. But, as the whole of the circumstances came to light, when Lady Francis was dragged away from the hotel in custody, on the charge of the Count's murder, Mme. de Vigny thought she had solved the riddle. She had no belief in Fenella's account of the defence of her honour. She sneered at the idea with an incredulous smile. But she *did* think that Lord Francis had found his wife and Count de Mürger together and had killed his rival before her eyes, or perhaps injured him so much with his muscular English fists that he had died from the effects. And then the wife, preferring to stand her trial for manslaughter sooner than confess her infidelity, had taken the crime, or the accident, or whatever you may like to call it, on her own shoulders, but for no love of the absent husband, who would probably refuse ever to see her again.

So far Mme. de Vigny's intelligence, which had not ripened in an entirely moral atmosphere, had led her pretty near the truth. But her conclusion was like a broken watch, useless because the mainspring was missing. For she did not stop there. She completed the story for herself. Lord Francis had flown, not for his wife's sake nor his own—but in order not to drag *her* (whom he loved) into the miserable tangle of his married life. He would remain away until

everything was concluded, and then he would seek her out again,
and they would be happy. Such a terrible scandal would surely be
followed by a divorce, after which he would be free to put her in
the place left vacant by his wife's infidelity. But the trial of Lady
Francis Onslow took place, as has been related, and yet no intelligence came of her missing husband. When she had left Harrogate,
and the child had been taken away, Mme. de Vigny became tired of
being left behind. She returned to London, and went down to Haslemere, thinking Lord Francis might be lying *perdu*, in his country
home. But all she found there was a large board stating that The
Grange was to be let, furnished, and that applications were to be
addressed to Mr. Abraham Hewett, of Chancery Lane.[2] Quick as
thought she resolved (if possible) to take it. She had no love for
the country, nor for a secluded life, but to settle in his very home
must be, she argued, the best way by which to come in contact
with Lord Francis Onslow. Even if he did not come there he must,
sooner or later, learn the name of his tenant, and be drawn into
the circle of her love again. She found no difficulty in the matter.
Her references were the best of all—ready cash—and Mr. Hewett
had been instructed to let The Grange as soon as possible. Her
foreign accent somewhat puzzled him, and he had mentioned her
to his client (as Onslow told Castleton) simply as a foreigner.

Perhaps she had tried to increase his mystification by speaking
as incoherently, and writing as illegibly, as she could. Any way, she
secured The Grange, and took possession of it.

How much she revelled at first in the thought that she was
living in the house which Lord Francis called his own, using the
same furniture, and walking in the same garden that he had been
used to walk in. Before long she hoped that he would be there
too, watching the moon rise above the summits of the fine old
trees. She searched the house for some memento of him—a cast-
off glove, a faded flower. But the housemaid's broom had been too
busy. The Grange was inviolate from attic to basement. Only in a
little drawer in his looking-glass stand she had found a few of his
visiting cards, evidently forgotten or overlooked.

"Lord Francis Onslow, The Grange, Chiddingford," and on the
other side, "The Corinthians, Pall Mall."[3] How sweet the words
looked! The enraptured woman raised them to her lips as she

thought that some day she might own a corresponding passport to society. Meantime, Madame de Vigny did not enjoy her solitude long. While the man she dreamed of was hiding himself in Paris, and on the *Seamew*, others of her acquaintance tracked her to The Grange, and intruded their presence upon her. Lucille de Vigny was too beautiful, and, unfortunately, too notorious, to conceal herself successfully. She had had many admirers besides Lord Francis Onslow, and before she had been many weeks at Chiddingford they commenced to run down from London to call upon her. And she was pleased to see them. She had not been used to the company of her own thoughts.

They proved ugly company to her on occasions—she had not always the courage to look back—and she earnestly hoped to make for herself a future on which the past should have no power to obtrude. So, pending the return of Lord Francis, she was glad to welcome the various friends who considered it worth their while to travel down to see her. Among them was Colonel Uriah B. Clutterbuck, a Senator from the United States, who had made a large fortune over railway iron, and was trying to spend it in the old country. He had been an ardent admirer of Madame de Vigny from the first day of their acquaintance, and would have proposed to her long before, had not Lord Francis Onslow's claims stood in his way. But now the Colonel thought he saw his opportunity. The first evening he dined with Lucille, and she took him after dinner into the garden, his heart overflowed, and he was able to contain himself no longer.

"Mrs. der Vin-yay," he commenced, "Loo-cill—if I may call you so—there is no man in the United States that can boast of a bigger pile than your obedient servant. I am not a lord, ma'am; I would disdain to be one. Neither am I, perhaps, an Apoller; but, in point of dollars, Mrs. der Vin-yay, you will not find my superior, and they and I are at your service, to-day, and for ever, if you will only say the word."

Madame de Vigny looked at him with surprise, mingled with a degree of contempt. She was a magnificent woman, towering several inches above the New York Senator, with a finely-moulded figure, large dark eyes, chiselled features, and a voluptuous mouth. She looked like a Juno[4] regarding a human rat.

"Colonel Clutterbuck," she replied, "you astonish me. Surely I have never encouraged you to address me in such an extraordinary manner. I have not the slightest intention of marrying again, and I must beg you never to refer to the subject."

"Very well, Mrs. der Vin-yay," replied the discomfited suitor, "say no more about it. I thought you might have liked the pile, ma'am, if you didn't admire the man; but it won't go begging, Mrs. der Vin-yay, you may bet your bottom dollar upon that."

"I do not wish to bet anything, Colonel Clutterbuck," said Lucille grandly, "nor should I take money into consideration on a question of marriage. But I am quite content with my life as it is, and have no desire to alter it."

"Ah! You're waiting for a title, Mrs. der Vin-yay," replied the Senator, "that's where it is. You'll never tell me that a fine woman like yourself means to remain single for the rest of her life. But you're gone on these English aristocrats, like the gals in my country, and nothing will satisfy you but to be a duchess or a countess."

"Colonel Clutterbuck, your remarks are positively offensive, and I must entreat you to turn your conversation to something else. I thank you for your offer, but I can never accept it. Come indoors and let me give you a song. I had a parcel of new ones down from London last week." She drew her lace wrap about her as she spoke, and turned to re-enter the house. Her handsome face looked proud and cold under the moonlight, but her heart was throbbing warmly against Lord Francis Onslow's card, which she carried in her bosom. She was not really faithful, or affectionate, but she had set her mind upon capturing and holding this man (as a woman sometimes sets her mind upon a spaniel or a bonnet), and would not rest until she had achieved her purpose. In like manner the American Senator had set his mind upon her, but he would not break his heart over her refusal. He had thought she would make a splendid picture at the head of his New York table, and an enviable wife to present to his friends, but if she couldn't accept his pile of dollars he concluded that some other lady would. So they parted on their usual terms, and Lucille even asked him to repeat his visit on the first opportunity.

The next morning, when her maid brought her letters into her room with her coffee, she was struck by the appearance among them of a pale buff letter, stamped on the top "On H. M. Service," and on the bottom, "Dead Letter Office."

"What is that, Rose?" she cried.

"I do not know, Madame, but it was left here with the other letters, so I thought I had better bring it up to you."

Lucille had by this time seized the envelope and read the superscription:

"Frank Doggie, Esq., The Grange, Chiddingford, Haslemere."

"How strange!" she laughed. "Who is Mr. Frank Doggie, and why do they send his letters here?"

"Shall I return it to the postman, Madame?"

"No! It would be useless. I will keep it a little while. It may be inquired for."

So the maid retired, leaving the letter behind her. It seemed to fascinate Lucille; though she had the morning papers and several letters of her own to peruse, her eyes kept turning towards the buff envelope with marked curiosity, until she took it up again and examined it carefully. What right had Mr. Doggie to have the name of Frank?—that name above all others so dear to her. The fact alone seemed to make the letter her property. It had come from the Dead Letter Office. That showed that all reasonable inquiries had been made for the owner without avail. There could be no harm, then, in her reading it, for the more she regarded it, the more curious she became to learn its contents; so without further ado, she tore it open. It contained an envelope addressed to "Mrs. Right, Prospect Hotel, Harrogate," and scribbled all over, both in red and black ink, and in various signatures, with the words, "Not known here," "Gone away," "No such person," etc. This was the letter (as may be remembered) that Lord Francis wrote with such a beating heart to his wife on the night of De Mürger's murder, and left, in his subsequent horror and confusion, on the table in his bedroom. When he had gone, the servants carried it to the land-lord, who, knowing no one of the name of "Right," had delivered it over to the Post Office. And so it had gone the round of Harrogate, being repudiated everywhere, and finally found its way to London, and was opened and returned to the address engraved on the note-paper. "Mrs. Right and Mr. Doggie." Madame de Vigny laughed at the strange conjunction of names, as she prepared to find out what

Doggie and Right had to say to each other. But she did not laugh long. The first words her eyes lit upon made the colour fade from her cheek, whilst her hand clenched savagely over the unoffending paper. They were the words Frank had poured forth in the anguish of his soul at Fenella's feet:—

"My darling—my own, *own* darling (for that you must ever be to me, let who will come between us), why will you make us both so unhappy? I know you are not happy, Fenella! I can read it in your face; hear it in each tone of your voice. Those were not the looks and tones that made the first years of our married life one long dream of bliss. And I am supremely miserable, more so than yourself, for I have sinned more against you than you have against me. I confess it, dear love. I prostrate myself before you, and I cry for forgiveness. Can you not forgive me? Will you not take me to your heart again, and let me try to atone for all the past? My life is so barren without you and my darling child. Do you suppose that anything can compensate me for your loss? As for Madame de V., she is *nothing* to me—less than nothing; a toy to pass away the time that goes so slowly without you; an opiate that for a moment makes me forget my pain, and sometimes, even while I seem to yield to her witcheries, I loathe her because she has come between us. But it shall never be again, dear love, if you but say the word. Come back to me, Fenella, and I will swear to wipe her (and all like her) out of my life, as surely as I would kill the viper that lay across your path. Oh, when I think of all that she has cost me, how bitterly I hate her!"

There was much more in the same strain, but this was sufficient for Lucille, who lay back on her pillow with the paper crushed in her hand, and jealousy and revenge gleaming from her eyes. *This* was how he thought of her, then. This was how he wrote and spoke of her to his wife—his faithless, flirting wife—the murderess, by her own account, of Count de Mürger, the unworthy mother of his child—the creature to whom he might, after all, return—so contemptible and despicable and mean-spirited were men. How could she be revenged on them both? On *him* for so deceiving herself; and on *her* for retaining her power over him?

Madame de Vigny did not weep. Her temperament was not of the weeping order, but she gnashed her teeth with impotent fury as she lay with her face buried in her pillow, and thought out her best means of revenge. Her maid was surprised to find how long a time elapsed before her usual services were required, but after the lapse of two hours she was summoned to her mistress's side.

Lucille was up and engaged in writing.

"Tell George to take this telegram into Chiddingford at once," she exclaimed, handing it to her.

It was addressed to Colonel Clutterbuck, and ran as follows:— "If not engaged, dine with me this evening."

When Madame de Vigny had arrived at this decision, she tried to calm herself, but it was a difficult task. All day she raved against Providence and the treachery of the man she had trusted in, but, when the evening came, she arrayed herself in her most becoming costume to meet the Senator. She had made up her mind by that time. She had refused him simply on account of her fatal passion for Lord Francis Onslow, but that was over now—quenched as effectually as though it had never been—and she was determined not to let the Colonel's dollars slip through her fingers a second time. For many reasons, too, America would suit her better than England. How could she have been such a fool as to think of giving it up for a foolish love dream?

She looked more than handsome—she looked bewitchingly seductive as she advanced with a soft, luminous gaze to meet Clutterbuck, and asked his pardon for the trouble she had given him.

"But something has occurred since last night, my dear friend," she said, "that makes it necessary for me to take a short sea voyage. My doctor is rather alarmed about my health, and insists on my obedience. So, as I have always had a supreme longing to visit your delightful country, I have decided to go to America for the autumn, and want you to tell me the best means of getting there. You must know so much," she concluded, as she slipped her arm confidingly through his.

"Ah! Mrs. der Vin-yay!" exclaimed the Colonel, patting her little hand, "why can't you make up your mind to let me take you there? You should travel like a queen, Loo-cill, and there's a house waiting for you in New York city that might satisfy an empress. Say the word, Mrs. der Vin-yay, say the word, and you'll make me the happiest man in the United States."

"But there is an obstacle to our marriage," she whispered, "perhaps an insuperable one. Had it not been so, I should have said 'yes,' last night."

"Dollars can overcome all obstacles," replied the Colonel. "What is it? I guess it'll make no difference between us."

"I have a little nephew—the orphan child of an only sister, now deceased, and I will marry no man who asks me to leave him behind."

"That man won't be myself, Mrs. der Vin-yay. Bring him along, by all means. There's room in the States for another boy or two, and I'll do by him as if he were my own."

"Oh, you are too good, *too* good," exclaimed Lucille fervently, as she pressed his hand.

The Senator was not young, and in no mind to wait, besides which he was anxious to get back to his own country, so, as the lady's wishes appeared to coincide with his own, they arranged matters to their mutual satisfaction that evening, and in a fortnight were married at a registrar's office in London, without any one but themselves being the wiser for the transaction. Lucille had pleaded for secrecy, lest her friends should interfere to prevent her leaving England, and the Colonel had arrived at that age when a man detests all publicity and fuss. So Madame de Vigny was transformed into Mrs. Colonel Clutterbuck as if by magic, and went home to the Langham Hotel[5] with her husband, as if they had been married for twenty years. Four days after the *Germanic* was to start from Liverpool for New York,[6] and their cabins were already secured on board of her.

"And now!" said Lucille, with a winning smile, the day before they started, "you must let me run down into Suffolk, Colonel, and fetch my little nephew."

"Suffolk? That's a long way," said Colonel Clutterbuck. "Hadn't I better go for you?"

"Oh, no, no! I couldn't hear of it. The little fellow would be frightened out of his senses at the sight of a stranger. He is terribly sensitive. I can never coax him away, but by pretending we are going to meet his poor, dear mother."

"Very well, Mrs. Clutterbuck, have it your own way," replied the Colonel, who was beaming with pride in the possession of so handsome a wife.

So Lucille, armed with Lord Francis Onslow's card, travelled down on the following day to Felixstowe,[7] where Jacynth's sister, Mrs. Grandison, was staying with her own son and little Ronny.

This was the Frenchwoman's revenge.

She had heard whilst at Harrogate of Ronny's destination, and knew that in so small a place she would experience little difficulty in finding out which house was occupied by Mrs. Grandison.

She disliked children (as most women of her stamp do), but she felt she could wreak no bitterer vengeance on Lord Francis Onslow and his wife than by depriving them of their son and heir, so dearly loved by both of them.

Her marriage had been conducted so secretly that she was most unlikely to be recognised as Mrs. Clutterbuck, and once she had got the boy to America she believed that (virtually) he would be lost. What was to follow after that, or whether the game would be worth the candle to her, she never stayed to consider.

Mrs. Grandison, whilst engaged over her mid-day meal with the children, was much surprised to hear that a lady wished to speak to her. Still more so when on entering the drawing room, she saw the fashionably-attired Mrs. Clutterbuck.

"You are doubtless surprised to receive a call from a perfect stranger, madam," commenced Lucille, with her charming accent; "but time did not permit me to prepare you for my appearance. I come as a messenger from Lord Francis Onslow. I am an intimate friend of his, and of his poor, dear wife!"

"Indeed!" said Mrs. Grandison gravely.

Her first opinion of Fenella's conduct had been intensified to horror when the news of the murder and the trial were made public, and she had only taken charge of Ronny under protest—at the urgent request of her brother—and because she had felt it to be a Christian duty to keep the poor child, as far as possible, from hearing the terrible things that were said of his mother. But her dislike of the subject was so great that when Lucille said she was an intimate friend of the Onslows, she shrunk from her with ill-concealed aversion.

"Indeed!" she reiterated slowly.

"Yes, and have been so for years. This has been a terribly sad affair for them both, but let us hope the worst is over. Lord Francis feels naturally that it is best they should spend the next few years, at least, out of England; therefore, they start for the Brazils to-morrow, and wish naturally to take Ronny with them."

"Lord Francis is, then, reconciled to his wife?"

"Oh, yes! Why should he not be? The unfortunate affair of Count de Mürger's death really redounds to her credit, and what preceded it was only a foolish misunderstanding!"

"Of course if Lord Francis is satisfied no one has a right to demur at his decision. You come from him, you say?"

"Yes. He asked me to fetch Ronny home for him. He would have come himself, but he had no time. Here is his card, which he begged me to present to you, with a thousand thanks for your kindness to his child."

Mrs. Grandison hardly knew what to do. She disliked delivering Ronny into the charge of a stranger, and yet she felt she had no right to keep the boy against his parents' wishes. She kept turning the card over and over in her hands as she considered the matter.

"Did you say they sailed to-morrow?" she asked, presently.

"Yes, to-morrow, at four in the afternoon."

"It is a very sudden resolution."

"Not at all. They have contemplated it for weeks past, but Lady Francis' health has prevented them carrying it out. Now they have a sudden opportunity, of which they wish to avail themselves. How long will it take to get Ronny ready to go back with me?"

"Oh, that can be done in half an hour. But I wish my brother (who put him in my charge) had written me word that his parents wished to resume their guardianship."

"I know nothing of that," snapped Lucille. "All Lord Francis told me was to come down to Felixstowe, and take back his boy to him at all costs; and I should think a parent's wish was imperative."

"Certainly," replied Mrs. Grandison, "and I should not dream of disputing it. If you will kindly wait here for a few minutes I will bring Ronny to you."

She left the room as she spoke, and Lucille felt that she had triumphed and her revenge would be complete. She remembered how Fenella had gloated over this boy, how Lord Francis had written of him as his "darling child," and smiled to herself as she thought what they would both say and do, when they found he had gone beyond recall. In a short time the door opened again, and Mrs. Grandison appeared with Ronny. He recognised Lucille at once as the lady he had seen at the *table d'hôte* at Harrogate.

"I know you!" he said, coming forward with a shy, outstretched hand; "you were with my papa at Harrogate."

"And with your mamma, Ronny, of course. We were all there together. But mamma wants you sadly. She has been fretting terribly for her boy. We are going back to her together."

"Going back to mummy? Oh, I *am* glad! I have wanted her so," said Ronny, trying hard to keep back his tears. "It's been very jolly with Harold, of course, and Mrs. Grandison's been ever so good to me—but I've missed mummy every day. Shall we go at once? I'm all ready, and my box is packed. And shall I see her to-day? Oh! do let us make haste and go."

He thrust his hand in that of Lucille as he spoke, who rose smiling, and addressed Helen Grandison.

"You see, madam, the ties of nature surmount those of friendship. Please to accept the best thanks of the parents of this boy, for your care of him at a very trying moment, to which I must add my own, and wish you farewell."

"Good afternoon," said Mrs. Grandison stiffly, as she watched them get into the fly which was in waiting, and drive away to the station.

And before she had time to acquaint Jacynth with the circumstance, Ronny (still with the expectation of meeting his mother) was far away on the broad Atlantic!

CHAPTER XII.

TO LIVE OR DIE?

BY FRANK DANBY.

"Row faster, man, row faster! Move—no, sit where you are, but give me the other oars. Pull, pull," he said, "as if you were getting away from hell." And feverishly, with white set lips, with gleaming eyes, Lord Francis accentuated his words by his actions, and propelled the boat with all the strength of which he was capable, across the blue waters that kept him from Fenella. His feet pressed against the wood, the muscles of his arms standing out like iron, the youth in him dying under the strain, his very brain ceasing to act, and his heart almost standing still; he tried by physical exertion to deaden that burning mental pain that seized him as he felt, saw, heard, and writhed under the sense that he had wronged her, wronged Fenella, wronged the woman who always was and always would be the one woman on earth for him; wronged the girl-love that had lain on his breast, believed and loved him; the child who had grown to womanhood in his arms—Fenella, his wife.

And at last the keel of the boat grated on the shore.

He had sat still while Lord Castleton had spoken of the trial. Once the stunning news had overwhelmed him, he had become an automaton and not a man. Sea and sky melted mistily into each other, and mechanically from his mouth issued the empty sentences. But then the hours passed on, Castleton slept, the yacht lay at its moorings, and then—then a glimmer of reason and sense penetrated the dull concussion of that first shock.

"Fenella," he said, "Fenella!" It was a moan, a cry, not a human being asking for his wife, but a soul in anguish crying to its God.

"Did you call, sir?" asked the mate, coming forward, touching his gold-braided cap; "did you call?" With blood-shot eyes Frank looked at him, saw beyond him: "Fenella."

"Any part of Guernsey, sir?"

"I must get back, I must get back."

All that he was capable of was a wish to get back, to see her face again, to fling himself down on his knees before her, see that fair sweet face, that child's face. Murderess they had called her, unfaithful he had called her. O Heaven! and she was his wife, and he——

And then he was in Guernsey again.

She sat at her window, still, white, silent. The hours had crushed heavily over her, and spared her nothing. Not until now did she know, not until now did she realise, all that her husband had been to her, all that she had looked for from him, all the hope that had illuminated the dark days of her imprisonment, lit up her bare cell, flushed its soft light over the courthouse that dreadful day, the day that until now had been the most dreadful day of all her life.

A hundred eyes had been upon her, had burnt greedily into her soul—curious eyes, searching eyes, eyes all around. All the air was alive with voices—voices that rose and fell monotonous, persistent, dreadful. What were they saying? Now a sentence disentangled itself, now another. "The prisoner pleads guilty, my lord." "The prisoner!" How curious it sounded. "The prisoner!" How should she know anything of prisoners, dreadful creatures, shameful, lowering, hideous? She had dreamed of them in her happy childhood, and awaking shuddering, had hidden her face in nurse's breast, or been soothed to rest again in father's arms.

"The prisoner is separated from her husband," went on that monotonous voice. How strange, *she* was separated from her husband; strange she should be like the *prisoner*, a shameful, disgraced prisoner. And dreaming she smiled, smiled in the dock, with a hundred opera-glasses scanning her fair, pale face, and a hundred naked eyes burning into her secrets.

But the smile woke her: she had always smiled; but now, now it was a long time since she had smiled. What was she smiling at? Then she woke to the knowledge of her surroundings, and she shuddered in the dock; the sweet face grew white and convulsed; suddenly she burst out crying. Crying aloud, poor child, poor wayward child, who had meant to play through life, and woke from her playing—here.

All alive and awake she was for the rest of that horrible day, quivering and trembling and sobbing, half child, half woman, as the trial wore on. Ever and again the crimson flushed into her cheek, her eyes suffused, her head bent, in a very agony of shame; she heard horrible questions, horrible answers. She felt herself undraped before these inquisitorial eyes, and shrinking, drawing her cloak round her with shaking hands, she would try and hide her poor hot face.

But as the day wore on, something of hope crept in warm about her heart. If Frank were here, he would not let them talk so—Frank, her lover. She heard again the passionate protestations of their short betrothal. She felt again his lips against hers. She was back again in the golden days when the sun-flush of love was over all her life, and sun-queen in those hours she had played with her happiness. And pitifully the tremulous lips murmured, "If Frank were here, he would not let them hurt me; if Frank were here!"

What a strange, complicated Fenella! Arraigned for murder, she pleaded "Guilty." "Guilty," though her hands were clean! With the unthinking generosity of a child she did a woman's deed with a man's heart. She took her husband's guiltless guilt upon herself, and cried, "It was I!" while yet the horror of his act was vibrating through her frame. She had not counted the cost, could not. But if all the sum of those dreadful hours and days had been spread out before her, with shining eyes she would have scanned it, and still have called out generously, "It was I."

But her heart was larger than her brain. Her brain failed her a little at the last. She was dim, confused, frightened. She forgot so much. These men who were there to judge her, noting the crouching, weeping girl, with golden hair dishevelled, bloodshot eyes, weak and shrinking, *thinking* her guilty, *pronounced* her innocent, and sent her forth free.

Free! but what a freedom! Where was Frank? Where was anybody? Who was there to take her in his strong arms, let her hide her face upon his breast, weep there until her shame had died away, and the memory of her degradation was washed clean. Who, indeed?

The man who had defended her, who had been her lover, who had been her friend, came to her and he—he would not take her hand. He had spoken to her of her boy, and the cold emptiness of her heart ached with the sudden rush of her emotion as she cried out, with outstretched arms: "My boy! bring me my boy!" To press the child in her arms, to feel the soft down of his cheek against hers, to hear the lisping, "Muzzer, muzzer dear!" from his lips, to have his arms about her—this, this would save her reason. She felt her reason going, felt her mind darkened, the path before her no longer clear. She was in a gloomy world, groping helplessly for a warm human clasp of fellowship. Jacynth, her friend, answered her mother-cry. Answered, and left her childless.

Then he brought her here, here to this beautiful, lonely, wind-girt, sea-girt island, and left her to strain her eyes out into the sea, that said nothing to her. The sky was empty for her, the flowers, it seemed to her, faded as she looked. Poor beauty! poor coquettish, light-hearted Fenella!

Then she met Frank in the street, and light flashed back to her, and memory and understanding. In a rush of emotion she saw him as lover, as husband, as murderer. She knew what he had done. She knew, too, what she had done to save him. "Frank"—the words rushed to her lips, words of love, of forgiveness, of—— and he repelled her. Ice-cold on her heart lay his dead love, his living contempt, and she who would have died for him, seemed as if she died by him. He killed her. Not physically; she still lived, moved, breathed, but her faith was dead, and her hope, and her youth. She staggered home to her old seat by the window. She felt sick, and giddy, and dazed as from an earthquake; all her world was in ruins. It was only now she realised the hope on which she had lived all this time. Only now she knew that Frank had been the bulwark on which she rested, the light toward which she had looked. That though she was past reason, and had not asked why he had delayed, she had felt he would come, and that in his eyes she would read his love for her that had never swerved, his faith in her that would answer for all things, his gratitude to her, gratitude that she would put away, and not let him linger over, but would banish and forget, and it should be forgotten. Nothing should be between them any more, but love. He would bring her back Ronny; he and she and Ronny would be together always.

And then they had met, and he had repulsed her, rejected her, looked upon her coldly! She was hopeless. She looked out over the blue sea, the rocks, the sails, the harbour, but there was a film before her eyes, all things were darkened. Even the face of Nature would never smile upon her again. Hope was dead.

Then he came back. He knelt at her feet, he called her by a thousand endearing names, he kissed her hands, the hem of her dress. She sat there dumb, stricken as a statue, the film darkening before her eyes, and her brain throb, throbbing, like the screw of a steam-engine.

"Fenella, my wife, my darling! For Heaven's sake, listen to me. Don't look at me like that, my darling; hear me. I never knew. I swear, I never knew. I was ill, I heard nothing, knew nothing until an hour ago. My sweet, what you must have suffered! Fenella, speak— a word, a little word. Sweetheart, think of our childhood."

And then a little moan came from her, a little sighing moan, and she fell half forward. He caught her in his arms. "Darling," he said again, passionately, "only hear me. Ah!"

It was too late! Was it too late? She lay in his arms white and cold and silent. Frank, kissing those pale, cold lips, chafing those dead hands, murmuring over her a thousand caressing names, dis-tracted with despair, desperately put away the fear, and called for help in anguished tones.

Then the women came in, and were busy about her, and there were moaning and lamentation, but still she heard not.

Fenella was not dead, but she was ill—terribly ill. The silver cord was not broken,[1] but it was strained to its last fibre. Weeks went by, weeks when she lay in the little cottage at Guernsey, and Frank crept about with anguished eyes, and lived on the bulletins from the sick-room. Weeks during which, with the gold locks short-cropped, and the sweet face fever-flushed and unrecognisable, Fenella lay in bed, and shrieked in her delirium that Frank did not do it, that she did; that Frank hated her because she had done it, but she had not done it. There was blood on her hands, horrible blood, human blood. There was blood on his hands, but she would kiss them. She was swimming in blood, drowning in blood; but Frank would save her. Ronny was on the shore, waiting for her—bright-faced Ronny, waiting to kiss away the stains from them both. And then she would call out again that she was drowning, and call for Frank, always for Frank, in agonised, delirious shrieks.

"Doctor! doctor!" He held him with hands grown thin and wasted, spoke to him in a voice all broken with tears, looked at him with eyes dim with wild, convulsive crying: "Will she live? will she live?"

The doctor was a man who had studied humanity as well as physic.

"I think so," he answered; "there is room for hope. Every day gained brings us nearer to it. If once she sleeps—sleeps naturally—I think she is saved." He hesitated, and Frank, hanging on his words, pressed him further.

"She will wake to reason—to mental restfulness?"

He was a man; he had heard his patient in her delirium. She had a history, this beautiful young woman who called herself Mrs. Orme, and over whom Lord Francis Onslow watched with such care. She had a history, but he did not know it, did not seek to know it. No idle curiosity prompted his question. But if she woke, and woke to trouble, then—then he could not answer for the consequences.

"Will you let me tell you?" Before Dr. Fairfax could say "Yes" or "No," Frank had dragged him back into the room, and was pouring out incoherently, quickly, the whole miserable story: their courtship, their married life, their bickerings, and the interference of relatives, their separation, his jealousy, the *murder* that even now he could not account for or remember—everything, everything.

The doctor listened, grave, sympathetic. Frank paused breathlessly.

"She has a child, you say, a little child? Did she care for that, did she love it?"

"She worships him as (fool that I have been not to have seen it!) only a good woman could love her child."

Frank's jealousy was dead for ever.

"Then bring her child here. Let her wake amid her natural surroundings—her husband by her side, her child's voice ringing in her ears, the life of the 'home' about her. Let the past be forgotten by her. Let peace be her healing, and love her medicine. You will be her doctor, not I, when there is recognition in her eyes, and she is struggling back to a world that has been so cruel to her."

He took up his hat. He had spoken. They must wait the hour.

CHAPTER XIII.

"THE SCARS REMAINED."

BY MRS. EDWARD KENNARD.

WHEN Lord Francis Onslow listened to Dr. Fairfax's advice, he resolved to act upon it without loss of time, especially as he sadly realised that in the present condition of affairs he could do nothing to expedite his wife's recovery. The issue lay in God's hands. He felt this keenly, chafing at his helplessness. During the many hours spent in the chamber of the sick woman, he reviewed his past life with bitter repentance. Little by little he distinctly perceived how unworthy had been his own conduct, and how much he was to blame for the terrible occurrences which had recently taken place. When he recalled Fenella as she was when they were first married, he found it impossible to hold himself guiltless. However wayward and childish she might have been, in those days no one could doubt her purity and innocence. Moreover, she loved him, and a man does not lose a woman's love without some cause. Now she lay stained and crushed upon a bed of pain, like a white lily stricken to earth. Her name was in all men's mouths. The spotlessness of her reputation had departed, never to return. She might have been a happy wife and mother, and now what was she? A creature shunned by her kind, fallen from her pedestal, and blackened by crime. Ah! it was pitiful to think of; still more pitiful to trace the folly, vanity, and wrong-doing which had brought about such a result. Why could they not have rested content with one another's love? What a fevered, unnatural existence theirs had been of late years! He smiled a wan smile, as it occurred to him that their histories contained an unwonted amount of sensation and melodrama. Their experiences would form a strange narrative. Once, long ago, Fenella had loved him truly and well. Of that he felt morally certain. If he had only exercised a little patience with his beautiful child-wife, and sought to correct her errors by example, rather than by preaching and criticism, how differently things might have turned out. She was young. Her faults were chiefly those of youth and ignorance, combined with the natural craving for admiration of a pretty woman. But there was no harm in her—then. She might have been guided. A girl in her teens is made of plastic material. Her character is not firmly set, as a rule, either for good or evil. It was in his power to have influenced her, and to have developed the finer side of her nature. But, instead of this, what had he done? In lieu of recognising the responsibility which he assumed, by taking the life of another into his keeping, he had sought to justify his own shortcomings by exaggerating hers and imitating them. If she flirted, he flirted. If she was foolish, he was doubly so. Was that the way for the head of a family to behave? When her coquetries irritated him, he looked for consolation elsewhere, and eventually allowed himself to fall completely under the spell of a middle-aged woman, remarkable rather for her beauty than her virtue. And then, when Fenella resented his conduct, and in forcible language pointed out that the marriage ceremony should be as binding for the husband as the wife, what reply did he make? He answered, in the false, unjust voice of the world, "No; you labour under a very great mistake in upbraiding me, and have no ground whatever to stand upon. Society has decreed that a man may do as he likes, be as unfaithful (within certain limits) as he pleases; but you are totally different. A woman cannot go out of bounds, without getting the worst of it. Therefore, once for all, you had better recognise your position."

He could see the hot blood rush to her cheek. "But this is monstrous, no matter what Society has decreed. May I ask, Frank, if such is the law by which you intend to shape your conduct in the future?"

With shame he remembered his answer. "Yes, Fenella. Right or wrong, it is the law of every man of the world."

And from that day they had become more and more estranged, until at last their unhappiness reached a culminating pitch, and by mutual desire, they determined to separate. But had they been happier apart than together? He, for one, could answer that question in the negative. In the midst of the wildest dissipation, the gayest scene, his heart had ached, and ever in his memory there dwelt the recollection of loving words and looks, which no effort on his part could banish. Looking back on the past, he saw that he was even more to blame than she. There had been faults on both sides, but mainly on his. As he sank on his knees by Fenella's bedside, he admitted the fact, freely and without reserve. And thus kneeling, a flood of tenderness and remorse swept over his spirit, and he who had not prayed for years, and was in the habit of denying the existence of a Deity, bowed down his head, humbly, meekly, like a little child, and prayed.

"Oh! good God!" he cried, "be merciful. Spare her to me, if only that I may atone for all my past errors by a life of devotion. We have stood on the brink of a precipice. Almost she and I have fallen into a bottomless pit, for in our blindness we turned our backs upon Thee,' but now, O great All-Father, strengthen us, and counsel us in this, our sore necessity."

He arose from his knees sobered, but calm. Then he stooped, kissed Fenella's burning brow, and went forth to seek his son—the little, innocent boy, with the curly head and clear eyes, the very thought of whom made his heart grow big.

There are seasons in the lives of all of us when the best of which we are capable rises to the surface—when the resolutions which we make for the future are not based on an insecure and worthless foundation, but on a fixed and permanent one. Such a time had come to Lord Francis. He left Guernsey a chastened, but a better man, determined henceforth to lead a new and purer life.

The journey seemed interminable. The tedious hours dragged on, and steam and machinery were unable to convey him fast enough to his destination. At last he reached Felixstowe, and hurried to Mrs. Grandison's residence. Philip Grandison was related to the Onslow family. Lord Francis had seen a great deal of his wife before his marriage, and they called each other by their Christian names.

"Helen," he cried, as Mrs. Grandison, taken aback by his unexpected visit and haggard appearance, stared at him as at an apparition, "where is Ronny? I want to see Ronny. Bring him to me at once! Fenella murmured in her delirium that he was with you."

"Have you not sailed? You and Lady Francis have not started, then, for Brazil, after all?" she asked in bewilderment.

"No," he answered, impatiently. "I haven't the least idea what you are talking about. There never was any question of our going to Brazil. Fenella is lying at death's door, and I have come here to fetch Ronny away."

"But, Frank, Ronny has gone. You yourself sent for him. Surely you must remember having done so."

"*I* sent to fetch *Ronny!* Helen! have you taken leave of your senses?" And he gripped her hard by the wrist.

"Don't, Frank!" shaking him off, and fearing for his reason as she looked into his wild eyes; "you hurt me."

"I sent no one to take Ronny away," he said, with increasing excitement. "Do you mean to say that the child is not here?"

"No, Ronny left us several days ago. I made sure that you knew."

Lord Francis staggered. The intelligence fairly prostrated him. For a moment or two he could not speak; then, in a hoarse voice, he said,—

"Of course you know where the boy has gone, Helen? You can tell me where to find him? It is of the utmost importance that I should take him back to Guernsey with me at once. His mother's life may depend upon Ronny's presence."

Mrs. Grandison's countenance assumed an expression of sore perplexity. She felt that Lord Francis held her responsible for his son.

"Unfortunately," she said, "I have not the least idea where he has gone. The other day a lady came here——"

"A lady!" he interrupted eagerly. "What kind of a one? Describe her personal appearance. It may give me a clue."

"She was not exactly a young woman, Frank; nevertheless she was very beautiful in a Southern, majestic style. Her eyes and hair were almost coal black, and she spoke with a foreign accent. In short, she looked like an Italian or Spaniard."

The wretched man groaned aloud. Too well he knew who his boy's abductor was, and his conscience told him that Lucille de Vigny's conduct was actuated by motives of revenge. She resented his desertion, and took this means of telling him so. He tottered to a chair, and sinking down on it, hid his face in his hands. Were the consequences of his imprudence ever to pursue him? Oh! it was horrible, horrible!

"Frank," said Mrs. Grandison, gazing at him in alarm, "do you know the lady? Is she an acquaintance of yours?"

He shuddered. "For my sins, yes! Would to God she were not! I have to thank Madame de Vigny for all my misery. If I had never set eyes on that woman, Fenella and I might have been living happily together at this moment. It was she who came between us, curse her!"

"Madame de Vigny!" exclaimed Helen, with a red flush mantling in her cheek, "Oh, Frank! if only I had known, nothing on earth would have induced me to give Ronny up into her charge. Poor, dear little Ronny! Why, she is an odious woman—an abominable woman!"

"I quite agree," he said moodily. "But abuse cannot alter the fact of her having stolen my boy. I can't think, though, how you let him go."

"She came here, Frank," continued Mrs. Grandison, in self-defence, "and some instinct warned me against her. I refused at first to accede to her request, but she was so urgent that at last I believed she was really empowered by you to take Ronny away. See, here is your card, which she produced in token of the genuineness of her errand." And so saying, Helen turned to the mantelpiece and showed Frank his card. He looked at it, then snatched up his hat and prepared to leave.

"This is a bad business," he said, tremulously. "A very bad business indeed; I would not have had it happen for a year's income. But perhaps you can tell me where Madame de Vigny is to be found?"

"Alas! no. She left no address, and I haven't the faintest notion where she resides. But stay," putting her hand up to her forehead, "if I remember rightly, Madame de Vigny did hint at travelling abroad and taking a long journey. Why, Frank, how impetuous you are!" as her visitor opened the door. "Where are you going?"

"Going!" he replied, his face all working with emotion. "I am going straight to London to engage a detective to hunt out Madame de Vigny's whereabouts, and after that I intend returning to Guernsey. Fenella is lying dangerously ill of brain fever.[2] We do not know what turn her illness may take. The doctor thought that the sight of Ronny might do her good, but now—now," breaking down suddenly, "I must go back alone, so help me God!" And without wishing Mrs. Grandison good-bye, he rushed downstairs.

Helen looked after his retreating form with the tears springing to her eyes. "Poor Frank!" she sighed, "how he loves Fenella. And yet she has completely spoilt his life. He was such a bright, nice boy once upon a time. It quite makes one's heart ache to see him as he is now."

CHAPTER XIV.

DERELICT.

BY RICHARD DOWLING.

WHEN Lord Francis found himself in the train, on his way up to London from Felixstowe, his mind was in a condition bordering on frenzy. The wife of his youth, the wife of his choice, the only woman to whom his heart had ever gone forth with unalloyed joy and limitless bounty, lay at death's door, from which one hope existed of beckoning her back—the touch of their child's tiny hand. And now, at this moment of supreme crisis, cursed Fate stepped in and took the child from his sight, snatched the possible deliverer from his arms!

Cursed Fate, or Nemesis,[1] or *lex talionis*, call it what one might, there was the maddening fact, the overwhelming act of that foreign woman whom once, in his malignant perversity, he thought he loved, who over and over again swore she loved him and only him! Granted he had treated her badly, had he attempted her life? Why, then, should she attempt his? Why should she seek to kill him through the hearts he held most dear? Because he had made love to her and ridden away? Great heavens! Was not his sin against her a mustard seed to the whole world in comparison to this attempt on Fenella's life?

From the beginning of their acquaintance, Lucille knew he was married; at no time of their acquaintance did he know much of her. She had her dark eyes, and her mystery, and her history—these were parts of her fascination. She had enslaved him, as a drug or wine might enslave him, for a time; but she had never touched the essence of his being—that was for Fenella, for Fenella only.

When he reached London he drove straight to Scotland Yard. If he had been in a normal state he would no doubt have paid a visit to his solicitors first, but he was in no normal state. He could not have told when he ate last, or where he had slept; what day of the week or month it was. All that was usual was worthless, and only the quest he was on worthy of heed.

At Scotland Yard he was at once shown into the presence of Inspector Brown. His father's position made his name illustrious; the murder trial had made himself notorious.

"My child—my boy of six—has been stolen. His mother, Lady Francis, is in danger of death from illness, and the instant recovery of the boy is a matter of life and death. She is in brain fever, and the doctor says if her boy is at her bedside when she recovers her senses it may save her life. Whatever sum of money may be necessary to recover the boy I'll double it, treble it, quadruple it, if you only find him for me, and at once!" he cried out to the inspector, all in a breath.

"The recovery of the child does not, unfortunately, depend on mere money, my lord."

"On what, then?"

"On possibility. If it is possible to be done it will be done; and whether we succeed or fail, you may rely on no time being lost. Will your lordship kindly give me all the particulars?"

The father told the history of the boy's abduction, as Mrs. Grandison had given it to him.

"And this foreign, handsome lady who took the child away, do you happen to know her name?"

Did he happen to know Lucille's name! Good Heavens, how strange such a question seemed! But it was one thing to know her name, and vow hatred of her, and another thing to give to the police the name of a woman he once made love to. He hesitated.

The inspector looked up from the sheet of paper on which he had been taking down the particulars.

The inspector, believing the other had not heard, repeated the question.

"Bah!" thought Lord Francis, "why should I hesitate? She has not hesitated to lie and to steal Ronny; and Fenella's life is in the scales." He said aloud: "The lady is French,"—the inspector recommenced writing,—"her name is Madame de Vigny."

The inspector looked up again, this time with a start, laid down his pen, and cleared his throat as though to clear his mind. "May I ask your lordship to repeat the name?"

"Madame de Vigny—Lucille de Vigny. Do you know anything of her?"

"Perhaps," said the inspector, touching an electric bell.

A policeman in uniform entered. The inspector handed the man a slip of paper. The constable withdrew. In a few moments he returned, handed some documents to his superior officer, and retired.

"Does your lordship happen to know anything of this Madame Lucille de Vigny before she came to England a few years ago?"

"Absolutely nothing."

"I suppose we are talking of the same lady"—the inspector looked down at his papers—"a tall, strikingly handsome, dark woman of about thirty-five or forty now. She was in the Prospect Hotel, Harrogate, at the time of the late tragic occurrence there, though she was not herself brought into the case."

"Yes, that is the lady."

"Well, we do know something of her here. We have been keeping an eye on her for a little time at the request of the French police. A French detective has been over here about her. It was not until the day before yesterday, when instructions came from Paris to act, that we knew she had left the country."

"Left the country!" cried Lord Francis, falling back on his chair in consternation.

"Sailed for New York in the *Germanic* four days ago. She is wanted in France for connection with some wholesale swindling of a bank in Lille² four or five years ago. We lost sight of her for a little while lately, but that we have just explained by the fact that she recently went through a form of marriage at a registry with a rich American Senator, Colonel Clutterbuck. I say, went through a form of marriage, for her husband, one of the clerks in the Lille bank, is now in the hands of the French police. My lord, you may make your mind easy about your boy. No doubt he is the child who sailed with Colonel and Mrs. Clutterbuck in the *Germanic* as Mrs. Clutterbuck's nephew, Roland Tyrrell, aged six."

"What is to be done now?" cried Lord Francis, relieved at getting a clue to his boy, and in despair at finding the child must already be half-way across the Atlantic.

"She will be arrested on landing, and brought back."

"But the boy—my son?"

"If you wish it we can cable and have him looked after for you. There will be a few days lost in legal formalities in New York."

"I'll follow the boy; I'll go by the next boat!" and with this resolution, and no thought of anything else, he rushed away from Scotland Yard for his chambers.

At his chambers he found everything as he had left it weeks ago. Into a couple of portmanteaux he bundled some clothes—any—no matter what he could put his hands on. Then he sat down to think. His brain was in a whirl. Only one thought had any value, any place in his mind—the recovery of Ronny. On that depended all. On that depended the life of Fenella, and his own power of making reparation to her for all she had gone through.

He had forgotten one thing at Scotland Yard. The inspector had said they could cable to have the boy taken care of for him. He had not asked the inspector to do so. He sat down, and with a hand that shook so that he could hardly hold the pen, he wrote to the inspector, begging that a message might be sent by cable, bidding them look after Ronny on his behalf in New York. He marked the envelope "Private," for there was plenty of time for the cable, and he wished the whole affair to be kept as quiet as possible.

Then he had nothing else to do but to get forward. He did not think of looking to see or of inquiring when the next boat left. Queenstown[3] was the point nearest to America, and, by the Irish mail[4] that night he started for Cork.

It was not until he had been six hours plunging through the Atlantic towards the New World, in the huge ocean steamer, that he remembered he had sent no word to Guernsey. But he dismissed the omission from his mind as a matter of no moment, "For," thought he, "all the messages in the world would not serve my poor girl as she now is, and I am going to fetch the elixir of life for her—our Ronny's voice."

At the moment that Lord Francis was soothing his mind and cheering his way with this encouraging reflection, Inspector Brown, of Scotland Yard, was writing to him, as follows:—

"My Lord,—I hasten to acknowledge the receipt of your note of the day before yesterday, which came after I left. It was marked 'Private,' and, consequently, was not opened in the ordinary course. I was absent on duty yesterday, and only got it just now. Hence I could not answer it sooner. The French authorities have decided that, having secured the so-called Madame Lucille de Vigny's husband, and she having got off to America, they will not follow her further for the present. She will therefore walk ashore free out of the *Germanic*, and, in the absence of formal instructions, we shall be powerless to stop her. Hoping this may reach you in time, I am, my lord, your humble servant,

"CHRISTOPHER BROWN, *Inspector.*"

Meanwhile the struggle for life in that cottage room in Guernsey had turned in favour of Fenella. The doctor had given a guarded opinion when Lord Francis made his frantic appeal to him. Before her husband fronted the western ocean the wasted sufferer opened her eyes, and once more looked out through the glance of reason on the world where she had endured so much.

For a day or two she hung between life and death. She looked too frail for this world. But she had store of the best of medicines in her own blood, youth, and she began to mend rapidly.

Happily, when she came to herself, she did not clearly remember the dreadful past. All was dim and shadowy. The doctor was careful to say nothing that could renew her sorrow. He was aware that her husband had set off to recover the boy, but since Lord Francis dashed out of the place no word had come from him, and as the patient made no inquiries the doctor held his peace. The nurse knew nothing, and Fenella herself had a vague feeling that the past, whatever was in it, had better be let alone. She was too weak for conflict, for even consecutive thought.

Hour after hour she lay weak and silent and gentle, the ghost of her former self, all the old audacious sprightliness vanished. She took what they gave her, and spoke when she was spoken to, and resisted nothing the attentive people around ordained for her. She did not ask questions. She had no memory of her husband's penitential visit; no means of knowing that he had gone to fetch their child.

The doctor, seeing that she was in no distress, left her in the hands of beneficent Nature. Peace was the finest cordial his patient could taste now, and if she showed no sign of joyousness, she was easy and at rest.

Fenella's brain being free of the fever, her splendid constitution and her youth asserted their prerogative to lead her to health, and the kindly doctor stood amazed at the progress she made towards convalescence. "You have nothing to do now but get well," said he, "and you are getting well as if getting well were a fever in full power. You are building up as fast—ay, faster—than you lost."

She answered only with a smile. She took no particular interest in getting well, or in anything else, for that matter. Although the brain may have been relieved from the ravages of active disease, it was inert, lifeless. The fountains of memory were still frozen, or dried up. She knew she lay at her cottage in Guernsey, but she did not actively realise why she was there. She felt that if she made a great effort, she could tell herself the story of her presence upon the island; but she was languid, and took no interest in anything, not even in herself.

"You may sit up for an hour to-morrow," said the doctor, one day.

She said: "Thank you, doctor."

He was careful not to call her by any name, and he told the nurse and maids not to address her as "Mrs. Orme." "Let us get the body strong first," thought he. "Until word comes from Lord Francis, we have nothing pleasant to say to her, and she may forget that she was ever 'Mrs. Orme.'"

So day slid into morrow, and brought no news—no word of any kind—and Lord Francis was a whole week gone, and the sufferer was allowed to move about a little. The good doctor concluded that Lord Francis had changed his intention again, and for some reason or other reverted to the condition of mind he had been in when he borrowed Lord Castleton's yacht, and took himself away into southern seas beyond the voice of England.

On the eighth day a letter came from London. It was addressed in a clerkly hand. It was the first letter that had come for Fenella since she had fallen ill. She was sitting in an arm-chair by the fire when she took it from the doctor, for he had given strict orders she was to get no letter except from his hand. The superscription was in such commonplace clerkly writing that the good doctor made sure that it was some ordinary business communication, one from her lawyer or trustee, or some other person connected with the routine of her affairs. She was now strong enough to stroll a short distance out of doors, and had taken a turn in the garden the day before, and was to walk a mile along the road later to-day when the sun grew stronger.

"A letter from some of your business people," said the man of science. "I hope it brings you good news." A little rousing would not come amiss to the lovely invalid.

It was addressed to "Mrs. Orme." She broke the cover. It contained a brief note from her lawyer and a letter enclosed, the writing of which, a woman's, was unfamiliar to her. The lawyer's letter ran:—

"DEAR MADAM,—I enclose a letter which reaches me from an unknown source, with an anonymous request that it may be forwarded to you.—I am, dear madam, yours faithfully,

"JOHN THORNHILL."

The letter enclosed was addressed to "Lady Francis Onslow." She broke the cover of that. It, too, was short. It ran:—

"Your husband has left you for ever, and I have taken care you shall never see your child again.

"LUCILLE DE VIGNY."

That was all.

CHAPTER XV.

ANOTHER RIFT.

BY MRS. HUNGERFORD.

FENELLA rose to her feet. There had been one terrible moment when all things faded from her, but she overcame that. She *would* not faint! She turned to the doctor, who, watching her anxiously, now came a step nearer to her. In truth, her face, always colour-less, was now ghastly; but there was a sudden strength in her eyes, her whole demeanour, that betokened, as it were, a new life within her. Lately, so weak she had been, she had fainted at any small thing that fell into her path threatening to annoy her; but now, when she had reached the most momentous point of her life, her hardihood returned to her, and the old, sweet, girlish gaiety, that might almost be termed audacity, developed into a courage true and noble.

This was no time for weakness. Now was the hour to rise and assert herself! If this devilish letter meant that evil machinations were at work to deprive her of her husband and her child, now was the time to fling aside all considerations and fight for her own.

Her own! *were* they her own? A terrible remembrance of the past when he, Frank, had been untrue to her, returned again. What if he should be untrue *again!* And again with that woman! Her heart for a second died within her, but another thought restored her to herself. Her child! Her darling! Her Ronny! He, at least, was all her own. She need fear no rival in his affections.

There was something so tragic in the expression of her young, beautiful face that the old doctor went closer to her and touched her arm as though to rouse her.

"What is it, my dear?" asked he, nervously. He had grown very fond of her during these past weeks, when she hovered between life and death.

"Read that!" said she, holding out to him the fatal letter. She let her eyes rest full on his—the lovely eyes now so much too large for the pale, small face. Her long white robe fell to her feet, showing but too plainly the attenuation of her figure. She looked like some tall, sad, mediæval saint, with her white clinging garments and her nimbus of red-brown hair.

"Good heavens!" said the kind little doctor, letting the letter flutter to his feet. "But what can this mean? Your husband—so devoted as he seemed—and—Who is this woman, then? This Madame de Vigny?"

"A fiend," said Fenella softly, bitterly. "But I shall overcome her yet. Give me a paper, a telegram form, ink; I"—excitedly—"I have a friend who will help me. *One* friend,"—she turned, and looked piteously at the old man. "I have only one friend in all the world," said she, "and he—distrusts me."

"You have another," said the good old doctor, stoutly, "in me. And I do not distrust you. Come! come now, my dear. Take courage. Here are pens and paper. Let us telegraph to this distrustful, if useful, friend of yours."

Fenella wrote rapidly, and handed the telegram to the doctor. He read it aloud:—

"Come to me at once. Great trouble! Make no delay, I implore you!"

Having read it, he went back to the address—"Clitheroe Jacynth!"

"Jacynth!—a distinguished man. One almost unconquerable, they say now. I congratulate you if you have *him* on your side."

"Ah! but you forget!"

"Tut—when he comes I shall speak to him. I shall dissolve all doubts," said the little man kindly. "And now to dispatch this at once. I shall take it myself, if you will promise to lie down and try to rest for a while."

"I promise," said she, meekly; but it was a promise vain indeed. The door once closed behind him, she began her dreadful walk up and down, up and down the room. She felt half mad. Her child— her little one, in that woman's power.

It was noticeable that in this hour all her thoughts went to the child.

* * * * *

"Hullo, Jacynth! This you? By Jove! what mad haste. Not even a word for an old friend?"

"Why, Castleton! What brings you here?"

"Folly! Folly only, if it must be told," said Lord Castleton, dismally. "Sentiment is folly; isn't it, Jacynth? Yet a sentimental desire to know how the Onslows are going on is driving me back to Guernsey—a spot I quitted a week ago."

"To Guernsey! Why, that is where I am going to. Have you heard anything?" He looked eagerly at his companion. "Do you know anything? I have had a telegram from—from her. Can *you* explain it?"

"A telegram! When?"

"A few hours ago. Look here, Castleton. I honestly think you are a friend of Lady Francis Onslow's—read this."

"I am a friend of both the Onslows," said Castleton, deliberately. He meant what he said. He took the telegram and glanced at it.

"Same old game!" said he at last, lifting his brows. "Another quarrel, I suppose. I thought when they came together this time that they meant business, but it seems not. How few married people are suited to each other!"

"I never thought much of Onslow," said Jacynth slowly. "A weak character at all times. I suppose nobody would dispute the fact of his having been unfaithful to his wife?"

"With Madame de Vigny? Pouf! There were faults on both sides."

"On Madame de Vigny's and his? Certainly."

"Not at all. On his and Lady Francis'. She certainly led him a life."

"A life he deserved! *He*—married to *her*." He looked suddenly at his companion, and the touch of passion in his eyes revealed *all* things. "To that poor, sweet, pretty girl. *He* to play fast and loose with her, a child just out of her schoolroom. It"—he paused and commanded himself—"In my opinion it was contemptible."

"You give yourself away a good deal," said Castleton, who looked amused—who looked, indeed, as if he would like to laugh.

He had a great affection for Jacynth, who was rather a special sort of man, and in spite of his mirth felt sorry for him. "You are, I presume, on the side of Lady Francis."

"That would be an impertinence from any man but you," said Jacynth moodily. "There is no need to go into it, however. Whether I love her or not is no matter. It"—miserably—"can *never* matter now. What I *do* is—to pity her with all my soul."

"Because of her marriage?"

Jacynth looked at him as if hesitating.

"For that, too," said he, deliberately. "She married, in my opinion, the last man in the world who would have made her really happy. But my pity did not run that way. I was thinking of that miserable trial and its consequences."

"Yes, she was a trifle too magnanimous there," said Castleton, believing the other knew all about it. "It would have been better, to my way of thinking, if she had told the broad truth, and let Onslow take his chance."

"His chance!" said Jacynth, staring at him.

"Certainly; it wasn't so bad a chance. He might, he positively *would*, have got off all right. But she chose to take the guilt on her own shoulders, and now she has created an enigma very difficult of solution."

"You mean——" Jacynth paused; he seemed gasping for breath.

"I mean——" Suddenly Lord Castleton grew silent, and gazed at his companion with a troubled countenance. "Do *you* mean," said he, "that you didn't know? Why, you conducted the case for *her.*"

"I know nothing," said Jacynth, with great agitation. "If you can throw any honest light on the matter, do it, I entreat you."

"I hardly know whether I should. I"—Castleton drew back from him—"I was so sure you knew that—— My dear fellow, *pray* forget what I have said."

"I shall forget nothing," said Jacynth sturdily. "I should advise you not to forget either. Look here, Castleton," catching his arm, "is it advisable to forget? Who knows what this telegram may mean? We are both friends of hers."

"Are you a friend of his?"

"No! Why should I disguise the truth? I have told you before how I regard him. But what has that got to do with it?"

"You are prejudiced."

"I am not. If you *have* anything to disclose, Castleton, disclose it! I may be of use to you——" He hesitated.

"Well, considering she has sent for you, I suppose she means to tell you herself," said Castleton. "And," reluctantly, "it is well you should know beforehand what there is to know, though I am surprised that she has not already told you." To him there was but one certainty, and that was that Fenella had betrayed to Onslow the part he took in the fatal night's work that murdered De Mürger. Probably Onslow had resented what she told him, and disbelieved it, and she had then sent for her lawyer. What else could demand so imperative a telegram? On the instant he opened his heart to Jacynth, and told him all his belief, all his doubts.

"I could never forget," said he, "how he looked in the last hypnotic fit; and hypnotic is the fashionable word for it, I know, but I call it madness. And his heart isn't sound, you know. He inherits disease in that direction. His father died of aneurism of the heart. Some day he will have a fashionable fit too strong for him, and there will be an end."

"The best thing that could happen for both of them," said Jacynth deliberately. He had been terribly upset by Castleton's revelation, and though hardly permitting himself to believe in it, still felt a wild, mad joy in the thought that she—*she*, the only woman the whole wide world contained for him—might be innocent of bloodshed after all. "See here," said he vehemently, "if this thing be true, if she saw him commit that crime—for crime it was—do you think they could ever live happily together in the future? Why, think, man, would she not see the colour of blood upon his hands, would she fail to rank him among murderers? And he——"

"Why, he knows nothing."

"True; and therein lies the real tragedy. Knowing nothing, he thinks of *her* as a murderess. There it lies, you see, in a nutshell. *He* thinks *her*, *she* thinks *him* guilty of a ghastly crime, and you madly believe they could live together happily."

"It need not go on like that; she might tell him the truth."

"She? Never!"

"At all events, he might learn it."

"And if so, what would be gained? The world would shun them both; and they were made for the world. We are all made for the world."

"True." A shrill whistle aroused them both. "Come on, the train is about to start," said Castleton.

* * * * *

As Jacynth entered her sitting-room, Fenella rose and ran toward him.

"At last, at last!" she said. The words came in a sort of gasp. Jacynth, holding her hands, stared at her, shocked at the change in her appearance. Every vestige of colour was gone from her face, her eyes looked wild, and her parted lips were very pale. She had pushed back her hair from her forehead with a quick gesture, just as he entered the room. She was at her worst this moment, but the man's love was so strong that he failed to see that. He thought her lovely—lovely always, and what was strange, even younger than she used to be.

"You know? you have heard?" she went on, her tone feverish.

"You forget!" said he gently, with a view to calming her agitation. "I know nothing. I have had only your telegram, and that was so vague."

"Ah! You shall see another telegram then. That——" thrusting Madame de Vigny's letter into his hand—"*that* is not vague, at all events."

Jacynth read it carefully. He frowned. "That woman again!" he said.

"Yes. Again." She stood back from him. "Do you believe he has gone back to her? *Do* you? *Do you?*" The very vehemence of her question conveyed to him the knowledge that she thought he had gone back.

"There is only this," said he, striking the paper. "And it is from *her.* She is not the woman to believe in."

"No! But I have thought it out for all that, and——" She paused and pressed her hands to her head. Jacynth gently led her to a seat. She looked exhausted. "He left me," said she presently—"to find my child and bring him to me. He came back, and there was no child with him. I was ill then—very ill. I could not think, but for all that, I *knew*. Then he went away again, and I waited—waited. Great Heaven!" said she, clasping her hands, "if you only knew what it was to wait like that for a sight of your child! and then there came—*that!*" She pointed to the telegram that he still held. "Well, what do you think?" asked she in a low voice, bending forward.

"It is hard to think——"

"No, it is not!" He was horrified by the change in her tone, and looked at her. She was still bending forward, her hands clasped, her young, sweet face as hard as misery could make it. "It is the easiest thing," she said. "He met her again, I suppose—I think, and together they have gone away, taking my child with them. Oh!" She sprang to her feet, and flung out her arms. "Oh! the child! He might have gone—gone for ever—it would be hard, for I loved him! but to take the child from me! The child! My darling! My baby! Do you know how many months I have lived without my little sweetheart? You, you of all men know!" She turned to him, and caught him by the arm. "Ever since that awful trial! I gave him up then, my little one: and for what?" she almost hissed out the words—"*to shield his father!*"

"You mean—" said Jacynth, his heart beating; was he now to hear the truth from her own lips? But the sound of his voice broke in upon her passion, and checked her.

"Nothing," said she, quickly, "except that—that he is false to me."

"I tell you again not to dwell too much on that," said Jacynth, slowly. Although his whole life seemed to depend upon it, he could not refrain from pleading his rival's cause. "You have only that woman's word for it. This telegram may be a fabrication from beginning to end."

"A curiously well-timed one." She laughed, in a cruelly miserable way. "If she knew nothing of him, how did she learn that my child and my husband were now away from me?"

"More curious things have been explained," said he.

"You! *you* talk to me like this?" cried she, passionately. "*You* would defend him! *You*, who knew he was once untrue? You"— faintly—"who once loved me?"

"I shall be your friend always," said he, putting a great con-straint upon himself. "It is because I *am* your friend that I speak thus: why not look at it in another light? You say your husband left you hurriedly; you say that Madame de Vigny must have known of his absence from you, and also of your boy's. It might be that she, out of revenge, stole the boy, and that your husband is now pursuing her with a view of restoring him to you."

He said this more to gain time than anything else, little thinking that he had guessed the truth, and had laid before her the exact facts of the case.

"A fairy tale," said she mournfully. "No! He lied to me the last time I saw him. When I asked him to bring me my child, he said he was tired—asleep. I too was tired, worn out from sickness and a broken heart, and too weak to do aught but believe him. The child was not here at all!" She stepped back from Jacynth, and covered her face with her hands. "Oh, my Ronny! my beloved! Oh, my little child!" She took down her hands. Her lips were trembling. "Mr. Jacynth, what shall I do?" said she.

"The first thing to do," said he, harshly, "is to keep up your courage." He spoke in a queer, grating tone. He knew if he once gave way, he should betray himself—betray the wild, mad longing he felt to take her in his arms, and press her poor, sweet, pretty head down upon his breast, and try with all his soul to comfort her. "You are condemning your husband unheard. Is that fair? Is it just?"

"He has not been just to me!"

"True! And, therefore, you find it difficult in such a crisis as this to believe in him." He looked at her suddenly. "Still you love him?" said he. The words were a question.

"Do I?" said she. *Her* words were also a question addressed to her own heart. "I feel so tired—so tired," she said. "It has been a struggle always, and through many things I loved him, I——" She hesitated. "I despise myself," she said, "but I think I love him still!" A pang shot through Jacynth's heart. He did not note the suggestion of doubt in her voice. "I love him, I think," she went on, slowly, "I *think*, but this I *know*, I distrust him."

"Distrust means ruin," said Jacynth.

"To what? To love?"

"To all things."

"To friendship?"

"Yes. To all things."

She went close to him.

"That is not true," she said. "You are befriending me now, yet you distrust me."

"I? No! You are thinking of that wretched trial!" He spoke with extreme agitation. "But I have heard all."

"*All?*"

"Yes! *All.* And if ever a man craved another's pardon upon his knees, I crave yours."

"*All?*" repeated she, faintly. She seemed to have heard that one word only.

"Yes," said he. He let his voice sink to a whisper; he leaned towards her. "Who killed De Mürger?" asked he.

* * * * *

"It is true!" said he presently, when she had told him all. "It is true that the world still produces heroines. It is now more imperative than ever that Lord Francis should be found."

"For what?" said she. "Do you think I should betray him now—even now? Ah! Mr. Jacynth, you do not know me. No! I shall go to my grave bearing this burthen. After all"—sadly—"he once *did* love me!"

"If he has gone off with that woman again I don't see why you should spare him," said Jacynth. "But, as I have said, I hope for the best about that. In the meantime——"

She interrupted him.

"In the meantime, find my child!" said she. She was still ghastly pale, but a little fire had come into her eyes. "Bring *him* back to me, get him back from that woman. Oh!" a little nervously, "I have no right to speak to you like this. Why should I order you about? Only—only—you are kind—kind always, and—I have now no friends! And Ronny—Ronny always hated strangers! Oh! my child, my little heart!" She broke down suddenly, and burst into violent weeping. "Oh, God!" cried she, "what shall I do? That woman! That woman, if she has him, she will kill him! He, who never knew anything but love! My little lamb! Oh! his eyes, his laugh! *You* saw him! Was there *ever* so pretty a boy? Oh! once—once"—passionately—"you said you loved me! *Help* me now! Tell me how I shall *begin* the search for Ronny."

"You would go yourself?"

"Oh, yes, yes! Oh, if you only *knew* what this last day and night have been!" She was sobbing violently, but now, by a supreme effort, she controlled herself; she took down her hands from her face, and pressed them against her throbbing bosom. "I will be calm," she said, "this is no time for tears, and you must not think me weak. I am strong—very strong. Tell me now how I shall begin."

"I will tell you," said he, "but you must try and see my plan as I see it. Now, it seems to me impossible that you, in your weak health, just recovered from a dangerous illness, could possibly institute such a troublesome search as this is likely to prove."

"And if not——" began she, despairingly.

"There is a substitute," said he. "*I* shall undertake this matter."

"You?"

"Yes. If you will entrust this affair to me, I will promise to bring you back your—husband."

"Bring me back my child!" said she.

"Fenella, your husband! You will want to have *him* back!"

"I have told you I am tired," said she, coldly. "I have borne a great deal, and——" she paused.

"There is something on your mind," said he.

"His hands!" she said. She seemed to shrink visibly. She shuddered. "*The blood!* I was unconscious then, I think——and it is only now—now—— But his hands! and his face! Great Heavens, how he *held* him. He choked him. It was as if he was over there now," staring wildly at the far part of the room. "His fingers closed round his throat, and there was such a sound—*a gurgle*—Heaven, what a sound! and then he stabbed, and stabbed, and *stabbed*—he was mad. Oh!" with a long-drawn, piercing sigh, "*I* shall go mad if I think of it!"

"Then don't think," said Jacynth. He caught hold of her arm and shook her sharply.

"Whenever I see him I see blood," said she, still trembling.

"Never mind him, think of your child," said he, with a desire to rouse her. "Am I to start now? and when I find him, what message am I to give him from his mother?"

He had roused her indeed. "A message!" she said. The old, sad, dreadful fear in her face died away. Hope lit it into a lovely life. "A message to Ronny!" she cried.

She fell on her knees before Jacynth and took his hand and laid her cold cheek upon it—a cheek wet with tears. "Tell him his mother loves him," said she. "Tell him, too, that his mother will for ever love the one who will restore him to her."

CHAPTER XVI.

IN NEW YORK.

BY ARTHUR A'BECKETT.

Mrs. CLUTTERBUCK, the newly-married wife of Colonel Clutterbuck, of New York, was not "at home"[1] to visitors. She had given orders to that effect, but the command was superfluous, as there were no callers. To tell the truth, Madame de Vigny had not been a great social success in the country of her adoption. The Senator, her husband, had married her to preside over his establishment and to gracefully adorn his dinner-table; and although she had accepted both duties, the result had been disappointment. Mrs. Clutterbuck's notion of looking after a house was to take the minimum amount of trouble, and order the maximum amount of goods. She had run up bills in all directions, giving a special preference to the stores of jewellers, dressmakers, and vendors of lace. Her idea of dispensing hospitality was scarcely in accord with the Colonel's notions on the same matter. The Senator, who was a power in Wall Street, firmly believed that more could be done over the viands and iced water than in the place of custom, and was in the habit of filling his dining-room with people who could be useful. His desire was, of course, to conciliate those he invited by adopting a tone of businesslike geniality, but he received no assistance from his wife, whose solitary aim seemed to be the unprovoked and contemptuous snubbing of her husband's guests.

"Loo-cille," said he one day, after a banquet had ended in disaster, "I guess you are not particular to company. Guess, Madame, you prefer solitude to some of the best known persons in the United States."

"If you mean by that," replied Mrs. Clutterbuck, admiring herself in a mirror, "I do not care for the vulgar crowd you ask to dinner, you are certainly right. They are neither polished nor amusing."

"Strikes me, madame, that you seem to feel the want of the

British aristocracy. You can't get on without them—that is so. It seems a pity that Lord Francis Onslow should be on the other side of the Atlantic. He would have been a decided acquisition to our family circle. See?"

"What do you mean?" asked Lucille, with her large eyes fixed upon the Colonel menacingly. "What do you mean?"

"What I say," retorted the Colonel. "I do not want, madame, any unpleasantness, but I give you fair warning that I know a thing or two. I have special sources of information."

"Do you want to insult me?" Lucille asked in a low tone, raising her head, and still keeping her steady gaze upon her husband, her eyes looking into his eyes, as if they would read his very soul.

"Come, come, Madame, none of that," cried Clutterbuck, waving her off. "I tell you, Loo-cille, I was not born yesterday, nor yet the day before. My will is a pretty strong one, and I tell you distinctly I am not a subject. I have been tried before, and it would not do. So take my word, madame, you are giving yourself a great deal of trouble for nothing. Take my advice, Madame, and drop it. Guess it won't do."

She seemed to concentrate her power of will into a supreme and final effort, and then she shrank back into a *fauteuil*²—conquered. Her husband laughed, and continued,—

"You see you cannot contrive it. No, madame, it won't do. So, if you take my advice, I would not try it again. You see it just riles me, and I am not a nice man to rile. I love and respect all ladies, but I have a sharp and short way of reckoning with snakes. See?"

She was silent for a moment and then burst into a hysterical laugh. "There," continued her husband, "you notice you are unhinged. It is not good for you, this kind of excitement. And now tell me, how is Ronny? Why did he not come down to give his uncle good-morning before I started for business to-day?"

"Ronny has gone," replied Lucille, shortly.

"Gone!" exclaimed the Senator. "Why, where have you sent him?"

"That is my business," returned Mrs. Clutterbuck. "Surely I have a right to do what I please with my own nephew."

"Nephew!" echoed he. "Whew!"

"Have you any reason for questioning the relationship?"

"Well, no," replied her husband, stroking his beard; "but it strikes me for so near a relative, the lad does not seem to care particularly about you. Why, I do believe he likes me better than he does you."

"Ronny has bad taste."

"Maybe, madame, maybe," returned her husband. "But you might keep a civil tongue in your head. It's that kind of thing that riles my guests."

"What kind of thing?"

"Oh, drop it! Now tell me, when do you expect Ronny's return?"

"I don't expect it at all."

"Ah! I see you are not in a communicative mood, so I shall take myself off. But see here, madame. You were intended by Nature for the leisured class, but in the States we haven't got the institution. Some day we may import it from Europe, and if we do, why then you will find yourself quite at home. But, until we do import it from Europe, take a word of advice. Climb down, Madame, climb down."

And with this parting shot the Colonel took his departure.

Mrs. Clutterbuck listened to the retreating steps, and then went to her desk. She sat down in front of the table and pondered. Had she acted wisely? Certainly it was advisable to quit England—Europe—but was not this a case of from the frying-pan into the fire? The Colonel was a man of violent passions, and she felt that she was absolutely without influence over him. He was too strong for her. She had been accustomed to do what she liked with members of the opposite sex; here was a man who set her at defiance, laughed her to scorn. What was she to do? She was absolutely dependent upon him for support. Unless she could get back to Europe (which was not a desirable spot for the moment), or find a travelling Englishman, she was powerless. Her husband's friends and acquaintances appeared to hold her in abhorrence. Besides, manners and customs on one side of the Atlantic seemed to differ from customs and manners on the other. It was not a cheerful prospect. However, there was nothing to be done but to submit, and to keep her eyes open to take immediate advantage of any chance that might offer itself. So she sat down before the little table, and unlocking her desk examined its contents. There were a few letters written in faded ink, and tears gathered in her eyes as she glanced at them.

"He loved me once," she said with a sigh, "and I absolutely loved him; yes, loved him. Well, that is past. He has abandoned me as he abandoned her, and I can strike them both through their boy."

Then she took out a letter that bore the New York postmark of the day before, and read it through from end to end. It was a long letter, and seemed to give her satisfaction. "I do not see how they can recover the boy," she murmured, "and, if this programme is carried out in the future, he should be as much lost to his family as a grain of sand in a desert, or a needle in a bundle of hay."

Then she considered whether she should burn the letter, or return it to her desk. She decided upon the latter course, and placed it for greater security in the concealed recesses of a secret drawer. The rest of the afternoon she spent listlessly in reading novels with yellow covers[3] and playing on the piano. She had no visitors. When the dinner hour arrived the Colonel had not reappeared. However, this did not greatly disturb her, as it was his custom on occasions to stay away from home; but when he decided to dine elsewhere he usually communicated through the telephone his intentions. He had neglected to do this, so Mrs. Clutterbuck decided upon her own responsibility to dine alone. She gave the necessary orders, and in due course the meal was served and discussed. After the things had been removed (she had taken her dinner in the boudoir) she lighted a cigarette.[4] It was not a habit which met with her husband's encouragement, but as he was not there to upbraid her she saw no reason why she should not indulge her taste for the fumes of nicotine. A little later the door was thrown open, and the Colonel entered. He was pale, and his features worked. Evidently, he was in a violent passion.

"You are quite a stranger," she said, with a little laugh, "and I have dined without you. I did not feel your loss, because the *suprême de volaille* was excellent. Take one?"

He deliberately seized the proffered cigarette case, and threw it with all his force against the wall. She shrugged her shoulders, and laughed again. "What a child you are! You remind me of Ronny, and yet you are no relative of his."

"Are you a relative of his?" asked the Colonel slowly, weighing every word as if he were afraid to trust his voice.

"Why, yes. Did I not tell you that he was my nephew?"

"And did you not tell me a lie?"

There was a pause, and they looked at one another as a duellist regards an opponent—neither anxious to begin, both on guard. Again she laughed.

"You are not very cheerful company this evening."

"Then I will make my visit as short as possible."

"Ah, you are paying me a visit, are you? You purpose obtaining a separation."

"There is no necessity for a separation."

"I see, then, you will obtain a divorce. I have always been told that in America there are special facilities for disjoining marriage ties.[5] Is New York a good place for that sort of thing?"

"There is no necessity, madame, to dissolve marriage ties."

"You are very, very serious this evening," said Lucille, putting the cigarette in her mouth. "I hate conundrums. All this afternoon I have been worrying myself to find an answer to the riddle, why I became your wife?"

"You never did become my wife," replied the Colonel shortly.

Lucille turned pale, and then her face was suffused with colour. She rose to her full height.

"And you have come to tell me this?"

"Now, madame, see here; I don't want any heroics. I am going to take it quietly, and I advise you to do the same. Now, what I have to say is just this. I made a mistake in marrying."

"The mistake was mutual."

"Now, madame, there is no cause for interruption. You shall have the story right away, and if you have not enough of it by the time I have done, it will be your fault and not mine. Look you here, if I made a mistake you made a greater. Have you ever heard of a crime called bigamy?"

"Yes," returned Lucille, coolly. "It is a weakness of mine—I committed bigamy when I married you."

"And you tell me that without turning a hair?" exclaimed the American, fairly taken aback at her audacity. "Then you know I could throw you into gaol, Madame?"

"You can do nothing of the sort," she returned. "Now stop further explanation; you see there is no necessity. I have saved you the trouble of inflicting a long story on me with your terrible nasal twang, and I am thankful."

"Look you here, madame!" returned the Colonel, white with passion, "don't you rile me too much. There is a limit, I tell you, and you have about reached it, and a bit over."

"Oh! I am not in the least afraid of you. For the reason that causes you not to hurl me into jail will prevent you from murdering me. And less than a murder would not do; even your countrymen don't care about wife—I beg your pardon—women-beaters."

The Colonel ground his teeth and clenched his hands, but kept tranquil.

"Madame, you are right," he said at last. "Quite right: I am not going to murder you. Anything of that sort I can leave to your husband—when he gets out of prison. But to come to business. If you take my advice you will make tracks. I have had private information that you have escaped by the skin of your teeth. They have got your husband and they wanted you, but the prosecutors seem to be economical, and they are satisfied with him. So instead of being taken to the Tombs[6] on your arrival in New York, you were allowed to come home with me. And a nice home you have made it, madame," and he looked round the room crammed with costly gimcracks. "It has cost me a pretty penny."

"Very likely," she replied calmly, "but you can afford it."

"Yes, fortunately I can, madame. Uriah Clutterbuck is good for millions."

"You had better not boast of your wealth, or you will make me avaricious."

"Avaricious! Why, what has my wealth to do with you, madame? All that is past and gone. We squared up when Mrs. Clutterbuck returned to Madame Vin-yay."

"Not quite," said Lucille with a cold smile. "You must be a bad man of business, and yet you have realised a fortune."

"Yes, I have made my pile, madame," he returned, with a vague feeling of uneasiness; "and as to my being a man of business, why, you just ask anyone who knows me."

"There is no necessity," said Lucille, "because I can test you

myself. As a man of business, how much do you intend to pay me
to go away?"

The Colonel indulged in a low whistle, and for a moment
regarded with absolute admiration the woman he had for a time
believed to be his wife. Then he slowly produced his pocket-book,
and taking out some notes, placed them before her. She took
them up, and reckoned the amount. "Not bad for a first bid," she
observed, "and I see you know how to deal. You are a better man
of business than I imagined. Say double, and we will call it done."

Again the Senator produced his pocket-book, and once more
extracted from its recesses some notes. He placed these before
Lucille, and she took them up as before. Once again she arrived at
a total.

"You are satisfied I shall not disturb you?" she asked. "You can
trust me?"

"Well, yes, madame, I can," replied the Colonel. "You think
quite rightly that I don't want a scandal.—I don't. But if there is to
be one, we may as well have it on a grand scale. If you come back,
Madame, to annoy me, why, then I shall know that I may as well
go in for the entire cucumber, and act accordingly."

"You will shoot me?"

"I guess it will come to that. You are a woman of great discrimi-
nation. I shall remove you, and I can do it with a better grace after
you have been away a bit. So you know what to expect. And now,
as we have had this friendly chat, there is no reason why we should
quarrel. Loo-cille, here's my hand."

She burst into a bitter laugh.

"Do you think I am going to take it? If by grasping it I could
make it wither, I would seize it and hold it to my heart."

"Why, what have I done, madame?"

"Why, you have robbed me of my last chance. If you had stood
by me I might have pulled through. Well, it will be pleasant reading
to see a report of your death."

"I daresay it will," said the Colonel, biting his lip until the blood
came. "In the meantime you can read this. And now, madame, I
have to bid you adoo."

And laying down a marked paper before her, he stalked away.

Lucille, left to herself, remained for some moments buried in the deepest thoughts. What should she do next? She had expected the storm, for she had felt that the discovery of her past was only a question of time. So she was not unprepared for the Colonel's desertion. She had taken care to supply herself with a goodly store of diamonds and precious stones, and accordingly for the moment was not within the reach of want. The bundle of notes she had extracted from the Senator's pocket-book represented a considerable sum, and added to the total of the value of her worldly goods. Then she had her beauty. She looked into the mirror and shuddered. What would her husband do when he escaped from the prison walls? It was the question she had asked herself a hundred times; it was the question that had been suggested to her not an hour ago. It would be a terrible day of reckoning.

"He will kill me," she muttered. "He has more pluck than this blustering American. He will kill me. Well, and if he does, what does it matter?"

And then she took up the marked paper that the Senator had left behind him, and glanced carelessly through it until she came to the column that bore the trace of ink. Then she started back as if stung by an adder. The marked passage told the world in general, and the American capital[7] in particular, that Lord Francis Onslow, the husband of the acquitted murderess, had lately arrived in New York.

★ ★ ★ ★ ★

It was night-time in the chief American police-station before Frank could find an opportunity for continuing his inquiries. On his arrival he had quickly learned that Mrs. Clutterbuck had not been arrested—that a telegram had been received warning the officials to do nothing, as their services were not required. And for the moment, the chief officer whom he consulted could tell him nothing more. He had been advised to let matters take their course.

"You see," said the chief, "we can't do much at present, sir. The Colonel is highly respected, and a Senator, and until we have authority to interfere with his arrangements we must hold our hands. You say that the boy that accompanies them is your son. Maybe it is so; but still the lad is under the Colonel's protection, and we don't want to lend ourselves to an abduction case. It would be giving ourselves away."

"But I tell you the boy belongs to me."

"Maybe he does and maybe he doesn't. The word of Colonel Clutterbuck is as good as yours, and while the lad is in his custody I don't see how we can help you. If you take our advice you will let matters slide for a while. We will keep our eyes upon the household, and if we find him taken out of the custody of the lady who says she is his aunt, why, then we will communicate with you, and then will be the time for you to come upon the scene. At present, you will pardon me, sir—I should say, my lord—you are what I may call a superfluity."

"Then you refuse to help me?" said Frank, angrily.

"Well, that is not quite as I want to put it," replied the officer of police, "but I guess it's about the true meaning. Don't be impatient, sir; many a bright undertaking has been ruined by too much impatience. I know it isn't pleasant advice to anyone to be told to take things coolly, but that's just the advice I would give to you. Let things slide a bit, and when the time is ripe for action, why then you shall know all about it."

"At least you will give me the Colonel's address?"

"Can't say I can; the Colonel is a man of business, and you will hear of him from every one in the proper quarter; but it is no part of my duty to act as a directory. You will run against him soon enough without my aid. So, sir, or as I should say, my lord, if you are not busy, I am, and I must wish you good-day."

With that, the official bowed and walked away. Frank, finding that nothing was to be done, turned also, and so the men separated.

In his hurry to leave England and reach the United States, Fenella's husband had neglected to arm himself with letters of introduction, and now he found the disadvantage of being in a strange city without a friend. He walked down Broadway, and paraded Fifth Avenue, but saw none but unfamiliar faces. He had put up at one of the large New York hotels, where he had advisedly given a false name. He was not particularly anxious to make the acquaintance of the American interviewer,—a gentleman who was unique until copied in England some few years ago.[8] So far he had been able to preserve his incognito, as the police official, who was a kind fellow at heart, had promised to preserve the secret of his identity. So, chafing at the delay, he wandered about listlessly, until, to his great delight, he received one evening a summons to attend at the bureau.

"You see I have not forgotten you," said the official. "Now I think we can set to work. The boy you have been looking for has left the custody of the Colonel—he is no longer in his care."

"And where is he?" asked Frank eagerly.

"That is a conundrum, my lord, that, for the moment, I cannot answer," was the reply. "The fact is, we have made a bit of a mess of it. A recruit—a sharp one, but still a recruit—was put upon your business, and he seems to have muddled it."

"What do you mean?"

"Well, look you here. He was ordered to keep his eye on the lad, and to report when the boy was removed from the Colonel's custody. Well, he did his duty, inasmuch as he gave us the notice the boy was off. That has been reported right enough, but——" he stopped.

"Don't you know where my son is at this moment?" said Frank angrily.

"Well, sir—I should say, my lord—that is exactly what I cannot say. Our man rushed off to tell us the news of departure; he would have done better had he followed up the track."

"And what do you propose to do?"

"Oh, we have made the best of it. We have sent a first-class officer, up to every move in the game, to take the matter up, and by this time you may be sure the country is being scoured high and low. When we come upon a track you shall hear of it. We can trust the Colonel. He is respected, and would not lend himself to any underhand piece of work. But it's the lady that is doing it. Now, we have not much of an opinion about her, and she is in it, that's the worst of it. However, don't you cry out yet; ours is the smartest service in the world, and we will do our best for you."

"But can I do nothing?"

"Well, no, sir—I should say, my lord—I don't see that you can. You had better look in to-morrow evening, and then I could report progress. In the meanwhile, keep an eye upon yourself. New York is a dangerous place for a stranger. I know you Englishmen are brave fellows, but such a thing as kidnapping, even an adult, is not unknown on this side of the Atlantic. So have a care, sir—I should say, my lord."

Smiling at the correction, Frank departed, determining to return on the following evening. On his way to the hotel, he had to pass a large house at the corner of a street, and as he walked along, he felt that there was someone gazing at him from one of the ground-floor windows. He turned his head in that direction, and immediately a blind was drawn down abruptly; but not until two piercing eyes had gazed for a moment into his own. He resumed his way, and then stopped suddenly. He was quite alone, for the street was empty. He raised his hand to his brow, and trembled as if he had an ague fit.[9] He seemed to be fighting some unseen, some terrible enemy. The perspiration ran down his face, and then of a sudden he became calmer, unnaturally calm. He appeared to be in a trance. He moved as if some power was controlling his actions. He hesitated, but only for a second, and then began to retrace his steps, and slowly, but surely, he walked along, as a somnambulist progresses. His eyes were wide open, but sightless; his arms hung listlessly by his side, until the time came for him to open a door, then slowly he extended his right arm, and his rigid hand seized the handle. He had passed through and entered the hall. Slowly he walked up the stairs, and slowly he made his way to the entrance of a large room. Again he opened a door, and again he walked on, until, seemingly exhausted, he sank into a chair.

When he returned to consciousness he still imagined he was taking part in some strange dream; for although he did not recognise the apartment in which he was resting, a familiar figure was bending over him. A woman had just taken her hand from his brow and was standing over him. He uttered an exclamation of horror, and tried to rise to his feet. The woman smiled and withdrew her hand, and once more he sank back in the chair in which he was resting.

Lord Francis Onslow and Madame de Vigny were face to face.

CHAPTER XVII.

CONFINED IN A MADHOUSE.

BY JEAN MIDDLEMASS.

LOVE was dead. There was no gainsaying the fact. With returning consciousness the expression of hatred became so fully developed on his face that Lucille de Vigny cowered before it. His wild blood-shot eyes looked as if they were ready to start from his head, and the desperation in his entire mien made her feel that there was no length to which he would not venture. Was he about to commit another murder?

Madame de Vigny knew naught of the previous one, or probably she would have run away in dire fear.

As it was, she was under the impression that the man she had once so loved and still cared for more than any one else in life, had suddenly become mad.

Rising at last to his feet with an effort, he began to speak gaspingly: "You fiend, you arch-demoness! where is my child?"

She laughed, and calling up her courage, tried to brave the matter out, though certainly she had never been so frightened in all her life before. Then, seeing that laughter irritated him, she said,—

"I believe he has gone back to his mummy, or at all events to Mrs. Grandison. Colonel Clutterbuck, my husband, would not stand him any longer."

"It is a lie, and you know it! Colonel Clutterbuck is not your husband, and the child has not left America. Where is he?"

"As you know so much, probably you know the rest. It is therefore useless for me to speak." Her tone and her manner were most aggravating, and in Lord Francis Onslow's then mood were positively dangerous. After the semi-somnolent, semi-stupid phase through which he had passed, an excitement had set in over which he had but little control.

He turned savagely on Madame de Vigny, and seized her by

the throat with his long, thin fingers; and yet she was the woman before whom he had once knelt in adoration.

"My boy—where is my boy? Tell me, where is Ronny?"

How could she tell him while he held her in a vice, even if she wished to do so. She tried vainly to utter some sound, possibly a scream, but nothing was heard save a gurgle, while her features became livid. The look of her to a degree sobered him, and he relaxed his grip; that is, he almost threw her from him with a force that caused her to fall with her head against the sharp edge of a sofa.

Even then he took no notice of her; it did not seem to trouble him that she was hurt, or that the handkerchief she held to her head was covered with blood.

He did not, however, attempt to touch her again, but walked up and down the room talking rapidly.

"Curse of my life that you have been! give me my child, that I may take him to the wronged Fenella, and forget that you ever existed. If it had not been for you, what a happy man I might have been with Fenella—my beautiful Fenella."

"And De Mürger?" asked Lucille, whose sting even fright and injury had not wholly killed.

"De Mürger—curse him too! But I forgot, he is dead—Fenella killed him to save her honour, even as I will kill you if you do not take me where I shall find Ronny."

But Madame de Vigny had not quite lost her wits, or her capacity for self-defence, though the pain in her head was intense, and the blood was still flowing freely. She managed, without his remarking it, to crawl from the sofa to the door, and then suddenly, before he had time to stop her, she jumped up, opened it, passed rapidly out, closed it, and locked him in.

Having done this, she could do no more, but fell in a dead faint on the mat.

Meantime, "cabined, cribbed, confined,"[1] Lord Francis was indeed "kept like a tiger in too small a cage."

She had thought him mad, and in truth it almost seemed as if she were right. He thumped at the door till the echoes in the house rang again; still no one came. The servants were all very far away, and were, moreover, amusing themselves with a game of poker, which was engrossing them far more at that moment than their mistress's visitors and quarrels. Not successful with the door, Lord Francis tried the window, but it was at least sixty feet from the ground—the jump was certain death; then he fell to smashing sundry bits of *bric-à-brac* that fell in his way—more to annoy Lucille than because he did not know what he was doing; and finally he rang the bell.

The bell brought Lucille's maid, but she did not open the door, though he loudly demanded that it should be unlocked.

The maid found her mistress faint and bleeding on the landing; it was scarcely likely she would open the door till she had tended her, especially as there was no cessation of the smashing inside.

Lucille was recovering her senses when the maid arrived, and thus by the help of an arm crawled into her own room, which was not very far distant. The first sentence she managed to pronounce was,—

"Do not let him out—he is mad. Poor man, he has a dreadful wife who has driven him mad. Set some one to watch the door in case he should force it, and send for Dr. Walton."

It was not for herself that Madame de Vigny desired the presence of Dr. Walton, for she washed her face, and put some plaster on the wound, which, after all, was not a very serious one, and she was a good deal revived by the time the doctor arrived.

Dr. Walton was a personal friend of Madame de Vigny; that is, she had made a friend of him since she had come to New York. She had a wonderful facility for fascinating the male sex and annexing their services, and she felt very certain she could depend on Dr. Walton, or she would not have sent for him.

When he did arrive, which was speedily, he was naturally aghast at the injury she had received. She would have allowed him to see it at its worst stage if she had not feared to disillusionise him by the aspect she had presented when the maid found her.

"Never mind me," she said, "I shall be all right in a day or two, but I cannot go on being subject to attacks from that madman. You must remove him; he says I have his child, whereas you know Ronny is my own nephew."

Dr. Walton did not know anything except what she had told him, but he believed in her, and therefore did not think of doubting her statement. "My dear madame, I will do the best I can for you; of course this must be stopped. Do you think it will be necessary to take—ahem!—extreme measures? I have some influence with the police."

"No police at all, if you please, Dr. Walton. The police are a body with which I wish to have no dealings. They have never done me any good. You have a house a little way out of town, where you keep patients who cannot control themselves. Take this man there as your guest, until I have time to communicate with his friends in England. He will be out of mischief and harm, and you will be doing a good action."

"You know his friends?" asked Dr. Walton, a little dubious whether he was not risking his professional reputation by taking this step.

"Well, I am most intimate with his wife. She is a most flighty, ill-behaved little person. I fancy it is her shortcomings that have driven this poor man to desperation. Still, of course, she is the proper person to communicate with. Hark! how he is knocking at that door again—there really is no time to be lost. I do not believe there is a bit of whole furniture in the room."

Thus urged, Dr. Walton proceeded to do what she wished; in fact, he began to think that it was the only thing that could be done. To get this man away quietly was, however, the difficulty—he did not want a scene and a scandal.

"Can you depend on the man on guard?" he asked.

"For coin—yes," she said, laughing, "money makes most people reliable—for a time."

"Well, stay where you are, and leave me to do the rest. I will return later, and let you know the result." So saying, Dr. Walton proceeded to the room where Lord Francis was still knocking clamorously. He said a few words in a low tone to the man at the door, and then he proceeded to interview the supposed lunatic.

To anyone less experienced than Dr. Walton, Lord Francis would certainly have seemed to be quite mad, but the doctor saw at once that he was merely suffering from excessive nervous excitement.

"A few days' seclusion would, however," he thought, "do him

no harm," as by that time, with a little judicious treatment, he would probably be quite himself again.

Was there something in Dr. Walton's touch or look that soothed Lord Francis, predisposed as he was to hypnotic influence, or was the doctor armed with some calming anæsthetic—who shall say? But, as if by magic, rage and excitement subsided, and as though insensible to what was passing around, Lord Francis sank down once more into the chair in which he was sitting when he first saw Lucille de Vigny.

Now he was entirely in the doctor's power, he could do with him as he liked. The servant, still outside the door, was called into the room, and in less than five minutes Frank Onslow was transported to the doctor's carriage, and was driven off to the private mad-house outside the city, of which Dr. Walton was the director.

From her bedroom window, by the aid of a gas lamp in the street, Lucille de Vigny saw him depart.

"Now," she said, "you are mine, to do as I like with. You will not leave that place until you have absolutely given up Fenella—for ever."

Madame de Vigny was an attractive woman, and she had, as in the instance of Dr. Walton, her slaves. She forgot that Fenella was quite as attractive, nay, more so, for she was younger than Lucille, and many thought her much better looking. She, too, had her devoted allies; Clitheroe Jacynth was no mean opponent for Walton, save that Walton was on his own ground. Still, if Madame de Vigny was not very much on the alert she might yet be balked.

For the moment, however, she decidedly held the trump cards in this terrible life game.

For some minutes after the carriage had driven off she stood by the window, thinking. The day had been an eventful one, and before the morrow dawned she must decide on some plan of action. A move out of her present quarters was inevitable, unless she wished to be turned out. Besides, since she no longer dared call herself Mrs. Clutterbuck, it was far better to reappear as Madame de Vigny in a new place. She did not, however, wish to leave the city till circumstances had shaped themselves somewhat; but New York was large enough for her to remain *perdu* for awhile if necessary. She counted her dollars. Colonel Clutterbuck's parting gift had been no mean one. She would not want money for some time to come. Having so far arranged her affairs, and told the maid to pack up, as they were going away for a few days, she went into the sitting room where Frank Onslow had been locked in for at least an hour, and, as she surveyed the *débris*, she smiled.

When Clutterbuck came back, as he doubtless would in a few days, when he thought she had had time to clear out, what would be his feelings, as, of course, he would attribute the breakages to her and call it petty revenge? But what matter? In fact, she felt rather glad that it had happened, especially as, casting her eyes round the room, she saw that the desk was uninjured. If Lord Francis had managed to dive into that, there is no saying what a pregnant change there might not have been effected in the course of events.

She opened it, took from it the papers which she considered of considerable importance to herself, sealed them up in some strong brown paper, and put the packet carefully into a dispatch box she intended to take with her.

For that night she would sleep under Colonel Clutterbuck's roof, and on the morrow she would take her departure. Before, however, she went to bed there was still work to be done. She told the servants, who did not yet know of the separation, that their master would not be in, and that they could shut up the house and go to bed. Having thus rid herself of them, she got ready to go out, tying a very thick veil over her hat in order to conceal the white plaster on her head, which might otherwise have been remarked. The servants' quarters were at the back of the house, so she slipped out unobserved. She took a tram, and went to an outlying part of the city. There she got out, and walked down two or three streets, looking carefully behind her to see if she were followed.

At last she knocked at the door of a tumbledown-looking house. It was opened by a slatternly foreigner, whose face lighted up into something like a smile when she saw Madame de Vigny. Not that she had any love for her, but her coming meant gold, and it was of the avaricious nature of this woman to do anything for money. "Is it all right?" asked Lucille, speaking French in a low tone.

"Yes, he went this morning, and if Satan himself sent his myrmidons on the quest,[2] they would not find him. Poor boy! it will be a hardish life that he will lead in the future. Have you ever read Daudet's 'Jack'?"

"Tush for Daudet's 'Jack!' Don't mix up sentiment with business."

"Business is done for the present, as far as I am concerned, only I quite understand I have to mother him in the future. Mercy, what a lot of money it does cost to keep a child, even in a poor way!"

"I know all about it; the terms are arranged. Here is six months' money in advance, as I am going away for a little. Not the slightest deviation in our compact, remember. You are in my hands; I know your past."

The woman made a cringing movement as she pocketed the money, and gave a promise of allegiance; but a few minutes later, as Madame de Vigny walked away, she muttered to herself,—

"I know as much of you as you of me, ma belle Lucille. Which of us has the most need to be afraid of the past, I wonder?"

Madame de Vigny adopted the same plan for returning home that she had done for coming to these purlieus. She took a tram to the Broadway, and from there started to walk to Colonel Clutterbuck's house.

She had not, however, proceeded far when, to her consternation and surprise, she met Lord Castleton and Clitheroe Jacynth strolling together arm in arm.

CHAPTER XVIII.

"WITHIN SIGHT OF HOME."

BY CLEMENT SCOTT.

"How will it end? In sorrow or in pain?
   It all depends, sweetheart, it all depends."
"We may be parted, we may meet again;
   It all depends, it all depends."

OF all forms of mental torture to which a sane human being can
be subjected, say which is the worst? to hear the door of your
prison cell close behind you, with hope gone, friends alienated,
love ruined, home wrecked, and the awful prospect of seven years'
unutterable silence and solitude, knowing before God you are an
innocent man? or to discover, and beat your brains into discord
with the knowledge that, being sane, you are the inmate of a
lunatic asylum; that, having reason, you are classed with idiots;
and that every explanation you can offer will be treated with a
mocking laugh?

The borderland between sanity and insanity is slighter than
many believe or would care to own. If ever man's brain had been
tested to its utmost limits of tension, that brain beat and throbbed
in the head of the wretched Frank Onslow. He had lost his adored
wife, and had found her; he had been granted the supreme hour
of reconciliation and rapture, and it was turned into the dull agony
of expected death. He had been told that if she awakened from
her dull brain stupor, and could mingle her kisses with those of
her husband and her child, her life might be spared, and he knew
that when she did awake she would discover that her lover and
her lord had vanished without a word. She might be dead even
now. He might have killed her. He who would have died to give
her life, might, for aught he knew, have struck her once more just
as she was tottering into the very arms of death. Everything had

failed—utterly, completely failed. Frank Onslow had become grey with grief.

The child who should have been in his arms was lost, God knew where; the wife whose life depended upon his honour was either dying or dead; the woman who had by him been changed from a companion into a fiend, was triumphant; and he, the hapless victim, was under lock and key, powerless to move, impotent for good or evil.

The more the poor creature protested his sanity, the more mad he seemed to be. The very situation, the ghastly surroundings, the hideous objects he met on every side, were enough to turn the brain of the strongest man. Insanity is bred in the air like a pestilence. Mad doctors become mad. Nurses, attendants, porters, and servants connected with lunatic asylums in time are devoid of reason. Put a madhouse, private or public, in any given neighbourhood, and in the course of years the surrounding villages and neighbours will become as cracked as King Lear himself, as suicidal as Ophelia.

When Frank Onslow awoke from the stupor of surprise he found to his horror that he was surrounded by gibbering madmen and crack-brained women. They sneaked round him, pulled him by the sleeve, and babbled nonsense into his ears. They believed that everyone was mad but themselves. They were deceitful, cruel, treacherous, hysterical, and maudlin.

Here was an old man driven mad by gluttony—a wild, weird, wolf-like man, who, after every meal, chattered for the next like a monkey. Scarcely had he swallowed his dinner before he stamped up and down the corridor muttering, "I want my nice tea and cut bread and butter. I tell you I want my nice tea and brown bread and butter." And after tea was swallowed he whined for his supper. Here was the young lover who was driven mad because he could not marry the girl he had met night after night in the stalls of the opera. Every night he dressed himself up in his evening clothes, put an artificial flower in his button-hole, and sitting on an old wooden chair, looked into space and warbled the music of *Faust's* love scene.[1] Here was a woman driven mad by the bad man who had deserted her, whose hair had turned grey in her long imprisonment, but who ever since wept tears all day over the love letters thrust into her bosom, and reduced to a pulp with much weeping. Here was the man who believed he had a millstone on his head; here the woman who was convinced that every means was being taken to accomplish her dishonour. Out they all came, mumbling, maundering, making faces at one another, pulling and picking at one another's coat sleeves; defiant, blasphemous, hysterical, howling, and weeping; men and women cursing; men and women rending the air with their piteous cries. Men glared at him with features distorted with rage; women hissed at him with lips polluted with blasphemies. It was enough to make anyone mad to talk to them. This was no home for the afflicted. It was a veritable hell upon earth.

The worst of it was that there was no humane desire to cure the insane. In public institutions they attempt to cure, too often in private homes they do not hesitate to kill the last vestige of reason. The doctors, instead of soothing their patients, irritated them. The mad point was not avoided, it was insisted upon. The consequence was that the wards, comparatively quiet before the medical attendants went their rounds, became a pandemonium after they left them. It would never have done to cure a paying patient. The object was to make him day by day madder and madder still.

In order to save his distracted brain, Frank Onslow relapsed into solemn and sullen silence. He was tortured with their mocking laughs. If he appealed to the doctors they laughed at him; if he consulted the attendants they turned away with a grin. If he hoped to obtain sympathy from the patients, the fitful gleam of intelligence turned into the animal laughter that was hideous.

"I shall go mad," said the wretched man to himself, "unless I hold my peace. Henceforward I will be dumb. It is my only safety."

There were regular visiting days at this particular establishment. The proprietor of it did not dare to run counter to public opinion, and he was artful enough to encourage these visits of inspection in order to show how admirable and infallible was his system. The patients were driven mad in private, and petted in public. They were literally fawned upon and thrashed.

Frank Onslow was saved by a miracle. In his darkest hour of distress he had lost hope in everything but prayer for help, prayer for deliverance, prayer that he might be rescued in order to protect the helpless. He was sitting moodily in his room, tortured with the sense that his reason would soon be lost to him, when he remembered that this was the day when visitors were admitted. He had prayed until his brow dripped with agony. His experience of the curious visitors so far had not been very encouraging. Whenever he attempted to get into conversation with any of them, or to pass a letter into their hands, he was greeted with a smile, or one of those mocking laughs. "Poor fellow," they whispered, "how dreadfully mad he is!" If not, they shrank from him as if he had been a wild beast.

The great iron bell pealed at the asylum gates. There were voices in the hall. Frank Onslow listened and listened again. It was an English voice talking to an American. Where had he heard that voice before? They were coming upstairs. The voices, indistinct before, became louder and louder. Yes; he knew both their voices. They were perfectly familiar to him.

"My God, is it possible? Can it be true? Are my unworthy prayers answered at last?"

The door of the room opened, and before the imprisoned man stood Lord Castleton and the very American detective who had been consulted when Frank arrived from England.

Here was an unexpected discovery. It was a miracle of miracles. There had been no search for the missing man. There was no hue and cry. Lord Castleton, like most Englishmen of an inquiring turn of mind, wanted to see the sights of New York, in order to record his impressions when he returned home. He had employed the services of one of the sharpest detectives in the city to show him round, and by a miracle he had discovered, and probably saved the life and reason of, his old friend.

In an instant the officer of police understood and grasped the situation. Once given the clue, and difficulties melt into thin air. It took very little time to procure an order for the release of the unfortunate Englishman, and before night time the medical proprietor of the fashionable mad-house was safely lodged in New York prison, and available for evidence on the subject of Mrs. Senator Clutterbuck, and, more important still, the safety and whereabouts of the unfortunate child Ronny.

At one time it appeared as if the troubles of Frank Onslow would end in an unsuspected manner. The drama was becoming a tragedy. He was released, it is true; he was safe once more. The discovery of his child was now more than probable. The discomfiture of his enemy, Mrs. Clutterbuck, was nearly complete, but the reaction after all this mental and physical strain nearly cost Frank Onslow his life. The strongest men break down at a given point, and now it was Frank's turn to succumb.

Once outside the asylum he appeared to be more insane than when he was in it. He wanted to face his enemy, and swore he would kill her. He pleaded to scour New York for the boy. He rushed off to the telegraph office to inform the wretched mother that he was true, and she might yet hope; but the strain was too much for even his strong constitution, and when he had placed in the hands of the detective every atom of information he possessed, and had almost imperatively been urged to leave the work of discovery to the hands of others, he went back reluctantly to his hotel, half-hysterical with excitement, but utterly dead beat. Lord Castleton found his friend next morning raging in the delirium of fever. At one time he cried piteously for Fenella, and kissed the pillow where he believed she had rested; in another instant he was twisting the bedclothes into a knot and imagined he was strangling Madame de Vigny. In the intervals he was sobbing, as if his heart would break, "Ronny, Ronny, my boy, my boy!"

No woman could have tended a sick man with greater devotion than did Lord Castleton. Night and day he never left his friend except to receive reports from the head office of the detectives, who once more proved themselves the finest officers in connection with any police service in the world. By constant care and devoted nursing the crisis was past. Reluctantly the doctors gave the permission for a move to be made, and on a certain bright morning Lord Castleton, with the aid of an invalid carriage,[2] took his worn and wasted friend down to the docks, where he had secured berths for England on board one of the fastest of the ocean liners. The journey to the sea seemed to revive the patient. As yet he had not been allowed to see any friends save Castleton, or to ask any questions. But the mists gradually disappeared from his eyes, and a smile of happiness played on his wan features.

"God bless you, old boy!" he said to Castleton as they drove slowly to the ship. "God reward you! Never did man find a truer friend. I should have been under the turf, old man, if it had not been for your tender care."

Castleton was anxious not to excite his friend too much. For the day was not over, and he knew that the drama of it was not yet complete.

On board they found Jacynth, who had been as loyal to his trust as Castleton.

The two men, when they met, whispered for a second to one another, and there was a look of distressed suspense on Frank Onslow's face.

"Is all well?" whispered Castleton.

"More than well," answered Jacynth.

"Where is he?"

"In the cabin."

"Do you think we dare risk it?"

"We must and shall," muttered Lord Castleton. "He can't break down now. It may save his life."

Gently these two brave gentlemen led their poor sick friend to his cabin, and placed him on his couch, but before they left him in a half-dream they uncovered the sleeping form of a little child who was resting in an opposite berth, the fingers of one hand twisted in his sunny locks and the others clasped over a woman's portrait. The faithful Jacynth had taken it from next his heart and placed it in the child's hands.

It was Ronny, who had gone to sleep kissing his mother's picture, which had fallen from his baby hands.

For hours the sick man slept, and his friends stood, sentinel-like, loyal hearts at the cabin door. The sun had sunk, the stars were out, and the steamer was already miles at sea, ploughing through the waves, lessening the journey between America and dear old England.

Still the true friends watched at the sick man's door. Suddenly they heard a passionate cry—a wild cry of pleasurable pain, a cry that faded into a moan of relief.

"Ronny, Ronny darling—my child, my son—oh! how good is God! Let us thank God together."

Quietly the two friends opened the cabin door and saw father and son on their knees in an attitude of prayer. The child was looking up into his father's eyes, and the wasted man, with streaming eyes was kissing his wife's portrait, and murmuring, "I have kept my oath. Beloved one, I'm bringing Ronny home to his mother's arms."

The stars went out and darkness fell upon the sea. There was silence in the cabin now, for father and boy were wrapped in a profound sleep. Castleton and Jacynth had finished their cigars and turned in.

Close upon midnight two figures came upon deck from the steerage part of the steamer, and walked backwards and forwards without exchanging a single word. But they never separated.

It was a detective from Scotland Yard, and Madame de Vigny was in his custody, cursing her fate.

As the huge ship plunged through the green Atlantic waves, bearing homewards the fatal lives of so many interested in this eventful history, poor Fenella, worn almost to a shadow, sat dreaming in her garden in "the island of carnations."

She knew, at any rate, that Frank was faithful, and that her boy was safe.

CHAPTER XIX.

A VISION FROM THE SEA.

BY CLO. GRAVES.

THE great ocean liner pushed her homeward way through the rolling surges of the Atlantic. Other yearning, tender hearts there doubtless were whose sole freight of hope the steamer carried; but the heart that beat so anxiously in the little Guernsey cottage had the most at stake. The ordeal of the past months had not lessened Fenella's beauty. The outlines of her features were sharper, their tints less vivid than of old. The tawny eyes looked wistfully out upon the world from orbits that were hollowed with grief and watching; the chestnut hair showed a thread of silver here and there. Would Ronny know his mother again? Fenella often asked herself that question. Meanwhile, for the child's sake, she husbanded her newly recovered strength with jealous care. She ate and drank, rose and slept, walked and rested, for Ronny. He must not find a peevish invalid in place of the old playfellow. None but her own hands should henceforth minister to the needs of this small idol of her heart. With these and other fond foolish fancies, she wore away the tedious hours of waiting.

One of her usual walks led in the direction of the village of St. Sampson's. The brown-faced quarrymen and fisher-folk grew accustomed to the sight of the pale, plainly-dressed lady with the wistful eyes, who so often paused to rest, or to smile at, and speak kindly to, the sturdy, sunburnt urchins that rolled in the dust by cottage thresholds, and pulled off their blue knitted caps as they passed her, in rude homage to her beauty, and respect for her loneliness.

One bright October afternoon she sat upon one of the rough wooden benches facing the wall of the little harbour, watching the progress of a child's game. There were five players, four of them hard-fisted, mop-headed urchins, with the brown skins and

blue eyes that seem indigenous to the island. The fourth was a
girl of nine or ten, a pale-faced, black-haired little creature, with
a shrewd, elfish manner and a voice of unchildish shrillness. The
game had to do with a wedding, of course—all the Guernsey children's games deal with marriages or christenings—and the song
that accompanied it was vocalised with immense vigour and zest
by all the performers:—

> "Jean, gros Jean, marryit sa fille,
> Grosse et grasse et bien habille.
> A un marchand d'sabots;
> Radinguette, Radingot!"[1]

The verse was repeated with even more shrillness. Then the
marriage procession tailed away round the corner with a clattering
of little wooden shoes, the sallow-faced girl gallantly supported on
the tattered jacket-sleeve of the most bullet-headed of the boys.
Fenella laughed, not with the ringing, careless music of the old
days, but still sweetly and clearly. She lifted her eyes and met the
melancholy glance of a shabby man, a stranger, whose attention,
like her own, had been attracted by the children.

The man was poorly dressed. He wore an old great-coat of grey
frieze,[2] and a peaked cap shadowed a lean, unshaven, sallow face.
The fringes of his ragged trousers fell over broken boots. No scare-
crow was ever more dingily attired than this strange man, who now
lifted his cap and bowed with something of foreign ceremonious-
ness, and looked at Fenella out of melancholy, hollow eyes.

"When the heart is heavy, madame, it is good to look at the
little people." He spoke in English, fluently, and with a strong
French accent. "They are so gay always; they know so little of care.
To sing and shout, and jump Gros Jean, that is the business of life.
Well! As good a business as any other, when all is said and done."

He shrugged his shoulders, and folded his arms upon his hollow
chest, shivering as the keen sea breeze crept in at the loop-holes of
his raggedness, and nipped his gaunt body. He did not beg, or seem
about to. The impulse was self-prompted that stretched Fenella's
hand to him with a silver coin in it.

"Take this. You look ill or hungry."

"Hungry, madame," said the man softly. "A thousand thanks." He hid the coin about him furtively, and saluted Lady Onslow again. The lifted cap revealed a narrow head shaved almost to the skin. Upon the temples was a livid scar, new-healed and ugly.

"You are a stranger to Guernsey?" Fenella hazarded.

"A stranger, Madame. I came from Cherbourg[3] yesterday. A fisherman brought me in his boat. I am not particular as to my accommodation, as madame will guess, nor was the boatman extortionate. Yet he took all my money, and left me without enough to buy a meal."

"You have friends in the island?"

"No and yes," the man returned. "The little daughter of one who was an old comrade of mine lives here in charge of a woman who was her foster-mother, and has married a foreman of the stone works. Madame has seen her playing with the children of the good *carrier*. She did not know who looked at her and questioned of her name just now. When last I saw her (five years ago) she was but four years old. At four years old the little Lucille could not be expected to understand—— Madame is cold?"

Fenella shrunk and shivered at the sound of that hated name. She recovered herself in another instant. She looked at the forlorn creature, who tried to interest her in his little story, with compassionate gentleness.

"Can the father not come himself to see his child?" she asked. "Is he an invalid or——"

The man answered her shortly and harshly.—

"The father is in prison."

He laughed a grating laugh, and ground the heel of his broken boot upon the pavement.

"Has madame patience to hear his story? Common enough, common enough. The father of the little black-haired one was once a clerk in a bank at Lille. He had assured prospects, enough for present wants; a charming—oh! yes, a charming—wife and a child. Charming women are apt to be vain; vain ones are apt to be extravagant, madame. She wanted money—always money. Her husband was like wax in her hands. *Hein!* She moulded her wax well—so well. She made of an honest man a rogue, madame, a forger, and a thief."

He broke off to wipe away the leaden drops that had gathered on his face with a miserable rag of a tattered handkerchief. His gaunt figure quivered, and the sinews started out like cords on the backs of his wasted hands.

Fenella spoke to him gently. "It distresses you to speak of it," she said.

"It relieves me to speak of it. Figure to yourself, madame, how this man must have loved that wretch, to sin so at her bidding. And she—she had not even the merit of being faithful to him. He found that out before the trial—for the frauds were discovered, and he was arrested. He denounced her as his accomplice. She fled before the law could lay hands on her—with one who had been, for long, her secret lover."

His face was frightful as he said the words. If he had been himself the wretched dupe, whose dreadful story he had upon his lips, he could not have looked and spoken with greater rancour. But he went on,—

"So my friend—always my friend, madame will remember—is found guilty and sentenced to imprisonment for eight years. He is sent to the 'Maison Centrale' at Clairvaux.[4] Compulsory labour, absolute silence; silence in the dormitory, silence in the work-shop, silence in the yard, silence in bed, from half-past six until six the next morning is the Clairvaux routine. Madame would never imagine how many cries of execration and despair, how many sobs of anguish, how many oaths of vengeance, can be packed into the space of one human breast that has the padlock of the law upon it."

He struck his own breast as he spoke, fiercely, and shook his clenched hand in the air.

"I have been a prisoner myself," he went on; "madame is not afraid of me? I knew that man at Clairvaux. Prisoners have methods of communication in spite of rules and punishments. I knew his sorrow as he my own. I promised him, when my hour of liberation came, I would visit the island to which his child had been taken, see her without speaking to her, and send him word. The last two years of his sentence have yet to expire before my friend can speak, unless he grows desperate, as a man does when the end is near, and escapes from prison. Clairvaux is a strong place, but there is a way

out of it. He has told me so. Chut! Here are the little ones returning. You are going, madame? Accept my thanks, the gratitude of a
poor man whom you have helped upon his way. I have not wearied
you with the story of my friend? A common criminal, no more.
And once having been in prison, as philanthropic people say, it is
twenty to one that he will eventually return there,—I myself also.
But the next crime of which that man is found guilty will not be
forgery."

Fenella yielded to an uncontrollable impulse. She looked full
into the hollow, glistening eyes. She put a question to the ragged
creature.

"Not forgery?" she said, repeating his words. "What then?"

The man bent toward her. She recoiled from the contact of
his foul and ragged garments. She shuddered as his hot breath
scorched her cheek. In a single word he gave the answer to her
question,—

"Murder!"

A dizziness came over her; she reeled, and put out her hands
to save herself from falling. They touched the cold stone of the
harbour wall. Her drooping lids lifted; she looked round vacantly.

The man was gone.

"The dreadful word!" she whispered—"oh, the cruel word! It
blights the present, it blackens the future. What can the future hold
for Frank—or for me? What does it promise to our child? A stained
title, a heritage of guilt and shame—a heavy, heavy weight for my
innocent love to bear. Oh, my heart, my heart is breaking!"

Tears came to her relief. She pulled down her veil hastily, and
hurried home, as the dusk October evening closed in. Late that
night she knelt by the open window of her bedroom, and looked
out upon the stormy heavens, upon the quiet sea. Herm loomed
near the horizon, a dark and shapeless mass upon the sleeping
ocean. The restless eye of the lightship[5] opened and shut; a bat flit-
tered noiselessly past, and vanished in the velvet darkness.

"Three days more," Fenella said—"only three days. Oh, my
son, my little son! Does the time seem as long to you as it does to
your mother?"

She closed the window, and went to her bed. Sleep would
not come at first. But towards the time of the flood tide she slept

and dreamed. She dreamed that she saw a great ship—an ocean steamer—ploughing homeward through a waste of waters. She knew that the vessel carried those three lives that were so dear to her. Friend, husband, child, lay sleeping in the cabins, lulled by the throbbing of the incessant screw. All peace, all security apparently. And yet a voice kept whispering in her ear, "Watch, watch! Danger!"

It seemed to the dreaming woman then that she stood upon the vessel's quiet deck. Not a sound broke the quiet except that throbbing of the screw. Not a sign of life appeared, until from the dark companion-hatch of the steerage deckhouse a solitary figure crept—the figure of a woman. And the white face it turned upon her, illumined by the pale rays of the moon, was the face of Madame de Vigny.

And the voice kept whispering, "Watch, watch! Danger!" She strove to shriek aloud and warn those on board, but her lips were sealed. She followed the creeping figure aft; followed it down a narrow brass-bound stairway, with no conscious movement of her feet; followed it through dusky passages, lighted by dim, swinging lanterns, and down stairways narrower still. Then it came to a halt, and she stood behind it, listening and watching.

A faint rasping sound. The striking of a match. A flickering light that revealed the place in which they stood together to be a place used for the keeping of ship's stores. Oil and tallow, firewood and candles, coils of dry rope, bundles of matches and other inflammable articles were gathered there. And then she knew, as another match struck and fired, and the pale blue flame lighted that evil face, the deadly purpose of her enemy. And even as she strove to burst the bonds of silence that held her, darkness fell upon the scene.

When she opened her eyes, still dreaming, the stately vessel was still gliding through the waters, herself removed from it by a distance that seemed impassable. But still the throbbing of the screw mingled with the whisper that warned her of danger to come. She strained her eyes and held her breath, and watched as she was bidden.

Then a little smoke began to curl upward from one of the aft hatchways. Thin and white, a narrow column of vapour slanting in the freshening breeze. Then a forked tongue of yellow flame shot out menacingly, and then a great bell began to clang furiously; and mingled with other sounds came the sound of voices shouting together. Only one word they kept repeating, and that word "Fire! Fire! fire! fire!"

The darkness was banished now by the fierce red glare that came from the burning vessel. Her deck was alive with orderly gangs of men, who came and went with hose and buckets, pouring water down the hatchways upon the roaring flames. Forward the passengers crowded together. And amongst those white faces which the quiet stars shone down upon, and the leaping flames illuminated with their own fierce glare, the dreaming woman saw the face of her child.

He was held, not in his father's arms, but in those of Jacynth. Frank was standing with his hand upon the shoulder of that true friend and staunch companion. The men spoke together with stern, grave looks; the child laughed and clapped his hands as the hissing tons of sea water fought with the fire that gnawed at the vitals of the brave vessel, deep below the water-line. And as the mother stretched her arms towards her boy the whole picture faded for the second time.

Another followed. Still the wide grey sea. No burning vessel on it now. Only a line of boats upon the waters, black against the background of a lurid, stormy dawn. The boats advanced towards the dreamer slowly. In the first only one familiar face—the face of Lord Castleton; in the second, none but strangers; in the third, strangers again; in the fourth, and last, a woman bound with cords lying at the bottom of the boat amidships, a grave, stern man keeping close watch and ward over the prisoner. In the stern-sheets, rough-handed, pitying men, dishevelled compassionate women, gathered round a little group of two. One of these in the uniform of an officer of the ship—the surgeon, perhaps, from the skilful way in which he supported the convulsed and trembling figure of the other on his arm, and held a restorative to the lips, and seemed to speak vain words of comfort. And the desolate creature to whose misery that kindly ministrance brought no relief lifted his head and looked at Fenella with eyes that were the eyes of her husband.

In her sudden agony of dread it seemed to her that she cried

out the names of the two who were missing. "Frank, where is
Jacynth? Where is Ronny? What have you done with my boy? Tell
me, for God's sake?"

And it seemed that her husband heard. He turned despairing
eyes on her. He shook his head and pointed to the sea.

She cried out then, and awoke as the first faint rays of daylight pierced through the blinds of her bedroom in the cottage
at Guernsey. And the woman who waited on her, roused by that
piercing cry, came running in.

CHAPTER XX.

THROUGH FIRE AND WATER.

BY H.W. LUCY.

SIX hours before the time Fenella beheld with fevered fancy the
light cast by the burning ship over the illimitable waters, the *Danic*,
with steam shut down, was slowly drifting outside Cork Harbour.
She was waiting for the tender to come alongside to take off the
mails and bear away the passengers who, having had enough of
the open sea, preferred to take the short cut by train across Ireland
and so home by Holyhead.[1]

There had not chanced to be any special cause for quitting snug
quarters on board the steamer. The *Danic* had made a splendid
voyage. Not once had the "fiddles" appeared on the dining-table to
the accompaniment of smashing crockery in the steward's pantry.
Day after day the passengers had been able to sit out on their deck-
chairs enjoying the sunshine, the fresh breeze and the sparkling
sea, through which for hours together the tireless dolphins swam,
emulous of the big ocean liner's volant speed. Two days out they
had passed close by a whale, who cheerily spouted farewell as they
speeded by.

Ronny looked on with grave eyes. He had often heard of a
whale, but never before seen one.

"Will Jonah[2] come out by-and-by?" he asked Jacynth, his constant companion, who held him standing on the rail.

"No, I think not," Jacynth answered gravely. "Jonah, you
remember, did not find the quarters so comfortable that he was
likely ever to seek them again of his own free will. Residence in a
whale, however temporary, is an experience that satisfies an ordinary man for a lifetime. The whale is only spouting, getting rid of
superfluous water taken in from the great depths."

"Well," said Ronny, his quick sympathies moved in another
direction, "he must get very thirsty if he does that often."

Ronny had thriven wondrously on the broad Atlantic, which had in no sense proved a disappointment to him. He was a prime favourite with all on board, the pet of the sailors, more particularly of the bos'n, whose whistle he was sometimes privileged to sound. Next to Jacynth he was fonder of the bos'n than anyone else, even than of his father, whose mood was less attuned to that of the light-hearted healthy lad, whom the stewards did their best to endow with dyspepsia by surreptitiously feeding him at unlawful hours with spoil from the dessert. He would sit by the hour on a coil of ropes, his big eyes fixed intently on the brown-visaged bos'n, who told him stirring tales (probably not all true) of seafaring life.

At first he had full run of the ship, and availed himself of the privilege.

"Father," he said, running breathlessly up to Lord Francis one morning when they were in mid-Atlantic, "what do you think? I've seen Mrs. Clutterbuck."

The little fellow, who in ordinary circumstances seemed to know no fear, trembled in every limb, and, as far as was possible with sun and wind-tanned face, was pitifully pale.

"Where?" asked Lord Francis, with signs of equal perturbation.

"Forrard," said Ronny, who had not in vain sat with the bos'n, and never now spoke of going downstairs when he should say going below. "I was standing by the rail at the end of the hurricane deck, looking at the passengers playing cards on the steerage deck, when she came along. She beckoned to me to go down to her, but I turned and bolted."

"Was she by herself?"

"No, there were a lot of people around. She wasn't speaking to any one, nor any one to her."

"Are you sure it was she?"

"Quite; she smiled just as she did when she came down in the country to take me away to join mother. I liked her smile then, but I don't now."

"Ronny," said his father, taking his hand and leading him aft, "I want you to promise me something; will you?"

"Yes, father," said the boy promptly, looking straight at him with eyes that never lied.

"Then you must never leave this deck for the lower one, whether in the steerage or amidships. It's quite big enough for a little fellow like you. You promise me?"

"Yes, father," said Ronny; and he kept his word to something more than the letter, limiting his excursions forward to the capstan, some distance from the steerage end. Perhaps he would not have gone so far, but it was here his friend the bos'n, when his turn came, kept his watch, and sitting there Ronny was careful to turn his back upon the bow, so that by no chance might he again see that evil face with the smile he, though all unused to the world, recognised as false.

On this bright evening off Queenstown Ronny was in a condition of special glee. Jacynth had put in the sweepstake on the day's run a sovereign in the name of Ronny, and Ronny had won the stake.

"Good gracious!" cried Jacynth, holding him at arm's length, "what on earth is a little mite like you going to do with £50?"

"I know," said Ronny, his eyes beaming with delight. "I remember when we were staying at Harrogate having a ride in a donkey chaise. It was very nice, but mother told me that the donkeys here are nothing like what grow in the streets of Cairo. When she was there she had two white donkeys as tall as a horse, with beautiful ears as long as my arm, and great brown eyes that look at you as if they wondered whether you could be so cruel as to want them to trot through dusty streets on a hot day. Mother often said she would like to have a pair of donkeys like she had in Cairo.—'Pharaoh and Rameses' were their names—together with a little carriage to hold her and me. I'll buy her the whole turn-out with my £50, and we'll go driving about all by ourselves through Jersey, Guernsey, Alderney, and Sark."

"Well, that's pretty selfish of you," said Jacynth, who keenly realised the joys of the situation as pictured by the boy, only he would like to have rearranged the company behind "Rameses and Pharaoh." They were all and always thinking of a woman waiting and watching in Guernsey. Lord Francis, with wistful eyes, thought of love; Jacynth with dumb, gnawing pain; Ronny with eager desire to see her smile, hear her voice, and feel her arms sheltering him;

Lord Castleton having some doubt as to whether she was worthy of it all; and Madame de Vigny——

Well, Madame de Vigny did not talk of the direction her thoughts took.

It was so near the dinner hour that it had been decided to postpone dinner till the mails and passengers bound for Queenstown had left. The tender[3] was close in sight, rolling and pitching in a manner that seemed inscrutable to the throng leaning over the taffrail. The magnificent *Danic* stood immovable as a stone pier on the rolling tide. The tender was speedily freighted with innumerable bags containing the mails, some thirty passengers followed amid hearty farewells from newly-made friends left behind, and many appointments were registered to meet again in London or Paris. With the last group there stepped toward the gangway a tall figure, a woman closely veiled, carrying a small bag in her hand. Just as she was stepping on the gangway the tender gave a lurch that dislodged the railed plank. Two passengers already on it narrowly escaped the disaster. They had just managed to skip on to the paddle-box of the tender, when, amid loud cries of "Stand back!" addressed to the group pressing forward on to the *Danic*, half a dozen ready hands hauled the gangway out of its aslant position, and made things smooth again. Once more the tall veiled figure pressed forward, when one of the steerage passengers roughly gripped her by the shoulder, and thrust her back. "Not this journey, madame," he said, seizing her wrist with a grip of iron. "Your passage is booked all the way to Liverpool, and we may as well make the most of the journey." The woman turned on her captor with the fury of a trapped lioness. For a moment it seemed as if she would grapple with him, and since she was nearly his height it would have been a desperate conflict, probably ending with a death grip under water.

For a moment the idea flashed over the mind of Madame de Vigny. She felt her game was up; wearied with the squalor of her unused condition, she did not care how soon she handed in the checks.

But she remembered that she had still one card to play, over which she had brooded in the dead, unhappy night as she lay wide awake in her narrow berth.

"Perhaps you'd better have let me go," she said to the man, whose plain clothes disguised his vocation of police serjeant. Then she sauntered slowly back, conscious that among the crowd on the hurricane deck, curiously watching this episode, was the man she really began to love with desperate affection now that her charms no longer lured him, and he was restlessly counting every mile that separated him from the white-curtained, rose-garlanded cottage in Guernsey where his wife awaited his coming.

"Jacynth, I wish I was certain to live for ten years or even for three," said Lord Francis Onslow, in the low, nerveless voice that had recently become habitual to him. The two friends were walking up and down the deck smoking their last cigar. Four bells had sounded, and they had the deck pretty much to themselves, save for the ghostly figures of the watch that moved with noise-less footsteps to and fro. When they came on deck after dinner the moon was shining, and far away on the starboard bow they could clearly discern the coast of Ireland, lying like a dark shadow on the moonlit water. Even as they walked and talked the scene changed. It had not at any time of the day been perfectly calm, as the passen-gers on the tender found as they made their way into Queenstown Harbour. Now it was blowing pretty fresh from the southwest, bringing up angry-looking clouds that from time to time hid the moon, promising presently finally to obscure its light. They were drawing up to Carnsore Point,[4] and were soon in the race of the channel. By this time they had found their sea legs, and though the wind played havoc with their cigars, as they paced about, and they gave up the attempt to keep pace in walking, they held on, Jacynth's spirits rising with the boisterous breeze.

"Ten years, old man? Why, you're only thirty at most, turned middle milestone—good for another thirty at least—and why should you not see threescore years and ten?"

"Because," said Lord Francis, "I'm pretty well played out at thirty. I've warmed both hands at the fire of life, and burnt them too. You remember when we were in Paris last year going to see 'Emile Angier,' from the play 'Jean de Thomeray'?[5] Often of late one scene comes back to me. The silent Quai Malaquais[6] which, on the eve of the beleaguering of Paris, the daylight even has deserted. Upon it *Jean* enters, sceptic and libertine, who jeers at his

friend, who has taken the trouble to get wounded in the struggle
with the Germans closing round the capital. Suddenly a military
band approaches, playing a march Thomeray knew when a child
in far off Brittany. At sight of the Breton Mobiles marching along
at quick step to meet the enemy of the country, Thomeray's heart
swells and bursts the bonds in which his scoffing nature has permitted itself to be bound. You remember how he steps forward,
and claims a place in the Breton ranks. 'Qu'êtes-vous?' they ask,
looking distrustfully at his fine gentleman's clothes. 'I am,' he said,
'a man who has lived ill and would die well.' That am I, Jacynth;
but it would not be meet that I should die just yet. I've been a fool
and worse. But if I had only three years, two years, one year, to
pay some of my long debt to Fenella, I wouldn't care about what
might follow. It's been all my fault from first to last. I want time to
tell her that, and to make some slight amends."

"Nonsense, Onslow; you are hipped;[7] perhaps seasick. Shall we
turn in?"

"You might, as we shall be in the Mersey early in the morning
and there's packing up to be done. But I'll take another turn.
Good-night."

"Well, if you send me to bed, good-night. I daresay another ten
minutes in the fresh air will take the blues out of you."

For another hour Lord Francis tramped up and down, unconscious of the unlit cigar in his mouth, thinking of the time when
he first met Fenella, of the years of idyllic happiness that followed
their wedding day, of Ronny's appearance on the scene, of the
little rift in the lute that, unwatched, broadened slowly, and made
all the music of their young lives mute.

Softly he sang to himself,—

> "Farewell, farewell,
> A river flows between."[8]

"Going to be a nasty night," said a tarpaulined figure, looming
out of the murk that enveloped the forepart of the deck, over which
the spray drifted as the Danic plunged her head into the angry sea,
and lifting it again, shook it as a retriever dashes the water off its
front.

"So it seems, bos'n," said Lord Francis. "But we're not far off port now. Good-night."

"Good-night, my lord. Better not leave things loose about in your stateroom to-night."

* * * * *

Jacynth slept the sleep of a man with a quiet conscience and a good digestion, who had passed the greater part of the day on deck of a ship over which swept strong air blown across the broad Atlantic. He rarely dreamt, but on this particular night, some two hours after he had bidden Lord Francis good-night, and turned into the stateroom he had all to himself, he began tossing about with a great weight on his mind. If he had a weakness in the matter of personal dress it was centered upon his stockings of rich red wool and ribbed as is the salt sea sand. He had a shapely leg, and missed no opportunity when out of town of displaying it with the advantage of knickerbocker dress.[9] He was dreaming now that a great calamity had befallen his treasured store of stockings. A spark from the funnel of the steamer, which, as he went below, he had seen streaming fire into the dark night, had, in the unaccountable way peculiar to dreams, fallen upon his bundle of stockings snugly ensconced in his box in the stateroom, and they were hopelessly smouldering; in vain he struggled to rise, seize a jug of water, and souse them. Something held him down by the chest, and he could not move. His terror seemed to have communicated itself to the passengers and crew. Hurried feet trampled on deck overhead. Voices sounded in eager talk, and the bos'n's whistle shrilly rose above the row of the waves that thunderously beat aft the shattered port-light. Possibly help would come in time and some of the stockings would be saved. A rattle at the door. Jacynth, almost awake, cried "Come in!" An invitation quite superfluous, for the door was burst open.

"Look alive, sir!" shouted the bos'n, entering hurriedly. "Ship's afire, and the boats are being got ready!"

"And Ronny?" said Jacynth, wide awake now, the nightmare of the burning stockings uplifted.

"The young un's all right; I seed to him first, and his father's got

him in tow. Better slue on as many things as you can. It'll be bad in
the boats till morning breaks."

Jacynth was not long in dressing, foregoing in his haste the
luxury of his worsted stockings, which he had full time to regret.
When he went on deck a strange sight met his eye. The passengers,
fully two hundred in number, were massed together aft of the
bridge, most of the women bareheaded and all showing signs of
hasty dressing. From one of the hatches near the wheel a dense
volume of smoke poured forth, now and then with increasing fre-
quency; lit up by tongues of flame on either side of the hatch, a line
of blue-jackets plied hose and bucket in ineffectual struggle with
the growing furnace. A singular quietness prevailed. There was a
murmur of conversation among the closely-packed crowd of passengers. A sharp word of command from the first officer in charge
of the fire brigade rose from time to time above the howling wind
and the war of the turbulent waves that dashed against the bulwarks, as if possessed with passionate desire to get at the flames.
Ronny, his father holding one hand and Lord Castleton the other,
stood on the outer fringe of the crowd aft, as near as he could
get to the fire, which he was evidently enjoying as the best thing
he had seen since the whale disappeared. The captain and second
officer stood on the bridge, and through the wheelhouse window
could be seen four grim faces of the blue-jacketed giants whose
curiously cheery voices answered the captain's signals with the cry
"Starboard!" "Steady it is, sir!" The captain, leaning over the rail of
the bridge and addressing the crowd of trembling but quiet passengers, said, "Friends below there, I hope you're all comfortably
wrapped up. This is a bad job, but there's no danger. If it had come
an hour later we should have made for Holyhead, and put in all
right. But with this wind, and the start the fire has got I don't think
we could carry on so far. The land is close by. If there were daylight
we could see it. The ship is now making for the spit of land at the
back of Pwllhely.[10] There is a smooth mile of beach there, which, if
I can make it, will bring the ship up comfortably, and you can walk
ashore in your slippers."

Jacynth led a cheer for the gallant captain, which was taken up
by the passengers, and seemed to do them an immense amount of
good. After this the wonderful quietness once more fell over the

doomed ship that sped onward swiftly through the sea that was now as rough as the bos'n's forecast had pictured. On the crowded deck all was as orderly as if, according to their daily habit, the passengers had mustered to take a look round before going down to dinner. The wind, now blowing what even a sailor would have admitted to be half a gale, whistled shrilly through the creaking spars. The course taken by the ship brought it more abaft, and sometimes a gust blew the smoke from the burning hatch under and across the bridge, choking the passengers and hiding the captain and second mate from view. But for the most part it blew clear away over the starboard side, leaving the vessel amidships and forward clear enough.

"Land ahead!" sung out the look-out man; the sing-song voice of the man throwing the lead showed how nearly they were approaching the coast, the outline of which was recognised in the deeper shadow on the horizon.

"Half-speed," the captain signalled to the engine-room. But the half-speed of an ocean liner soon bridges space, and nearer and nearer came the dark line of the coast. Straining eyes looking out from beneath the bridge could make out the outline of a mountain, at the foot of which nestled the smooth beach that was to give them safety and rest. Nearer and nearer it came, and higher and higher rose hope. Nothing between it and them but the sea, rough enough, but nothing to the majestic liner even with its hatches full of fire. The water steadily shallowed, as the monotonous cry of the leadsman marked minute by minute the lessening fathoms.

Suddenly, even as the leadsman sang out his last record, a crash resounded through every fibre of the ship. The *Danic* came as suddenly to a halt as if she had run up against Penmaenmawr.[11] The crowd amidships were knocked down pell-mell over each other, as if a giant hand had swept across them at the level of the chin. The captain, leaning against the rail of the bridge on the starboard side, was pitched headlong into the sea.

That proved the worst thing of all. The second officer, left in command on the bridge at this critical moment, signalled to the engine room, "Go astern full speed." That seemed an order natural enough, though the veteran Captain Irving would not have been led into so fatal a mistake. The *Danic* had run on to a jagged rock, which rose like a spear-head out of the sea, and had literally embedded itself in the hull of the steamer. Had the ship been kept head on, it might have hung suspended, the jagged rock serving to staunch the wound it had made, at least long enough for the boats to be launched and every one to quit the ship.

The mighty screw, reversing its action in obedience to the word of command, slowly but irresistibly drew the ship back. The terrified passengers could hear the iron plates ripped open, and barely was the vessel free from the rock than she began to go down by the head.

There was a rush for boats. They were ready and in perfect order. But with the sea rushing in in tons through the great gap in the hull, there was neither time nor opportunity for the marshalling of the now terrified passengers. It was not generally known that the captain had gone overboard, and the officers, expecting him to issue instructions, hesitated. Somehow boats filled, and four were safely launched. The two last had not far to fall from the height of the davits, the bulwarks being now almost level with the water. Just as their keels touched the sea, the great steamer went down by the head, sucking them under.

As soon as the collision came Jacynth had darted forward to the spot where he had seen Ronny standing, fearing no evil, for his hand was in his father's. When he came up to them Lord Castleton had disappeared—swept away, they surmised, in the rush for the boats. Jacynth, as he made his way aft, caught sight of Madame de Vigny and her escort clambering into one of the boats.

"Come along, Onslow; I'll carry Ronny," said Jacynth.

"Yes, but let the women go first."

"So we will; but not all the men," said Jacynth, grimly eyeing the crowd fighting round the nearest boat.

"My lord, and you, sir," said the bos'n, coming by, "take my advice. Don't be in a hurry about the boats. She's settling down. In five minutes there won't be a bulwark above water-line, but the masts and spars will be aloft safe and dry till morning. Fetch young un' along, and I'll give you a hand up the mainmast. There's nothing more I can do below. Look alive! and hold on tight. You'll feel a bump in another moment."

With a final lurch forward the ship went down, and the waves at last had their will on the seething mass in the hatchway. From secure, if not comfortable, quarters in the maintop Lord Francis, Jacynth, and Ronny saw the two boat-loads swamped, heard the seething roar of the waters as they closed over the burning hatch, and listened with chilled hearts to the shrieks of drowning men and women that filled the air.

It seemed a long night, but it was really only three hours, before, with the morning light, a steam-tug bound for Liverpool, after giving a fair start down channel to its charge, caught sight of the wreck and took off what at first seemed to be the only survivors.

"And," said Jacynth, as he sat in the captain's cabin, forgetful of his own stockingless state, and chafed Lord Onslow's numbed hands and feet, "if we had been four strings of priceless pearls hanging on to the yardarm, they couldn't have been more delighted to have plucked us off."

CHAPTER XXI.

"ALIVE OR DEAD?"

BY ADELINE SERGEANT.

THE Liverpool streets were, as usual, muddy, crowded, and malodorous; but had they been bowers of Elysian bliss they could not be traversed by men with gladder hearts than those of Onslow and Jacynth when they set foot on English soil. The gladness was of a sober sort, and tinged, perhaps, by anxiety for the future and sorrow for the past; but there was a natural elation, brought about by the recollection of the peril that they had escaped, and triumph in the thought of Ronny's restoration to his mother's arms. They took a friendly leave of the captain and officers of the ship which had brought them to Liverpool, and then proceeded to the nearest hotel, where they intended to stay for a few hours only, in order to replenish their pockets and wardrobes.

"Shall we telegraph to Fenella?" Frank asked wistfully; and Jacynth replied, in a brisker tone—

"Why, of course, or she will be hearing some garbled version of the shipwreck story, and will imagine that she has lost Ronny for ever."

"Don't put too much in the telegram," said Lord Francis, still in an uncertain voice. "'Ronny safe and well; we are bringing him back to you to-day.' And Jacynth, old man, sign it with both our names. She owes his safety to you rather than to me. Sign it by your name alone, if you like. I have no right" (a little bitterly) "to claim her gratitude."

Jacynth stood silent for a moment. Onslow was generous, but did he not, after all, speak truth? Surely he—Jacynth—had some right to Fenella's gratitude; it was all that would be left to him when the husband and wife were reconciled. He felt sure that that reconciliation would take place, and no place would then be left for him save that of a useful friend. Yes, he was tempted for a moment to claim the whole of Fenella's gratitude for the safety of her boy. But how could he let Frank Onslow be more generous than himself?

He laughed slightly when that little pause was ended, and shook his head.

"Lady Francis will question me pretty closely, and will soon find out where credit is due," he said. "There is no question as to which of us has suffered most in her cause and Ronny's." And he signed the telegram with Onslow's name alone.

They had thought of going south that evening, but an unexpected delay arose. Ronny developed symptoms of a severe cold, verging on bronchitis, and the doctor, who was immediately summoned, declared that it would be the height of folly to let him travel for a day or two. "It's nothing serious, but you cannot be too careful where children are concerned," he said, "and the boy has had a chill. You, too" (glancing at Lord Francis), "don't look quite fit for a long journey."

"I am fit for anything; all I want is to be with my wife again," Onslow averred feverishly.

The doctor glanced at him in a dubious way, and shook his head. He knew something of the Onslows' history—as who did not?—and did not understand the young man's anxiety to seek out his presumably erring wife. "Even for yourself I should not recommend the journey until you have had a rest," he said; "and as your little boy is so unwell, you cannot do better than keep yourselves quiet and warm, for a day or two until he is recovered."

He spoke privately to Jacynth afterwards. "The little fellow is not seriously ill; you need not be alarmed," he said. "I am making a trifle worse of his case than I need in order to detain Lord Francis for a short time. I suppose you see for yourself how much he is in need of rest and care. The fire must have given him a severe nervous shock."

"He is not strong, but I hoped that he would be better if I could get him to Guernsey, and leave him in good hands."

"Do you mean his wife's hands?" the doctor asked abruptly.

"I do. He will never be happy till he has seen her."

"Then why not telegraph to her to come here? The great thing just now with Lord Francis is to keep his mind easy. If her presence

would soothe and calm him you had better send for her at once,
especially as the boy is unwell. If he should be unduly excited or
agitated, however, I would not answer for the consequences."

Jacynth hesitated. "I do not know," he said slowly, "whether she
could travel so far. She has been ill—and——"

"And, perhaps—she may not care to come, eh?" said the shrewd
old doctor. "You must excuse me if she is a friend of yours, but the
fact is, everything I have heard of Lady Francis Onslow leads me
to conclude that she will not put herself much out of her way for
her husband's sake."

"You do not know her," said Jacynth, warmly; then, controlling with some difficulty a feeling of offence, he added, "I believe
that she is very much attached to Lord Francis, and would come at
once if she thought that he was ill."

"Then telegraph," said the doctor. "Anything rather than let
him travel in his present state of nerves and heart. It might be the
death of him." And with a brusque nod he took himself off, leaving
Jacynth more than ever perplexed by the duty that devolved on
him.

What could he say to Fenella that would neither frighten nor
repel? If he told her that Ronny was ill, she would be frantic with
alarm. If he said that Lord Francis needed her she might shrink
away with wounded pride. He thought of the way in which she
had spoken to him of her husband, and decided that he could not
hope to conjure by his name. As he had said to the doctor, she
would come if he told her that Lord Francis were ill; but if he
summoned her on that account, how explain her appearance to
Onslow himself? Every way seemed to be surrounded by difficulties. At last, in desperation, he wrote and dispatched the following
telegram,—

"Ronny knocked up by travelling; Lord Francis also unwell; can
you come to us in order to save delay?"

"The mother's heart in her," said Jacynth to himself, "will
supply all that is ambiguous in this message, and we shall have her
with us to-morrow."

He felt so much more at ease when the message was sent off,
that he turned into the smoking-room to glance at the papers and
smoke a cigar before going back to Onslow. Ronny was under

the care of a nurse, and Onslow was probably resting; he had no special responsibility with respect to either of them at present, and he was glad to feel himself free.

The papers already contained long accounts of the fire, of the swamping of the boats, and of the rescue of the four survivors found clinging to the wreck. A list of the drowned passengers and crew was appended, and here Jacynth caught sight of the name of Madame de Vigny. "So she went back to her old title, did she?" he mused. "Well, one obstacle to Fenella's happiness has been removed now that that woman is dead. Let us hope that she is dead indeed. It would be no kindness to her or to others to hope for her safety."

His eye had fallen on a short paragraph, which at first he had overlooked. Here it was stated that three or four of the crew had managed, by clinging to floating spars or other pieces of wreckage, to come safe to land, and that it was possible that more lives had been preserved in this way than could at present be ascertained. There was no mention, however, of any woman among the survivors: and, uncharitable as the wish might sound, it must be confessed that Jacynth heartily desired to be assured that Lucille de Vigny would trouble no man's peace again.

The rest of the day dragged slowly by—slowly because he and Onslow were both fretting at the delay caused by poor Ronny's illness. They were longing to reach the sunny shores of Guernsey, to enter that rose-wreathed cottage, and to pour their stories—each in his own way—into the ears of the woman dearer to them than any other in the world. And Onslow was not upheld by the hope that Jacynth cherished—namely, that Fenella, forgetting her past injuries in the love of her child, would fly at once to nurse him, and to clasp her newly-rescued husband in her arms. Painful as this consummation might be to Jacynth personally, he was unselfish enough to rejoice in the prospect of Fenella's future happiness; but Lord Francis, who did not know of the later telegram, grew irritable in his state of suspense and anxiety, and could neither rest by day nor sleep by night.

Jacynth had counted confidently on a return telegram from Fenella as soon as possible, and he was annoyed and disappointed when another day dragged slowly by without any news of her. Did she harbour so much resentment against Lord Francis, that

she would not even come to him when their child was in danger?
Jacynth's anger burned a little at the thought. He could not believe
that Fenella would be thus implacable. And Ronny was distinctly
worse: he was feverish, and wandered in his talk, calling out for
"Mummy," and imploring to be taken away from Mrs. Clutterbuck
in a way that was pitiful to hear. There were hints, too, of that
darker time when he had been left alone with men and women of
a coarser type—brutes in human guise, who starved and beat him,
and swore at him because he would neither lie nor steal. This part
of his story his friends had striven to make him forget, but when
his brain was clouded by fever, the frightful images of those terrible weeks in a New York slum came back to him with redoubled
force, and it sometimes seemed as though only the presence of the
mother for whom he cried so constantly could chase them away.

And yet Fenella did not come.

On the third day Jacynth waxed desperate, and resolved to
telegraph again. He had seen in the newspapers some accounts of
a gale which had been raging in the Channel, and it occurred to
him that the Guernsey boats might perhaps have ceased running,
which would of course give a reason for Fenella's silence; and yet
it seemed to him impossible that she should have heard nothing
yet, or been unable to send him any answer. He would telegraph
again, but he would go to Onslow first; it was possible—just possible—that she might have written to *him*.

From the look of agitation on Frank's face, and the convulsive tightness with which he grasped a letter in his hand, Jacynth
fancied at first that his conjecture had been correct. "What is it?"
he said hurriedly. "Your wife—is she coming? Does she know that
you are safe?"

"Heaven knows! She makes no sign. No, the letter is not from
her."

His face was so pale, his aspect so disordered, that Jacynth could
only gaze at him in surprise. And seeing his expression, Frank suddenly thrust the letter into his hand.

"See there!" he said. "What does it mean? Do you think there is
anything in it? If it should be true—of Fenella, my darling—what
have we done?" And he sank down in a chair beside the table, and
buried his face in his hands.

Jacynth opened the letter, which was written on coarse blue paper, and enclosed in a common envelope. Outside it looked like a tradesman's circular. There was no stamp, no postmark; it was simply superscribed with Onslow's name, and addressed to the hotel. The writing was evidently disguised—many of the words were printed, others written in a sloping hand.

"I will not tell you who I am," the letter began, "or you may not believe me; nevertheless, I speak the truth. I am the only person, except Lady Francis Onslow, who can unravel the mystery of Count de Mürger's death. From her lips you will never hear it: will you hear it from mine?

"She is innocent of his death; I can convince you of that. She is screening another. Do you not want to know his name? I was in the corridor on the night when the murder took place; I saw and heard all that occurred.

"If you want to clear your wife's name, come at four o'clock this afternoon to No. 10, Pearson's Row, Merslet Street, then I will tell you all.

                    "ONE WHO KNOWS THE TRUTH."

The paper dropped from Jacynth's hands. "If Madame de Vigny were living I should say that she wrote this letter," he remarked. "But how," he added, rather to himself than to Frank, "how could she know?"

Onslow looked up. His face was haggard, and there was a wild light in his eyes. "If she lives," he said brokenly, "she shall pay for all that she has done——"

"There is no likelihood that she has been saved," Jacynth broke in. "I don't think a single woman was rescued. No, Frank, this is a plant; and of course you will take no notice of it."

"No notice of it! But do you think that I would leave a stone unturned where Fenella's honour is in question?"

"For Heaven's sake, don't go!" cried Jacynth hotly. "There can be no possible good in it. What can there be for you to hear, unless you doubt your wife's story?"

His brow became dark and menacing as he spoke, but he was more anxious than angry. He and Fenella knew the truth, and he was bound by her wishes to keep it secret from Lord Francis. Was it possible that anyone else should know? Surely, he said to himself, no other soul on earth now living had an inkling of the truth. But at all hazards he would try to prevent Onslow from keeping so suspicious and so unworthy a tryst.

Frank Onslow, however, had made up his mind, and did not respond to any of Jacynth's somewhat ineffective arguments. And when the clock struck three he took up his hat and went out without saying whither he was bound. But Jacynth was only too certain that he had gone to the place mentioned in the letter.

While he still stood hesitating whether to follow, and force his company on him whether he would or no, there was a sound outside the door which made him start—the rustle of a woman's dress, the well-known intonation of a woman's voice.

"My Ronny; is he here? And Frank—Frank?"

Fenella had arrived.

She came in radiant with hope and joy, holding out her hands to Jacynth, who came slowly forward, and clasped them in his own.

"My Ronny!" she repeated. "Ah, how happy you have made me! I shall have both Ronny and Frank again. Take me to them at once; I cannot bear another instant of delay."

CHAPTER XXII.

RETRIBUTION.

BY GEORGE MANVILLE FENN.

"Merslet Street, sir? Oh, yes; first to the right, second to the left, and then third to the right."

Frank Onslow nodded his thanks and hurried away, trying hard to retain the sequence of rights and lefts in his confused brain; while the policeman whom he had questioned stood looking after him and beating his gloves.

"What does he want down Merslet Street? No accounting for these swells."[1]

Onslow had not noticed the man's manner, but he could not help hesitating for a moment as he reached the street named; and he hesitated again as he paused at the open door of No. 10—open, as he thought, like a trap.

But the intense desire to test the value of the promised information bore down everything else; and, forgetting the aspect of the coarse-looking women and ruffianly men loafing about at public-house doors and the corners of the streets, he knocked sharply.

"I will not go in," he said to himself. "Ronny—Fenella—my life may be of value to them if it is little to me."

A hard-faced, showily-dressed woman of about forty came to the door, looked him sharply up and down, and before he could speak exclaimed,—

"Oh, you're the gent, are you?"

"What do you mean? Yes, I am the gentleman who was to come here by appointment."

"Then you're too late," said the woman sourly. "She's gone!"

"She—has—gone?" faltered Onslow. "The appointment was at four o'clock. It is not ten minutes past."

"I can't help that. She came back in a hurry in a cab, fetched her bag, and she's gone."

"But the—the lady—is coming back?"

"Not likely. If you came you was to be shown into the room she took. Want to wait?"

"No," said Onslow shortly, as a strange suspicion flashed through his brain, and he turned and hurried away.

Had Lucille been saved, and was this some fresh scheme on her part, some fresh web spinning to entangle him, and keep him and Fenella apart?

He shivered slightly as he walked sharply away, feeling that he must by an accident have escaped from some new peril; and as he walked rapidly on through the crowded streets he saw nothing but the face of his fair young wife gazing at him reproachfully, but with a yearning look of forgiveness in her eyes.

"Yes, there must be forgiveness now," he muttered feverishly; "I do not deserve it, but for Ronny's sake. And she is waiting for me—waiting till I go to her, and on my knees beg her to come, and she will come, for the sake of our darling boy."

He was hurrying on with the busy tide of life eddying by his side, but his eyes had once more assumed their fixed, hypnotic look as he gazed straight before him, seeing the chamber in which his child lay dying, as it seemed, his little head tossing from side to side, while his monotonous, ceaseless cry was for his mother.

He had room but for one thought now, and that was to fetch Fenella to her boy's bedside; and as the mental vision faded, and his countenance resumed its wonted aspect, the influence remained.

He hesitated for a few moments, thinking that he would first return to the hotel, but feeling that if the boy were worse he would not have the strength of mind to leave him, he forced himself in the other direction, and made straight for the great station.

"It was madness to expect her to come here," he kept on muttering. "It was my duty to fetch her to our child."

His actions were almost mechanical, but throughout he felt as if some force other than his own natural impulse was urging him on in all that followed, though there seemed nothing unusual in the aspect of the careworn man who spoke to the inspector on the spacious platform, learned that the next London express started in half an hour, and then paced the flags slowly till he could take a ticket and his place in a corner of one of the *coupés*.[2]

The rest was dreamlike, and there were times when he became unconscious. It could hardly be called sleep. And at those moments, mingled with the rush and roar of the swift train, he could hear Ronny's plaintive cry for her who would bring him back to life and health, while in the faint distance, as if beckoning him onward, there was Fenella's sweet, half-reproachful face, waiting, always waiting, until he should come.

Ever the same, whether sunk in repose or awake and staring out at the blurred landscape, there was Fenella with her great eyes, silently calling him to her feet.

Yes, all dreamlike—visionary—of a great station, of a short journey through the great city; then of the rail once more, and then of the steamer calmly gliding down Southampton Water. The lights here and there, then the darkness and the cool, soft, light breeze fanning his burning temples, as he leaned over the bulwarks staring forward, with fixed eyes, waiting for the morning and the first glimpse of the sunny island which he loved.

Always confused and dreamlike, but there were memories of the dancing waters, of dimly seen white rocks, and of a great blaze of light flashing out at intervals with electric glare, and seeming to sweep the sea. Then a long, long period of darkness in a rough, tossing sea, whose cool spray ever dashed in his face, and at last a pale pearly grey, changing to a warm glow; then broad sunshine, and at last the rocky islets and his destination looking a very paradise set in the deep blue sea.

The sight of the island gave him hope, and his brain cleared for the time. He saw Fenella placing her hands in his, eager to follow him to their child, and for one moment he closed his eyes and clung fast to the vessel's side, for there was a sensation of joy that turned him giddy. It seemed greater than he could bear.

The port at last and the tedious landing, for it was low water; but he sprang down into the first boat that came alongside, and feeling calmer now, he landed, but, as he stepped ashore, staggered and nearly fell.

A curious feeling of irritation came over him as he saw a man smile, and he turned upon him resentfully.

"Don't be cross, sir," said the man. "You're not the first who has felt dizzy after being seasick. You'll be all right after breakfast."

"Breakfast!" The man's words rang in his ears and he remembered that it was many hours since anything had passed his lips. But he thought no more of his growing weakness, and had himself driven to the rose-hung cottage where Fenella was waiting for him with outstretched hands.

How long the time seemed, and how misty and dim everything looked! The sun shone brilliantly, but there was a something pressing, as it were, upon his brain; a strange pain too at his heart, and that feeling of faintness which seemed to overcome him from time to time.

At last! The cottage where he had left her—his darling—yes, the only woman he had ever loved; and he sat up eager to spring out—to tell her that his mission had been faithfully performed. But he had to avail himself of the driver's arm and totter up to the door, his eyes wildly searching the window for Fenella's face.

Then once more, as in a dream, some one meeting him, and a voice speaking: "The lady? No, sir, she left here in the bad weather, two days ago, by the boat."

Onslow heard no more, for a black cloud closed him in, and when he recovered consciousness he was looking in the pleasant face of the elderly little doctor who had attended his wife.

"That's better, my dear sir," he said. "You are suffering from exhaustion. That's right—no, no, you must drink this. You are not used to the sea, I suppose. It does prostrate some people, and leave them weak."

"Mrs.—Lady Francis Onslow—my wife?" gasped the wretched man.

"She has left the island, my dear sir, and really you must—— Good Heavens! what are you going to do?"

"Return at once," said Onslow, trying to rise.

"Impossible. You are not fit to travel."

"Must travel."

"But there is no boat till to-morrow morning between nine and ten, and even if there were, believe me, my dear sir, it would be madness. It is my duty to tell you that you seem to me to be developing symptoms that——"

The doctor said no more, for Frank Onslow had sunk on the couch insensible once more, and the next day's boat had gone when, weak so that he had to support himself with a stick, he made his way slowly along the cliffs after despatching a telegram to Jacynth at the hotel at Liverpool, telling him of his state, of his failure, and imploring him to send news.

He knew that it would be hours before an answer could come, and to try and calm himself he was slowly walking along the path, gazing out to sea at the swiftly coming tide, and thinking of the long period that had to be got over before he could take boat the next morning, and escape from what now seemed to him a prison.

Sick at heart and angry at his weakness, he sat down upon one of the blocks of stone that rose from amongst the heather just as footsteps approached from the direction in which he had come, and a strange, foreign-looking man, thin, ghastly, and whose ragged garments were hardly hidden under a rough pea-jacket,[3] looked at him sharply as he passed, and raised his cap, showing his closely cut hair.

Onslow acknowledged his salute, saw in him a beggar, and his hand involuntarily went to his pocket; but the man made a quick gesture, and passed on.

"One as wretched, perhaps, as I," thought Onslow; and then, as if moved by some strange impulse, he rose and followed the man, who somehow had a strange fascination for him.

The path turned there, and the man disappeared beyond a projecting rock, but reappeared, sheltering behind the rock, as if to avoid being seen.

It was curious, but Onslow passed on, and left the man bending downward, as if to fill a pipe. But the man and his gestures passed out of Onslow's thoughts instantly, for, as he went on past the rock in turn, he stopped short, paralysed at the sight of a well-dressed lady approaching him rapidly, leaning down and talking to a little elfish, sharp-faced peasant child, whom she was leading by one hand, while she carried a small travelling bag in the other.

"Lucille!" gasped Onslow, as a great dread of some fresh complication assailed him.

She started, drew herself up erect, and then, with a look of wonder in her eyes which gave place to a look of delight—

"Ah! *mon chéri!*" she cried. "Then you have followed me?" Then to the wondering child, "Go back to the cottage, *petite*. I do not want you yet. I will fetch you soon. The little one of an old friend, Frank," she continued.

The handsome, smiling face suddenly turned livid, the jaw dropped, and, with her eyes dilated, Lucille de Vigny stood gazing past Onslow as if at some spectral object at his back. Then, clutching the bag to her breast as if to protect herself, she uttered a wild, animal-like cry of dread, turned, and dashed down among the rocks where a precipitous track led to the sea.

Almost at the same moment a hoarse voice cried to Onslow in French,—

"Take care! The poor child! Do not let her see!"

But as the man literally plunged down the track, the child uttered a piercing shriek, covered her little face with her hands, and dropped down upon her knees.

Onslow was paralysed for the moment, and then, as he heard another cry from below, he forgot his weakness, a thrill of vigour ran through him, and he staggered to the commencement of the track. The woman was hateful to him now; he had looked upon her as a serpent in his path, but still she had loved him in her way. She was a woman, and he could not stand supine and not raise a hand to defend her from the attack of the savage-looking wretch whose aspect had filled her with such horror. He looked to right and left: there was not a soul in sight, while at his feet the sea came rushing and swirling in amid the wild, jagged rocks, a wave every now and then rising up and falling with a roar, scattering the spray high in air.

In his weak state it was madness to attempt the descent, one at which he would have hesitated even when well and strong, while now, as he lowered himself down, clinging to rock after rock and grasping at a handful of the tangled growth amongst their interstices, he felt that the thrill of strength was passing rapidly away.

But still he went on, with the thought in his mind that even had Fenella been present, and known of her enemy's peril, she would have urged him to try and save her from this man.

But now he felt that it could not be robbery; it must be something more; and again, as from below there arose a hoarse, despairing cry for help, he asked himself, Was this another of Lucille's victims, and—— Good Heavens! the thought chilled him with horror. The man refused his alms—he was no common beggar— did it mean some terrible revenge?

The idea thrilled him with another wave of strength, and he went on lowering himself down, feeling that those who had gone before must have fallen. For there was no track now; he was on a precipitous slope, where a false step would have sent him headlong down to where the waves were racing in among the broken crags of granite crusted with limpet and barnacle, and amber-clinging fucus, and amongst which every now and then were the long strands of ruddy or olive sea-wrack tossed here and there, like the shaggy hair of strange sea monsters, coming in with the tide.

Onslow had lowered himself down till his strength totally failed, and he sank upon a ledge, giddy with weakness and excitement, as he looked about him in vain for those he sought.

At that moment a huge wave broke with a heavy, booming roar, and in the following noise and rush of the waters, he lay down on his chest, reaching out over the edge of the shelf to peer below, for the chilling thought came upon him now that both must have reached the bottom, and have been swept away.

A thrill ran through him again for there, not thirty feet below him, in a complete *cul de sac* among the rocks, stood Lucille, her face toward him, her wrist thrust through the handle of the bag, and her fingers, with her delicate gloves all torn, cramped as it were into the rough rock on either side, as, with her head thrown back and her body bowed, she seemed to be at one and the same time clinging desperately to the rock and forcing herself as far back as she could from the bareheaded man who stood a couple of paces away, his arms crossed upon a breast-high stone between them, and his chin upon them as he gazed with a grim satisfaction at the terror-convulsed face before him.

Onslow grasped the position, and he saw, too, something glitter,—it was the point of a knife which appeared between the rock and the man's elbow.

"And I can do no more," groaned Onslow to himself.

At that moment he made an effort to try and climb down, and a terrible spasm at his breast made him sink down again, panting.

But his movement had caught Lucille's eye, and she glanced up wildly, and uttered a shriek.

"Frank! Frank!" she cried; "help, help! He is mad!"

The man looked up and uttered a loud laugh, as he said calmly, in good English,—

"No, monsieur, I am not mad. I am this woman's fate."

"No, no!" shrieked Lucille, about whose feet the waves were now surging; but she dared not stir, lest the man should spring upon her with that knife. "Frank, for God's sake, help! He will kill me."

"Yes," said the man, "as you killed me, body and soul, and buried me in a dungeon that was like a tomb."

"No, no!" shrieked Lucille. "Help, Frank! You loved me once."

"Ha! ha!" cried the man, unfolding his arms, and glaring at Frank. "Another lover! Poor wretch, I pity you! She has wrecked you as she wrecked me."

"No, no!" cried the wretched woman hoarsely. "Help! help!"

"There is no help, woman!" thundered the man. "The end has come. Monsieur, I claim the right of punishment. I am her husband. Bah! you can do nothing. It is her fate.

"And so," he continued, as he turned his terrible eyes on the shrinking woman, "you saw me away there yonder, and fled here. Fool! I knew you would come here to steal away my little Lucille—curse you! Why did I let her bear your name? You would have stolen her away; not that you loved her—you never loved, you cannot—and it was to plant another sting, another poisoned arrow in the breast of the poor trusting wretch who loved you, idolised you, and committed crime for your sake. But you could not escape me longer. I followed you from yonder town; I tracked you step by step till I have you here before me, dying—do you hear, wretch?—dying before my eyes."

"No, no, for pity's sake!" she shrieked, her thin voice hardly rising above the roar of the coming tide. "Frank, call for help; he will murder me!"

"Yes—call, monsieur, call aloud. There is none to hear. No one can help her now. This is the time for which I prayed in the cold,

silent dungeon at Clairvaux—for which I prayed as I toiled; and it
has come—come at last. Lucille, dearest wife—ah, how beautiful
you are!—will you embrace me once again? Thus, with the knife
between us, the hilt to my breast, the point to thine? Shall we clasp
each other in our arms once more, or shall I wait, and see the
waves slowly rise—and rise—and rise till they sweep above your
head?"

She uttered no sound now for the moment, but kept her eyes
fixed upon him, while Onslow strove vainly to call for help—to go
to the woman's aid; but every nerve seemed chained, and he could
only gaze down as the man glided round the rock which parted
him from his wife, holding the knife-hilt against his breast.

Then, heard above the roar of the waves, Lucille's voice rang
out inarticulately as she still clung there, her back to the rock, her
arms outstretched. It was the cry of the rat driven to the corner
from which there is no escape, and in his agony Onslow lay there,
watching the *dénouement* of the tragedy, perfectly helpless to save.

CHAPTER XXIII.

SICK UNTO DEATH.

BY "TASMA."

OUR nineteenth century, as we are all aware, is nothing if not analytical. Chemists spend days and nights in examining into the properties of some apparently unimportant compound, and do not abandon their task until they have ascertained the exact proportions in which primal gases are blended in its composition. In the same way, men of science, dissectors of motives, and these curious lay-preachers, the French novelists, take some complicated sentiment of the human heart, and twist it round, and turn it inside out, and expend themselves in efforts to trace it back to its origin through the influences of heredity or idiosyncrasy, or a predominance of white or red globules in the blood. Their researches are not always as fertile in results as those of the chemists, for in every human organisation there enters an unknown quantity which upsets the calculations of all the physiologists and psychologists combined. Nevertheless, they carry on their labours undaunted, and it may be said of them, as of the alchemists of old, that if they do not find the philosopher's stone, they make at least occasional discoveries which help to bring about a better understanding of human needs and weaknesses. It is unnecessary to say that the sentiment of love, or the condition of a man or woman under the influence of this sentiment, is the favourite object of their investigations; and the more it is entangled with other sentiments—such, for instance, as those of duty, or honour, or pride, or passion, the better they are pleased; for, like the chemists with their unknown compound, they can give full vent to their analytical skill in pulling it to pieces, and proving to their own satisfaction that it is made up of all manner of minor mingled sentiments, and is, in fact, nothing but a mere jumble of inherited instincts and impulses.

The state of Jacynth's mind during his friend's absence upon his fruitless and bootless quest in Guernsey was just such as a scientific French novelist would have loved to fathom and explain. In so doing he would have performed a feat of which the object of his investigation was himself utterly incapable, for Jacynth, for reasons best known to himself, shrank from making too close an examination of his feelings and desires at this particular period. It might have been that he was afraid of facing the conclusion which lurked at the bottom of them. There was a small balcony at the Liverpool hotel, just outside the room wherein Ronny was being coaxed into convalescence by his mother, where our hero would sit smoking his cigar until late in the afternoon, following out a train of disjointed thoughts that he essayed to drive away upon the circling wreaths of smoke drifting before him into the void. Perhaps they were more impressions than thoughts, half sad, half pleasant musings that it was safer not to reduce to coherent shape. He was conscious throughout of a dominant wish that the present time could be prolonged into an indefinite future; not at the cost of sickness and suffering to his unfortunate friend, but only, perhaps, at the cost of a timely prolongation of the actual gales which prevented the Guernsey boats from putting to sea. He had not willed that his signature should appear upon the telegram to Fenella in connection with her husband's; but since fate and (to say the truth) Frank's folly in running off upon a wild goose chase of his own had combined to leave him in charge, he could not but feel that there was a certain poetical justice in the situation, which it was allowable to enjoy to the full while it lasted. He pondered a good deal upon Fenella's character, which seemed to have revealed itself to him latterly in a new light. He remembered that her first question, her first cry, as she rushed into the hotel, had been for her child. It was only afterwards that she had shown any solicitude concerning the fate of Ronny's father. Then, had she not resigned herself to the lot—nay, had she not wilfully chosen it—of a self-constituted grass-widow' for years unnumbered? Her child, however, she had kept by her side, and, as far as could be seen, he had satisfied all the needs of her heart, for Jacynth was of those who believed that the train-attendant of Fenella's adorers had had nothing to say to her heart, thought they might have amused her vanity. Could she belong, he asked himself, to the order of women

of whom Dumas *fils*² speaks, when he says that in certain natures
the instinct of maternity overcomes the instinct of wifehood,
and that the woman ceases to be wife and mother, and becomes
mother and wife, or possibly mother only? In that case, any man
who should prove himself a true friend and protector of her little
boy might be sure of having a warm second place in her heart. It
was certainly to be deplored that Ronny's natural protector was
not better fitted for his responsible office. Though Lord Francis
had shown spasmodic bursts of affection for the lad and had undergone in New York a useless martyrdom in his behalf, which a man
who, to speak familiarly, had kept his head upon his shoulders,
would have known how to avoid, he had not been a father to him
in the true sense of the word. He had not once essayed to reach
the mother's heart through the child's during all the years that he
had been separated from her. How differently Jacynth would have
acted in his place! but then, as he reflected, he would never have
parted from Fenella at all. He would have given her no reason,
no excuse for desiring to leave him; and as for those flirtations of
her juvenile matronhood, he would not have taken them too seriously, for he would have felt convinced that she would outgrow
them—would leave them behind, very likely, with the cutting of
her wisdom teeth. Well, life's experience had done for her what a
husband's guidance had failed to do. She was amazingly reasonable
now, and might develop into a delightful companion for a man of
sense. It was a pity, Jacynth thought again—but I do not believe he
avowed the thought—that Frank should have been so wanting in
this quality. A fine fellow without doubt—a man to lead a forlorn
hope in an emergency; only forlorn hopes are unfortunately rare as
everyday occurrences. A grain of common sense would have been
much more to the purpose, and this grain was unhappily just what
Fenella's husband lacked. When his friend's deficiencies were not
vaguely outlining themselves upon the smoke wreaths before him,
the recollection of a certain episode would take their place, which
never failed to bring a curious half smile upon the smoker's face—
not a smile of the lips, but an unconscious wrinkling of the skin in
the neighbourhood of the eyes, which conveyed the impression of
some inward pleasure. The episode had occurred the first morning
that Ronny had been well enough to be taken out in a bath chair to

Sefton Park,[3] his mother and Jacynth walking on either side. The little boy had espied a sailor sitting on a bench with a smoked-out pipe in his hand (lacking, perhaps, the means of replenishing it), and having the vision of his friend the bos'n before his eyes, and a full comprehension, gathered from his night upon the mast, of the dangers that lie in wait for those who go down to the sea in ships, had asked that his bath-chair might be stopped, while he pulled out his new purse and extracted one of the sixpences his mother had put into it for the tobaccoless sailor. The man's gratitude had been unbounded. He had taken off his hat to all the group under the evident impression that it was a family party, and "May all your progeny, sir, and my lady, take after this 'ere little chap," he had said at parting; "it's the best wish a grateful heart can salute ye with." Fenella had blushed a deep rose colour, and Jacynth had felt an unreasoning pang of elation and regret as he walked away. He would have liked to come across the sailor again, not to correct him of his error, but to reward him for it.

Another point connected with the present aspect of affairs, which it was pleasant to be reminded of, was the way in which Fenella seemed to lean upon him. She would open the door that communicated with the balcony at all hours of the day to ask him to decide this or that question for her. Might not Ronny be "let off" his tonic, which he hated, and have some roast chicken? Did Mr. Jacynth think it would hurt him to have his sofa wheeled on to the balcony—and oh! would he mind just tasting the tiniest drop of the new cough mixture, which was quite a different colour from the last, and telling her whether he thought the apothecary might not have made some mistake? And all these questions Jacynth settled with a pseudo-marital authority it was delightful to exercise. He unhesitatingly prescribed roast chicken in the place of the tonic; he wheeled Ronny's sofa himself on to the balcony; and he swallowed a whole teaspoonful of magenta cough mixture without a murmur, inwardly flattered that Fenella should assign him the *rôle* of a slave of the worst of the Roman Emperors (for was he not her slave in all things?). Her smile took away all the bitter flavour from the drug, and the subsequent hours, during which she sat by the side of Ronny's sofa, seemed to pass like a pleasant dream. What he most enjoyed was the atmosphere of domestic retirement and

freedom that pervaded them. Fenella would insist upon his continuing to smoke his cigar, and so at home did he feel in her presence that it had actually happened to him to close his eyes behind
the *Times* he was pretending to read, and to allow himself the full
measure of the traditional forty winks (though why forty, more
than fifty or a hundred, I for one have never been able to discover)
before he opened them again. Fenella, for her part, would remain
silent or speak, just as the spirit moved her. Sometimes she would
read a sentence out loud from her book—an old copy of "Sartor
Resartus," as it happened, taken from the hotel library, and ask
him if he could make it clear for her. At other times she would take
no notice of his presence, but would occupy herself entirely with
Ronny. Jacynth loved to watch her at these moments from behind
his paper, and seek fresh proofs of the infinite variety of her charm.
He did not wonder that the little boy adored his mother. She was
his playmate and companion, as well as his nurse and guardian.
The stories she told him, when he was tired of playing at spilikins,[4]
with transparent little fingers that trembled from weakness, were
delightful. There was always some point in them which provoked
a duet of laughter from both together, that Jacynth found it good
to listen to. There were times, too, when the conversation would
become general: that is to say, when Ronny would be the chief
speaker, and when he would tell, in his quavering little voice, of
the wonderful and terrible things he had seen in the New York
slums. Jacynth, moved with pity for the white terror portrayed on
Fenella's face, would essay to divert his attention to other topics.
He could not, however, prevent the child from narrating to his
mother the manner in which he had been ultimately found and
rescued. "They wouldn't let me go out of the room," he said earnestly; "we was all together in a room upstairs—oh! up such a lot
of stairs—Mick, that was the man's name, and Bridget and me. It
was only one room, and that was all our house; the other people
only had one room for all their house, too, and they gave me a
horrid old mattress in the corner to sleep on, and I had no toys,
not the least little bit of a toy to play with, and I did get so tired all
day long, and it smelt so horrid in the room, you can't think. And
one day Bridget thumped me on the head with a plate—there was
only two plates she had—and it broke all to pieces; and I cried so,

you can't think; I cried, and I cried, and I asked God to send you to me, mummy; I went on asking Him and begging Him all the time. But I don't think He heard me, for there was lots more rooms and more ceilings—oh! ever so many over ours before you got to the roof. And one day there was someone knocked at the door; a great loud knock, and Bridget called out, 'There's the black man come for you; hide for your life, you spalpeen'⁵—she often called me a spalpeen—and I was so frightened, I ran to my mattress, and Bridget threw a horrid old dress over me and nearly smothered me. Mick wasn't there, and what do you think? When the men came in I heard a voice that wasn't a bit like a black man's voice. I'd often heard the black men talking, you know. There was a black butler where I was staying before in New York, but this voice wasn't a bit like that; and so I just peeped, like this, from under the clothes; and, oh! mummy, there was Mr. Jacynth and a lot of policemen standing inside the room, and I gave a great shriek—didn't I, Mr. Jacynth?—and I kicked away the dress, and I rushed right to where Mr. Jacynth was standing, and I held to his legs—I did; and he took me right up and kissed me. I put my arms round his neck, and I cried and sobbed fit to break my heart; and what do you think, mummy?" (Ronny's voice conveyed unnumbered notes of emphatic exclamation.) "Mr. Jacynth was crying, too; he was; I *seed him.*" He might have added "as you are crying now, mother," for as the climax of the narrative was reached, Fenella broke down completely, and instinctively held out her hand to the saviour of her little boy. Jacynth could not refrain from pressing his lips to it, and the action conveyed a thousand times more than the courtly old custom is wont to convey under ordinary circumstances. Ronny, overcome by the recollections of the scene he had conjured up, flung his arms round his mother's neck, and then held up his face to Jacynth to be kissed. "Let's kiss all together," he said, in the effusiveness of the moment, and Fenella was fain once more to turn away her head lest Jacynth should see her blushes.

In connection with all this portion of the disastrous chances that Ronny had experienced, it will be noticed that no mention of his father crossed his lips. It was only when the moving accident on board the *Danic* was under discussion that Frank's share in the strange eventful history came to be narrated; and even then,

whether for the reason that Jacynth's presence recalled his behaviour on that dreadful night more strongly to Ronny's mind than
that of his absent father, or whether because his personality was
in point of fact so much the stronger of the two, it is certain that
the child persistently assigned the *rôle* of the principal hero to his
friend, notwithstanding the well-intentioned efforts of the latter to
transfer a portion of his laurels to Lord Francis. *Les absents ont toujours tort*, says the French proverb,[6] and in a modified sense Ronny
was unconsciously proving the truth of the proverb.

It must not be supposed, however, that Fenella neglected to
inform herself in so far as was possible of her husband's movements. The telegram from Guernsey had apprised her of his
safe arrival, and of his enforced detention through bad weather.
The three days' gale had grown into a five days' gale, and every
morning Jacynth notified to Fenella, with an expression of
becoming gravity, the deplorable reports that had reached him
from the meteorological authorities; and insisted upon the inad-
visability of risking a Channel crossing until the present tempes-
tuous winds should have abated. As Ronny was growing hourly
better, and had been promoted by the doctor from roast chicken to
mutton chops, and, indeed, to "anything he fancied," which was a
larger order, perhaps, than the worthy man could have imagined,
Lady Francis accepted the delay in her husband's return with com-
mendable philosophy. I am not sure that she would have shown
equal resignation if there had been no one at hand to participate in
her delight at Ronny's recovery; but Jacynth's interest in the event
seemed almost to equal her own, and his skilful suggestion that
the longer Frank remained away the greater would be the joyful
surprise that awaited him, as regarded the amount of flesh that
Ronny would have put on during his absence, seemed the best of
reasons for taking patience.

It is an ill wind, says the old proverb, that blows nobody any
good. The wind that retarded the Guernsey boats was blowing the
roses into Ronny's cheeks and joy into Jacynth's heart, when it suddenly lifted, and a great calm fell upon land and sea. Looking from
the balcony Fenella saw the lake in the opposite park shining in
the distance like a silver shield, and reflected that at the same time
next evening she would probably be watching it with her husband

by her side. Ronny was now running about in the full exercise of a convalescent's privileges, and tyrannizing over his mother and his friend upon the principle that he was to live at his ease, to do as he pleased, and "not to be worried, the doctor says." With the recuperative force of childhood, he seemed hourly to grow and expand, and many were the conversations that Fenella had with Jacynth upon the subject of his future training. She noticed that a word from the latter went farther than a whole chapter of expostulations from herself, and fell unconsciously into the habit of referring the little boy to his friend upon every occasion. It may be that as she watched the sky this evening she was wondering what Ronny would do when the firm and gentle influence that was so beneficial to him was removed; and altogether so absorbed was she in her thoughts that she did not even hear Jacynth's step approaching until he was by her side. Then she turned her face, transfigured by the sunlight glow, and looked at him with questioning eyes. Jacynth's face was very grave; there was bad news written in every line. He held a telegram in his hand, and Fenella, with a sudden sense of icy chilliness invading her forehead and cheeks, took it from him without a word. Jacynth, seeing her so white, thought she was about to faint, and forced her gently back into a chair. The telegram was brief, as telegrams are wont to be, even when infinite joy and sorrow are compressed into them. "Lord Onslow seriously ill," it said. "Advise Lady Francis to come at once."

"Oh, why," was Fenella's first thought, "had she not gone sooner? Why had she allowed herself to take it for granted that the winds and the waves were the cause of the long delay? Might not her heart have told her that some stronger power than those was holding her husband back? Had she even once taken the trouble to verify for herself the list of the arrivals and departures on the Guernsey boats? What selfishness, what apathy, what *indifference*, alas! she had been guilty of." These were the self-upbraidings that pursued her all the time she was making her hurried and eager preparations for departure. Jacynth had essayed, in his usual calm and kindly fashion, to reassure her against her worst fears, but he could not enter into the subtler causes of her remorse. Ronny, in morbid terror of being taken to sea again, behaved, nevertheless, like a man when Jacynth showed him that it was his duty to take

care of his mother. That very night he, Fenella, and the child, who
were so used by this time to passing for Monsieur, Madame, et
Bébé that they almost felt like the personages they simulated, left
Liverpool for London.

A privilege children share with animals is their inability to
realise the meaning of sickness and sorrow, or suffering at a distance. Though Ronny knew that he was being taken to see "poor
papa, who was ill," the knowledge did not bring home to him in
any way the fact that he was in danger of losing his father. Fenella's
prescience was keener; the words "seriously ill" pursued her like
a maddening refrain throughout the whole long journey. In vain
Jacynth represented to her that "seriously" did not signify the same
thing as "dangerously." For the first time since he had known her,
she showed a disposition to resent his consolatory speeches. On
the steamer she hid herself away in the ladies' cabin—a proceed-
ing which Jacynth knew to be contrary to all her instincts—and
left him to smoke his cigar forlornly on the deck. She would not
even give him the solace of taking charge of Ronny, but carried
the little boy below into the petticoat atmosphere of the unwhole-
some stronghold she had selected. Jacynth, therefore, battled with
his thoughts alone. He was better able than Ronny to realise the
import of the telegram which had summoned him to Guernsey,
and it must be admitted that he did his utmost to bring himself to
hope that the issue would be such as his conscience and his sense
of honour demanded that he should hope, for the consideration
that Frank's death would transform the "might have been" into the
"might be" was one that he strove manfully to put away. It must
not be as a Judas, he told himself, that he approached the bedside
of his friend, sick, perhaps, unto death at this very moment.

Ay! sick unto death, though even the doctor who attended poor
stricken Frank would have told you there was hope still. What did
the doctor know of the last terrible scene in a life's tragedy to which
his patient had been a helpless witness, before he dragged himself
back, quaking with fever and affright, to the cottage wherein he
had taken up his temporary abode? What if the love that had linked
him for a space with Lucille de Vigny had had little in common
with the "holy flame that for ever burneth"? What if it had been
nothing but the evanescent and unholy outcome of "fantasy's hot

fire"? It had yet left a recollection behind it which rendered it more terrible for him to see her tortured and slain than another and a better woman. That second during which the lunatic's knife had been pressed against her heart, the second during which she had shrieked aloud to him for help, a hideous, unmelodious shriek, more like a squeal of far-gone animalish agony than a woman's shriek, had utterly unmanned him. He had realised in that short space all the horrors of a Dantesque hell whence rescue is impossible. Yielding to the mad impulse of the moment, he would have flung himself down from the rock, a useless victim, had not the mighty ocean, or possibly some stronger power still, taken the matter into its hands and rendered all intervention useless. Frank was conscious of a loud booming noise accompanied by a mighty swish and whirl of water that seemed to cover the whole tragic scene from his view. The salt spray dashed aloft and closed his smarting eyes. When he opened them again Lucille and her husband were gone; only a monster wave curling back into the ocean was sounding their dirge. Whether the knife had entered her heart before the sea took her into its merciful embrace, whether in her death struggle she had clutched at her murderer, and dragged him down with her to her doom; whether some mighty wave had risen unexpectedly and swept both combatants away at the same instant, could never be known. The ocean seemed to be lashed into a sudden fury. For a moment Frank dimly discerned some object that might have been a woman's hair floating under the liquid green. But was it Lucille's hair? For all he knew it might have been only one of those waving tangles of brown seaweed that the mighty Atlantic surges wash into the English Channel. With trembling knees and a reeling brain he staggered away from the scene of the tragedy. It was fully two hours before he succeeded in dragging himself back to the cottage, where he terrified the inmates by the aspect of his drawn white face and hollow eyes. What had become of Lucille's sobbing child, orphaned in one short, fateful instant, he could not have told. Tended and put to bed by kindly hands, he lay like the Israelitish king with his face to the wall, in the torpor that followed upon the too great tension he had endured.[7] Even the zest for life seemed to be leaving him. There was only one thing left, for which he would fain have endured a few hours longer, and no one could

give him the assurance that this thing he yearned for was coming
closer and closer to him with every vibration of the screw that
drove the Guernsey boat, with its freight of passengers, nearer and
nearer to its destination.

CHAPTER XXIV.

"WHOM THE GODS HATE DIE HARD."[1]

BY F. ANSTEY.

IT seemed that the doctor was right after all. Frank Onslow was feeling better, distinctly, undeniably better, as he lay on the chintz couch in the little sitting-room of the rose-hung cottage at Guernsey. The pain about the region of the heart had entirely disappeared under skilled medical treatment; not for many a day had he felt more vigorous and hopeful, reclining there with his eyes fixed upon the door in momentary expectation that it would open and admit the slight girlish form of the wife from whom he had been so long and cruelly separated. Yes, Fenella was on her way to him; he would see her, hold her in his arms! There might be years of happiness yet in store for them—years in which to atone, to forget. Surely the boat must have arrived by this time! What was that sound? He had not deceived himself; there *was* a light step on the gravel outside. She had come—she was here; in another instant she would be at his side! The door was gently opened; he rose to his feet with a smothered cry of joy, rose—and the next instant sat down again heavily, with a groan of irrepressible disappointment, for the woman who stood there, dazzling yet in her faded Southern beauty, was not Fenella; it was Lucille de Vigny, whom, as he fondly imagined, he had last beheld drowning in the blue-green waves, clasped in the fierce embrace of her injured and revengeful husband, the blade of whose dagger was deeply embedded in her bosom!

The shock of the surprise was considerable; it was some time before he could recover sufficiently to express himself adequately.

"Witch, demoness, arch-fiend that you are!" he groaned, "how came you here? Has the sea given you up once more?"

"Ah, Frank!" she said, with a soft musical accent of reproach, "I

did not expect that question (to say nothing of the form in which
it was put) from you, of *all* men. Who should know how I escaped
what seemed a well-nigh inevitable doom, if not the man who preserved my life?"

"I—*I* preserve your life?" gasped Onslow, in a bewilderment
which, under the circumstances, was not unnatural.

"You forget soon, sooner than I. I can see the whole scene yet:
my horrible husband holding me closer, closer still; the steely glitter
of the blade as it touched my breast; you on the rock thirty feet
above, gazing with eyes that are fixed—oh, but fixed!" (she closed
her own as she spoke, with a flicker like the instantaneous shutter
of a camera) "and next, without warning, with a sudden bound
you leapt the distance between us, hurled, with a strength that in
your shattered state seemed almost supernatural, my would-be
executioner into the sea with one hand, while you supported my
half-fainting form with the other, and then strode away up the cliff
like one in a dream. Surely you remember?"

Frank shook his head; he had no recollection whatever of the
incident. That this should be so will not surprise the reader, who is
already aware that he was subject, under certain mental conditions,
to hypnotic trances. In one of them he had, as we know, destroyed
a life; in another he had preserved one—with an equal lack of voli-
tion of consciousness in either case. Even now he could not bring
himself to credit her account, any more than he could affect a
decent degree of satisfaction at so untimely a resuscitation.

Still, there she stood, alive—whoever had rescued her; and it
occurred to him presently that he might at least profit by the fact to
obtain some light upon a point which had cost him several anxious
thoughts of late. Had she, or had she not, written that mysterious
letter from Pearson's Row? If she had, could she indeed prove that
Fenella was guiltless of Count de Mürger's blood?

Despite his intrinsic loyalty to his wife, he could not help preferring that her fair little hand should be unstained even by a justifiable homicide. It was weakness, no doubt; but man is built up of
prejudices which can neither be defended or overcome.

"Lucille," he said, more mildly, though in a voice which
betrayed his harrowing emotion, "for long months past you have
persecuted me with a relentlessness that I can only characterise

as demoniacal. You did your utmost to alienate my poor wife's heart from me, and sow mistrust and suspicion between us. Not content with that, and actuated by no conceivable motive but blind and wanton malevolence, you abducted our only son—my little Ronny; and when, with a very natural desire to rescue him from such a guardian, I followed you to New York, you procured my incarceration in a lunatic asylum, where, but for a happy accident, I might have remained to this day! Worse still, when all our perils seemed at an end, and I, with my boy restored to me, was on board the *Danic*, within a few hours of home and happiness, it was your malignity, I have only too much reason to suspect, that fired the ill-fated vessel, in the hope of involving us all in one common doom! And yet—and yet, Lucille, I cannot but think that you still retain a lingering spark of true womanliness somewhere, in spite of all! By that spark, I adjure you solemnly, to tell me, as you hope for mercy, whether you did or did not write that letter signed 'One who knows the truth'?"

"I did," she answered; "I *do* know it. I have come here with the full intention of telling it."

"And you can clear Fenella?" asked Frank. "Then I forgive you freely all the wrong you have done. Only speak, Lucille. Tell me all at once; keep me no longer in suspense!"

"Wait," she said, calmly, and almost soothingly; "are you quite sure that you can bear to know the truth?"

"Sure?" he exclaimed. "If only Fenella did not stab the Count, what care I what other hand dealt the fatal blow?"

Lucille de Vigny smiled a dark and mystic smile, as she said slowly, "Not even if the hand should prove to be *your own*?"

Frank Onslow fell back with blue and writhing lips. "It is a lie!" he said hoarsely, "a cruel lie!"

"It is the truth, my poor Frank. I can prove it."

Now, as has been already stated, this was mere conjecture on her part. In spite of the assertion in her letter, she had *not* been in the corridor of the Prospect Hotel when the tragic occurrence had taken place. On the contrary, she had been, perhaps, the most perplexed by Frank's disappearance the next morning. It was only subsequently that her feminine intuition had supplied a partial solution of the mystery. However, her shot told with terrible effect.

"Prove it!" he repeated incredulously. "Why, after I had seen the Count enter Fenella's room, I went straight to my own; I sat up in a stupor till daylight—I did, indeed, Lucille!"

"And at daylight you fled," said Madame de Vigny softly.

"Only as far as Paris," he rejoined, "and I did not fly. I travelled in my ordinary manner."

"At least you left your wife to go through the inquest and trial alone."

"I did not know of either until weeks afterwards, when Castleton showed me the reports."

"Not know of a sensation that was convulsing all England? Paris is scarcely Kamschatka,[2] my dear Frank. English papers are procurable at the hotels."

"I—I was ill," he said feebly, "or else I was yachting for weeks in the Bay of Biscay. Or both—*I* don't know!" Even to his sick and bewildered brain his story began to seem rather a lame and improbable one. "But my wife," urged the wretched Frank, with a pitiful return of hopefulness, "expressly admitted, when she was examined and cross-examined on her trial, that she had done the deed herself in defence of her life. I have never yet known Fenella, with all her faults, stoop to a direct falsehood. How do you get over *that*, Lucille?"

"I am a foreigner," was the chilling response, "and, as such, imperfectly acquainted with your criminal procedure. Still, I have always understood that persons indicted for such offences are not entitled to give evidence in their own defence. I may be wrong."[3]

It should be explained here that Madame de Vigny *was* wrong— or partly so. There certainly is some such rule, but it would be strange, indeed, if an advocate of Clitheroe Jacynth's position and influence could not succeed in getting it set aside in favour of his fair client, when, as his legal acumen had divined, the effect of such an admission would inevitably insure the prisoner's triumphant release, even on a trial for manslaughter. And the result, as has been stated, amply justified his calculations.

But the diabolical plausibility of Lucille's rejoinder destroyed the last vestige of hope for Frank, who was less familiar with the laws of his country than every well-educated Briton should be.

"You are right," he groaned; "I did it—I *must* have done it. And—what on earth shall I do *now*, Lucille?"

Her face, past its first youth as it was, became rapt and transfigured with tenderness as she bent over him and laid one slight burning hand on each of his shoulders.

"I will tell you," she said, in her low, cooing accents; "if you stay here you are lost! For ever since your rash visit to Inspector Brown at Scotland Yard, nay, before that, the detectives have been upon your track. It cannot be many years, or months, perhaps, before they hunt you down, even in such a remote island as Guernsey. And if you are arrested and brought to trial, Fenella will be powerless to screen you any longer. As your wife she will be unable to give her testimony in your behalf, as you are doubtless aware. I alone know your guilt, but do you think that I would betray you? Why, I love you, Frank; I think I have always loved you, even when I seemed to hate you most. And now that you have saved me from a hideous death, oh! my dear, my dear, how can I give you up? No, fly with me at once. We will go to South Africa, where society is freer and healthier than here, and conventional prejudices do not exist. Come, Frank, come ere it is too late."

The miserable man wavered on the couch; he did not love this woman—not at least with any passion deserving the name, but he was in her power. And how, how could he face his lovely innocent Fenella with the consciousness that he was a murderer?

As he still hesitated, there came a resounding knock at the trellised door which made them both start.

"The detectives!" whispered Lucille de Vigny, "*already!* Quick, Frank, the back door!"

But Frank Onslow had not lost all his manliness; he drew himself to his full height with a proud dignity.

"Back doors are not exactly in my way, Lucille," he said, "let them take me. I am ready to atone with the last remnant of my miserable, ill-spent life."

And the door flew open as he spoke—but it was no detective that entered. Fenella came in, in her pretty light frock, her small cheeks flushed with a now unaccustomed rose tint, and something of the old, merry, mischievous sparkle in her tan-coloured hazel eyes, for she had been laughing and talking on the way up with Jacynth, and telling him how she had fascinated the steward of the steamer, until, with her customary light-heartedness, she had almost forgotten the gravity of the errand on which she came. Jacynth's dark, clean-shaven face, with the imperturbable expression and the firmly-moulded jaw, was visible over her slim shoulder.

But at the sight of Madame de Vigny, her old enemy and rival, all the merriment and infantile innocence in Fenella's lovely audacious face faded suddenly; her tawny eyes flashed with the tigerish gleam Frank remembered so well, her soft red mouth grew hard and set.

"I perceive," she said icily, "that I am *de trop*.⁴ I was not aware that you were well enough to receive a *visitor*, Lord Francis. Mr. Jacynth, will you please take me away?"

"Fenella!" cried Frank in an agony, "let me explain! This—this she-fiend, this mocking devil, has come to try and persuade me that it was I—*I* who stabbed Count de Mürger with my own hand! Tell me, for pity's sake, that you at least do not believe it!"

In spite of herself, Fenella's first and very natural resentment was somewhat appeased by the evident sincerity in her husband's manner, and it was with a pitying reluctance that she answered.

"Frank," she said, "I would spare you this if I could, but the time for silence has gone by. Since you appeal to me, I am bound to tell you that I *do* believe it. I have no alternative, for—although it comes from the lips of Madame de Vigny—it is the simple truth. Remember, I was *there*, I saw it all with my own eyes. It *was* your hand, and no other's, that sent the Count de Mürger to his doom!"

The unhappy Frank staggered at these terrible words.

"My own wife! *She* says she saw me do this thing! How you must *loathe* me, Fenella! *How* you must loathe me!"

"But I *don't*, Frank," she assured him, earnestly. "I don't loathe you in the least, you poor unhappy boy! Because—oh! listen, Frank—when you killed him, I knew from your expression that you were in a hypnotic trance, and, therefore, neither morally nor legally responsible for your actions. Had it been otherwise, do you think I should have screened you as I did?"

Frank wiped his brow; an immense load was lifted from his soul.

"That accounts for it," he said, slowly, "I felt sure I could not have committed such an act in an ordinary state without retaining *some* recollection of the circumstance. And yet," he added moodily, "if I am accused, who can prove that I did it in this unconscious state? Not you, Fenella—according to Madame de Vigny, at least."

"Just so," said Lucille, speaking for the first time. "You are his wife, Lady Francis, and the law will not accept you as a witness.[5] There is no one who can prove it, and therefore, the deduction I leave to you."

"Pardon me," said Jacynth, stepping calmly forward. "There *is* somebody—Lord Castleton, who was, like us, rescued from the wreck. He has lately told me so. It appears, my dear Onslow, that he saw you subsequently, when you were suffering from a precisely similar attack. You stabbed madly, blindly, without being in the least aware of your actions."

"*Another* murder!" cried the horrified Frank. "Oh, the horror, the black, hopeless horror of it! To be doomed to these deeds of blood, and never to suspect it till too late! Jacynth, I think I shall go mad."

"There is no necessity, my dear boy," said the barrister kindly. "Fortunately, on this particular occasion you were armed with no more formidable weapon than a roll of paper, or else, had there been a victim at hand, which providentially there was not, the consequences might indeed have been disastrous."

Frank's countenance cleared once more. He could embrace his wife now with a clear conscience, and he turned to her accordingly with extended arms. "Fenella!" he cried. "*Mrs. Right!*"

"*Doggie, my own Doggie!*" was the ringing response, and the pair were folded in one another's arms. Jacynth had turned away. Pardon him, reader, if at that supreme moment of reconciliation his own heart was too sore and bitter to bear the sight of the happiness which had been mainly his own work. Devoted friend, self-contained, distinguished barrister as he was, he was still many removes from an angel. But the sound of the old pet names—the names she remembered on the envelope returned to Chiddingford from the Dead Letter Office—seemed to exasperate Lucille de Vigny to a fury that would not have disgraced a fiend. It must be remembered, in justice to her, that she had loved this man with all the ardour of a passionate, undisciplined nature; she had lost him, had been on the verge of recapturing him, and now he had escaped her once more, and something told her that this time it was for ever!

"Very pretty, my faith!" she said, with a bitter laugh of mingled rage and despair. "*Quelle innocence, mon Dieu!* You have defenders—is it not?—who combine military duties with a naval footing? How do you call them, *hein?* I forget."

"Possibly, madame," suggested Jacynth gravely, "you refer to the Marines?"[6]

"The Marines—it is that, yes. Well, tell this fine story to them—to your Marines.[7] Or, better still—for I hear them, they are here at last—to your detectives, and see what they will say to you!"

Her fine instinct had not deceived her this time; almost before she had finished speaking a couple of men in plain clothes came into the room. They had the sharp, roving eye of the trained sleuthhound, and one of them carried a pair of steel handcuffs.

"There is the man you seek!" cried Lucille, pointing to Frank, who stood quietly awaiting his captors in the centre of the room. "Ah, my poor Doggie, you have had your day!"

"Begging your pardon, madame," said one of the men, not uncivilly slipping the handcuffs over Lucille's slender wrists, "but *you're* the party we're after. You have given us the slip often enough, but I think we've got you safe this time."

Madame de Vigny's face changed; for an instant she seemed to contemplate resistance, and then she submitted to the inevitable, and followed her captors to the door. On the threshold she paused and looked back with a gaze of concentrated hate upon the party. "Bah!" she ejaculated, and then, with an indescribable gesture of defiant contempt, she walked out of the room, and out of the lives her baleful influence had done so much to perturb.

As soon as she was gone, Frank, with a sudden recollection, inquired, "And the boy, our Ronny, Fenella? He is not ill—not *again?* Tell me the worst. I—I can bear it!"

"Ronny," said Fenella, with one of her little spasms of silent mirth, "Ronny is quite well; only he insisted in driving up to the door in a goat-chaise. What is the matter, Frank—you are not unwell?"

"No," said Frank, faintly—"no, only the dread of some new disaster. We have gone through so many!"

"They are all over now," she said, sweetly and confidently—"all over. Ronny will be here soon, and then we three will live here happily together, and poor Mr. Jacynth, whose time I am afraid I have really monopolised quite shamefully, can go back to his chambers and his clients again."

"Yes," said Jacynth dully. "I can go back. I—I have neglected them too long."

It was the end, he realised; she needed him no longer. He should see her no more—he would go. But before he could carry out his intention, he was startled by a sudden change in Onslow's expression, and, shocked beyond words, he saw him throw his arms above his head, turn sharply round three times, and totter heavily against a wire flower-stand full of hyacinths in bloom, which he brought down with him in his fall. It was all over! The long-standing heart trouble, combined with the excitement of the varied events of the past months, and especially of the last hour, had brought poor Frank Onslow's chequered career to a sudden and tragic close, and the form that lay there among the bared bulbs, crushed bells, scattered earth, and broken pots was already itself nothing but lifeless clay.

Fenella felt too much for tears; she stood there in a kind of stupor, wondering what had happened to her, and how it would affect her when she was able to think of it. It was Jacynth who, with his never-failing tact and consideration, came to her relief.

"This is no place for you now," he said, in his grave, gentle tones. "Let me lead you away, Fenella."

Fenella allowed herself to be guided by him; she had got so much into the habit of depending entirely upon him lately that somehow it seemed the natural thing to do. Only when they reached the fresh air and sunshine outside she looked up at him with childlike, appealing eyes. "Where are we going?" she inquired dreamily.

"We are going," he said, "to meet Ronny and the goat chaise."

It was strange, perhaps, but this simple remark gave Fenella a vague comfort. It would be some time—weeks, or even months— she knew, before happiness returned to her, and she was her own wayward, light-hearted self again; but that happiness *was* in store for her—that, in days to come, she would look back on the heart-rending trials, the conflicting emotions, the gloom, anxiety and despair it had been her fate to ensure, and see in them only a confused nightmare, too wildly improbable to excite even a reminiscent shudder—she knew as surely as that she was walking down the road, and leaning upon Clitheroe Jacynth's strong right arm.

And so these two went down to meet the goat-chaise.

THE END.

EXPLANATORY NOTES

EDITOR'S NOTE

1 (p. 2) The novelist and journalist, who himself enjoyed a successful
period of collaboration with James Rice, had published a discussion
of the topic in *The New Review* 6 (February 1892), 200-209.

CHAPTER I

1 (p. 3) *And dinna ye mind, love Gregory... thee thine?*: Lines from "The
Lass of Roch Royal," no. 76 in *The English and Scottish Popular Ballads*
(1882) by Francis James Child (1825-1896), a collection of 305 traditional (mainly Scottish) songs. In this ballad a young mother searches
for the man she claims as her husband but is cast out by respectable
society only to die.

2 (p. 3) *Harrogate*: A small spa town in Yorkshire, in the North of England,
celebrated for its restorative waters drawn from a sulphur well, and
its 87 different springs. In the nineteenth century it became a popular
resort for wealthy invalids. The Prospect Hotel on James Street was
built in 1814 by Nicholas Carter. A palatial Italianate building, it was
part demolished in 1936 and now trades as "The Imperial."

3 (p. 3) *Stray*: An expanse of grassland which wraps around the older
part of Harrogate, a popular spot for walking, sports, kite-flying and
picnicking.

4 (p. 3) *Nigger minstrel*: An enormously popular form of live entertain-
ment in the nineteenth and early-twentieth centuries, dependent on
racist caricature. White entertainers put on black make-up and cari-
catured African-American speech, singing and dancing.

5 (p. 4) *Pump-room*: The building which houses one of Harrogate's
sulphur wells, and where visitors drink the restorative waters. Patron-
ised by Queen Victoria, it became known as the "Royal Pump Room."

6 (p. 5) *Lucretius ... better for being abroad*: Lines from "On the Nature of
Things" by the Roman poet Titus Lucretius Carus (d. ca. 50 B.C.).

7 (p. 5) *Crown Hotel*: Large hotel situated in the old part of the town,
next to the Royal Pump Room; an exclusive place to stay.

8 (p. 6) *Bogs Valley Gardens*: Public flower gardens, first laid out in 1880;
part of it was originally known as Bogs Field and contained 36 of the
town's springs.

9   (p. 8) *Sulphur baths*: Supposedly useful for the removal of impurities and the relief of skin conditions such as psoriasis and eczema.

10   (p. 10) *Lady Caroline Lamb*: Born 1785, daughter of Lord Duncannon, she married politician William Melbourne at 17. A by-word for unconventional behavior, she gained notoriety in 1812 thanks to an extramarital affair with the poet Lord Byron which lasted four months. Lamb's novel *Glenarvon* (1816) is semi-autobiographical, prompted by her relationship with Byron. Caroline was sent away in disgrace by her family to Europe, dying aged 43 in 1828, with her husband by her bedside.

CHAPTER II

1   (p. 12) *Kismet*: Derived from the Arabic, "fate".

2   (p. 12) *But, ah, that Spring should vanish ... close*: From verse 96 of *The Rubaiyat of Omar Khayyam*, popularized in Britain thanks to an 1859 translation by Edward FitzGerald (1809-1883) of the Persian (Iranian) verses.

3   (p. 12) *Shepheard's*: A well-known hotel in Cairo. Opened in 1841 it was the haunt of royalty, celebrities, and members of the upper-classes.

4   (p. 13) *Levantine*: Originating from Levant, *i.e.* the Mediterranean coastal area covered by Syria, Jordan, Lebanon, and Palestine.

5   (p. 13) "Pasha" was the title bestowed on a distinguished palace official (along the lines of an English knighthood or ennobling); the award was in the gift of the Sultan of Turkey or the "khedive" (governor) of Egypt who was subject to his jurisdiction.

6   (p. 14) *Thackeray's ballad ... forty year*: A reference to "The Age of Wisdom" by the novelist and humorist W. M. Thackeray (1811-1863). The ballad celebrates the maturity that comes with middle-age: "HO! pretty page, with the dimpled chin / That never has known the barber's shear, / All your wish is woman to win; / This is the way that boys begin, — / Wait till you come to forty year."

CHAPTER III

1   (p. 19) *"How it Strikes a Contemporary"*: The title of a poem by Robert Browning (1812-1889) in the collection *Men and Women* (1855). The poem is a dramatic monologue which gives a portrait of a famous poet as the ignorant, gossiping public mistakenly see him. The public are incapable of understanding the real personality of the poet.

2   (p. 19) *"But this case is so plain..."*: From "A Dissuasive from Popery" (1650), a tract by the Protestant clergyman and theologian Jeremy Taylor (1613-1667), notable for his attacks on Roman Catholicism.

3 (p. 20) *Crimean*: In the Crimean War (1853-1856), Britain and France
attempted to bolster up the dying Turkish (Ottoman) empire against
an aggressive Russia. The conflict was widely reported and thanks
to advances in technology, news from the front did not take long to
appear in the press. The Crimean has been seen as the first "media
war," bringing the public closer than ever before to the events and its
personalities.

4 (p. 22) *Master*: Master of Fox Hounds, the chief representative of the
sport in a particular county or district.

5 (p. 23) *Garrison*: The city of Portsmouth on the south coast was extensively fortified against attack in the fifteenth century with a series of
forts and towers, and became the base for a standing army until the
1960s.

6 (p. 23) *Prussic acid*: One of the most rapidly acting toxins; also the basis
for cyanide.

7 (p. 23) *Can't expect to marry a lady from Chicago or New York with millions of dollars in pigs or petroleum*: In the boom industrial years after
the American Civil War, powerful families in American high society
increasingly came to be defined by wealth, rather than by birth.
Snubbed by older families descended from Dutch settlers but aware
of their own value, many families started looking abroad for husbands for their daughters, notably European aristocrats. Money could
be traded for birth, especially if the aristocrat was in need of funds to
maintain his country estates. Notable among these Anglo-American
marriages was that of Consuelo Vanderbilt and the Duke of Marlborough in 1896.

8 (p. 24) *She had been presented on her marriage, of course*: It was the custom
in British high society for young wives to be formally presented to the
Queen during the first year of their marriage at a special ceremony at
Buckingham Palace.

9 (p. 25) *Tartar's*: From the ethnic group of Central Asia and Mongolia;
thanks to Genghis Khan they had a reputation as violent invaders.

CHAPTER IV

1 (p. 28) *"Happier is he who standeth betwixt the fire and the flood, than
he who hath a jealous woman on either side of him.—Fourth Veddah"*:
Chanted poetry of the Veddahs—the ancient aboriginal inhabitants
of Sri Lanka.

2 (p. 31) *Row*: "Rotten Row," running along the edge of London's Hyde
Park; a fashionable place to take exercise, either on foot or horseback.
Something of a tourist attraction, according to *Crutchley's New Guide*

to London (1866), not least for the sight of the well-heeled and socially ambitious parading round the two main circuits of the Park. "During the season, Hyde Park attracts within its precincts all the wealth, fashion and beauty of London, and in no other civilized country can be seen such a spectacle as is then presented by the Lady's Mile and 'Rotten Row' ... the long bridle-road stretching from Apsley House to Kensington Gardens." (264).

CHAPTER V

1   (p. 34) *Weep not, my wanton ... sorrow hide*: Opening lines of "Sephestia's Lullaby" by Robert Greene (1560-1592).

2   (p. 35) *And divorce is no such easy matter*: Before 1857 divorce was a lengthy, expensive, and very public process; administered through the ecclesiastical courts, it could only be obtained via private act of Parliament. There were two types of divorce. First, *a mensa et thoro* (from bed and board) granted for adultery, extreme cruelty, or desertion. Second, *a vinculo* (from the bonds of marriage), by which the marriage was declared null and void, but permitted only the grounds of mental incapacity, impotence, or fraud. See Mary Lyndon Shanley, "Divorce," in Sally Mitchell (ed.) *Victorian Britain: An Encyclopedia* (New York: Garland, 1988), 223. The 1857 Matrimonial Causes Act made divorce easier but petitioners still faced having details of their private lives made public. By the terms of the new Act, a husband could divorce his wife on the grounds of adultery; his wife, however, had to prove not only adultery but also additional charges—incest, cruelty, bigamy, or bestiality.

3   (p. 35) *Knaresborough Rocks*: Knaresborough is a small picturesque town to the east of Harrogate, situated in a deep gorge formed by the River Nidd.

4   (p. 38) *Tom Dory*: Possibly John Dory; large sea fish common in northern waters, notable for stalking their prey head on before using an extending tube to suck in their victim.

5   (p. 38) *Cotillions*: A brisk dance, performed by eight persons in a square.

6   (p. 38) *Prater*: Vienna's biggest fun-fair, established in the fifteenth century.

7   (p. 38) *la ville la plus dévergondée*: (French) The most shameless town.

8   (p. 39) *Eton*: Eton School in Windsor, founded in 1440; one of the country's most exclusive, fee-paying schools. The reference is a swipe at the fact that for most of the nineteenth century its curriculum was dominated by ancient languages, *e.g.*, Latin and Greek, rather than modern ones.

9   (p. 39) *Suckie-pig*: A young piglet roasted and stuffed with herbs. Considered a special delicacy.

10 (p. 40) *Jezebel*: The wife of King Ahab of Israel, her history is recounted in the Biblical "Book of Kings" in which she is a by-word of pagan female evil.

11 (p. 40) *Bottle imp*: A reference to the short story by Robert Louis Stevenson, "The Bottle Imp," first published in the fashionable magazine *Black and White* (April 1891). Set in Hawaii, the story centers on Keawe who is offered the opportunity to buy a bottle containing an "imp" or genie who will fulfill every desire—except the wish for a longer life. The bottle can only be sold at a loss; if the owner dies before he sells it, he is sentenced to burn in hell.

CHAPTER VI

1   (p. 43) *lex talionis*: The ancient law of equal and direct retribution: in the words of Hebrew scriptures, "an eye for an eye, a tooth for a tooth, an arm for an arm, a life for a life."

2   (p. 44) *Esclandre*: (French) scandal.

3   (p. 45) *partie carrée*: (French) surprise party.

CHAPTER VII

1   (p. 52) *Charing Cross*: Charing Cross railway station, south of Trafalgar Square in central London, was opened in 1864, the result of Southern Eastern Railway's wish to get its commuting passengers to and from Kent into the heart of the city. At Dover passengers could catch a ship to Calais and then continue their journey by train Paris.

2   (p. 52) *"Pall Mall!" "St. James Gazette!"* or *"Star!"*: London evening papers, no longer in existence. *The Pall Mall Gazette* was founded in February, 1865 with the idea of publishing reports on political and social questions. Its most sensational story was W.T. Stead's "Maiden Tribute of Modern Bablyon" (1883) about the trafficking of child prostitutes. Although founded with the aim of imitating *The Pall Mall*, *The St. James's Gazette* (1880) was slightly more up-market. It was noted for its conservative political stance and literary reviews whilst providing a snapshot summary of the daily papers. *The Star* (founded in 1788) was a cheaper evening paper, price one halfpenny; it boasted of having the capital's largest circulation thanks to its detailed coverage of many scandalous events.

CHAPTER VIII

1   (p. 54) *Out, out, damned spot!*—*Shakespeare*: From *Macbeth*; words

spoken by the guilt-ridden Lady Macbeth in the celebrated sleepwalking scene: "Out, damned spot! out, I say!" (V, i, 38)

2   (p. 54) *Scientists have found in this hypnological condition ... stranger
    than fiction*: In the 1800s the Austrian physician Franz Anton Mesmer
    claimed to be able to remove the regulatory power of the will. It was
    claimed that by putting the subject into a trance and by inducing
    "artificial somnambulism" mesmerism could help with much needed
    pain relief. According to Joel Eigen "medical practitioners and soon
    hypnotists alike exploited the possibility that an idea 'suggested from
    the outside'—that is, not from a person's own consciousness—could
    produce behavior beyond the individual's control and even aware-
    ness." (*Unconscious Crime: Mental Absence and Criminal Responsibility in
    Victorian London* [Baltimore: Johns Hopkins University Press, 2003],
    15). However, mesmerism was also one of a number of "pseudo-sci-
    ences" which aroused the interest of both intellectuals and popular
    audiences, for whom it could be a form of entertainment. Hypno-
    tism (from the ancient Greek for "sleep") was also hailed as a modern
    science. It, too, provoked controversy because it gave one person
    unlimited control over another; Daniel Pick argues that through the
    1890s: "Victorian hypnotism [like mesmerism] continued to exist on
    the border between the medically sober and the erotically intoxicated,
    science and theatre, work and abandon, treatment and amusement."
    See Daniel Pick, *Svengali's Web: The Alien Enchanter in Modern Culture*,
    New Haven: Yale University Press, 2000, p. 100.

3   (p. 55) *Classic virtue*: Of the steadfast, selfless kind celebrated in the
    patriotic Roman epic "The Aeneid" by Virgil (70 B.C. – 19 B.C.) and by
    the violated Roman matron Lucrece.

4   (p. 56) *"The Dead Heart"*: In 1889 the celebrated actor-manager Henry
    Irving revived *The Dead Heart*—a spectacular melodrama by Watts
    Phillips, taken from Charles Dickens's novel *A Tale of Two Cities*. First
    produced at the Adelphi Theatre in 1859, the play's thrilling scenes
    included the fall of the Bastille, a duel, and the hero's self-sacrifice at
    the guillotine.

5   (p. 56) *Louis Stevenson has confessed that he dreams his stories, and then
    writes them out*: In an article in *The New York Herald* (6 September
    1887), "Evolved in Dreams," Stevenson explained that, "I am quite in
    the habit of dreaming stories." Stevenson elaborated on this idea in
    an essay "A Chapter on Dreams," written for *Scribner's Magazine* in
    1888. Here he described how elements of *The Strange Case of Dr. Jekyll
    and Mr. Hyde* (1886) and *Deacon Brodie* had come to him whilst he was
    asleep. As he cried out, his wife thought he was having a nightmare

and woke him up—"much to his indignation." Stevenson told her that he had dreamt "a fine bogey tale." The next morning he hurriedly started to write the story down. This anecdote was well-known and gained new currency just as *The Fate of Fenella* was being serialized. "Evolved in Dreams" was republished in 1892 in *Across the Plains*, and William Archer discussed the topic again in the *Pall Mall Gazette* (20 April 1892).

6   (p. 56) *There was in a recent Academy the picture of a young girl walking with closed eyes amid poppies and hemlocks*: A reference to "Poppyland," by A.W. Redpath, exhibited at London's annual Royal Academy Exhibition in April 1892.

7   (p. 57) *Dream sleep ... mind*: There was a good deal of interest in the conscious and unconscious behavior behind crime. In *Unconscious Crime* Eigen notes its appearance in a number of high profile trials in London's Old Bailey courthouse. These include cases in which defendants displayed evidence of mental aberration but were not classified as insane by the Victorian legal system—a sleepwalking homicidal nursemaid, a juvenile poisoner and a man who committed arson by a "lesion of the will." Eigen's research investigates the differences between legal and medical perceptions of defendant sanity. Between 1853 and 1876, 198 defendants put forward a defence of aberrant mental state at the time of the crime (Eigen 11).

8   (p. 59) *Nihilistic vengeance*: Emerging in Russia in the 1860s Nihilism was originally a reaction against the harsh absolutism of Czarist rule. Revolutionary ideas were fostered amongst university students and workers and secret societies sprang up. In 1881 Czar Alexander II received horrific injuries as a result of a bomb being thrown in front of his carriage and died two days later. The Nihilists demanded civil liberties from his successor Alexander III, whose response was to instill a climate of repression and retaliation. Many activists sought exile abroad, including London where cells continued to spring up, watched anxiously by the police. To outsiders Nihilists were easily confused with anarchists and socialists and their calls for the establishment of a new social order seemed very similar and equally threatening. See "The Anarchist Movements," *St. James Gazette* (21 April 1892), 9.

9   (p. 60) *Inquest*: Under the British legal system, the Coroner's Court holds an inquest when a cause of death remains in doubt, for example, the deceased died a violent death, or a sudden death and the cause is unknown. Coroners are appointed as independent judicial officers. An inquest aims to discover where, when, and how the deceased died.

10 (p. 61) *French novels*: French novels were considered to be dangerous reading for women and girls of good character, largely because of their freer discussion of male-female relations. Kate Flint writes that the "French Novel was a topos familiar in Victorian reviews and other cultural forms, carrying with it ... the generic assumptions of its power to corrupt." (*The Woman Reader, 1837-1914*. Oxford: Clarendon, 1993, 138). Honoré de Balzac, Alexandre Dumas *fils*, Eugène Sue and Paul de Kock were seen as particularly suspect, whilst Gustave Flaubert's *Madame Bovary* (1857) was "the quintessential work of French fiction in the mid-century" (Flint 140).

11 (p. 61) *Vanity Fair*: The term "vanity fair" originates from the allegorical story *The Pilgrim's Progress*, published in 1678 by John Bunyan, where there is a town fair held in a village called Vanity. Taken up by W. M. Thackeray as the title of his satiric novel of 1847-8, it became associated with a grubby world of fortune-hunting, worldly ambition, licentiousness and casual cruelty on the part of those who see themselves as part of "high-society."

12 (p. 62) *Tarquin*: The Tarquin dynasty were kings of ancient Rome. In the mid sixth century B.C., Lucius Tarquinius was king. His son, also called Tarquin, raped the wife of a fellow army officer, a virtuous woman called Lucrece. After asking her husband and father to avenge her, she stabbed herself. Her death prompted rebellion against the Tarquin family, who were deposed and banished, after which Rome became a republic. A version of the story is told by the Roman historian Livy (59 B.C.–17 A.D.) in his *History of Early Rome* and by Shakespeare in his poem "The Rape of Lucrece" (1594).

13 (p. 62) *"Justifiable homicide" is a verdict not unknown to the English law*: William Blackstone, author of the influential *Commentaries on the Laws of England* (1765-9) noted that in eighteenth century English law, homicide could be judged justifiable if a husband killed a man raping his wife (p. 391). This statute was intended to protect the sanctity of marriage but was also a reminder that a wife was her husband's property.

14 (p. 62) *Scotland Yard*: In 1829, in London, Robert Peel oversaw the passage of the Metropolitan Police Act, thereby establishing a regular police force in London. The Force's headquarters were based at 4 Whitehall Place. The rear of the building opened onto a courtyard which according to legend had once been the site of a house owned by the Kings of Scotland and was therefore known as "Scotland Yard." In 1890 the organization moved to the Victoria Embankment by the River Thames and this became known as "New Scotland Yard."

CHAPTER IX

1 (p. 63) *And my soul from out that shadow that lies floating on the floor / Shall be lifted—Nevermore!*: The final ominous lines from Edgar Allan Poe's "The Raven" (1845).

2 (p. 65) *Dover Street*: Situated just off Piccadilly in London's West End, an area noted for its exclusive hotels and gentlemen's clubs.

3 (p. 66) *Brand of Cain*: Cain has traditionally been invoked as the personification of the sin of murder. In the Book of Genesis, Cain and Abel were the sons of Adam and Eve. Cain killed Abel out of jealousy, believing that God favoured his brother. The mark of Cain, bestowed by God as protection thus became part of his stigma and he was cast out. "And now thou art cursed from the earth." "And Cain said unto the Lord, My punishment is greater than I can bear. Behold thou hast driven me this day from the face of the earth; and from thy face shall I be hid; and I shall be a fugitive and a vagabond in the earth; and it shall come to pass, that every one that findeth me shall slay me" (4: 11-14).

4 (p. 67) *Channel Islands*: Situated closer to the coast of France than Britain but under British rule, the Channel Islands comprise five different islands: Jersey and Guernsey are the biggest; Alderney, Sark and Herm, much smaller.

5 (p. 68) *St. Peter's Port*: The capital of Guernsey; a busy stopping point for ships.

6 (p. 70) *Serge*: a stiff woollen cloth, used to make overcoats and suits.

CHAPTER X

1 (p. 75) *something like that last moment after death in Wiertz's picture*: Antoine Wiertz (1806-1865), A Belgian artist noted for his treatment of dark, morbid subjects: "La Belle Rosine" (1847) and "The Suicide" (1854). The reference here seems to be to "Last Thoughts and Visions of a Decapitated Head" (1853), a graphic image of death by guillotine and inspired by scientific discussions of the period about whether a severed head still experienced a brief moment of consciousness.

2 (p. 76) *Chiddingford, near Haslemere*: Small, picturesque town in the county of Surrey, south of London.

CHAPTER XI

1 (p. 79) *Revenge is sweet—especially to women.—Byron*: Misquotation of lines spoken by the amorous hero of "Don Juan," the epic poem by the celebrated poet and *roué* George Gordon, Lord Byron (1788-1824): "Sweet is revenge—especially to women" (Canto 1, stanza 124).

2   (p. 80) *Chancery Lane*: Famous as a main thoroughfare of London's legal district, and the site of numerous attorneys' offices.

3   (p. 80) *Pall Mall*: West London street, famous in the nineteenth century for its proliferation of private gentlemen's clubs. Today the Reform Club, the Athenæum, and the Carlton Club remain. The Corinthians appears to be fictional.

4   (p. 81) *Juno*: the wife of Jupiter; immortalized in countless classical statues; appears in Roman mythology as the vengeful Queen of the gods.

5   (p. 86) *Langham Hotel*: a luxury London hotel, situated near Regent's Park. It opened in 1865 and counted visiting royalty and celebrities amongst its clientele.

6   (p. 86) *Liverpool to New York*: Liverpool in the north-west of England was the embarkation point for several Oceanic liners; the White Star Line and the Cunard Line were both based at the port. The *Germanic* was a steamship built in 1874 at Belfast for the White Star Line company. It could make an Atlantic crossing in seven days.

7   (p. 87) *Felixstowe*: a sea port in Suffolk.

CHAPTER XII

1   (p. 94) *silver cord was not broken*: The silver cord connects the astral body to the physical. See Ecclesiastes 12:6.

CHAPTER XIII

1   (p. 98) *Almost she and I have fallen into a bottomless pit; for in our blindness we turned our backs upon thee*: In the Book of Revelation, the place into which Satan and his followers were cast (Revelation 20:2-3). The bottomless pit is Hell but it is also seen as a state of mind dominated by sin (Romans 8:6).

2   (p. 100) *Brain fever*: Possibly a form of meningitis. A popular literary device in nineteenth century novels, through which the hero or heroine is purged or purified.

CHAPTER XIV

1   (p. 102) *Nemesis*: The ancient Greek goddess of retribution.

2   (p. 104) *Lille*: City in northern France; in the nineteenth century an industrial textile centre.

3   (p. 105) *Queenstown*: Irish port on the west (Atlantic) coast; for many years the embarkation point for Irish emigrants setting out for America. Queenstown was the last port of call of the *Titanic* in 1912.

4   (p. 105) *Irish mail*: Originally a postal route between London and

Dublin. By the 1890s an overnight train service ran from London's Euston Station to Dublin, the journey taking ten hours.

CHAPTER XVI

1   (p. 120) *"at home"*: In polite Victorian society, the designated hours of the day (usually the afternoon) during which the lady of the house would be willing to be receive visitors.

2   (p. 121) *fauteuil*: elegant arm chair with wooden frame, originating from eighteenth century France.

3   (p. 123) *novels with yellow covers*: French novels—considered risqué and "unhealthy"—had long appeared in yellow covers. When Oscar Wilde was arrested in 1895 he was carrying a French novel.

4   (p. 123) *Cigarette*: Popularized in Britain in the 1850s by soldiers returning from the Crimean War who had picked up the habit of "Papirossi" (tobacco rolled in paper) from their Turkish allies. The habit was controversial and the implications for health were regularly debated in the medical journal *The Lancet*. Smoking was initially deemed to be for men. Only "loose" women did so; the first women to smoke publicly were "Lorettes," prostitutes near the Notre Dame de Lorette church in Paris.

5   (p. 124) *in America there are special facilities for disjoining marriage ties*: A common misconception in 1890s Britain—and a source of press discussion in 1892. It was the subject of a lengthy article in *Blackwood's Magazine*: "Civilization, Morality and Social Order in the United States" (April 1892). The *St. James's Gazette* ran an article "The Land of Divorces" (2 May 1892, p.6) in which it wrote of "a poisonous atmosphere" in America—the result of a lax attitude towards marriage and morality. By mid-century most U.S. states allowed divorce but only in extreme situations involving the breaking of the marital contract—adultery, physical abuse, and desertion. Although by 1900 there were still only 4 divorces for every 1000 marriages, the country had the highest divorce rate in the world. See Tiffany K. Wayne, *Women's Roles in Nineteenth Century America* (Westport: Greenwood Press, 2007), 5-6.

6   (p. 125) *The Tombs*: New York's Halls of Justice (built 1835-40), comprising male, female, and children's prisons, as well as offices and courts. Mainly used as a holding place for those awaiting trial or for those on Death Row.

7   (p. 127) *American capital*: New York was the American capital until 1790.

8   (p. 128) *He was not particularly anxious ... some few years ago*: A reference, perhaps, to the journalist Edmund Yates (1831-1894), credited—

not least by himself—with importing to Britain "that style of personal journalism which is so very much to be deprecated and so enormously popular" (*Fifty Years of London Life. Memoirs of a Man of the World.* New York: Harper, 1885, I, 278). Yates was the editor of *The World*, a magazine successful partly as a result of its series of interviews with well-known men and women called "Celebrities at Home." This was part of a wider trend in the 1880s and 1890s towards a more intrusive, personality-based writing, sometimes labeled "the New Journalism." Yates was a divisive character. Algernon Swinburne called him a "blackguard" whilst Harry Furniss wrote of his "repulsive manner and repellent pen" (quoted in P. D. Edwards, *Dickens's "Young Men": George Augustus Sala, Edmund Yates and the World of Victorian Journalism.* Aldershot: Ashgate, 1997, p.10). James Comyns Carr noted that "Yates had many enemies in those days and the features he introduced into English journalism were in many quarters profoundly resented..." (*Some Eminent Victorians.* London: Duckworth, 1908, p.38).

9   (p. 130) *ague fit*: A fever marked by chills and sweating.

CHAPTER XVII

1   (p. 132) In Act 3, scene iv, when Macbeth receives the news that Banquo is killed, but Banquo's son, Fleance, has escaped, he cries: "'Then comes my fit again: I had else been perfect;/Whole as the marble, founded as the rock,/As broad and general as the casing air:/But now I am cabined, cribbed, confined, bound in/To saucy doubts and fears."

2   (p. 137) *Satan himself sent his myrmidons*: Satan's demons who are taught by him to seek out and possess men's souls. See the Biblical Gospel according to Mark (5:1-13).

3   (p. 137) *Jack* (1876), a novel by Alphonse Daudet (1840-1897) which details the sadistic treatment of a child and of a mother caught between sexual desire and maternal love.

CHAPTER XVIII

1   (p. 139) *Faust's love scene*: Reference to *Faust*, the opera by Charles Gounod, which premiered in 1859. In Act 3 Marguerite sings a famous aria, the "Jewel Song"; she is joined by Faust who seduces and then deserts her.

2   (p. 142) *Invalid carriage*: A wheel chair which can be steered by the invalid.

CHAPTER XIX

1   (p. 146) *Jean, gros Jean*: Colloquial French, loosely translated as: "John,

fat John, married his fat and greasy daughter in her old clothes, to a clog seller, miserly, in his old overcoat."

2   (p. 146) *Frieze*: coarse, woollen cloth.

3   (p. 147) *Cherbourg*: Northern French port, located in Normandy, on the English Channel.

4   (p. 148) *Maison Centrale at Clairvaux*: A high-security prison in the Champagne-Ardenne region of northeastern France, built on the site of the abbey of Clairvaux.

5   (p. 149) *Lightship*: A ship with a tall light or beacon which patrolled the coastline in order to protect shipping.

CHAPTER XX

1   (p. 153) *Holyhead*: Sea port on Anglesey, North Wales. A favoured crossing point to Ireland.

2   (p. 153) *Jonah*: From the Old Testament Book of Jonah: Jonah is thrown into the sea but does not drown because God sends a whale to swallow him alive and thus protect him.

3   (p. 156) *Tender*: A boat used to transport supplies and passengers from the shore to larger ships unable to get into the harbour.

4   (p. 157) *Carnsore Point*: Carnsore Point in County Wexford, on the south-eastern tip of Ireland.

5   (p. 157) *'Emile Angier,' from the play 'Jean de Thomeray'*: Emile Angier (1820-1889) was a renowned French dramatist and poet known for taking a moral and patriotic stance in his works, many of which offer scathing indictments of contemporary sexual and familial behavior. *Jean de Thommeray* was premiered in 1873 after the privations of the siege of Paris (1870-1) during the Franco-Prussian War. The city was surrounded by Prussian troops and its inhabitants reputedly ate rats and dogs in order to survive. This was followed by the humiliating cessation of Alsace Lorraine to Prussia and the emergence of Germany as the dominant power in continental Europe. In Angier's play there is a call for patriotism and action as well as an emphasis on the importance of home as the bedrock of society.

6   (p. 157) *Quai Malaquais*: in the heart of Saint-Germain-des-Près, just across from the Louvre museum.

7   (p. 158) *Hipped*: distracted or preoccupied.

8   (p. 158) *Farewell, farewell*: Paraphrase of "A Farewell" by Alfred, Lord Tennyson (1809-1892), a poem in which death provides the final parting.

9   (p. 159) *knickerbocker dress*: knee-length breeches or trousers, worn with stockings or gaiters.

10 (p. 160) *Pwllhely*: seaside town of Pwllheli on the Llŷn Peninsula, north-west Wales.

11 (p. 161) *Penmaenmawr*: Welsh coastal town situated between Llanfair-fechan and Conwy. Popular as a seaside resort since the nineteenth century.

CHAPTER XXII

1 (p. 171) *Swells*: slang; a person of rank or wealth; sometimes showily dressed.

2 (p. 173) *Coupés*: The front compartment of a railway carriage.

3 (p. 175) *pea-jacket*: a navy-coloured heavy wool jacket originally worn by sailors or manual workers.

CHAPTER XXIII

1 (p. 181) *grass widow*: A wife whose husband is often away, leaving her on her own.

2 (p. 182) *Dumas, fils*: Alexandre Dumas, *fils* (1824-1895), illegitimate son of Alexandre Dumas, père. His most famous (risqué) work was *The Lady of the Camellias* (1848), the story of a Parisian courtesan; later the basis for the opera *La Traviata*.

3 (p. 183) *Sefton Park*: One of Britain's largest public parks; it opened in Liverpool in 1872 and contained a cricket ground, lake and a famous iron bridge which was a popular meeting place.

4 (p. 184) *Spilikins*: A board with small pegs of wood, used for counting the score in a game of cribbage, or played as a variety of backgammon.

5 (p. 185) *spalpeen*: An Irish term for a wastrel or ruffian.

6 (p. 186) *Les absents ont toujours tort, says the French proverb*: The absent are always wrong.

7 (p. 189) *Israelitish king with his face to the wall ... endured*: In the Biblical Book of Kings (21.4) King Ahab was angry when his offer to buy land from his neighbor, Naboth, was refused. The king went to bed with his face to the wall and refused to eat. His wife Jezebel arranged for Naboth to be executed and Ahab obtained the land. Jezebel is invoked as the epitome of female evil.

CHAPTER XXIV

1 (p. 191) *"Whom the gods hate die hard"*: Possibly a paraphrase of the classical proverb "whom the gods love die young" recorded by the Roman playwright Plautus (c. 254-184 B.C.).

2 (p. 194) *Kamschatka*: One of the largest, most desolate, regions of Russia, situated in the east towards the Pacific Ocean.

3 (p. 194) *I have always understood that persons indicted for such offences...*: Until the passing of the Criminal Evidence Act (1898) defendants were not permitted to testify in their own defence from the witness box. Some changes had taken place before this, however. For example, from 1883 defendants were allowed to give an unsworn statement.

4 (p. 196) *de trop*: (French) in the way.

5 (p. 197) *the law will not accept you as a witness*: The law saw husband and wife as one person. William Blackstone, author of *Commentaries on the Laws of England*, wrote that because of this "the very being or legal existence of the woman is suspended during the marriage, or at least is incorporated and consolidated into that of the husband; under whose wing, protection, and cover, she performs everything . . . [I]n trials of any sort they are not allowed to be evidence for, or against, each other: partly because it is impossible their testimony should be indifferent, but principally because of the union of person. . . . But, where the offence is directly against the person of the wife, this rule has been usually dispensed with; and therefore, by statute 3 Hen. VII, c. 2, in case a woman be forcibly taken away, and married, she may be a witness against such her husband, in order to convict him of felony. For in this case she can with no propriety be reckoned his wife; because a main ingredient, her consent, was wanting to the contract: and also there is another maxim of law, that no man shall take advantage of his own wrong; which the ravisher here would do, if, by forcibly marrying a woman, he could prevent her from being a witness, who is perhaps the only witness to that very fact. (Vol. 1., 1765, pp. 442-445).

6 (p. 198) *Marines*: Troops drawn from the army and navy to form a special amphibious unit, and forming part of the crew of warships.

7 (p. 198) *Well, tell this fine story to them—to your Marines*. According to Brewer's *Dictionary of Phrase and Fable* marines are supposed by other sailors to be so gullible that they will believe anything.

ABOUT THE AUTHORS

Helen Mathers (1851-1920)

Helen Mathers was the pen name of Helen Buckingham Reeves. She gained renown with her debut novels *Comin' Thro' the Rye* (1875) and *Cherry Ripe* (1878). "Miss Helen Mathers . . . may not know much of the world, but she knows a good deal about young ladies, and she has depicted some members of that large class with fidelity," noted the *Liverpool Mercury*.[1] Mathers became noted for her modish literary style—lots of slang and slightly risqué behaviour on the part of her heroines—which spawned a host of imitators. In 1877, Mathers married a surgeon, Henry Reeves, but remained a high-profile member of the London literary scene, "very deaf," as *Winter's Magazine* reported in 1892, "a very winning woman, with a charming speaking voice and never looking so well as when dressed in pure white. Mrs. Reeves has a perfect passion for flowers and always has them about herself and lavishly decking her rooms."[2] "Famed for the elegance of her dress,"[3] Mathers wrote to fund this comfortable lifestyle. She worked energetically through the 1880s and 1890s producing a steady stream of novels, mostly love stories but mixed with a smattering of crime. In public, however, she presented herself as a gifted amateur: "I can't say in the least how my books get written," she told an interviewer, "I just jot down anything that I especially observe, or think of, on a bit of paper, and when I have a great many pieces I sort them out, and usually pin them together in some sort of sequence."[4] The system seemed to work and she was much in demand.

Mathers's last years were unhappy; her only son died in 1907; her husband's poor health meant that he was unable to earn

[1] "The Minor Novelists," *Liverpool Mercury* (4 Feb 1885), 7.
[2] "Mrs. Gadabout," "Indoors and Out," *Winter's Magazine* (15 October 1892), 372.
[3] "Lady Novelists at Home," *Western Mail*, (18 May 1895), 4.
[4] Helen C. Black, *Notable Women Authors of the Day* (Glasgow: D. Bryce & Son, 1906), 72.

money and her own popularity started to diminish in the early
1900s. Novels which had once seemed daring started to appear out-
dated and she was forced to apply to the Royal Literary Fund for
charitable support, increasingly irked that she had sold the rights
to *Comin' Thro' the Rye* for a mere 30 guineas and that it was still
making profits for her publishers. She died virtually penniless in
lodgings in 1920. An obituary in *The Times* observed that for most
of her career her work "always commanded a public, for she could
always be depended upon to produce an agreeable love story with
a strong outdoor interest and to tell it with vivacity and charm."[1]

Justin H. McCarthy (1859-1936)

Justin H. McCarthy was the son of a well-known Irish Nation-
alist MP (also called Justin McCarthy) and followed his father into
Parliament in 1885. By 1892, McCarthy Jr. was a popular "man-
about-town," capable of performing the part of the humorous
Irishman on demand. A writer for *Winter's Magazine* described him
as: "a slight fair, good-looking young man, with a pretty taste in
writing and an almost limitless admiration for the fair sex! Most
people like Justin McCarthy extremely and his Irish accent is one
of his greatest charms."[2] McCarthy combined his duties as MP
with writing—journalism, popular history, poetry, novels, and
plays. His many works include: *An Outline of Irish History* (1883);
Serapion and other Poems (1883) and *England under Gladstone* (1884)
At his death in 1936, *The Times* noted that "whatever else he might
be doing he always found time to be engaged on a play or on a
novel . . . full of real, full-blooded melodramatic situations."[3]

Frances Eleanor Trollope (1835-1913)

Frances Eleanor Trollope (not to be confused with her novelist
mother-in-law, also called Frances Trollope) was the second wife
of Thomas Adolphus Trollope. Born Frances Eleanor Ternan, she

---

[1] "Helen Mathers," *The Times* (13 March 1920), 18.
[2] "Indoors and Out," by "Mrs. Gadabout." *Winter's Magazine*, 23 October
1892 p. 387.
[3] "Mr. Justin H. McCarthy," *Times* (23 March 1936) p. 18

was an actress whose childhood was spent working in British thea-
tres with her mother and two sisters. Her youngest sister Ellen is
now best known as Charles Dickens's mistress. In the early 1860s
Frances went to Italy to study opera. She broke off her studies to
take employment as a governess in the expatriate Trollope household based in Florence. Thomas Trollope was a widower with
a small daughter, and twenty-five years her senior. The couple
married in 1866. A historian and novelist, Thomas was the brother
of the more famous Anthony. Frances Eleanor also began writing
fiction. Dickens helped her by publishing two early works, *Aunt
Margaret's Trouble* (1866) and *Mabel's Progress* (1867), as serials in his
magazine *All the Year Round*.

As well as collaborating on historical works with Thomas Trollope, Frances Eleanor went on to publish twelve novels on sensational themes, often involving abusive men and mistreated wives.
These include *A Charming Fellow* (1876) and *An Unfortunate Marriage* (1888). Like Florence Marryat and Arthur Conan Doyle (see
below), she had an interest in spiritualism and this also makes itself
felt in her work, notably *Black Spirits and White* (1877). She also
wrote a biography of her famous mother-in-law (1895). Widowed
in 1892, Frances Eleanor returned to Britain, setting up home with
her sister Ellen in Southsea, on the south coast.

Arthur Conan Doyle (1859-1930)

Born in Edinburgh in 1859, Doyle trained as a doctor at Edinburgh University and practiced in Southsea in England, but in his
spare time started writing stories. His most successful creation
Sherlock Holmes made his first appearance in *A Study in Scarlet*
(1887) and then again in The *Sign of Four* (1890). Doyle gave up
medicine and devoted himself full-time to writing, alternating
Sherlock Holmes stories with longer historical novels which he
saw as being more serious work. Offered large sums of money
from the *Strand Magazine* to carry on writing about Holmes,
Doyle produced a string of short stories, *The Adventures of Sherlock
Holmes*, before killing off Holmes in *The Final Problem* (1893). This,
he believed, would leave him free to concentrate on other—more
"literary"—writing but the demand for more Holmes stories led

Doyle to write *The Hound of the Baskervilles* (1902). He returned to Holmes again in *The Return of Sherlock Holmes* (1905) and finally in 1927 in the collection *The Case-Book of Sherlock Holmes*. After World War I Doyle became very interested in spiritualism, and investigated many (apparently) psychic phenomena. His output remained considerable—poetry, short stories, and novels, including *The Lost World* (1912) and the Brigadier Gerard stories. Doyle was knighted in 1902 and died in 1930.

May Crommelin (c. 1850-1930)

Maria Henrietta de la Cherois was born in County Down, Ireland, into a large Protestant family which had fallen on hard times. When her brother took over the family estate, she and her sister moved to London. By this time she had already published several novels—much to her father's disapproval. These include *Queenie* (1874), *My Love, She's But a Lassie* (1875) and *In the West Countrie* (1883). Crommelin's Irish background, the clash of Catholic and Protestant, together with the need to support herself and her sisters makes itself felt in her work.

Interviewing Crommelin for the *Ladies Pictorial* in 1893, Helen Black observed her "faultless figure," "unusually large workman-like-looking writing-table" but also a life full of "anxieties." It was no surprise, Black concluded, that "[t]o the readers of May Crommelin's novels it is quite apparent that the idea of Duty is the keynote."[1] "Whilst all her works are remarkable for their refinement and purity of thought and style, she almost unconsciously makes her heroes and heroines (though they are no namby-pamby creatures) struggle through life doing the duty nearest to hand, however disagreeable the consequences or doubtful the reward."[2]

As she became more successful Crommelin spent long periods on foreign travel, ostensibly seeking local colour but also taking a break from an exhausting writing schedule which left her, she told one interviewer, feeling "like a limp rag."[3] Her work met a mixed

---

[1] Helen C. Black, *Notable Women Authors of the Day*, 211, 209.
[2] Ibid, 222.
[3] "Mrs. Gadabout," "Indoors and Out," *Winter's Magazine* (15 October 1892), 372.

response from the critics; she was invariably treated patronisingly and her work viewed as suitable only for domestic servants and the wives of clerks. Of *Dust Before the Wind* (1894), Crommelin's attempt at a fashionable story of infidelity, the *Graphic* reckoned her out of her depth: "the authoress does not realise in the least the character of her own story and has only a general idea that this is the sort of thing that the public likes—an idea which is certainly not altogether without warrant."[1] At various periods Crommelin struggled to make ends meet; she applied for assistance to the Royal Literary Fund in 1891 and 1909. At her death in 1930 *The Times* noted how "in the course of a long life she had to bear many heavy sorrows and trials, but her pluck never failed . . . ."[2]

F[rancis] C[harles] Philips (1849-1921)

After experimenting with a variety of professions—army officer (via Sandhurst military training college), actor (using the surname "Fairlie"), theatre-manager, barrister, journalist—Philips announced his arrival on the literary scene with *As in a Looking Glass* (1885). The novel scandalised critics on account of its graphic violence but nonetheless sold 40,000 copies. The novel, written in the first person, from the point of view of a woman, was later dramatized for the celebrated French actress, Sarah Bernhardt. Philips followed this hit with similarly lurid works at the rate of at least one a year to the end of the century, although none had quite the impact of the first. Later novels include: *A Lucky Young Woman* (1886), *The Strange Adventures of Lucy Smith* (1888), *A French Marriage* (1890), *Extenuating Circumstances* (1891), and *A Devil in Nun's Veiling* (1895). Philips also worked as a dramatist; his plays include *The Dean's Daughter* (1891) and *One Never Knows* (1909).

Philips seems not to have taken himself too seriously and his autobiography *My Varied Life* (1914) is a cheerful account of this multifarious activity, and famous people he came into contact with. Summing up Philips's career in 1921, *The Times* found it difficult to think of any long-lasting achievement, merely noting "he

---

[1] "New Novels," *The Graphic* (21 April 1894), 12.
[2] "May Crommelin," *The Times* (14 August 1930), 15.

had at any rate an ingenious invention, a pleasant wit, and a sub-
acid humour . . . ."[1]

"Rita" [Margaret Jane Humphreys] (1856-1938)

Margaret Gollan, who wrote as "Rita," was born in Scotland,
but it was her childhood in Australia which formed the basis for
her hit novel *Sheba* (1889), the story of an unruly young girl and
her growth to maturity. Ill-educated and neglected, Sheba gets
much of her knowledge of life from the sensation novels of Mary
Braddon and Ellen Wood. The ingredients of Humphreys's plot—
extramarital sex, seduction, hidden spouse, miscarriage, disappear-
ances—set the tone for much of the work that followed.

Mr. Humphreys—"Rita's" second husband—was an invalid and
the task of supporting the family fell on his wife—a task which she
carried out with some skill, producing over 60 books by the time of
her death. A necessarily prolific writer of novels and plays, Humphreys was at her peak of popularity in the 1890s and early 1900s
thanks to risqué romantic novels like *A Husband of No Importance*
(1894), *Souls* (1903)—a vicious satire of society women—and *Saba
Macdonald* (1906). She was not always popular with her contemporaries and seems to have disappointed an interviewer for *Winter's
Magazine* who, in 1892, described her as "a little dark and ruddy
shy woman, with a rather ungracious manner, and very little to
say for herself! She is not a good hostess, nor much addition to
any society in which she happens to be . . ."[2] To Rita's thousands
of fans—amongst whom was Queen Mary—this didn't seem to
matter, and this is not the impression given in Rita's very gossipy
autobiography *Recollections of a Literary Life* (1936)—a revealing
take on the Victorian and Edwardian literary scene.

Joseph Hatton (c. 1841-1907)

By his own account a child prodigy in music, Hatton worked

---

[1] "F.C. Philips," *The Times* (22 April 1921), 13.
[2] "Mrs. Gadabout," "Indoors and Out," *Winter's Magazine* (15 October
1892), 373.

initially as a lawyer's clerk before getting work as a journalist on a local paper, *The Derbyshire Times*, owned by his father. By a combination of hard work, talent, luck, and opportunism, Hatton became editor of *The Bristol Mirror* at the age of 22, and spent most of his twenties working for a series of provincial papers, becoming proprietor of two: *The Worcester Journal* and *The Illustrated Midland News*. From 1868 he was based in London as editor of *The Gentleman's Magazine* and *The People* but left these posts in 1874 to act as roving reporter for *The New York Times* and *The Sydney Morning Herald*. He wrote down his impressions of the United States in *Today in America: Studies for the Old World and the New* (1881).

Hatton was like many energetic and supremely confident mid-Victorian men of letters in that he kept up a sideline in novel writing. One observer described him as "as sturdy as a bull dog."[1] His early novels were *Bitter Sweets* (1865), *Christopher Herick* (1869), and he followed these with his most successful, *Clytie* (1874) and his most controversial *By Order of the Czar: The Tragic Story of Anna Klostock* (1890) in which a Jewish woman is raped and whipped by a sadistic local governor. In *Pen and Pencil* Helen Black described Hatton as "an eminent novelist" possessing "vivid imagination and a deep poetic strain [which], combined with much foreign travelling and close observation of human nature, have given his versatile pen the ease and fluency, the profound interest and instructiveness, that distinguish his works." According to Black, Hatton adhered to the notion of the novelist as teacher: "Mr. Hatton says 'there is always a lesson in a good story, always a moral in the conclusion of the adventures of a man or woman, either in fact or fiction.'"[2]

Mrs. [Emily] Lovett Cameron

Born Caroline Emily Sharp in 1844 in London, Emily Cameron was the daughter of a successful businessman. Little else is known of her early life save that she was sent to Paris at the age of six

---

[1] Ibid, 386-388.
[2] Helen C. Black, *Pen, Pencil, Baton and Mask* (London: Spottiswoode, 1896), 274; 281.

and married Henry Lovett Cameron in 1874. The couple settled in Montpelier Square, a smart address in west London. *Juliet's Guardian* (1877) was well-received and was the first in a string of novels detailing love-affairs among the middle and upper-classes, of women betrayed and abandoned and dying of grief. In *Juliet's Guardian* the plot centres on the love affair between Juliet Blair (age seventeen) and her guardian, Colonel Fleming. Later novels included: *A Dead Past* (1885), *A Lost Will* (1889), *A Sister's Sin* (1893). *A Soul Astray* (1895), *A Bad Lot* (1895), *A Fair Fraud* (1899), and *Bitter Fruit* (1914).

Despite her subject matter, Cameron emerges overall as a fairly conservative writer, working to strict hours, a strong supporter of domesticity, and an opponent of the "New Woman"—a subject she deals with robustly in *The Man Who Didn't* (1895). She could appear a fairly forbidding figure but contemporary accounts make much, too, of her softer side, "a slight, fair woman a little past forty, with lovely golden hair (real) and one of the prettiest and cosiest drawing-rooms I was ever in" gushed one interviewer.[1] One of her publishers, William Tinsley, assigned her to the top of the second rank novelist writing, suggesting that she "should have a top place for always better diction and homely sentiment."[2]

Bram Stoker (1847-1912)

Born Abraham Stoker into a modest Irish-Protestant family at Clontarf, Dublin, Stoker began his working life as a civil servant but in 1878 was asked by the celebrated actor Henry Irving to become business manager of London's Lyceum Theatre. Stoker threw in his respectable job and hurriedly married his fiancée, Florence Balcombe (who numbered Oscar Wilde among her former suitors but clearly reckoned Stoker a better bet). Stoker "looked after" Irving (the "Guvnor") for twenty-eight years, a devotion which it is often claimed cost Stoker his relations with Florence who resented her husband's being at Irving's beck and call. Somehow Stoker also

---

[1] "Mrs. Gadabout," "Indoors and Out," *Winter's Magazine* (15 October 1892), 373.

[2] William Tinsley, *Random Recollections of an Old Publisher*, 2 vols. (London: Simpkin, Marshall, 1900,) II, 300

found time to make an active literary career for himself, writing over thirty short stories and twelve novels. *The Primrose Path*, a violent anti-alcohol story about Irish immigrants in London, was published in 1875. The adventure story *The Snake's Pass* was published in 1890, followed by *The Watter's Mou'* (1894), *The Shoulder of Shasta* (1895), *Dracula* (1897), *Miss Betty* (1898), *The Mystery of the Sea* (1902), *The Jewel of Seven Stars* (1903), *The Man* (1905), *Lady Athlyne* (1908), *The Lady of the Shroud* (1909), and his swan song, *The Lair of the White Worm* (1911). The quality of these works varies enormously but the diversity of these achievements suggests that Stoker was an adaptable writer who could move between different sub-genres.

By the early 1900s Stoker's health had begun to fail. It has been suggested that he was a victim of Bright's Disease (a degenerative kidney disease) as early as 1897; in 1906 he suffered a paralyzing stroke and died in 1912 aged sixty-four.

Florence Marryat (1833-1899)

Praised by the *New York Times* as "one of the most prolific writers of our time,"[1] Marryat was the daughter of Captain Frederick Marryat, a former naval officer and celebrated writer of seafaring novels. She was educated at home on her father's Norfolk estate and in 1854 married Thomas Ross Church, an army officer. The couple settled in India where Marryat lived the leisured life of an officer's wife in the Raj. However in 1860, the collapse of Marryat's health (apparently the result of the Indian climate, combined with her fourth pregnancy) forced her and her children to return to England without Thomas Ross Church. Marryat turned to novel writing, bringing out *Love's Conflict* in 1865. This first novel of murder and unhappy marriages was rapidly followed by two more within next twelve months: *Too Good for Him* and *Woman Against Woman*. Marryat was never again without a writing project, going on to publish novels for the next thirty-five years. To read these lurid stories of seduction, murder, insanity, extramarital sex, incest, and the exploits of the *demi-monde—Woman Against Woman* (1866), *The Confessions of Gerald Escourt* (1867), *Nelly*

---

[1] "Florence Marryat," *New York Times* (28 October 1899), 7.

Brooke (1868), *Veronique* (1868), *The Girls of Feversham* (1869)—is to watch a novelist mining a profitable sensational seam. Although reviewers admitted Marryat's "readableness" and the power of her "graphic, nervous, vital" and [by implication] "sensational" style, some, like George Saintsbury, pictured the typical Marryat reader as a person "of easy faith and unfastidious taste."[1] *The Academy* called her cynical and "third-rate," too dependent for her plots on "the stock in trade of fourth-rate solicitors."[2] Despite this hostility Marryat's popularity usually ensured that her sales were unaffected (or perhaps improved) by the critical disapproval.

In the 1890s, despite being increasingly plagued by ill health, Marryat's career continued at a hectic pace. Between 1885 and 1897, she produced another forty novels, all "very unequal" as publisher William Tinsley remembered.[3] She was active in the newly formed Society of Authors and took to breeding bulldogs and terriers. Separated from Colonel Lean, she also set up a "School of Literary Art" with the express purpose of training people for "a literary profession" and "turning talent to best account."[4]

In 1892 an interviewer described her as "very tall, fair and Scotch-looking . . . a little bizarre in dress, and a devout believer in all sorts and conditions of 'spooks.'"[5] By this time Marryat had become an advocate for spiritualism, an interest which she gave voice in *The Clairvoyance of Bessie Williams* (1893) and in the sensational *There is No Death*, a book which caused a considerable stir when it appeared in 1891 and ran to six editions in the first four years.

"Frank Danby" [Julia Frankau] (1859-1916)

Julia Frankau *née* Davis (1859-1916) was born in Dublin, the

---

[1] George Saintsbury, "Her Father's Name," *The Academy* (6 February 1877), 7.

[2] [Unsigned Review], "On Circumstantial Evidence," *The Academy* (25 May 1889), 355.

[3] William Tinsley, *Random Recollections of an Old Publisher*, II, 251.

[4] Florence Marryat, "Prospectus. The School of Literary Art. Conducted by Florence Marryat." British Library Mss.C/194.a.117.

[5] "Mrs. Gadabout," "Indoors and Out," *Winter's Magazine* (15 October 1892), 374.

daughter of a Jewish artist who had been forced to become a photographer. The family's finances were tight and their daughters were expected to work—or find a husband. Julia married cigar merchant Arthur Frankau in 1883; the couple had several children.

Frankau's first novel *Dr. Phillips, A Maida Vale Idyll* in which a Jewish doctor who murders his wife with morphine caused considerable offence for its unflattering depiction of middle-class Jewish life when it was published in 1887. Its successor *A Babe in Bohemia* (1899) which centres on a syphilitic, epileptic girl, was judged equally distasteful and was boycotted by Mudie's Circulating Library. Such *succès de scandale* encouraged Frankau's public persona, that of "a bright clever woman of the world"[1] as one gossip columnist noted in 1889, a modern woman who admitted to smoking and who got Oscar Wilde and George Moore to her literary parties. Frankau's novel *Pigs in Clover* (1903) contains a thinly-disguised portrait of Wilde. Other works mix social commentary with melodrama; often they focus on a crime or immoral behaviour such as *The Copper Crash* (1890), in which a hypnotist tries to use his influence to ruin a defenceless girl. *The Graphic* condemned the novel as "repulsive" and an example of how Frankau aimed at "bidding for sensational popularity by unpleasant events."[2] Equally "morbid" were *Baccarat* (1904), the story of a gambling-addicted wife, and *Joseph in Jeopardy* (1912) in which a husband is tempted to commit adultery.

At the time of Frankau's death in 1916 *The Times* suggested that her novels could be characterised by their "accomplished, very shrewd and very unpleasant studies of ill-behaved and disagreeable people"[3] and she was compared to the French novelist Emile Zola. A fonder account of her life is given by her son Gilbert in the posthumously published collection of short stories *Mothers and Children* where he suggests that his mother's work was hampered by her devotion to her children.[4]

---

[1] "Personal Gossip," *Birmingham Daily Post* (18 May 1889), 9.

[2] "New Novels," *The Graphic* (22 February 1890), 15.

[3] "Death of Frank Danby: A Clever Novelist," *The Times* (18 March 1916), 11.

[4] Frank Danby," *Mothers and Children. Hitherto Unpublished Stories by the late "Frank Danby"*. *With a "Preface" by her eldest son, Gilbert Frankau*. London: William Collins, 1918.

Mary [Mrs. Edward] Kennard (1850-1936)

Born Mary Laing in 1850, the novelist best known as "Mrs. Edward Kennard" was the daughter of a successful railway investor and MP. In 1870 she married Edward Kennard, a sometime journalist and lived at their estate at Clack Hill, in Northamptonshire. Nicknamed "the Diana of fiction"[1] after the Roman goddess of hunting, her novels tend to be set in the leisured country environment in which she lived, a world of fox-hunting, shooting, and fishing. Explaining her reliance on these settings she told an interviewer: "Marrying very young, it has since been my fate to reside in a hunting country, and therefore, I have few opportunities for gratifying my love for travel and seeing fresh scenes."[2] These novels include *The Right Sort* (1883), *Killed in the Open* (1886), *The Girl in the Brown Habit* (1887), *Glorious Gallop* (1888), *A Hunting Girl* (1894), and *At the Tail of the Hounds* (1897). When asked about her career, Kennard, like Helen Mathers, tended to downplay it; her writing was mere "scribbling," done to kill time.[3] Some critics agreed about her lack of artistry, complaining that the novels were verbose, having nothing to distinguish them. "Everybody talks, very much alike, expressing the same commonplace ideas in the same would-be smart language"[4]

In spite of this, Kennard quickly made a name for herself with her "horsey" fiction, later diversifying into other sports. She was a keen motorist and cyclist and published *A Guidebook for Lady Cyclists* (1896). Those who interviewed her were quick to point out that she was not at all "mannish" or "unfeminine" herself: "Mrs. Edward Kennard is perhaps the least horsey-looking woman imaginable in morning or evening dress and yet when she is in her habit, you see the thorough horsewoman in a moment, perfect in every detail, cool, quiet, and self possessed-looking; she is above medium height, slim of figure, and not especially good looking though she

---

[1] "New Fiction," *Penny Illustrated Paper* (10 February 1894), 4.
[2] Helen C. Black, *Notable Women Authors of the Day*, 176-177.
[3] Ibid, 174.
[4] "Literature," *Glasgow Herald* (1 April 1885), 6.

has beautiful eyes."[1] When she died in 1936 *The Times* noted that this prolific novelist had long since been forgotten: "Large sums were earned by her publications; then came complete oblivion, which was viewed by the formerly popular favourite with serene detachment. Her many works, though without pretensions to literature were 'rattling good yarns' and suited particularly to the young. Moreover they give a very good picture of the society of their time . . . Mrs. Kennard who before the fashion for open air women had been a noted sportswoman . . . had become practically a cripple and blind, which afflictions were borne with unfailing stoicism. Her interests in old age were in housework, the wireless programmes and the doings of her grandchildren"[2]

Richard Dowling [Marcus Fall] (1846-1898)

Richard Dowling was a good example of a writer who never quite "made it." Born Marcus Fall in 1846 at Clomel, Ireland, he worked as a ship-broker's clerk before getting a post on the Dublin-based paper *The Nation*. He then edited *Zozimus* and *Ireland's Eye* before emigrating to London in 1874, getting a post on the staff of the *Illustrated Sporting and Dramatic News* where he contributed a well-received series of sketches, "Mr. Andrew O'Rourke's Ramblings." Fall wanted to be regarded as a serious writer but, his contemporaries noted, found himself living the life of the hack writer, churning out "innumerable short stories," and "obliged to cater for the general reading public." "There are only two kinds of literature that pay now: the religious and the unclean. I am," he added, "adopting the latter." Privately Fall expressed the "wish . . . that I could obtain a connection with an established paper" which would provide him with a regular income.[3] Instead he turned to writing lurid novels for the circulating library market: *The Sport of Fate* (1880), *A Husband's Secret* (1881), *The Weird Sisters* (1883), *The Hidden Flame* (1885), *The Dark Intruder* (1895). *The Mystery of Killard* (1879)

---

[1] "Mrs. Gadabout," "Indoors and Out," *Winter's Magazine* (15 October 1892), 370.
[2] "Mrs. Kennard," *The Times* (9 March 1936), 8.
[3] Father Matthew Brown, "Richard Dowling," *Freeman's Journal* (28 December 1898), 8.

about a deaf mute fisherman who develops a jealousy of his son who can hear was his best known work. Dowling also developed a line in crime stories, notably *The Skeleton Key* (1886) and *Old Corcoran's Money* (1897) and in the last twenty years of his life he produced sixty volumes. Although some contemporaries flatteringly compared him to Victor Hugo, Fall saw himself as both hack and failure and reckoned the collection of documentary essays *While London Sleeps* (1892) his best work. Not surprisingly the relentless workload took its toll and he died prematurely in 1898.

Margaret [Mrs.] Hungerford (1855-1897)

The writer known as "Mrs. Hungerford" was born Margaret Hamilton in Cork, Ireland, in 1855. She was the daughter of a clergyman and began to write as a child, producing at the age of ten a ghost story which was reputedly so terrifying that it frightened even herself. At eighteen she wrote *Phyllis*, a big seller when published in 1877, and many of her novels were subsequently advertised as "by the author of *Phyllis*." The death of her first husband left Hamilton with three daughters to support. In 1883 she married and took her name from her second husband Harry Hungerford, owner of a large estate in Bandon, Cork. Between the mid-seventies and her death from typhoid in 1897, Hungerford wrote upwards of thirty-five novels, many set Ireland. These include *Molly Bawn* (1878) and *A Little Irish Girl* (1891). Some, such as *Nor Wife Nor Maid* (1892), are sensational in tone, others, like *Lady Verner's Flight* (1893) about a wife trapped in an abusive marriage, are much darker and more outspoken about women's experience of marriage.

Hungerford, who also wrote as "The Duchess," was extremely successful. In 1889, U.S. publisher John W. Lovell claimed that Hungerford was the most popular British writer in the States, selling 30,000 copies easily. In 1893, Helen Black described her as "over-full of work, sells as fast as she can write, and has at present more commissions than she can get through during the next few years."[1] Her prolific output led to a rumour that she didn't write the novels herself but merely sold her name; this idea was vigor-

---

[1] Helen C. Black, *Notable Women Authors of the Day*, 112.

ously refuted.[1] Hungerford cast herself as an enthusiastic amateur never writing more than two hours a day and irregularly. Some reviewers decided that she was not only amateurish but shallow. *The Daily News* wrote that Hungerford's stories were "devoid of ethical purpose," old-fashioned, and "safe," taking no note of the real issues of the modern world: "The New Woman has not yet been born, and 'Marriage a Failure' has not yet been breathed."[2] In 1897, at the height of her success, Hungerford died of typhoid fever. Her novels remained in print until the 1920s.

Arthur à Beckett (1844-1909)

Arthur à Beckett was a son of Gilbert Abbott à Becket, a some-time-journalist and friend of Charles Dickens. He claimed to have inherited his father's "strong literary bias."[3] As a young man he was employed at the War Office and the Post Office and in his spare time helped set up a new journal, *The Glow Worm*, of which he became editor at twenty-one. This was the start of a very successful journalistic career: he served on the staff of the humorous magazines *Punch* and *The Tomahawk* and later edited the *Sunday Times* (1891-94) and the magazine *John Bull* which he established in 1902. In 1893, he was elected President of The Newspaper Society, and in 1900 President of the Institute of Journalism. In 1899 he was responsible for organising public festivities for Queen Victoria's eightieth birthday.

Beckett's charm and good connections clearly helped him get on, but he also possessed some talent, writing plays and novels in his spare time. Most of the novels fit into the category of detective fiction: *Fallen Among Thieves* (1870), *The Mystery of Mostyn Manor* (1878), *Hard Luck; or, A Murder at Monte Carlo* (1890), and *The Tunnel Mystery* (1905). Overall, Beckett's career and achievements are difficult to sum up. As *The Times* noted on his death from complications following the amputation of a leg: "His activities were so wide and his ingenuity in finding scope for them so great that it is hard to keep count of his enterprises."[4]

---

[1] "English Novels in America," *Pall Mall Gazette* (19 September 1889), 14.
[2] "Some New Novels," *Daily News* (4 February 1897), 9.
[3] Helen C. Black, *Pen, Pencil, Baton and Mask*, 322.
[4] "Arthur à Beckett," *The Times*, 15 Jan 1909 p.11: d.

Jean Middlemass (1834-1919)

Born Mary Jane Middlemass, into an affluent Scottish family, Middlemass was the last surviving member of her immediate family (her four brothers predeceased her). When interviewed by Helen Black for *The Ladies' Pictorial* in 1892, she was living alone in Brompton Square, a fashionable district of west London. "She is above the middle height," Black reported, "very upright, with a good figure, fair complexion, grey curly hair, and keen, bright-blue, short-sighted eyes. She is dressed in black . . . sprightly and merry in nature, full of pleasant conversation, and genial in manner."[1]

Middlemass had wanted to be an actress and made successful appearances in Brighton. But at a time when any woman taking to the stage faced charges of sexual looseness, and the common association of actress with prostitute, she had decided not to take the risk. Instead, adopting the pseudonym "Myrtle," she started writing for magazines. Her first novel, *Lil*, was published in 1872. She was immediately popular, not least, as *The Times* noted, because "her work was promptly recognised as most suitable for the young person, for it combined abundant excitement and profundity of mystery with the strictest correctitude of morality. Even the worst of her characters is never guilty of any but the more reputable forms of villainy, such as murder and forgery, which would never bring a blush to the most innocent cheek."[2] Middlemass carried on writing for the next forty years mixing alternating sentimental stories of young women struggling against the odds with sensational stories of wrong-doing. These include *Poisoned Arrows* (1884), *A Felon's Daughter* (1885), and *His Lawful Wife* (1901). The *Pall Mall Gazette*, in a review of *Hush Money* (1896) summed up the typical Middlemass story as "a tale of incident. Hidden crimes, detectives, sudden death, villains, French phrases, bad women and bad grammar darken the air in a surging throng . . . dashed off at an alarming rate and never revised. In reading it one becomes quite breathless, not from excitement, but by reason of strange labyrinthine constructions, eccentric punctuation, and sudden jumps from

---

[1] Helen C. Black, *Notable Women Authors of the Day*, 264.
[2] "Jean Middlemass," *The Times* (7 November 1919), 15.

one tense to another and back again"[1] Readers, however, did not seem to mind and as *The Times* observed, Middlemass "maintained a considerable vogue" in the libraries.[2] Others saw a more subtle writer trying to break out, "a clever character painter"[3] particularly in the novels where she tackles social problems. *Dandy* (1881) is a study of poverty; *Patty's Partner* (1882) is set in a porcelain manufacturing district in the west of England. Middlemass claimed to "prefer" writing stories of middle or working-class life, claiming to get her inspiration from watching people on street corners.[4]

Clement Scott (1841-1904)

The son of an East End clergyman, Scott was educated at an expensive public school, Marlborough College, and began writing pieces for a local paper whilst still a schoolboy. He began his working life as a clerk in the War Office in 1860 but made a move into journalism via a friend who worked on *The Era*, an influential magazine with a strong theatrical emphasis. From 1863-65 Scott served as drama critic for *The Sunday Times*, and then moved to *The Weekly Dispatch;* in 1871 he became a drama critic for the *Daily Telegraph*. Although he wrote extensively on other subjects, Scott came to be seen as the most powerful—and hated—voice in British theatre, a supporter of the "well-made play," but a vociferous opponent of plays he judged "immoral"—particularly the work of Henrik Ibsen. Towards the end of his career Scott caused an uproar when in an interview he claimed that it was "impossible for a woman to remain pure who adopts the stage as a profession . . . [or] to preserve that simplicity of manner which is after all her greatest charm."[5] He was forced to retract the comments but to many in the theatrical profession it suggested that Scott was out of touch.

Scott was primarily a critic but he also wrote poetry and short

---

[1] "New Novels," *Pall Mall Gazette* (23 June 1896), 9.

[2] "Jean Middlemass," *The Times* (7 November 1919), 15.

[3] Alfred Pratt, *People of the Period*, 2 vols. (London: Beeman, 1897), II, 166.

[4] *Lloyd's Weekly Newspaper* 19 July 1891.

[5] "Mr. Clement Scott on the Stage," *Reynolds' Newspaper* (6 February 1898), 8.

stories. A writer for *People of the Period* described him as "a brilliant descriptive writer"[1] and he was best known for his championing of the Norfolk countryside around the town of Cromer, which he nicknamed "Poppyland." This is celebrated in the lyrics to "The Garden of Sleep"—a very popular song at the time—and in *Blossom Land and Fallen Leaves* (1890). His *Lays of a Londoner*—a collection of poems about the London slums—were praised for their sentiments if not their construction. He was also a successful playwright and the rather stilted and excruciatingly stagey dialogue in his chapter of *The Fate of Fenella* perhaps owes something to Scott's experience as a (melo)dramatist with plays such as *Off the Line* (1871), *Peril* (1876), *The Vicarage* (1877) *Diplomacy* (1878), *Sister Mary* (1886), and *The Swordsman's Daughter* (1895).

Clo Graves (1863-1932)

Clotilde Inez Mary Graves was born in Buttevant, Ireland. As a young woman she trained as a painter and worked as an actress. By the late 1880s she had gained reputation as a West End dramatist; her first play *Nitocris*, a verse tragedy, was performed at Drury Lane in 1887; the following year she wrote a pantomime *Puss in Boots*. Her play *Rachel*, about the celebrated tragedienne of the same name, was premiered by the celebrated actor-manager Herbert Beerbohm Tree in 1890. *Dr. and Mrs. Neill*, in which a young wife forms a romantic attachment to her husband's ward was produced in 1894; her biggest success, the cross-dressing comedy *A Mother of Three* played to packed houses in 1896. Later works included *The Matchmaker* (1896) and *Nurse* (1900). The spectre of a successful female playwright was unusual enough to provoke a good deal of comment. Graves was praised for her "smart writing"[2] and held up by progressive critics as "a striking example of what can be achieved by industry."[3]

By 1895 Graves was recognised as the pre-eminent female playwright of her day. In person, she cut an appropriately striking and independent figure; the *Era* reported that she was "an enthusiastic

---

[1] Alfred Pratt, *People of the Period*, 2 vols. (London: Beeman, 1897), II, 365.
[2] "Theatrical Gossip," *Era* (9 May 1896), 3.
[3] "Female Dramatists of the Past," *Era* (23 May 1896), 4.

fly fisher and rides a tricycle"; she smoked in public and adopted masculine-looking dress.[1] *The Belfast Newsletter* described her as "one of the cleverest women writers of the day."[2] When she turned to fiction she chose to take independently minded women as her central characters—a predatory *femme fatale* trying to regain her place in society in *Dragon's Teeth* (1891) and the enterprising female farmers of *In A Market Garden* (1894). In *Katherine Kavanagh* (1892) the heroine is the bait to attract customers to a seedy gambling house. Her biggest fictional success, however, came later. This was *Dop Doctor* (1911). Set in South Africa during the Boer War and published under the pseudonym Richard Dehan the novel went through thirty reprints. Between 1911 and her death Graves published another sixteen works of fiction, mostly short stories. When she died in a convent in Middlesex, in 1928, *The Times* suggested her long career as "an example of what can be achieved by force of character, resourcefulness and hard work. She was practically self-taught and her unconventional beginnings continued throughout her life."[3]

H[enry] W[illiam] Lucy (1845?-1924)

"Henry Lucy," recalled Thomas Anstey Guthrie, "wrote the descriptive sketches of Parliament whilst it was in session, and his comments were both dreaded and courted by ambitious members . . . witty in a quiet dry way, with a thorough knowledge of Parliamentary intrigues and manœuvres which made him a power."[4] Such power at the heart of the Parliamentary establishment was all the more remarkable given Lucy's relatively humble beginnings as the son of a watchmaker. He worked for both *Punch* (writing as "Toby MP") and the *Daily News* and was much admired for his industry and energy. At heart, Lucy wanted to be a politician. Unable to achieve this he, like Anthony Trollope before him, chan-

---

[1] "Theatrical Gossip," *Era* (10 March 1900), 3.
[2] "Literary Gossip," *Belfast Newsletter* (16 March 1896), 7.
[3] "Clo Graves," The Times (5 December 1932), 17.
[4] T.A. Guthrie, *A Long Retrospect* (Oxford: Oxford University Press, 1936), 176-177.

nelled his frustrated parliamentary ambitions into fiction. *Gideon Fleyce*, his first novel, published when he was thirty-seven, is about a man's unsuccessful struggle to get elected. A year later he published an account of his trip round the world, "East by West." He also edited speeches of notable orators of the day including Joseph Chamberlin and William Gladstone. In *The Diary of a Journalist* Lucy noted that part of his fame rested on his connections with other people: "the vastness of the stage before which I was privileged to occupy a seat in the pit, and of the multiplicity of star actors who trod it. For myself I was merely a looker-on."[1]

Adeline Sergeant (1851-1904)

Adeline Sergeant was noteworthy in her own day as one of the first women to attend university. However, this did not mean greater career opportunities and her studies were followed by several years in the traditional career for middle-class working women—governessing. Her break came in 1882 when her novel *Jacobi's Wife* won a competition organised by a provincial newspaper, the *Dundee People's Friend*. On this basis she was invited to become a staff writer and moved to Scotland in 1885, returning to London in 1887. Sergeant never married and supported herself entirely from what she could earn as a writer; looking at her vast output it is difficult not to think that she simply abandoned one life of drudgery (that of the governess) for another (that of the second-division writer for hire). She suffered a breakdown from overwork in 1892. The life of the single literary woman is something she writes about in her novel *Esther Dennison* (1889).

Elsewhere, Sergeant's novels are a mixture of the commercial and the personal. "My works seem to me to fall into two classes: the one of incident . . . and the one of character, with the minimum of story. I like to analyze a character 'to death,' so to speak, and I look on my stories of this sort as the best I have written."[2] "Every now and then I feel the necessity of escaping from the trammels

---

[1] H.W. Lucy, *Diary of a Journalist*, 3 vols. (London: John Murray 1922), vi.
[2] Helen C. Black, *Notable Women Authors of the Day*, 166.

imposed by publishers, editors and the supposed taste of the public. I want to say my own say, to express what I really mean, and feel, to deliver my soul."[1] Thus some novels—*An Open Foe* (1884), *Deveril's Diamond* (1889) and *Dr. Endicott's Experiment* (1894), a tale of bodysnatching—are recognisably thrillers. Others are slightly tamer domestic romances: *Christine* (1894), *Cynthia's Ideal* (1903), *The Choice of Emelia* (1904). A few reflect Sergeant's individual concerns. In *The Common Lot* (1899) the heroine puts her ungrateful relatives' interest before her own, whilst *No Saint* (1886) and *The Story of a Penitent Soul* (1892), written in ten days, were admitted to contain "many transcripts from her personal experiences."[2] *Alison's Ordeal* (1903) likewise contains something of Sergeant's own struggles with religious faith.

Meeting her in 1892, the gossip-columnist for *Winter's Magazine*, "Mrs. Gadabout," saw "a wee little woman, rather buxom, with a mass of fair hair turned loosely back from her face, a fair skin, ruddy complexion, keen bluish grey eyes and as wide-awake as a pure-bred Skye terrier. A natty little woman: she, too, uses a stenographer and has a great ambition to do six thousand words in a day."[3] This ambition led to a nervous breakdown in 1892, just after Sergeant had submitted her chapter for *The Fate of Fenella*. Thereafter her health was always fragile, presumably not helped by her punishing schedule. In her own day, Sergeant's admirers compared her to George Eliot; she could have been as good, it was suggested, if she had the time and space. Instead, she wrote unceasingly, recognising "few limits to the privileges of invention and possess[ing] one of the most fluent of pens."[4]

George Manville Fenn (1831-1909)

One of the most prolific of Victorian novelists, Fenn came from a well-to-do family who lost all their money when he was ten. Fenn

---

[1] Ibid, 167.
[2] Ibid, 165.
[3] "Mrs. Gadabout," "Indoors and Out," *Winter's Magazine* (15 October 1892), 373.
[4] "New Novels," *The Graphic* (10 December 1892), 14.

trained as a teacher and got his first post in Lincolnshire. Once married, Fenn decided that a literary career would serve his family better and moved to London where he struggled to find work. Initially he worked in printing offices as a compositor. Gradually he started to write and in 1864 achieved something of a lucky break when he sent his novel *In Jeopardy* to *All the Year Round* where it was accepted by the magazine's owner, Charles Dickens. This led to more work and Fenn gradually got a foothold in journalism via his much-admired sketches of working class life appearing in *The Morning Star* (later collected as *Readings by Starlight* [1867]). Fenn then joined the staff of another popular family magazine, *Chambers's Journal*, eventually becoming its editor. This was the start of a massive outpouring of stories. Many are works of "the blood and thunder type," as one reviewer put it in an 1886 review of *Double Cunning*. "Love, murder, suicide, poison, shooting, madhouses, strait-jackets, snake-like aristocratic villains, unscrupulous Yankee rogues, gambling, night watches, horrible discoveries—these are the heterogeneous, but attractive elements of which this novel is composed."[1]

Fenn alternated stories of crime with "boy's own" adventures—patriotic stories of manly deeds of derring-do. Titles included *Devon Boys: A Tale of the North Shore* (1887), *The Crystal Hunters: A Boy's Adventures in the Higher Alps* (1892), *Fix Bay'nets!* (1899). As a writer he was acknowledged to have ability but as the *Graphic* noted went to work "in the spirit rather of a craftsman than of an artist."[2]

By the 1890s Fenn was living in some style at Syon House, near the River Thames. Meeting him there, "Mrs. Gadabout," gossip columnist for *Winter's Magazine*, described him "as good a worker as any scribe in England," adding that "Mr. Fenn is light in complexion and always reminds me strongly in appearance of the late Charles Dickens . . ."[3]

"Tasma" [Jessie Catherine Couvreur] (1848-1897)

---

[1] "Literature," *Aberdeen Weekly Journal* (4 February 1886), 6.
[2] "New Novels," *The Graphic* (20 March 1886), 17.
[3] "Mrs. Gadabout," "Indoors and Out," *Winter's Magazine* (23 October 1892), 387.

Born Jessie Huybers in Highgate, north London, the author known as "Tasma" moved with her family to Tasmania at the age of four. In 1873, she left her husband, Charles Fraser, and went to Europe, supporting herself by writing. Her first story, "Barren Love," appeared in 1877. She had also begun to publish articles and reviews in the *Australasian*, many based on her European travels. In 1879 she left Australia permanently, divorcing her husband and travelling first to London and then Paris, where she settled in 1880. Unusually for the time, she made her living as a lecturer, billed as "Madame Jessie Tasma," and became known for her radical political views and socialist inclinations. One observer described her as: "A tall and very handsome lady. She had not only consider-able conversational powers but a genuine gift for platform oratory which she turned to account in various lecturing tours."[1] After her divorce, she married Auguste Couvreur in 1885.

"Tasma" was thus already famous when she began writing novels in the late 1880s. Her first—*Uncle Piper of Piper's Hill: An Australian Novel*—met with great acclaim when it appeared in 1888. The *Pall Mall Gazette* suggested that Tasma would "take her place among the first and best of Australian writers of fiction"; *The Spectator* called it only "the third novel of remarkable merit to come from the Antipodes."[2] This was followed by *In Her Earliest Youth* (1890) the story of a young Melbourne woman married to a drunk-ard and a gambler. Unhappy marriages are a prominent feature of Tasma's work—notably *The Penance of Portia James* (1891) and *A Knight of the White Feather* (1892)—but her work is also striking for its presentation of independent women who are much stronger and more admirable than the weak men to whom they are shack-led. *Not Counting the Cost* (1895), about a woman who leaves her husband in a Tasmanian mental asylum, was also well-received, although some reviewers baulked at the "taint of 'New Womanish-ness'" pervading it.[3] Despite her success, Tasma was always short

---

[1] "Jottings," *Northern Echo* (27 October 1897), 3.

[2] *Pall Mall Gazette* (1 February 1889), *Spectator* (2 February 1889). Cited in Patricia Clark, *Tasma: The Life of Jessie Couvreur* (London: Allen and Unwin, 1994), 115.

[3] "Literature," *The Scotsman* (August 1895). Cited in Clark, 149.

of money. When her husband died in 1894, he left little money, and she took over his post as Belgian correspondent for *The Times*. Stress and overwork were given as some of the reasons for her decline in health, but by 1896 she had developed angina and died of a heart attack in July 1897, her death coinciding with the publication of her last novel *A Fiery Ordeal*.

F. Anstey [Thomas Anstey Guthrie] (1856-1934)

The son of a London tailor, Anstey studied to be a lawyer (though he never practised). Instead he started publishing stories in the late 1870s. He had an early 'hit' with the comic—and subsequently much-filmed—novel *Vice Versa* (1882) in which a father and son magically change bodies for a week. (The name "F. Anstey" is sometimes thought to be a play on the word "fantasy.") On the basis of this Anstey was invited to become a contributor for *Punch* by its editor F. C. Burnand and this became the centre of his literary work. *Burglar Bill* (1882) and *Mr. Punch's Model Music Hall* (1892) both appeared in the magazine. Anstey found his niche with a series of humorous novels: *The Tinted Venus* (1885), *A Fallen Idol* (1886) and *The Brass Bottle* (1900). Anstey also wrote some serious fiction: *The Pariah*, about a well-off but low born young man who tries to enter high-society but encounters only disdain, and *The Statement of Stella Maberly* (1897), a psychological thriller about schizophrenia and hallucination. In later life, Anstey spent a good deal of time overseeing dramatizations of his works, and later film adaptations.

Anstey had no pretensions to being seen as a "great" author. In *A Long Retrospect* he wrote: "my life has had no adventures, and no vicissitudes; such incidents as have happened in it have been the experiences of any author who has been fairly popular in his day and has enjoyed his work."[1] He died of pneumonia in 1934.

---

[1] T.A. Guthrie, *A Long Retrospect* (Oxford: Oxford University Press, 1936), v.

LaVergne, TN USA
07 March 2010
175198LV00002B/70/P